THREE
Great African-American Novels

THREE
Great African-American Novels

The Heroic Slave
FREDERICK DOUGLASS

Clotel
WILLIAM WELLS BROWN

Our Nig
HARRIET E. WILSON

DOVER PUBLICATIONS, INC.
Mineola, New York

Copyright

Bibliographical Note

Three Great African-American Novels, first published in 2008, is a new compila-
tion of unabridged works from standard editions. *The Heroic Slave* was originally
published in 1853 by John P. Jewett, Cleveland; *Clotel, or, The President's
Daughter* was originally published in 1853 by Partridge & Oakey, London; and *Our
Nig; or, Sketches from the Life of a Free Black* was originally published in 1859 by
Geo. C. Rand & Avery, Boston.

The spelling and punctuation found in the original material have been retained
here for the sake of authenticity. The publisher's note has been specially prepared
for this edition.

Library of Congress Cataloging-in-Publication Data

Three Great African-American Novels.
    p. cm.
   "A new compilation of unabridged works from standard editions."
   ISBN-13: 978-0-486-46851-8 (pbk.)
   ISBN-10: 0-486-46851-8
   1. African Americans—Fiction. I. Douglass, Frederick, 1818–1895. Heroic
slave. II. Brown, William Wells, 1814?–1884. Clotel. III. Wilson, Harriet E.,
1825–1900. Our Nig.

PS508.N3T476 2008
813'.4—dc22

                                                                    2008028453

Manufactured in the United States of America
Dover Publications, Inc., 31 East 2nd Street, Mineola, N.Y. 11501

Note

IN THE 1830s, the slave narrative appeared in fictional form. By the middle of the nineteenth century, African-American writers made notable contributions, like the three novels in this edition, to the literature of the United States.

The Heroic Slave (1853) is a fictional account based on a real event. On November 7, 1841, nineteen slaves on board the *Creole* seized control of the ship and redirected it to the British free port of Nassau. Upon entering the harbor, the slaves threw away their weapons and asked the British authorities for freedom. Despite complaints from the Americans, the British refused to reprimand the slaves and eventually set them free. By 1852, the incident was largely forgotten by the public and erased from American history. Frederick Douglass (1818–1895) resurrected it in this, his only work of fiction. Through the noble protagonist Madison Washington (who starkly contradicted the degraded images of slaves and refuted the charge of inferiority), Douglass tapped the American conscience by alluding to the American Revolution, compelling readers to re-examine the nation's mission and identity. The greatest lesson of the *Creole*, not long ago learned by the Americans, was that the only match for tyranny was revolt.

Whereas the protagonist in *The Heroic Slave* is a black man, the main character in *Clotel* (1853) is a woman of mixed race. Author William Wells Brown (1814?–1884) identifies Clotel as the illegitimate child of Thomas Jefferson. (Throughout the 1840s, Brown would have been familiar with accounts of Jefferson's relationship with Sally Hennings.) The novel literary genre liberated Brown from the rigid chronology of narrative.

Although *Clotel* is fiction, the pervasive cruelty toward slaves, the instances of children being born and sold into sexual slavery, and the widespread victimization of black women are not.

Our Nig (1859) blends the genres of autobiography and fiction in a uniquely American tale of an individual struggling against all odds. Author Harriet E. Wilson (1825–1900) adhered closely to the painful details of suffering that were part of her life (and by extension, the experience of African Americans in the antebellum North). Pain, not sexuality, determined the experiences of the protagonist, Alfrado. More so than Douglass's Madison and Wells's Clotel, Afrado's spirit and intellect mature in the ceaseless struggle of her life.

Contents

The Heroic Slave
Frederick Douglass

PART I

Oh! child of grief, why weepest thou?
  Why droops thy sad and mournful brow?
Why is thy look so like despair ?
  What deep, sad sorrow lingers there?

THE STATE OF VIRGINIA is famous in American annals for the multitudinous array of her statesmen and heroes. She has been dignified by some the mother of statesmen. History has not been sparing in recording their names, or in blazoning their deeds. Her high position in this respect, has given her an enviable distinction among her sister States. With Virginia for his birth-place, even a man of ordinary parts, on account of the general partiality for her sons, easily rises to eminent stations. Men, not great enough to attract special attention in their native States, have, like a certain distinguished citizen in the State of New York, sighed and repined that they were not born in Virginia. Yet not all the great ones of the Old Dominion have, by the fact of their birth-place, escaped undeserved obscurity. By some strange neglect, *one* of the truest, manliest, and bravest of her children,—one who, in after years, will, I think, command the pen of genius to set his merits forth, holds now no higher place in the records of that grand old Commonwealth than is held by a horse or an ox. Let those account for it who can, but there stands the fact, that a man who loved liberty as well as did Patrick Henry,—who deserved it as much as Thomas Jefferson,—and who fought for it with a valor as high, an arm as strong, and against odds as great, as he who led all the armies of the American colonies through the great war for freedom and independence, lives now only in the chattel records of his native State.

Glimpses of this great character are all that can now be presented. He is brought to view only by a few transient incidents, and these afford but partial satisfaction. Like a guiding star on a stormy night, he is seen through the parted clouds and the howling tempests; or, like the gray peak of a menacing rock on a perilous coast, he is seen by the quivering flash of angry lightning, and he again disappears covered with mystery.

Curiously, earnestly, anxiously we peer into the dark, and wish even for the blinding flash, or the light of northern skies to reveal him. But alas! he is still enveloped in darkness, and we return from the pursuit like a wearied and disheartened mother, (after a tedious and unsuccessful search for a lost child,) who returns weighed down with disappointment and sorrow. Speaking of marks, traces, possibles, and probabilities, we come before our readers.

In the spring of 1835, on a Sabbath morning, within hearing of the solemn peals of the church bells at a distant village, a Northern traveller through the State of Virginia drew up his horse to drink at a sparkling brook, near the edge of a dark pine forest. While his weary and thirsty steed drew in the grateful water, the rider caught the sound of a human voice, apparently engaged in earnest conversation.

Following the direction of the sound, he descried, among the tall pines, the man whose voice had arrested his attention. "To whom can he be speaking?" thought the traveller. "He seems to be alone." The circumstances interested him much, and he became intensely curious to know what thoughts and feelings, or, it might be, high aspirations, guided those rich and mellow accents. Tieing his horse at a short distance from the brook, he stealthily drew near the solitary speaker; and, concealing himself by the side of a huge fallen tree, he distinctly heard the following soliloquy:—

"What, then, is life to me? it is aimless and worthless, and worse than worthless. Those birds, perched on yon swinging boughs, in friendly conclave, sounding forth their merry notes in seeming worship of the rising sun, though liable to the sportsman's fowling-piece, are still my superiors. They *live free*, though they may die slaves. They fly where they list by day, and retire in freedom at night. But what is freedom to me, or I to it? I am a *slave*,—born a slave, an abject slave,—even before I made part of this breathing world, the scourge was platted for my back; the fetters were forged for my limbs. How mean a thing am I. That accursed and crawling snake, that miserable reptile, that has just glided into its slimy home, is freer and better off than I. He escaped my blow, and is safe. But here am I, a man,—yes, *a man!*—with thoughts and wishes, with powers and faculties as far as angel's flight above that hated reptile,— yet he is my superior, and scorns to own me as his master, or to stop to take my blows. When he saw my uplifted arm, he darted beyond my reach, and turned to give me battle. I dare not do as much as that. I neither run nor fight, but do meanly stand, answering each heavy blow of a cruel master with doleful wails and piteous cries. I am galled with irons; but even these are more tolerable than the consciousness, the *galling* consciousness of cowardice and indecision. Can it be that I *dare* not run away? *Perish the thought*, I *dare* do any thing which may be done by another. When that young man struggled with the waves *for life*, and others stood back appalled in helpless horror, did I not plunge in, forgetful of life, to save his? The raging bull from whom all others fled, pale with fright, did I not keep at bay with a single pitchfork? Could a coward do that? *No,—no,*—I wrong myself,—I am no coward. *Liberty* I will have, or die in the attempt to gain it. This working that others may live in idleness! This cringing submission to insolence and curses! This living under the constant dread and apprehension of being sold and transferred, like a mere brute, is *too* much for me. I will stand it no longer. What others have done, I will do. These trusty legs, or these sinewy arms shall place me among the free. Tom escaped; so can I. The North Star will not be less kind to me than to him. I will follow it. I will at least make the trial. I have nothing to lose. If I am caught, I shall only be a slave. If I am shot, I shall only lose a life which is a burden and a curse. If I get clear, (as something tells me I shall,) liberty, the inalienable birthright of every man, precious and priceless, will be mine. My resolution is fixed. *I shall be free.*"

At these words the traveller raised his head cautiously and noiselessly, and caught, from his hiding-place, a full view of the unsuspecting speaker. Madison (for that was the name of our hero) was standing erect, a smile of satisfaction rippled upon his expressive countenance, like that which plays upon the face of one who has but just solved a difficult problem, or vanquished a malignant foe; for at that moment he was free, at least in spirit. The future gleamed brightly before him, and his fetters lay broken at his feet. His air was triumphant.

Madison was of manly form. Tall, symmetrical, round, and strong. In his movements he seemed to combine, with the strength of the lion, a lion's elasticity. His torn sleeves disclosed arms like polished iron. His face was "black, but comely." His eye, lit with emotion, kept guard under a brow as dark and as glossy as the raven's wing. His whole appearance betokened Herculean strength; yet there was nothing savage or forbidding in his aspect. A child might play in his arms, or dance on his shoulders. A giant's strength, but not a giant's heart was in him. His broad mouth and nose spoke only of good nature and kindness. But his voice, that unfailing index of the soul, though full and melodious, had that in it which could terrify as well as charm. He was just the man you would choose when hardships were to be endured, or danger to be encountered,—intelligent and brave. He had the head to conceive, and the hand to execute. In a word, he was one to be sought as a friend, but to be dreaded as an enemy.

As our traveller gazed upon him, he almost trembled at the thought of his dangerous intrusion. Still he could not quit the place. He had long desired to sound the mysterious depths of the thoughts and feelings of a slave. He was not, therefore, disposed to allow so providential an opportunity to pass unimproved. He resolved to hear more; so he listened again for those mellow and mournful accents which, he says, made such an impression upon him as can never be erased. He did not have to wait long. There came another gush from the same full fountain; now bitter, and now sweet. Scathing denunciations of the cruelty and injustice of slavery; heart-touching narrations of his own personal suffering, intermingled with prayers to the God of the oppressed for help and deliverance, were followed by presentations of the dangers and difficulties of escape, and formed the burden of his eloquent utterances; but his high resolution clung to him,—for he ended each speech by an emphatic declaration of his purpose to be free. It seemed that the very repetition of this, imparted a glow to his countenance. The hope of freedom seemed to sweeten, for a season, the bitter cup of slavery, and to make it, for a time, tolerable; for when in the very whirlwind of anguish,—when his heart's cord seemed screwed up to snapping tension, hope sprung up and soothed his troubled spirit. Fitfully he would exclaim, "How can I leave her? Poor thing! what can she do when I am gone? Oh! oh! 'tis impossible that I can leave poor Susan!"

A brief pause intervened. Our traveller raised his head, and saw again the sorrow-smitten slave. His eye was fixed upon the ground. The strong man staggered under a heavy load. Recovering himself, he argued thus aloud: "All is uncertain here. To-morrow's sun may not rise before I am sold, and separated from her I love. What, then, could I do for her? I should be in more hopeless slavery, and she no nearer to liberty,— whereas if I were free,—my arms my own,—I might devise the means to rescue her."

This said, Madison cast around a searching glance, as if the thought of being overheard had flashed across his mind. He said no more, but, with measured steps, walked away, and was lost to the eye of our traveller amidst the wildering woods.

Long after Madison had left the ground, Mr. Listwell (our traveller) remained in motionless silence, meditating on the extraordinary revelations to which he had listened. He seemed fastened to the spot, and stood half hoping, half fearing the return of the sable preacher to his solitary temple. The speech of Madison rung through the chambers of his soul, and vibrated through his entire frame. "Here is indeed a man," thought he, "of rare endowments,—a child of God,—guilty of no crime but the color of his skin,—hiding away from the face of humanity, and pouring out his thoughts and feelings, his hopes and resolutions to the lonely woods; to him those distant church bells have no grateful music. He shuns the church, the altar, and the great

congregation of christian worshippers, and wanders away to the
gloomy forest, to utter in the vacant air complaints and griefs,
which the religion of his times and his country can neither console nor relieve. Goaded almost to madness by the sense of the
injustice done him, he resorts hither to give vent to his pent up
feelings, and to debate with himself the feasibility of plans, plans
of his own invention, for his own deliverance. From this hour I
am an abolitionist. I have seen enough and heard enough, and I
shall go to my home in Ohio resolved to atone for my past indifference to this ill-starred race, by making such exertions as I
shall be able to do, for the speedy emancipation of every slave
in the land.

Part II

The gaudy, blabbing and remorseful day
Is crept into the bosom of the sea;
And now loud-howling wolves arouse the jades
That drag the tragic melancholy night;
Who with their drowsy, slow, and flagging wings
Clip dead men's graves, and from their misty jaws
Breathe foul contagions, darkness in the air.
　　　　　　　　　　　　　　—*Shakspeare*

FIVE YEARS AFTER the foregoing singular occurence, in the winter of 1840, Mr. and Mrs. Listwell sat together by the fireside of their own happy home in the State of Ohio. The children were all gone to bed. A single lamp burnt brightly on the centretable. All was still and comfortable within; but the night was cold and dark; a heavy wind sighed and moaned sorrowfully around the house and barn, occasionally bringing against the clattering windows a stray leaf from the large oak trees that embowered their dwelling. It was a night for strange noises and for strange fancies. A whole wilderness of thought might pass through one's mind during such an evening. The smouldering embers, partaking of the spirit of the restless night, became fruitful of varied and fantastic pictures, and revived many bygone scenes and old impressions. The happy pair seemed to sit in silent fascination, gazing on the fire. Suddenly this *reverie* was interrupted by a heavy growl. Ordinarily such an occurrence would have scarcely provoked a single word, or excited the least apprehension. But there are certain seasons when the slightest sound sends a jar through all the subtle chambers of the mind; and such a season was this. The happy pair started up, as if some sudden danger had come upon them. The growl was from their trusty watch-dog.

"What can it mean? certainly no one can be out on such a night as this," said Mrs. Listwell.

"The wind has deceived the dog, my dear; he has mistaken the noise of falling branches, brought down by the wind, for that of the footsteps of persons coming to the house. I have several times to-night thought that I heard the sound of footsteps. I am sure, however, that it was but the wind. Friends would not be likely to come out at such an hour, or such a night; and thieves are too lazy and self-indulgent to expose themselves to this biting frost; but should there be any one about, our brave old Monte, who is on the look-out, will not be slow in sounding the alarm."

Saying this they quietly left the window, whither they had gone to learn the cause of the menacing growl, and re-seated themselves by the fire, as if reluctant to leave the slowly expiring embers, although the hour was late. A few minutes only intervened after resuming their seats, when again their sober meditations were disturbed. Their faithful dog now growled and barked furiously, as if assailed by an advancing foe. Simultaneously the good couple arose, and stood in mute expectation. The contest without seemed fierce and violent. It was, however, soon over,—the barking ceased, for, with true canine instinct, Monte quickly discovered that a friend, not an enemy of the family, was coming to the house, and instead of rushing to repel the supposed intruder, he was now at the door, whimpering and dancing for the admission of himself and his newly made friend.

Mr. Listwell knew by this movement that all was well; he advanced and opened the door, and saw by the light that streamed out into the darkness, a tall man advancing slowly towards the house, with a stick in one hand, and a small bundle in the other. "It is a traveller," thought he, "who has missed his way, and is coming to inquire the road. I am glad we did not go to bed earlier,—I have felt all the evening as if somebody would be here to-night."

The man had now halted a short distance from the door, and looked prepared alike for flight or battle. "Come in, sir, don't be alarmed, you have probably lost your way."

Slightly hesitating, the traveller walked in; not, however, without regarding his host with a scrutinizing glance. "No, sir," said he, "I have come to ask you a greater favor."

Instantly Mr. Listwell exclaimed, (as the recollection of the Virginia forest scene flashed upon him,) "Oh, sir, I know not your name, but I have seen your face, and heard your voice before. I am glad to see you. *I know all.* You are flying for your liberty,—be seated,—be seated,—banish all fear. You are safe under my roof."

This recognition, so unexpected, rather disconcerted and disquieted the noble fugitive. The timidity and suspicion of persons escaping from slavery are easily awakened, and often what is intended to dispel the one, and to allay the other, has precisely the opposite effect. It was so in this case. Quickly observing the unhappy impression made by his words and action, Mr. Listwell assumed a more quiet and inquiring aspect, and finally succeeded in removing the apprehensions which his very natural and generous salutation had aroused.

Thus assured, the stranger said, "Sir, you have rightly guessed, I am, indeed, a fugitive from slavery. My name is Madison,—Madison Washington my mother used to call me. I am on my way to Canada, where I learn that persons of my color are protected in all the rights of men; and my object in calling upon you was, to beg the privilege of resting my weary limbs for the night in your barn. It was my purpose to have continued my journey till morning; but the piercing cold, and the frowning darkness compelled me to seek shelter; and, seeing a light through the lattice of your window, I was encouraged to come here to beg the privilege named. You will do me a great favor by affording me shelter for the night."

"A resting-place, indeed, sir, you shall have; not, however, in my barn, but in the best room of my house. Consider yourself, if you please, under the roof of a friend; for such I am to you, and to all your deeply injured race."

While this introductory conversation was going on, the kind lady had revived the fire, and was diligently preparing supper; for she, not less than her husband, felt for the sorrows of the oppressed and hunted ones of earth, and was always glad of an opportunity to do them a service. A bountiful repast was quickly prepared, and the hungry and toil-worn bondman was cordially invited to partake thereof. Gratefully he acknowledged the favor of his benevolent benefactress; but appeared scarcely to understand what such hospitality could mean. It was the first time in his life that he had met so humane and friendly a greeting at the hands of persons whose color was unlike his own; yet it was impossible for him to doubt the charitableness of his new friends, or the genuineness of the welcome so freely given; and he therefore, with many thanks, took his seat at the table with Mr. and Mrs. Listwell, who, desirous to make him feel at home, took a cup of tea themselves, while urging upon Madison the best that the house could afford.

Supper over, all doubts and apprehensions banished, the three drew around the blazing fire, and a conversation commenced which lasted till long after midnight.

"Now," said Madison to Mr. Listwell, "I was a little surprised and alarmed when I came in, by what you said; do tell me, sir, *why* you thought you had seen my face before, and by what you knew me to be a fugitive from slavery; for I am sure that I never was before in this neighborhood, and I certainly sought to conceal what I supposed to be the manner of a fugitive slave."

Mr. Listwell at once frankly disclosed the secret; describing the place where he first saw him; rehearsing the language which he (Madison) had used; referring to the effect which his manner and speech had made upon him; declaring the resolution he there formed to be an abolitionist; telling how often he had spoken of the circumstance, and the deep concern he had ever since felt to know what had become of him; and whether he had carried out the purpose to make his escape, as in the woods he declared he would do.

"Ever since that morning," said Mr. Listwell, "you have seldom been absent from my mind, and though now I did not dare to hope that I should ever see you again, I have often wished that such might be my fortune; for, from that hour, your face seemed to be daguerreotyped on my memory."

Madison looked quite astonished, and felt amazed at the narration to which he had listened. After recovering himself he said, "I well remember that morning, and the bitter anguish that wrung my heart; I will state the occasion of it. I had, on the previous Saturday, suffered a cruel lashing; had been tied up to the limb of a tree, with my feet chained together, and a heavy iron bar placed between my ankles. Thus suspended, I received on my naked back forty stripes, and was kept in this distressing position three or four hours, and was then let down, only to have my torture increased; for my bleeding back, gashed by the cow-skin, was washed by the overseer with old brine, partly to augment my suffering, and partly, as he said, to prevent inflammation. My crime was that I had stayed longer at the mill, the day previous, than it was thought I ought to have done, which, I assured my master and the overseer, was no fault of mine; but no excuses were allowed. 'Hold your tongue, you impudent rascal,' met my every explanation. Slave-holders are so imperious when their passions are excited, as to construe every word of the slave into insolence. I could do nothing but submit to the agonizing infliction. Smarting still from the wounds, as well as from the consciousness of being whipt for no cause, I took advantage of the absence of my master, who had gone to church, to spend the time in the woods, and brood over my wretched lot. Oh, sir, I remember it well, and can never forget it."

"But this was five years ago; where have you been since?"

"I will try to tell you," said Madison. "Just four weeks after that Sabbath morning, I gathered up the few rags of clothing I had, and started, as I supposed, for the North and for freedom. I must not stop to describe my feelings on taking this step. It seemed like taking a leap into the dark. The thought of leaving my poor wife and two little children caused me indescribable anguish; but consoling myself with the reflection that once free, I could, possibly, devise ways and means to gain their freedom also, I nerved myself up to make the attempt. I started, but ill-luck attended me; for after being out a whole week, strange to say, I still found myself on my master's grounds; the third night after being out, a season of clouds and rain set in, wholly preventing me from seeing the North Star, which I had trusted as my guide, not dreaming that clouds might intervene between us.

"This circumstance was fatal to my project, for in losing my star, I lost my way; so when I supposed I was far towards the North, and had almost gained my freedom, I discovered myself at the very point from which I had started. It was a severe trial, for I arrived at home in great destitution; my feet were sore, and in travelling in the dark, I had dashed my foot against a stump, and started a nail, and lamed myself. I was wet and cold; one week had exhausted all my stores; and when I landed on my master's plantation, with all my work to do over again,—hungry, tired, lame, and bewildered,—I almost cursed the day that I was born. In this extremity I approached the quarters. I did so stealthily, although in my desperation I hardly cared whether I was discovered or not. Peeping through the rents of the quarters, I saw my fellow-slaves seated by a warm fire, merrily passing away the time, as though their hearts knew no sorrow. Although I envied their seeming contentment, all wretched as I was, I despised the cowardly acquiescence in their own degradation which it implied, and felt a kind of pride and glory in my own desperate lot. I dared not enter the quarters,—for where there is seeming contentment with slavery, there is certain treachery to freedom. I proceeded towards the great house, in the hope of catching a glimpse of my poor wife, whom I knew might be trusted with my secrets even on the scaffold. Just as I reached the fence which divided the field from the garden, I saw a woman in the yard, who in the darkness I took to be my wife; but a nearer approach told me it was not she. I was about to speak; had I done so, I would not have been here this night; for an alarm would have been sounded, and the hunters been put on my track. Here were hunger, cold, thirst, disappointment, and chagrin, confronted only by the dim hope of liberty. I tremble to think of that dreadful hour. To face the deadly cannon's mouth in warm blood unterrified, is, I think, a small achievement, compared with a conflict like this with gaunt starvation. The gnawings of hunger conquers by degrees, till all that a man has he would give in exchange for a single crust of bread. Thank God, I was not quite reduced to this extremity.

"Happily for me, before the fatal moment of utter despair, my good wife made her appearance in the yard. It was she; I knew her step. All was well now. I was, however, afraid to speak, lest I should frighten her. Yet speak I did; and, to my great joy, my voice was known. Our meeting can be more easily imagined than described. For a time hunger, thirst, weariness, and lameness were forgotten. But it was soon necessary for her to return to the house. She being a house-servant, her absence from the kitchen, if discovered, might have excited suspicion. Our parting was like tearing the flesh from my bones; yet it was the part of wisdom for her to go. She left me with the purpose of meeting me at midnight in the very forest where you last saw me. She knew the place well, as one of my melancholy resorts, and could easily find it, though the night was dark.

"I hastened away, therefore, and concealed myself, to await the arrival of my good angel. As I lay there among the leaves, I was strongly tempted to return again to the house of my master and give myself up; but remembering my solemn pledge on that memorable Sunday morning, I was able to linger out the two long hours between ten and midnight. I may well call them long hours. I have endured much hardship; I have encountered many perils; but the anxiety of those two hours, was the bitterest I ever experienced. True to her word, my wife came laden with provisions, and we sat down on the side of a log, at that dark and lonesome hour of the night. I cannot say we talked; our feelings were too great for that; yet we came to an understanding that I should make the woods my home, for if I gave myself up, I should be whipped and sold away; and if I started for the North, I should leave a wife doubly dear to me. We mutually determined, therefore, that I should remain in the vicinity. In the dismal swamps I lived, sir, five long years,—a cave for my home during the day. I wandered about at night with the wolf and the bear,—sustained by the promise that my good Susan would meet me in the pine woods at least once a week. This promise was redeemed, I assure you, to the letter, greatly to my relief. I had partly become contented with my mode of life, and had made up my mind to spend my days there; but the wilderness that sheltererd me thus long took fire, and refused longer to be my hiding-place.

"I will not harrow up your feelings by portraying the terrific scene of this awful conflagration. There is nothing to which I can liken it. It was horribly and indescribably grand. The whole world seemed on fire, and it appeared to me that the day of judgment had come; that the burning bowels of the earth had burst forth, and that the end of all things was at hand. Bears and wolves, scorched from their mysterious hiding-places in the earth, and all the wild inhabitants of the untrodden forest, filled with a common dismay, ran forth, yelling, howling, bewildered amidst the smoke and flame. The very heavens seemed to rain down fire through the towering trees; it was by the merest chance that I escaped the devouring element. Running before it, and stopping occasionally to take breath, I looked back to behold its frightful ravages, and to drink in its savage magnificence. It was awful, thrilling, solemn, beyond compare. When aided by the fitful wind, the merciless tempest of fire swept on, sparkling, creaking, cracking, curling, roaring, out-doing in its dreadful splendor a thousand thunderstorms at once. From tree to tree it leaped, swallowing them up in its lurid, baleful glare; and leaving them leafless, limbless, charred, and lifeless behind. The scene was overwhelming, stunning,—nothing was spared,—cattle, tame and wild, herds of swine and of deer, wild beasts of every name and kind,—huge night-birds, bats, and owls, that had retired to their homes in lofty tree-tops to rest, perished in that fiery storm. The long-winged buzzard, and croaking raven mingled their dismal cries with those of the countless myriads of small birds that rose up to the skies, and were lost to the sight in clouds of smoke and flame. Oh, I shudder when I think of it! Many a poor wandering fugitive, who, like myself, had sought among wild beasts the mercy denied by our fellow men, saw, in helpless consternation, his dwelling-place and city of refuge reduced to ashes forever. It was this grand conflagration that drove me hither; I ran alike from fire and from slavery."

After a slight pause, (for both speaker and hearers were deeply moved by the above recital,) Mr. Listwell, addressing Madison, said, "If it does not weary you too much, do tell us something of your journeyings since this disastrous burning,—we are deeply interested in everything which can throw light on the hardships of persons escaping from slavery; we could hear you talk all night; are there no incidents that you could relate of your travels hither? or are they such that you do not like to mention them."

"For the most part, sir, my course has been uninterrupted; and, considering the circumstances, at times even pleasant. I have suffered little for want of food; but I need not tell you how I got it. Your moral code may differ from mine, as your customs and usages are different. The fact is, sir, during my flight, I felt myself robbed by society of all my just rights; that I was in an enemy's land, who sought both my life and my liberty. They had transformed me into a brute; made merchandise of my body, and, for all the purposes of my flight, turned day into night,— and guided by my own necessities, and in contempt of their conventionalities, I did not scruple to take bread where I could get it."

"And just there you were right," said Mr. Listwell; "I once had doubts on this point myself, but a conversation with Gerrit Smith, (a man, by the way, that I wish you could see, for he is a devoted friend of your race, and I know he would receive you gladly,) put an end to all my doubts on this point. But do not let me interrupt you."

"I had but one narrow escape during my whole journey, " said Madison.

"Do let us hear of it," said Mr. Listwell.

"Two weeks ago," continued Madison, "after travelling all night, I was overtaken by daybreak, in what seemed to me an almost interminable wood. I deemed it unsafe to go farther, and, as usual, I looked around for a suitable tree in which to spend the day. I liked one with a bushy top, and found one just to my mind. Up I climbed, and hiding myself as well I could, I, with this strap, (pulling one out of his old coat-pocket,) lashed myself to a bough, and flattered myself that I should get a *good night's* sleep that day; but in this I was soon disappointed. I had scarcely got fastened to my natural hammock, when I heard the voices of a number of persons, apparently approaching the part of the woods where I was. Upon my word, sir, I dreaded more these human voices than I should have done those of wild beasts. I was at a loss to know what to do. If I descended, I should probably be discovered by the men; and if they had dogs I should, doubtless, be *'treed.'* It was an anxious moment, but hardships and dangers have been the accompaniments of my life; and have, perhaps, imparted to me a certain hardness of character, which, to some extent, adapts me to them. In my present predicament, I decided to hold my place in the tree-top, and abide the consequences. But here I must disappoint you; for the men, who were all colored, halted at least a hundred yards from me, and began with their axes, in right good earnest, to attack the trees. The sound of their laughing axes was like the report of as many well-charged pistols. By and by there came down at least a dozen trees with a terrible crash. They leaped upon the fallen trees with an air of victory. I could see no dog with them, and felt myself comparatively safe, though I could not forget the possibility that some freak or fancy might bring the axe a little nearer my dwelling than comported with my safety.

"There was no sleep for me that day, and I wished for night. You may imagine that the thought of having the tree attacked under me was far from agreeable, and that it very easily kept me on the look-out. The day was not without diversion. The men at work seemed to be a gay set; and they would often make the woods resound with that uncontrolled laughter for which we, as a race, are remarkable. I held my place in the tree till sunset,—saw the men put on their jackets to be off. I observed that all left the ground except one, whom I saw sitting on the side of a stump, with his head bowed, and his eyes apparently fixed on the ground. I became interested in him. After sitting in the position to which I have alluded ten or fifteen minutes, he left the stump, walked directly towards the tree in which I was secreted, and halted almost under the same. He stood for a moment and looked around, deliberately and reverently took off his hat, by which I saw that he was a man in the evening of life, slightly bald and quite gray. After laying down his hat carefully, he knelt and prayed aloud, and such a prayer, the most fervent, earnest, and solemn, to which I think I ever listened. After reverently addressing the Almighty, as the all-wise, all-good, and the common Father of all mankind, he besought God for grace, for strength, to bear up under, and to endure, as a good soldier, all the hardships and trials which beset the journey of life, and to enable him to live in a manner which accorded with the gospel of Christ. His soul now broke out in humble supplication for deliverance from bondage. 'O thou,' said he, 'that hearest the raven's cry, take pity on poor me! O deliver me! O deliver me! in mercy, O God, deliver me from the chains and manifold hardships of slavery! With thee, O Father, all things are possible. Thou canst stand and measure the earth. Thou hast beheld and drove asunder the nations,—all power is in thy hand,—thou didst say of old, "I have seen the affliction of my people, and am come to deliver them,"—Oh look down upon our afflictions, and have mercy upon us.' But I cannot repeat his prayer, nor can I give you an idea of its deep pathos. I had given but little attention to religion, and had but little faith in it; yet, as the old man prayed, I felt almost like coming down and kneeling by his side, and mingle my broken complaint with his.

"He had already gained my confidence; as how could it be otherwise? I knew enough of religion to know that the man who prays in secret is far more likely to be sincere than he who loves to pray standing in the street, or in the great congregation. When he arose from his knees, like another Zacheus, I came down from the tree. He seemed a little alarmed at first, but I told him my story, and the good man embraced me in his arms, and assured me of his sympathy.

"I was now about out of provisions, and thought I might safely ask him to help me replenish my store. He said he had no money; but if he had, he would freely give it me. I told him I had *one dollar*; it was all the money I had in the world. I gave it to him, and asked him to purchase some crackers and cheese, and to kindly bring me the balance; that I would remain in or near that place, and would come to him on his return, if he would whistle. He was gone only about an hour. Meanwhile, from some cause or other, I know not what, (but as you shall see very wisely,) I changed my place. On his return I started to meet him; but it seemed as if the shadow of approaching danger fell upon my spirit, and checked my progress. In a very few minutes, closely on the heels of the old man, I distinctly saw *fourteen men*, with something like guns in their hands."

"Oh! the old wretch!" exclaimed Mrs. Listwell, "he had betrayed you, had he?"

"I think not," said Madison, "I cannot believe that the old man was to blame. He probably went into a store, asked for the articles for which I sent, and presented the bill I gave him; and it is so unusual for slaves in the country to have money, that fact, doubtless, excited suspicion, and gave rise to inquiry. I can easily believe that the truthfulness of the old man's character compelled him to disclose the facts; and thus were these blood-thirsty men put on my track. Of course I did not present myself; but hugged my hiding-place securely. If discovered and attacked, I resolved to sell my life as dearly as possible.

"After searching about the woods silently for a time, the whole company gathered around the old man; one charged him with lying, and called him an old villain; said he was a thief; charged him with stealing money; said if he did not instantly tell where he got it, they would take the shirt from his old back, and give him thirty-nine lashes.

"'I did *not* steal the money,' said the old man, 'it was given me, as I told you at the store; and if the man who gave it me is not here, it is not my fault.'

"'Hush! you lying old rascal; we'll make you smart for it. You shall not leave this spot until you have told where you got that money.'

"They now took hold of him, and began to strip him; while others went to get sticks with which to beat him. I felt, at the moment, like rushing out in the midst of them; but considering that the old man would be whipped the more for having aided a fugitive slave, and that, perhaps, in the *melée* he might be killed outright, I disobeyed this impulse. They tied him to a tree, and began to whip him. My own flesh crept at every blow, and I seem to hear the old man's piteous cries even now. They laid thirty-nine lashes on his bare back, and were going to repeat that number, when one of the company besought his comrades to desist. 'You'll kill the d—d old scoundrel! You've already whipt a dollar's worth out of him, even if he stole it!' 'O yes,' said another, 'let him down. He'll never tell us another lie, I'll warrant ye!' With this, one of the company untied the old man, and bid him go about his business.

"The old man left, but the company remained as much as an hour, scouring the woods. Round and round they went, turning up the underbrush, and peering about like so many bloodhounds. Two or three times they came within six feet of where I lay. I tell you I held my stick with a firmer grasp than I did in coming up to your house to-night. I expected to level one of them at least. Fortunately, however, I eluded their pursuit, and they left me alone in the woods.

"My last dollar was now gone, and you may well suppose I felt the loss of it; but the thought of being once again free to pursue my journey, prevented that depression which a sense of destitution causes; so swinging my little bundle on my back, I caught a glimpse of the *Great Bear* (which ever points the way to my beloved star,) and I started again on my journey. What I lost in money I made up at a hen-roost that same night, upon which I fortunately came."

"But you didn't eat your food raw? How did you cook it?" said Mrs. Listwell.

"O no, Madam," said Madison, turning to his little bundle;— "I had the means of cooking." Here he took out of his bundle an old-fashioned tinder-box, and taking up a piece of a file, which he brought with him, he struck it with a heavy flint, and brought out at least a dozen sparks at once. "I have had this old box," said he, "more than five years. It is the *only* property saved from the fire in the dismal swamp. It has done me good service. It has given me the means of broiling many a chicken!"

It seemed quite a relief to Mrs. Listwell to know that Madison had, at least, lived upon cooked food. Women have a perfect horror of eating uncooked food.

By this time thoughts of what was best to be done about getting Madison to Canada, began to trouble Mr. Listwell; for the laws of Ohio were very stringent against any one who should aid, or who were found aiding a slave to escape through that State. A citizen, for the simple act of taking a fugitive slave in his carriage, had just been stripped of all his property, and thrown penniless upon the world. Notwithstanding this, Mr. Listwell was determined to see Madison safely on his way to Canada. "Give yourself no uneasiness," said he to Madison, "for if it cost my farm, I shall see you safely out of the States, and on your way to a land of liberty. Thank God that there *such* a land so near us! You will spend to-morrow with us, and to-morrow night I will take you in my carriage to the Lake. Once upon that, and you are safe."

"Thank you! thank you," said the fugitive; "I will commit myself to your care."

For the *first* time during *five* years, Madison enjoyed the luxury of resting his limbs on a comfortable bed, and inside a human habitation. Looking at the white sheets, he said to Mr. Listwell, "What, sir! you don't mean that I shall sleep in that bed?"

"Oh yes, oh yes."

After Mr. Listwell left the room, Madison said he really hesitated whether or not he should lie on the floor; for that was *far* more comfortable and inviting than any bed to which he had been used.

We pass over the thoughts and feelings, the hopes and fears, the plans and purposes, that revolved in the mind of Madison during the day that he was secreted at the house of Mr. Listwell. The reader will be content to know that nothing occurred to endanger his liberty, or to excite alarm. Many were the little attentions bestowed upon him in his quiet retreat and hiding-place. In the evening, Mr. Listwell, after treating Madison to a new suit of winter clothes, and replenishing his exhausted purse with five dollars, all in silver, brought out his two-horse wagon, well provided with buffaloes, and silently started off with him to Cleveland. They arrived there without interruption, a few minutes before sunrise the next morning. Fortunately the steamer Admiral lay at the wharf, and was to start for Canada at nine o'clock. Here the last anticipated danger was surmounted. It was feared that just at this point the hunters of men might be on the look-out, and, possibly, pounce upon their victim. Mr. Listwell saw the captain of the boat; cautiously sounded him on the matter of carrying liberty-loving passengers, before he introduced his precious charge. This done, Madison was conducted on board. With usual generosity this true subject of the emancipating queen welcomed Madison, and assured him that he should be safely landed in Canada, free of charge. Madison now felt himself no more a piece of merchandise, but a passenger, and, like any other passenger, going about his business, carrying with him what belonged to him, and nothing which rightfully belonged to anybody else.

Wrapped in his new winter suit, snug and comfortable, a pocket full of silver, safe from his pursuers, embarked for a free country, Madison gave every sign of sincere gratitude, and bade his kind benefactor farewell, with such a grip of the hand as bespoke a heart full of honest manliness, and a soul that knew how to appreciate kindness. It need scarcely be said that Mr. Listwell was deeply moved by the gratitude and friendship he had excited in a nature so noble as that of the fugitive. He went to his home that day with a joy and gratification which knew no bounds. He had done something "to deliver the spoiled out of the hands of the spoiler," he had given bread to the hungry, and clothes to the naked; he had befriended a man to whom the laws of his country forbade all friendship,—and in proportion to the odds against his righteous deed, was the delightful satisfaction that gladdened his heart. On reaching home, he exclaimed, "*He is safe,—he is safe,—he is safe,*"—and the cup of his joy was shared by his excellent lady. The following letter was received from Madison a few days after.

"Windsor, Canada West, Dec. 16, 1840.
My dear Friend,—for such you truly are:—

Madison is out of the woods at last; I nestle in the mane of the British lion, protected by his mighty paw from the talons and the beak of the American eagle. I am free, and breathe an atmosphere too pure for *slaves*, slave-hunters, or slave-holders. My heart is full. As many thanks to you, sir, and to your kind lady, as there are pebbles on the shores of Lake Erie; and may the blessing of God rest upon you both. You will never be forgotten by your profoundly grateful friend,

Madison Washington.

PART III

—His head was with his heart,
And that was far away!
—*Childe Harold*

JUST UPON THE EDGE of the great road from Petersburg,
Virginia, to Richmond, and only about fifteen miles from the
latter place, there stands a somewhat ancient and famous public
tavern, quite notorious in its better days, as being the grand resort for most of the leading gamblers, horse-racers, cock-
fighters, and slave-traders from all the country round about.
This old rookery, the nucleus of all sorts of birds, mostly those
of ill omen, has, like everything else peculiar to Virginia, lost
much of its ancient consequence and splendor; yet it keeps up
some appearance of gaiety and high life, and is still frequented,
even by respectable travellers, who are unacquainted with its
past history and present condition. Its fine old portico looks well
at a distance, and gives the building an air of grandeur. A nearer
view, however, does little to sustain this pretension. The house
is large, and its style imposing, but time and dissipation, unfailing in their results, have made ineffaceable marks upon it, and
it must, in the common course of events, soon be numbered
with the things that were. The gloomy mantle of ruin is, already,
out-spread to envelop it, and its remains, even but now remind
one of a human skull, after the flesh has mingled with the earth.
Old hats and rags fill the places in the upper windows once occupied by large panes of glass, and the moulding boards along
the roofing have dropped off from their places, leaving holes
and crevices in the rented wall for bats and swallows to build
their nests in. The platform of the portico, which fronts the

highway is a rickety affair, its planks are loose, and in some places entirely gone, leaving effective man-traps in their stead for nocturnal ramblers. The wooden pillars, which once supported it, but which now hang as encumbrances, are all rotten, and tremble with the touch. A part of the stable, a fine old structure in its day, which has given comfortable shelter to hundreds of the noblest steeds of "the Old Dominion" at once, was blown down many years ago, and never has been, and probably never will be, rebuilt. The doors of the barn are in wretched condition; they will shut with a little human strength to help their worn out hinges, but not otherwise. The side of the great building seen from the road is much discolored in sundry places by slops poured from the upper windows, rendering it unsightly and offensive in other respects. Three or four great dogs, looking as dull and gloomy as the mansion itself, lie stretched out along the door-sills under the portico; and double the number of loafers, some of them completely rum-ripe, and others ripening, dispose themselves like so many sentinels about the front of the house. These latter understand the science of scraping acquaintance to perfection. They know every-body, and almost every-body knows them. Of course, as their title implies, they have no regular employment. They are (to use an expressive phrase) *hangers on,* or still better, they are what sailors would denominate *holders-on to the slack, in every-body's mess, and in nobody's watch.* They are, however, as good as the newspaper for the events of the day, and they sell their knowledge almost as cheap. Money they seldom have; yet they always have capital the most reliable. They make their way with a succeeding traveller by intelligence gained from a preceding one. All the great names of Virginia they know by heart, and have seen their owners often. The history of the house is folded in their lips, and they rattle off stories in connection with it, equal to the guides at Dryburgh Abbey. He must be a shrewd man, and well skilled in the art of evasion, who gets out of the hands of these fellows without being at the expense of a treat.

It was at this old tavern, while on a second visit to the State of Virginia in 1841, that Mr. Listwell, unacquainted with the fame of the place, turned aside, about sunset, to pass the night.

Riding up to the house, he had scarcely dismounted, when one of the half dozen bar-room fraternity met and addressed him in a manner exceedingly bland and accommodating.

"Fine evening, sir."

"Very fine," said Mr. Listwell. "This is a tavern, I believe?"

"O yes, sir, yes; although you may think it looks a little the worse for wear, it was once as good a house as any in Virginy. I make no doubt if ye spend the night here, you'll think it a good house yet; for there aint a more accommodating man in the country than you'll find the landlord."

Listwell. "The most I want is a good bed for myself, and a full manger for my horse. If I get these, I shall be quite satisfied."

Loafer. "Well, I alloys like to hear a gentleman talk for his horse; and just because the horse can't talk for itself. A man that don't care about his beast, and don't look arter it when he's travelling, aint much in my eye anyhow. Now, sir, I likes a horse, and I'll guarantee your horse will be taken good care on here. That old stable, for all you see it looks so shabby now, once sheltered the great *Eclipse,* when he run here agin *Batchelor* and *Jumping Jemmy.* Them was fast horses, but he beat 'em both."

Listwell. "Indeed."

Loafer. "Well, I rather reckon you've travelled a right smart distance to-day, from the look of your horse?"

Listwell. "Forty miles only."

Loafer. "Well! I'll be darned if that aint a pretty good *only.* Mister, that beast of yours is a singed cat, I warrant you. I never see'd a creature like that that was'nt good on the road. You've come about forty miles, then?"

Listwell. "Yes, yes, and a pretty good pace at that."

Loafer. "You're somewhat in a hurry, then, I make no doubt? I reckon I could guess if I would, what you're going to Richmond for? It would'nt be much of a guess either; for it's rumored hereabouts, that there's to be the greatest sale of niggers at Richmond to-morrow that has taken place there in a long time; and I'll be bound you're a going there to have a hand in it."

Listwell. "Why, you must think, then, that there's money to be made at that business?"

Loafer. "Well, 'pon my honor, sir, I never made any that way myself; but it stands to reason that it's a money making business; for almost all other business in Virginia is dropped to engage in this. One thing is sartain, I never see'd a nigger-buyer yet that hadn't a plenty of money, and he wasn't as free with it as water. I has known one on 'em to treat as high as twenty times in a night; and, ginerally speaking, they's men of edication, and knows all about the government. The fact is, sir, I alloys like to hear 'em talk, bekase I alloys can learn something from them."

Listwell. "What may I call your name, sir?"

Loafer. "Well, now, they calls me Wilkes. I'm known all around by the gentlemen that comes here. They all knows old Wilkes."

Listwell. "Well, Wilkes, you seem to be acquainted here, and I see you have a strong liking for a horse. Be so good as to speak a kind word for mine to the hostler to-night, and you'll not lose anything by it."

Loafer. "Well, sir, I see you don't say much, but you've got an insight into things. It's alloys wise to get the good will of them that's acquainted about a tavern; for a man don't know when he goes into a house what may happen, or how much he may need a friend." Here the loafer gave Mr. Listwell a significant grin, which expressed a sort of triumphant pleasure at having, as he supposed, by his tact succeeded in placing so fine appearing a gentleman under obligations to him.

The pleasure, however, was mutual; for there was something so insinuating in the glance of this loquacious customer, that Mr. Listwell was very glad to get quit of him, and to do so more successfully, he ordered his supper to be brought to him in his private room, private to the eye, but not to the ear. This room was directly over the bar, and the plastering being off, nothing but pine boards and naked laths separated him from the disagreeable company below,—he could easily hear what was said in the bar-room, and was rather glad of the advantage it afforded, for, as you shall see, it furnished him important hints as to the manner and deportment he should assume during his stay at that tavern.

Mr. Listwell says he had got into his room but a few moments, when he heard the officious Wilkes below, in a tone of

disappointment, exclaim, "Whar's that gentleman?" Wilkes was
evidently expecting to meet with his friend at the bar-room, on
his return, and had no doubt of his doing the handsome thing.
"He has gone to his room," answered the landlord, "and has
ordered his supper to be brought to him."

Here some one shouted out, "Who is he, Wilkes? Where's he
going?"

"Well, now, I'll be hanged if I know; but I'm willing to make
any man a bet of this old hat agin a five dollar bill, that that gent
is as full of money as a dog is of fleas. He's going down to
Richmond to buy niggers, I make no doubt. He's no fool, I warrant ye."

"Well, he acts d—d strange," said another, "anyhow. I likes to
see a man, when he comes up to a tavern, to come straight into
the bar-room, and show that he's a man among men. Nobody
was going to bite him."

"Now, I don't blame him a bit for not coming in here. That
man knows his business, and means to take care on his money,"
answered Wilkes.

"Wilkes, you 're a fool. You only say that, becase you hope to
get a few coppers out on him."

"You only measure my corn by your half-bushel, I won't say
that you're only mad becase I got the chance of speaking to him
first."

"O Wilkes! you're known here. You'll praise up any body that
will give you a copper; besides, 'tis my opinion that that fellow
who took his long slab-sides up stairs, for all the world just like
a half-scared woman, afraid to look honest men in the face, is a
Northerner, and as mean as dish-water."

"Now what will you bet of that," said Wilkes.

The speaker said, "I make no bets with you, 'kase you can get
that fellow up stairs there to say anything."

"Well," said Wilkes, "I am willing to bet any man in the company that *that* gentleman is a *nigger*-buyer. He did'nt tell me so
right down, but I reckon I knows enough about men to give a
pretty clean guess as to what they are arter."

The dispute as to *who* Mr. Listwell was, what his business,
where he was going, etc., was kept up with much animation for

some time, and more than once threatened a serious disturbance of the peace. Wilkes had his friends as well as his oppo-
nents. After this sharp debate, the company amused themselves
by drinking whiskey, and telling stories. The latter consisting of
quarrels, fights, *rencontres,* and duels, in which distinguished
persons of that neighborhood, and frequenters of that house,
had been actors. Some of these stories were frightful enough,
and were told, too, with a relish which bespoke the pleasure of
the parties with the horrid scenes they portrayed. It would not
be proper here to give the reader any idea of the vulgarity and
dark profanity which rolled, as "a sweet morsel," under these
corrupt tongues. A more brutal set of creatures, perhaps, never
congregated.

Disgusted, and a little alarmed withal, Mr. Listwell, who was
not accustomed to such entertainment, at length retired, but not
to sleep. He was *too* much wrought upon by what he had heard
to rest quietly, and what snatches of sleep he got, were interrupted by dreams which were anything than pleasant. At eleven
o'clock, there seemed to be several hundreds of persons crowding into the house. A loud and confused clamour, cursing and
cracking of whips, and the noise of chains startled him from his
bed; for a moment he would have given the half of his farm in
Ohio to have been at home. This uproar was kept up with undu-
lating course, till near morning. There was loud laughing,—loud
singing,—loud cursing,—and yet there seemed to be weeping
and mourning in the midst of all. Mr. Listwell said he had heard
enough during the forepart of the night to convince him that a
buyer of men and women stood the best chance of being respected. And he, therefore, thought it best to say nothing which
might undo the favorable opinion that had been formed of him
in the bar-room by at least one of the fraternity that swarmed
about it. While he would not avow himself a purchaser of slaves,
he deemed it not prudent to disavow it. He felt that he might,
properly, refuse to cast such a pearl before parties which, to
him, were worse than swine. To reveal himself, and to impart a
knowledge of his real character and sentiments would, to say the
least, be imparting intelligence with the certainty of seeing it
and himself both abused. Mr. Listwell confesses, that this rea-

soning did not altogether satisfy his conscience, for, hating slavery as he did, and regarding it to be the immediate duty of every man to cry out against it, "without compromise and without concealment," it was hard for him to admit to himself the possibility of circumstances wherein a man might, properly, hold his tongue on the subject. Having as little of the spirit of a martyr as Erasmus, he concluded, like the latter, that it was wiser to trust the mercy of God for his soul, than the humanity of slave-traders for his body. Bodily fear, not conscientious scruples, prevailed.

In this spirit he rose early in the morning, manifesting no surprise at what he had heard during the night. His quondam friend was soon at his elbow, boring him with all sorts of questions. All, however, directed to find out his character, business, residence, purposes, and destination. With the most perfect appearance of good nature and carelessness, Mr. Listwell evaded these meddlesome inquiries, and turned conversation to general topics, leaving himself and all that specially pertained to him, out of discussion. Disengaging himself from their troublesome companionship, he made his way towards an old bowling-alley, which was connected with the house, and which, like all the rest, was in very bad repair.

On reaching the alley Mr. Listwell saw, for the first time in his life, a slave-gang on their way to market. A sad sight truly. Here were one hundred and thirty human beings,—children of a common Creator—guilty of no crime—men and women, with hearts, minds, and deathless spirits, chained and fettered, and bound for the market, in a christian country,—in a country boasting of its liberty, independence, and high civilization! Humanity converted into merchandise, and linked in iron bands, with no regard to decency or humanity! All sizes, ages, and sexes, mothers, fathers, daughters, brothers, sisters,—all huddled together, on their way to market to be sold and separated from home, and from each other *forever*. And all to fill the pockets of men too lazy to work for an honest living, and who gain their fortune by plundering the helpless, and trafficking in the souls and sinews of men. As he gazed upon this revolting and heart-rending scene, our informant said he almost doubted the existence of a God of justice! And he stood wondering that the earth did not open and swallow up such wickedness.

In the midst of these reflections, and while running his eye up and down the fettered ranks, he met the glance of one whose face he thought he had seen before. To be resolved, he moved towards the spot. It was MADISON WASHINGTON! Here was a scene for the pencil! Had Mr. Listwell been confronted by one risen from the dead, he could not have been more appalled. He was completely stunned. A thunderbolt could not have struck him more dumb. He stood, for a few moments, as motionless as one petrified; collecting himself, he at length exclaimed, "*Madison! is that you?*"

The noble fugitive, but little less astonished than himself, answered cheerily, "O yes, sir, they've got me again."

Thoughtless of consequences for the moment, Mr. Listwell ran up to his old friend, placing his hands upon his shoulders, and looked him in the face! Speechless they stood gazing at each other as if to be doubly resolved that there was no mistake about the matter, till Madison motioned his friend away, intimating a fear lest the keepers should find him there, and suspect him of tampering with the slaves.

"They will soon be out to look after us. You can come when they go to breakfast, and I will tell you all."

Pleased with this arrangement, Mr. Listwell passed out of the alley; but only just in time to save himself, for, while near the door, he observed three men making their way to the alley. The thought occurred to him to await their arrival, as the best means of diverting the ever ready suspicions of the guilty.

While the scene between Mr. Listwell and his friend Madison was going on, the other slaves stood as mute spectators,—at a loss to know what all this could mean. As he left, he heard the man chained to Madison ask, "Who is that gentleman?"

"He is a friend of mine. I cannot tell you now. Suffice it to say he is a friend. You shall hear more of him before long, but mark me! whatever shall pass between that gentleman and me, in your hearing, I pray you will say nothing about it. We are all chained here together,—ours is a common lot; and that gentleman is not less *your* friend than *mine*." At these words, all mys-

terious as they were, the unhappy company gave signs of satisfaction and hope. It seems that Madison, by that mesmeric
power which is the invariable accompaniment of genius, had
already won the confidence of the gang, and was a sort of
general-in-chief among them.

By this time the keepers arrived. A horrid trio, well fitted for
their demoniacal work. Their uncombed hair came down over
foreheads *"villainously low,"* and with eyes, mouths, and noses
to match. "Hallo! hallo!" they growled out as they entered. "Are
you all there!"

"All here," said Madison.

"Well, well, that's right! your journey will soon be over. You'll
be in Richmond by eleven to-day, and then you'll have an easy
time on it."

"I say, gal, what in the devil are you crying about?" said one
of them. I 'll give you something to cry about, if you don't mind."
This was said to a girl, apparently not more than twelve years
old, who had been weeping bitterly. She had, probably, left behind her a loving mother, affectionate sisters, brothers, and
friends, and her tears were but the natural expression of her
sorrow, and the only solace. But the dealers in human flesh have
no respect for such sorrow. They look upon it as a protest against
their cruel injustice, and they are prompt to punish it.

This is a puzzle not easily solved. *How* came he here? what
can I do for him? may I not even now be in some way compro-
mised in this affair? were thoughts that troubled Mr. Listwell,
and made him eager for the promised opportunity of speaking
to Madison.

The bell now sounded for breakfast, and keepers and drivers,
with pistols and bowie-knives gleaming from their belts, hurried
in, as if to get the best places. Taking the chance now afforded,
Mr. Listwell hastened back to the bowling-alley. Reaching
Madison, he said, "Now *do* tell me all about the matter. Do you
know me?"

"Oh, yes," said Madison, "I know you well, and shall never
forget you nor that cold and dreary night you gave me shelter. I
must be short," he continued, "for they'll soon be out again.
This, then, is the story in brief. On reaching Canada, and getting

over the excitement of making my escape, sir, my thoughts turned to my poor wife, who had well deserved my love by her virtuous fidelity and undying affection for me. I could not bear the thought of leaving her in the cruel jaws of slavery, without making an effort to rescue her. First, I tried to get money to buy her; but oh! the process was *too slow*. I despaired of accomplishing it. She was in all my thoughts by day, and my dreams by night. At times I could almost hear her voice, saying, 'O Madison! Madison! will you then leave me here? can you leave me here to die? No! no! you will come! you will come!' I was wretched. I lost my appetite. I could neither work, eat, nor sleep, till I resolved to hazard my own liberty, to gain that of my wife! But I must be short. Six weeks ago I reached my old master's place. I laid about the neighborhood nearly a week, watching my chance, and, finally, I ventured upon the desperate attempt to reach my poor wife's room by means of a ladder. I reached the window, but the noise in raising it frightened my wife, and she screamed and fainted. I took her in my arms, and was descending the ladder, when the dogs began to bark furiously, and before I could get to the woods the white folks were roused. The cool night air soon restored my wife, and she readily recognized me. We made the best of our way to the woods, but it was now *too* late,—the dogs were after us as though they would have torn us to pieces. It was all over with me now! My old master and his two sons ran out with loaded rifles, and before we were out of gunshot, our ears were assailed with '*Stop! stop! or be shot down.*' Nevertheless we ran on. Seeing that we gave no heed to their calls, they fired, and my poor wife fell by my side dead, while I received but a slight flesh wound. I now became desperate, and stood my ground, and awaited their attack over her dead body. They rushed upon me, with their rifles in hand. I parried their blows, and fought them 'till I was knocked down and overpowered."

"Oh! it was madness to have returned," said Mr. Listwell.

"Sir, I could not be free with the galling thought that my poor wife was still a slave. With her in slavery, my body, not my spirit, was free. I was taken to the house,—chained to a ring-bolt,—my wounds dressed. I was kept there three days. All the slaves, for miles around, were brought to see me. Many slave-holders came with their slaves, using me as proof of the completeness of their power, and of the impossibility of slaves getting away. I was taunted, jeered at, and berated by them, in a manner that pierced me to the soul. Thank God, I was able to smother my rage, and to bear it all with seeming composure. After my wounds were nearly healed, I was taken to a tree and stripped, and I received sixty lashes on my naked back. A few days later, I was sold to a slave-trader, and placed in this gang for the New Orleans market."

"Do you think your master would sell you to me?"

"O no, sir! I was sold on condition of my being taken South. Their motive is revenge."

"Then, then," said Mr. Listwell, "I fear I can do nothing for you. Put your trust in God, and bear your sad lot with the manly fortitude which becomes a man. I shall see you at Richmond, but don't recognize me." Saying this, Mr. Listwell handed Madison ten dollars; said a few words to the other slaves; received their hearty "God bless you," and made his way to the house.

Fearful of exciting suspicion by too long delay, our friend went to the breakfast table, with the air of one who half reproved the greediness of those who rushed in at the sound of the bell. A cup of coffee was all that he could manage. His feelings were too bitter and excited, and his heart was too full with the fate of poor Madison (whom he loved as well as admired) to relish his breakfast; and although he sat long after the company had left the table, he really did little more than change the position of his knife and fork. The strangeness of meeting again one whom he had met on two several occasions before, under extraordinary circumstances, was well calculated to suggest the idea that a supernatural power, a wakeful providence, or an inexorable fate, had linked their destiny together; and that no efforts of his could disentangle him from the mysterious web of circumstances which enfolded him.

On leaving the table, Mr. Listwell nerved himself up and walked firmly into the bar-room. He was at once greeted again by that talkative chatter-box, Mr. Wilkes.

"Them's a likely set of niggers in the alley there," said Wilkes.

"Yes, they're fine looking fellows, one of them I should like to purchase, and for him I would be willing to give a handsome sum."

Turning to one of his comrades, and with a grin of victory, Wilkes said, "Aha, Bill, did you hear that? I told you I know'd that gentleman wanted to buy niggers, and would bid as high as any purchaser in the market."

"Come, come," said Listwell, "don't be too loud in your praise, you are old enough to know that prices rise when purchasers are plenty."

"That's a fact," said Wilkes, "I see you knows the ropes—and there's not a man in old Virginy whom I'd rather help to make a good bargain than you, sir."

Mr. Listwell here threw a dollar at Wilkes, (which the latter caught with a dexterous hand,) saying, "Take that for your kind good will." Wilkes held up the dollar to his right eye, with a grin of victory, and turned to the morose grumbler in the corner who had questioned the liberality of a man of whom he knew nothing.

Mr. Listwell now stood as well with the company as any other occupant of the bar-room.

We pass over the hurry and bustle, the brutal vociferations of the slave-drivers in getting their unhappy gang in motion for Richmond; and we need not narrate every application of the lash to those who faltered in the journey. Mr. Listwell followed the train at a long distance, with a sad heart; and on reaching Richmond, left his horse at a hotel, and made his way to the wharf in the direction of which he saw the slave-coffle driven. He was just in time to see the whole company embark for New Orleans. The thought struck him that, while mixing with the multitude, he might do his friend Madison one last service, and he stept into a hardware store and purchased three strong *files*. These he took with him, and standing near the small boat, which lay in waiting to bear the company by parcels to the side of the brig that lay in the stream, he managed, as Madison passed him, to slip the files into his pocket, and at once darted back among the crowd.

All the company now on board, the imperious voice of the captain sounded, and instantly a dozen hardy seamen were in the rigging, hurrying aloft to unfurl the broad canvas of our Baltimore built American Slaver. The sailors hung about the ropes, like so many black cats, now in the round-tops, now in the cross-trees, now on the yard-arms; all was bluster and activity. Soon the broad fore topsail, the royal and top gallant sail were spread to the breeze. Round went the heavy windlass, clank, clank went the fall-bit,—the anchors weighed,—jibs, mainsails, and topsails hauled to the wind, and the long, low, black slaver, with her cargo of human flesh, careened and moved forward to the sea.

Mr. Listwell stood on the shore, and watched the slaver till the last speck of her upper sails faded from sight, and announced the limit of human vision. "Farewell! farewell! brave and true man! God grant that brighter skies may smile upon your future than have yet looked down upon your thorny pathway."

Saying this to himself, our friend lost no time in completing his business, and in making his way homewards, gladly shaking off from his feet the dust of Old Virginia.

PART IV

Oh, where's the slave so lowly
Condemn'd to chains unholy,
    Who could he burst
    His bonds at first
Would pine beneath them slowly?
                    —*Moore*

—Know ye not
Who would be free, *themselves* must strike the blow.
                    —*Childe Harold*

WHAT A WORLD of inconsistency, as well as of wickedness, is suggested by the smooth and gliding phrase, AMERICAN SLAVE TRADE; and how strange and perverse is that moral sentiment which loathes, execrates, and brands as piracy and as deserving of death the carrying away into captivity men, women, and children from the *African coast*; but which is neither shocked nor disturbed by a similar traffic, carried on with the same motives and purposes, and characterized by even *more* odious peculiarities on the coast of our MODEL REPUBLIC. We execrate and hang the wretch guilty of this crime on the coast of Guinea, while we respect and applaud the guilty participators in this murderous business on enlightened shores of the Chesapeake. The inconsistency is so flagrant and glaring, that it would seem to cast a doubt on the doctrine of the innate moral sense of mankind.

Just two months after the sailing of the Virginia slave brig, which the reader has seen move off to sea so proudly with her human cargo for the New Orleans market, there chanced to

meet, in the Marine Coffee-house at Richmond, a company of
ocean birds, when the following conversation, which throws
some light on the subsequent history, not only of Madison
Washington, but of the hundred and thirty human beings with
whom we last saw him chained.

"I say, shipmate, you had rather rough weather on your late
passage to Orleans?" said Jack Williams, a regular old salt, taunt-
ingly, to a trim, compact, manly looking person, who proved to
be the first mate of the slave brig in question.

"Foul play, as well as foul weather," replied the firmly knit
personage, evidently but little inclined to enter upon a subject
which terminated so ingloriously to the captain and officers of
the American slaver.

"Well, betwixt you and me," said Williams, "that whole affair
on board of the Creole was miserably and disgracefully managed. Those black rascals got the upper hand of ye altogether;
and, in my opinion, the whole disaster was the result of ignorance of the real character of *darkies* in general. With half a
dozen *resolute* white men, (I say it not boastingly,) I could have
had the rascals in irons in ten minutes, not because I'm so
strong, but I know how to manage 'em. With my back against
the *caboose*, I could, myself, have flogged a dozen of them; and
had I been on board, by every monster of the deep, every black
devil of 'em all would have had his neck stretched from the
yard-arm. Ye made a mistake in yer manner of fighting 'em. All
that is needed in dealing with a set of rebellious *darkies*, is to
show that yer not afraid of 'em. For my own part, I would not
honor a dozen niggers by pointing a gun at one on 'em,—a good
stout whip, or a stiff rope's end, is better than all the guns at Old
Point to quell a *nigger* insurrection. Why, sir, to take a gun to a
nigger is the best way you can select to tell him you are afraid of
him, and the best way of inviting his attack."

This speech made quite a sensation among the company, and
a part of them indicated solicitude for the answer which might
be made to it. Our first mate replied, "Mr. Williams, all that
you've now said sounds very well *here* on shore, where, perhaps,
you have studied negro character. I do not profess to understand
the subject as well as yourself; but it strikes me, you apply the

same rule in dissimilar cases. It is quite easy to talk of flogging niggers here on land, where you have the sympathy of the community, and the whole physical force of the government, State and national, at your command; and where, if a negro shall lift his hand against a white man, the whole community, with one accord, are ready to unite in shooting him down. I say, in such circumstances, it's easy to talk of flogging negroes and of negro cowardice; but, sir, I deny that the negro is, naturally, a coward, or that your theory of managing slaves will stand the test of *salt* water. It may do very well for an overseer, a contemptible hireling, to take advantage of fears already in existence, and which his presence has no power to inspire; to swagger about whip in hand, and discourse on the timidity and cowardice of negroes; for they have a smooth sea and a fair wind. It is one thing to manage a company of slaves on a Virginia plantation, and quite another thing to quell an insurrection on the lonely billows of the Atlantic, where every breeze speaks of courage and liberty. For the negro to act cowardly on shore, may be to act wisely; and I've some doubts whether *you*, Mr. Williams, would find it very convenient were you a slave in Algiers, to raise your hand against the bayonets of a whole government."

"By George, shipmate," said Williams, you're coming rather *too* near. Either I've fallen very low in your estimation, or your notions of negro courage have got up a button-hole too high. Now I more than ever wish I'd been on board of that luckless craft. I'd have given ye practical evidence of the truth of my theory. I don't doubt there's some difference in being at sea. But a nigger's a nigger, on sea or land; and is a coward, find him where you will; a drop of blood from one on 'em will skeer a hundred. A knock on the nose, or a kick on the shin, will tame the wildest *'darkey'* you can fetch me. I say again, and will stand by it, I could, with half a dozen good men, put the whole nineteen on 'em in irons, and have carried them safe to New Orleans too. Mind, I don't blame you, but I do say, and every gentleman here will bear me out in it, that the fault was somewhere, or them niggers would never have got off as they have done. For my part I feel ashamed to have the idea go abroad, that a ship load of slaves can't be safely taken from Richmond to New

Orleans. I should like, merely to redeem the character of Virginia sailors, to take charge of a ship load on 'em to-morrow."

Williams went on in this strain, occasionally casting an imploring glance at the company for applause for his wit, and sympathy for his contempt of negro courage. He had, evidently, however, waked up the wrong passenger; for besides being in the right, his opponent carried that in his eye which marked him a man not to be trifled with.

"Well, sir," said the sturdy mate, "you can select your own method for distinguishing yourself;—the path of ambition in this direction is quite open to you in Virginia, and I've no doubt that you will be highly appreciated and compensated for all your valiant achievements in that line; but for myself, while I do not profess to be a giant, I have resolved never to set my foot on the deck of a slave ship, either as officer, or common sailor again; I have got enough of it."

"Indeed! indeed!" exclaimed Williams, derisively.

"Yes, *indeed*," echoed the mate; "but don't misunderstand me. It is not the high value that I set upon my life that makes me say what I have said; yet I'm resolved never to endanger my life again in a cause which my conscience does not approve. I dare say *here* what many men *feel*, but *dare not speak*, that this whole slave-trading business is a disgrace and scandal to Old Virginia."

"Hold! hold on! shipmate," said Williams, "I hardly thought you'd have shown your colors so soon,—I'll be hanged if you're not as good an abolitionist as Garrison himself."

The mate now rose from his chair, manifesting some excitement. "What do you mean, sir," said he, in a commanding tone. *"That man does not live who shall offer me an insult with impunity."*

The effect of these words was marked; and the company clustered around. Williams, in an apologetic tone, said, "Shipmate! keep your temper. I mean't no insult. We all know that Tom Grant is no coward, and what I said about your being an abolitionist was simply this: you *might* have put down them black mutineers and murderers, but your conscience held you back."

"In that, too," said Grant, "you were mistaken. I did all that any man with equal strength and presence of mind could have done. The fact is, Mr. Williams, you underrate the courage as well as the skill of these negroes, and further, you do not seem to have been correctly informed about the case in hand at all."

"All I know about it is," said Williams, "that on the ninth day after you left Richmond, a dozen or two of the niggers ye had on board, came on deck and took the ship from you;—had her steered into a British port, where, by the by, every woolly head of them went ashore and was free. Now I take this to be a discreditable piece of business, and one demanding explanation."

"There are a great many discreditable things in the world," said Grant. "For a ship to go down under a calm sky is, upon the first flush of it, disgraceful either to sailors or caulkers. But when we learn, that by some mysterious disturbance in nature, the waters parted beneath, and swallowed the ship up, we lose our indignation and disgust in lamentation of the disaster, and in awe of the Power which controls the elements."

"Very true, very true," said Williams, "I should be very glad to have an explanation which would relieve the affair of its present discreditable features. I have desired to see you ever since you got home, and to learn from you a full statement of the facts in the case. To me the whole thing seems unaccountable. I cannot see how a dozen or two of ignorant negroes, not one of whom had ever been to sea before, and all of them were closely ironed between decks, should be able to get their fetters off, rush out of the hatchway in open daylight, kill two white men, the one the captain and the other their master, and then carry the ship into a British port, where every 'darkey' of them was set free. There must have been great carelessness, or cowardice somewhere!"

The company which had listened in silence during most of this discussion, now became much excited. One said, I agree with Williams; and several said the thing looks black enough. After the temporary tumultuous exclamations had subsided,—

"I see," said Grant, "how you regard this case, and how difficult it will be for me to render our ship's company blameless in your eyes. Nevertheless, I will state the fact precisely as they

came under my own observation. Mr. Williams speaks of 'ignorant negroes,' and, as a general rule, they are ignorant; but had
he been on board the *Creole* as I was, he would have seen cause
to admit that there are exceptions to this general rule. The
leader of the mutiny in question was just as shrewd a fellow as
ever I met in my life, and was as well fitted to lead in a dangerous enterprise as any one white man in ten thousand. The name
of this man, strange to say, (ominous of greatness,) was MADISON
WASHINGTON. In the short time he had been on board, he had
secured the confidence of every officer. The negroes fairly wor-
shipped him. His manner and bearing were such, that no one
could suspect him of a murderous purpose. The only feeling
with which we regarded him was, that he was a powerful, good-
disposed negro. He seldom spake to any one, and when he did
speak, it was with the utmost propriety. His words were well
chosen, and his pronunciation equal to that of any schoolmaster.
It was a mystery to us *where* he got his knowledge of language;
but as little was said to him, none of us knew the extent of his
intelligence and ability till it was too late. It seems he brought
three files with him on board, and must have gone to work upon
his fetters the first night out; and he must have worked well at
that; for on the day of the rising, he got the irons *off eighteen*
besides himself.

"The attack began just about twilight in the evening.
Apprehending a squall, I had commanded the second mate to
order all hands on deck, to take in sail. A few minutes before this
I had seen Madison's head above the hatchway, looking out
upon the white-capped waves at the leeward. I think I never saw
him look more good-natured. I stood just about midship, on the
larboard side. The captain was pacing the quarter-deck on the
starboard side, in company with Mr. Jameson, the owner of
most of the slaves on board. Both were armed. I had just told
the men to lay aloft, and was looking to see my orders obeyed,
when I heard the discharge of a pistol on the starboard side; and
turning suddenly around, the very deck seemed covered with
fiends from the pit. The nineteen negroes were all on deck, with
their broken fetters in their hands, rushing in all directions. I
put my hand quickly in my pocket to draw out my jack-knife; but

before I could draw it, I was knocked senseless to the deck. When I came to myself, (which I did in a few minutes, I suppose, for it was yet quite light,) there was not a white man on deck. The sailors were all aloft in the rigging, and dared not come down. Captain Clarke and Mr. Jameson lay stretched on the quarter-deck,—both dying,—while Madison himself stood at the helm unhurt.

"I was completely weakened by the loss of blood, and had not recovered from the stunning blow which felled me to the deck; but it was a little too much for me, even in my prostrate condition, to see our good brig commanded by a *black murderer*. So I called out to the men to come down and take the ship, or die in the attempt. Suiting the action to the word, I started aft. You murderous villain, said I, to the imp at the helm, and rushed upon him to deal him a blow, when he pushed me back with his strong, black arm, as though I had been a boy of twelve. I looked around for the men. They were still in the rigging. Not one had come down. I started towards Madison again. The rascal now told me to stand back. 'Sir,' said he, 'your life is in my hands. I could have killed you a dozen times over during this last half hour, and could kill you now. You call me a *black murderer*. I am not a murderer. God is my witness that LIBERTY, not *malice*, is the motive for this night's work. I have done no more to those dead men yonder, than they would have done to me in like circumstances. We have struck for our freedom, and if a true man's heart be in you, you will honor us for the deed. We have done that which you applaud your fathers for doing, and if we are murderers, *so were they.*'

"I felt little disposition to reply to this impudent speech. By heaven, it disarmed me. The fellow loomed up before me. I forgot his blackness in the dignity of his manner, and the eloquence of his speech. It seemed as if the souls of both the great dead (whose names he bore) had entered him. To the sailors in the rigging he said: 'Men! the battle is over,—your captain is dead. I have complete command of this vessel. All resistance to my authority will be in vain. My men have won their liberty, with no other weapons but their own BROKEN FETTERS. We are nineteen in number. We do not thirst for your blood, we demand only our rightful freedom. Do not flatter yourselves that I am ignorant of chart or compass. I know both. We are now only about sixty miles from Nassau. Come down, and do your duty. Land us in Nassau, and not a hair of your heads shall be hurt.'

"I shouted, *Stay where you are, men,*—when a sturdy black fellow ran at me with a handspike, and would have split my head open, but for the interference of Madison, who darted between me and the blow. 'I know what you are up to,' said the latter to me. 'You want to navigate this brig into a slave port, where you would have us all hanged; but you'll miss it; before this brig shall touch a slave-cursed shore while I am on board, I will myself put a match to the magazine, and blow her, and be blown with her, into a thousand fragments. Now I have saved your life twice within these last twenty minutes,—for, when you lay helpless on deck, my men were about to kill you. I held them in check. And if you now (seeing I am your friend and not your enemy) persist in your resistance to my authority, I give you fair warning, YOU SHALL DIE.'

"Saying this to me, he cast a glance into the rigging where the terror-stricken sailors were clinging, like so many frightened monkeys, and commanded them to come down, in a tone from which there was no appeal; for four men stood by with muskets in hand, ready at the word of command to shoot them down.

"I now became satisfied that resistance was out of the question; that my best policy was to put the brig into Nassau, and secure the assistance of the American consul at that port. I felt sure that the authorities would enable us to secure the murderers, and bring them to trial.

"By this time the apprehended squall had burst upon us. The wind howled furiously,—the ocean was white with foam, which, on account of the darkness, we could see only by the quick flashes of lightning that darted occasionally from the angry sky. All was alarm and confusion. Hideous cries came up from the slave women. Above the roaring billows a succession of heavy thunder rolled along, swelling the terrific din. Owing to the great darkness, and a sudden shift of the wind, we found ourselves in the trough of the sea. When shipping a heavy sea over the starboard bow, the bodies of the captain and Mr. Jameson were washed overboard. For awhile we had dearer interests to look after than slave property. A more savage thunder-gust never swept the ocean. Our brig rolled and creaked as if every bolt would be started, and every thread of oakum would be pressed out of the seams. To the pumps! to the pumps! I cried, but not a sailor would quit his grasp. Fortunately this squall soon passed over, or we must have been food for sharks.

"During all the storm, Madison stood firmly at the helm,—his keen eye fixed upon the binnacle. He was not indifferent to the dreadful hurricane; yet he met it with the equanimity of an old sailor. He was silent but not agitated. The first words he uttered after the storm had slightly subsided, were characteristic of the man. 'Mr. mate, you cannot write the bloody laws of slavery on those restless billows. The ocean, if not the land, is free.' I confess, gentlemen, I felt myself in the presence of a superior man; one who, had he been a white man, I would have followed willingly and gladly in any honorable enterprise. Our difference of color was the only ground for difference of action. It was not that his principles were wrong in the abstract; for they are the principles of 1776. But I could not bring myself to recognize their application to one whom I deemed my inferior.

"But to my story. What happened now is soon told. Two hours after the frightful tempest had spent itself, we were plump at the wharf in Nassau. I sent two of our men immediately to our consul with a statement of facts, requesting his interference in our behalf. What he did, or whither he did anything, I don't know; but, by order of the authorities, a company of *black* soldiers came on board, for the purpose, as they said, of protecting the property. These impudent rascals, when I called on them to assist me in keeping the slaves on board, sheltered themselves adroitly under their instructions only to protect property,—and said they did not recognize *persons as property*. I told them that by the laws of Virginia and the laws of the United States, the slaves on board were as much property as the barrels of flour in the hold. At this the stupid blockheads showed their *ivory*, rolled up their white eyes in horror, as if the idea of putting men on a footing with merchandise were revolting to their humanity.

When these instructions were understood among the negroes, it was impossible for us to keep them on board. They deliberately gathered up their baggage before our eyes, and, against our remonstrances, poured through the gangway,—formed themselves into a procession on the wharf,—bid farewell to all on board, and, uttering the wildest shouts of exultation, they marched, amidst the deafening cheers of a multitude of sympathizing spectators, under the triumphant leadership of their heroic chief and deliverer, MADISON WASHINGTON."

Clotel,

or,

The President's Daughter

WILLIAM WELLS BROWN

Contents

Contents

I. The Negro Sale

"Why stands she near the auction stand,
  That girl so young and fair?
What brings her to this dismal place,
  Why stands she weeping there?"

WITH THE growing population of slaves in the Southern States of America, there is a fearful increase of half whites, most of whose fathers are slaveowners, and their mothers slaves. Society does not frown upon the man who sits with his mulatto child upon his knee, whilst its mother stands a slave behind his chair. The late Henry Clay, some years since, predicted that the abolition of negro slavery would be brought about by the amalgamation of the races. John Randolph, a distinguished slaveholder of Virginia, and a prominent statesman, said in a speech in the legislature of his native state, that "the blood of the first American statesmen coursed through the veins of the slave of the South." In all the cities and towns of the slave states, the real negro, or clear black, does not amount to more than one in every four of the slave population. This fact is, of itself, the best evidence of the degraded and immoral condition of the relation of master and slave in the United States of America.

In all the slave states, the law says:—"Slaves shall be deemed, sold, taken, reputed, and adjudged in law to be chattels personal in the hands of their owners and possessors, and their executors, administrators and assigns, to all intents, constructions, and purposes whatsoever. A slave is one who is in the power of a master to whom he belongs. The master may sell him, dispose of his person, his industry, and his labour. He can do nothing, possess

51

nothing, nor acquire anything, but what must belong to his master. The slave is entirely subject to the will of his master, who may correct and chastise him, though not with unusual rigour, or so as to maim and mutilate him, or expose him to the danger of loss of life, or to cause his death. The slave, to remain a slave, must be sensible that there is no appeal from his master." Where the slave is placed by law entirely under the control of the man who claims him, body and soul, as property, what else could be expected than the most depraved social condition? The marriage relation, the oldest and most sacred institution given to man by his Creator, is unknown and unrecognised in the slave laws of the United States. Would that we could say, that the moral and religious teaching in the slave states were better than the laws; but, alas! we cannot. A few years since, some slaveholders became a little uneasy in their minds about the rightfulness of permitting slaves to take to themselves husbands and wives, while they still had others living, and applied to their religious teachers for advice; and the following will show how this grave and important subject was treated:—

"Is a servant, whose husband or wife has been sold by his or her master into a distant country, to be permitted to marry again?"

The query was referred to a committee, who made the following report; which, after discussion, was adopted:—

"That, in view of the circumstances in which servants in this country are placed, the committee are unanimous in the opinion, that it is better to permit servants thus circumstanced to take another husband or wife."

Such was the answer from a committee of the "Shiloh Baptist Association"; and instead of receiving light, those who asked the question were plunged into deeper darkness!

A similar question was put to the "Savannah River Association," and the answer, as the following will show, did not materially differ from the one we have already given:—

"Whether, in a case of involuntary separation, of such a character as to preclude all prospect of future intercourse, the parties ought to be allowed to marry again."

Answer—

"That such separation among persons situated as our slaves are, is civilly a separation by death; and they believe that, in the sight of God, it would be so viewed. To forbid second marriages in such cases would be to expose the parties, not only to stronger hardships and strong temptation, but to church-censure for acting in obedience to their masters, who cannot be expected to acquiesce in a regulation at variance with justice to the slaves, and to the spirit of that command which regulates marriage among Christians. The slaves are not free agents; and a dissolution by death is not more entirely without their consent, and beyond their control, than by such separation."

Although marriage, as the above indicates, is a matter which the slaveholders do not think is of any importance, or of any binding force with their slaves; yet it would be doing that degraded class an injustice, not to acknowledge that many of them do regard it as a sacred obligation, and show a willingness to obey the commands of God on this subject. Marriage is, indeed, the first and most important institution of human existence—the foundation of all civilisation and culture—the root of church and state. It is the most intimate covenant of heart formed among mankind; and for many persons the only relation in which they feel the true sentiments of humanity. It gives scope for every human virtue, since each of these is developed from the love and confidence which here predominate. It unites all which ennobles and beautifies life,—sympathy, kindness of will and deed, gratitude, devotion, and every delicate, intimate feeling. As the only asylum for true education, it is the first and last sanctuary of human culture. As husband and wife through each other become conscious of complete humanity, and every human feeling, and every human virtue; so children, at their first awakening in the fond covenant of love between parents, both of whom are tenderly concerned for the same object, find an image of complete humanity leagued in free love. The spirit of love which prevails between them acts with creative power upon the young mind, and awakens every germ of goodness within it. This invisible and incalculable influence of parental life acts more upon the child than all the efforts of education, whether by means of instruction, precept, or exhortation. If this be a true picture of the vast influence for good of the institution of marriage, what must be the moral degradation of that people to whom marriage is denied? Not content with depriving them of all the higher and holier enjoyments of this relation, by degrading and darkening their souls, the slaveholder denies to his victim even that slight alleviation of his misery, which would result from the marriage relation being protected by law and public opinion. Such is the influence of slavery in the United States, that the ministers of religion, even in the so-called free states, are the mere echoes, instead of the correctors, of public sentiment.

We have thought it advisable to show that the present system of chattel slavery in America undermines the entire social condition of man, so as to prepare the reader for the following narrative of slave life, in that otherwise happy and prosperous country.

In all the large towns in the Southern States, there is a class of slaves who are permitted to hire their time of their owners, and for which they pay a high price. These are mulatto women, or quadroons, as they are familiarly known, and are distinguished for their fascinating beauty. The handsomest usually pays the highest price for her time. Many of these women are the favourites of persons who furnish them with the means of paying their owners, and not a few are dressed in the most extravagant manner. Reader, when you take into consideration the fact, that amongst the slave population no safeguard is thrown around virtue, and no inducement held out to slave women to be chaste, you will not be surprised when we tell you that immorality and vice pervade the cities of the Southern States in a manner unknown in the cities and towns of the Northern States. Indeed most of the slave women have no higher aspiration than that of becoming the finely-dressed mistress of some white man. And at negro balls and parties, this class of women usually cut the greatest figure.

At the close of the year—the following advertisement appeared in a newspaper published in Richmond, the capital of the state of Virginia:—"Notice: Thirty-eight negroes will be offered for sale on Monday, November 10th, at twelve o'clock, being the entire stock of the late John Graves, Esq. The negroes are in good condition, some of them very prime; among them are several mechanics, able-bodied field hands, plough-boys, and women with children at the breast, and some of them very prolific in their generating qualities, affording a rare opportunity to any one who wishes to raise a strong and healthy lot of servants for their own use. Also several mulatto girls of rare personal qualities: two of them very superior. Any gentleman or lady wishing to purchase, can take any of the above slaves on trial for a week, for which no charge will be made." Amongst the above slaves to be sold were Currer and her two daughters, Clotel and Althesa; the latter were the girls spoken of in the advertisement as "very superior." Currer was a bright mulatto, and of prepossessing appearance, though then nearly forty years of age. She had hired her time for more than twenty years, during which time she had lived in Richmond. In her younger days Currer had been the housekeeper of a young slaveholder; but of later years had been a laundress or washerwoman, and was considered to be a woman of great taste in getting up linen. The gentleman for whom she had kept house was Thomas Jefferson, by whom she had two daughters. Jefferson being called to Washington to fill a government appointment, Currer was left behind, and thus she took herself to the business of washing, by which means she paid her master, Mr. Graves, and supported herself and two children. At the time of the decease of her master, Currer's daughters, Clotel and Althesa, were aged respectively sixteen and fourteen years, and both, like most of their own sex in America, were well grown. Currer early resolved to bring her daughters up as ladies, as she termed it, and therefore imposed little or no work upon them. As her daughters grew older, Currer had to pay a stipulated price for them; yet her notoriety as a laundress of the first class enabled her to put an extra price upon her charges, and thus she and her daughters lived in comparative luxury. To bring up Clotel and Althesa to attract attention, and especially at balls and parties, was the great aim of Currer. Although the term "negro ball" is applied to most of these gatherings, yet a majority of the attendants are often whites. Nearly all the negro parties in the cities and towns of the Southern States are made up of quadroon and mulatto girls, and white men. These are democratic gatherings, where gentlemen, shopkeepers, and their clerks, all appear upon terms of perfect equality. And there is a degree of gentility and decorum in these companies that is not surpassed by similar gatherings of white people in the Slave States. It was at one of these parties that Horatio Green, the son of a wealthy gentleman of Richmond, was first introduced to Clotel. The young man had just returned from college, and was in his twenty-second year. Clotel was sixteen, and was admitted by all to be the most beautiful girl, coloured or white, in the city. So attentive was the young man to the quadroon during the evening that it was noticed by all, and became a matter of general conversation; while Currer appeared delighted beyond measure at her daughter's conquest. From that evening, young Green became the favourite visitor at Currer's house. He soon promised to purchase Clotel, as speedily as it could be effected, and make her mistress of her own dwelling; and Currer looked forward with pride to the time when she should see her daughter emancipated and free. It was a beautiful moonlight night in August, when all who reside in tropical climes are eagerly gasping for a breath of fresh air, that Horatio Green was seated in the small garden behind Currer's cottage, with the object of his affections by his side. And it was here that Horatio drew from his pocket the newspaper, wet from the press, and read the advertisement for the sale of the slaves to which we have alluded; Currer and her two daughters being of the number. At the close of the evening's visit, and as the young man was leaving, he said to the girl, "You shall soon be free and your own mistress."

As might have been expected, the day of sale brought an unusual large number together to compete for the property to be sold. Farmers who make a business of raising slaves for the market were there; slave-traders and speculators were also numerously represented; and in the midst of this throng was one who felt a deeper interest in the result of the sale than any other of the bystanders; this was young Green. True to his promise, he was there with a blank bank check in his pocket, awaiting with impatience to enter the list as a bidder for the beautiful slave. The less valuable slaves were first placed upon the auction block, one after another, and sold to the highest bidder. Husbands and wives were separated with a degree of indifference that is unknown in any other relation of life, except that of slavery. Brothers and sisters were torn from each other; and mothers saw their children leave them for the last time on this earth.

It was late in the day, when the greatest number of persons were thought to be present, that Currer and her daughters were brought forward to the place of sale. Currer was first ordered to ascend the auction stand, which she did with a trembling step. The slave mother was sold to a trader. Althesa, the youngest, and who was scarcely less beautiful than her sister, was sold to the same trader for one thousand dollars. Clotel was the last, and, as was expected, commanded a higher price than any that had been offered for sale that day. The appearance of Clotel on the auction block created a deep sensation amongst the crowd. There she stood, with a complexion as white as most of those who were waiting with a wish to become her purchasers; her features as finely defined as any of her sex of pure Anglo-Saxon; her long black wavy hair done up in the neatest manner; her form tall and graceful, and her whole appearance indicating one superior to her position. The auctioneer commenced by saying, that "Miss Clotel had been reserved for the last, because she was the most valuable. How much gentlemen? Real Albino, fit for a fancy girl for any one. She enjoys good health, and has a sweet temper. How much do you say?" "Five hundred dollars." "Only five hundred for such a girl as this? Gentlemen, she is worth a deal more than that sum; you certainly don't know the value of the article you are bidding upon. Here, gentlemen, I hold in my hand a paper certifying that she has a good moral character." "Seven hundred." "Ah, gentlemen, that is something like. This paper also states that she is very intelligent." "Eight hundred." "She is a devoted Christian, and perfectly trust-worthy." "Nine hundred." "Nine fifty." "Ten." "Eleven." "Twelve hundred." Here the sale came to a dead stand. The auctioneer stopped, looked around, and began in a rough manner to relate some anecdotes relative to the sale of slaves, which, he said, had come under his own observation. At this juncture the scene was indeed strange. Laughing, joking, swearing, smoking, spitting, and talking kept up a continual hum and noise amongst the crowd; while the slave-girl stood with tears in her eyes, at one time looking towards her mother and sister, and at another towards the young man whom she hoped would become her purchaser. "The chastity of this girl is pure; she has never been from under her mother's care; she is a virtuous creature." "Thirteen." "Fourteen." "Fifteen." "Fifteen hundred dollars," cried the auctioneer, and the maiden was struck for that sum. This was a Southern auction, at which the bones, muscles, sinews, blood, and nerves of a young lady of sixteen were sold for five hundred dollars; her moral character for two hundred; her improved intellect for one hundred; her Christianity for three hundred; and her chastity and virtue for four hundred dollars more. And this, too, in a city thronged with churches, whose tall spires look like so many signals pointing to heaven, and whose ministers preach that slavery is a God-ordained institution!

What words can tell the inhumanity, the atrocity, and the immorality of that doctrine which, from exalted office, commends such a crime to the favour of enlightened and Christian people? What indignation from all the world is not due to the government and people who put forth all their strength and power to keep in existence such an institution? Nature abhors it; the age repels it; and Christianity needs all her meekness to forgive it.

Clotel was sold for fifteen hundred dollars, but her purchaser was Horatio Green. Thus closed a negro sale, at which two daughters of Thomas Jefferson, the writer of the Declaration of American Independence, and one of the presidents of the great republic, were disposed of to the highest bidder!

> "O God! my every heart-string cries,
>   Dost thou these scenes behold
> In this our boasted Christian land,
>   And must the truth be told?
>
> "Blush, Christian, blush! for e'en the dark,
>   Untutored heathen see
> Thy inconsistency; and, lo!
>   They scorn thy God, and thee!"

II. Going to the South

"My country, shall thy honoured name,
 Be as a bye-word through the world?
 Rouse! for, as if to blast thy fame,
 This keen reproach is at thee hurled;
 The banner that above thee waves,
 Is floating o'er three million slaves."

DICK WALKER, the slave speculator, who had purchased Currer
and Althesa, put them in prison until his gang was made up, and
then, with his forty slaves, started for the New Orleans market.
As many of the slaves had been brought up in Richmond, and
had relations residing there, the slave trader determined to
leave the city early in the morning, so as not to witness any of
those scenes so common where slaves are separated from their
relatives and friends, when about departing for the Southern
market. This plan was successful; for not even Clotel, who had
been every day at the prison to see her mother and sister, knew
of their departure. A march of eight days through the interior of
the state, and they arrived on the banks of the Ohio river, where
they were all put on board a steamer, and then speedily sailed
for the place of their destination.

Walker had already advertised in the New Orleans papers,
that he would be there at a stated time with "a prime lot of able-
bodied slaves ready for field service; together with a few extra
ones, between the ages of fifteen and twenty-five." But, like
most who make a business of buying and selling slaves for gain,
he often bought some who were far advanced in years, and
would always try to sell them for five or ten years younger
than they actually were. Few persons can arrive at anything like
the age of a negro, by mere observation, unless they are well

acquainted with the race. Therefore the slave-trader very frequently carried out this deception with perfect impunity. After
the steamer had left the wharf, and was fairly on the bosom of
the Father of Waters, Walker called his servant Pompey to him,
and instructed him as to "getting the negroes ready for market."
Amongst the forty negroes were several whose appearance indicated that they had seen some years, and had gone through
some services. Their grey hair and whiskers at once pronounced
them to be above the ages set down in the trader's advertisement. Pompey had long been with the trader, and knew his
business; and if he did not take delight in discharging his duty,
he did it with a degree of alacrity, so that he might receive the
approbation of his master. "Pomp," as Walker usually called
him, was of real negro blood, and would often say, when alluding to himself, "Dis nigger is no countefit; he is de genewine
artekil." Pompey was of low stature, round face, and, like most
of his race, had a set of teeth, which for whiteness and beauty
could not be surpassed; his eyes large, lips thick, and hair short
and woolly. Pompey had been with Walker so long, and had
seen so much of the buying and selling of slaves, that he appeared perfectly indifferent to the heartrending scenes which
daily occurred in his presence. It was on the second day of the
steamer's voyage that Pompey selected five of the old slaves,
took them in a room by themselves, and commenced preparing
them for the market. "Well," said Pompey, addressing himself
to the company, "I is de gentman dat is to get you ready, so dat
you will bring marser a good price in de Orleans market. How
old is you?" addressing himself to a man who, from appearance,
was not less than forty. "If I live to see next corn-planting time
I will either be forty-five or fifty-five, I don't know which." "Dat
may be," replied Pompey; "But now you is only thirty years old;
dat is what marser says you is to be." "I know I is more den dat,"
responded the man. "I knows nothing about dat," said Pompey;
"but when you get in de market, an anybody axe you how old
you is, an you tell 'em forty-five, marser will tie you up an gib
you de whip like smoke. But if you tell 'em dat you is only thirty,
den he wont." "Well den, I guess I will only be thirty when dey
axe me," replied the chattel.

"What your name?" inquired Pompey. "Geemes," answered the man. "Oh, Uncle Jim, is it?" "Yes." "Den you must have off dem dare whiskers of yours, an when you get to Orleans you must grease dat face an make it look shiney." This was all said by Pompey in a manner which clearly showed that he knew what he was about. "How old is you?" asked Pompey of a tall, strong-looking man. "I was twenty-nine last potato-digging time," said the man. "What's your name?" "My name is Tobias, but dey call me 'Toby.'" "Well, Toby, or Mr. Tobias, if dat will suit you better, you is now twenty-three years old, an no more. Dus you hear dat?" "Yes," responded Toby. Pompey gave each to understand how old he was to be when asked by persons who wished to purchase, and then reported to his master that the "old boys" were all right. At eight o'clock on the evening of the third day, the lights of another steamer were seen in the distance, and apparently coming up very fast. This was a signal for a general commotion on the Patriot, and everything indicated that a steamboat race was at hand. Nothing can exceed the excitement attendant upon a steamboat race on the Mississippi river. By the time the boats had reached Memphis, they were side by side, and each exerting itself to keep the ascendancy in point of speed. The night was clear, the moon shining brightly, and the boats so near to each other that the passengers were calling out from one boat to the other. On board the Patriot, the firemen were using oil, lard, butter, and even bacon, with the wood, for the purpose of raising the steam to its highest pitch. The blaze, mingled with the black smoke, showed plainly that the other boat was burning more than wood. The two boats soon locked, so that the hands of the boats were passing from vessel to vessel, and the wildest excitement prevailed throughout amongst both passengers and crew. At this moment the engineer of the Patriot was seen to fasten down the safety-valve, so that no steam should escape. This was, indeed, a dangerous resort. A few of the boat hands who saw what had taken place, left that end of the boat for more secure quarters.

The Patriot stopped to take in passengers, and still no steam was permitted to escape. At the starting of the boat cold water was forced into the boilers by the machinery, and, as might have been expected, one of the boilers immediately exploded. One dense fog of steam filled every part of the vessel, while shrieks, groans, and cries were heard on every hand. The saloons and cabins soon had the appearance of a hospital. By this time the boat had landed, and the Columbia, the other boat, had come alongside to render assistance to the disabled steamer. The killed and scalded (nineteen in number) were put on shore, and the Patriot, taken in tow by the Columbia, was soon again on its way.

It was now twelve o'clock at night, and instead of the passengers being asleep the majority were gambling in the saloons. Thousands of dollars change hands during a passage from Louisville or St. Louis to New Orleans on a Mississippi steamer, and many men, and even ladies, are completely ruined. "Go call my boy, steward," said Mr. Smith, as he took his cards one by one from the table. In a few moments a fine looking, bright-eyed mulatto boy, apparently about fifteen years of age, was standing by his master's side at the table. "I will see you, and five hundred dollars better," said Smith, as his servant Jerry approached the table. "What price do you set on that boy?" asked Johnson, as he took a roll of bills from his pocket. "He will bring a thousand dollars, any day, in the New Orleans market," replied Smith. "Then you bet the whole of the boy, do you?" "Yes." "I call you, then," said Johnson, at the same time spreading his cards out upon the table. "You have beat me," said Smith, as soon as he saw the cards. Jerry, who was standing on top of the table, with the bank notes and silver dollars round his feet, was now ordered to descend from the table. "You will not forget that you belong to me," said Johnson, as the young slave was stepping from the table to a chair. "No, sir," replied the chattel. "Now go back to your bed, and be up in time to-morrow morning to brush my clothes and clean my boots, do you hear?" "Yes, sir," responded Jerry, as he wiped the tears from his eyes.

Smith took from his pocket the bill of sale and handed it to Johnson; at the same time saying, "I claim the right of redeeming that boy, Mr. Johnson. My father gave him to me when I came of age, and I promised not to part with him." "Most certainly, sir, the boy shall be yours, whenever you hand me over a cool thousand," replied Johnson. The next morning, as the passengers

were assembling in the breakfast saloons and upon the guards of
the vessel, and the servants were seen running about waiting
upon or looking for their masters, poor Jerry was entering his
new master's state-room with his boots. "Who do you belong to?"
said a gentleman to an old black man, who came along leading a
fine dog that he had been feeding. "When I went to sleep last
night, I belonged to Governor Lucas; but I understand dat he is
bin gambling all night, so I don't know who owns me dis morning." Such is the uncertainty of a slave's position. He goes to bed
at night the property of the man with whom he has lived for
years, and gets up in the morning the slave of some one whom
he has never seen before! To behold five or six tables in a steamboat's cabin, with half-a-dozen men playing at cards, and money,
pistols, bowie-knives, &c. all in confusion on the tables, is what
may be seen at almost any time on the Mississippi river.

On the fourth day, while at Natchez, taking in freight and passengers, Walker, who had been on shore to see some of his old
customers, returned, accompanied by a tall, thin-faced man,
dressed in black, with a white neckcloth, which immediately
proclaimed him to be a clergyman. "I want a good, trusty woman
for house service," said the stranger, as they entered the cabin
where Walker's slaves were kept. "Here she is, and no mistake,"
replied the trader. "Stand up, Currer, my gal; here's a gentleman
who wishes to see if you will suit him." Althesa clung to her
mother's side, as the latter rose from her seat. "She is a rare cook,
a good washer, and will suit you to a T, I am sure." "If you buy
me, I hope you will buy my daughter too," said the woman, in
rather an excited manner. "I only want one for my own use, and
would not need another," said the man in black, as he and the
trader left the room. Walker and the parson went into the saloon,
talked over the matter, the bill of sale was made out, the money
paid over, and the clergyman left, with the understanding that
the woman should be delivered to him at his house. It seemed as
if poor Althesa would have wept herself to death, for the first two
days after her mother had been torn from her side by the hand
of the ruthless trafficker in human flesh. On the arrival of the
boat at Baton Rouge, an additional number of passengers were
taken on board; and, amongst them, several persons who had

been attending the races. Gambling and drinking were now the order of the day. Just as the ladies and gentlemen were assembling at the supper-table, the report of a pistol was heard in the direction of the Social Hall, which caused great uneasiness to the ladies, and took the gentlemen to that part of the cabin. However, nothing serious had occurred. A man at one of the tables where they were gambling had been seen attempting to conceal a card in his sleeve, and one of the party seized his pistol and fired; but fortunately the barrel of the pistol was knocked up, just as it was about to be discharged, and the ball passed through the upper deck, instead of the man's head, as intended. Order was soon restored; all went on well the remainder of the night, and the next day, at ten o'clock, the boat arrived at New Orleans, and the passengers went to the hotels and the slaves to the market!

> "Our eyes are yet on Afric's shores,
>   Her thousand wrongs we still deplore;
>   We see the grim slave trader there;
>   We hear his fettered victim's prayer;
>   And hasten to the sufferer's aid,
>   Forgetful of *our own 'slave trade.'*

> "The Ocean 'Pirate's' fiend-like form
>   Shall sink beneath the vengeance-storm;
>   His heart of steel shall quake before
>   The battle-din and havoc roar:
>   *The knave shall die,* the Law hath said,
>   While it protects our own *'slave trade.'*

> "What earthly eye presumes to scan
>   The wily Proteus-heart of man?—
>   What potent hand will e'er unroll
>   The mantled treachery of his soul!—
>   O where is he who hath surveyed
>   The horrors of *our own 'slave trade?'*

> "There is an eye that wakes in light,
>   There is a hand of peerless might;
>   Which, soon or late, shall yet assail
>   And rend dissimulation's veil:
>   Which *will* unfold the masquerade
>   Which justifies *our own 'slave trade.'"*

III. The Negro Chase

WE SHALL now return to Natchez, where we left Currer in the hands of the Methodist parson. For many years, Natchez has enjoyed a notoriety for the inhumanity and barbarity of its inhabitants, and the cruel deeds perpetrated there, which have not been equalled in any other city in the Southern States. The following advertisements, which we take from a newspaper published in the vicinity, will show how they catch their negroes who believe in the doctrine that "all men are created free."

"NEGRO DOGS.—The undersigned, having bought the entire pack of negro dogs (of the Hay and Allen stock), *he now proposes to catch runaway negroes.* His charges will be three dollars a day for hunting, and fifteen dollars for catching a runaway. He resides three and one half miles north of Livingston, near the lower Jones' Bluff Road.

"WILLIAM GAMBREL."

"Nov. 6, 1845."

"NOTICE.—The subscriber, living on Carroway Lake, on Hoe's Bayou, in Carroll parish, sixteen miles on the road leading from Bayou Mason to Lake Providence, is ready with a pack of dogs to hunt runaway negroes at any time. These dogs are well trained, and are known throughout the parish. Letters addressed to me at Providence will secure immediate attention. My terms are five dollars per day for hunting the trails, whether the negro is caught or not. Where a twelve hours' trail is shown, and the negro not taken, no charge is made. For taking a negro, twenty-five dollars, and no charge made for hunting.

"JAMES W. HALL."

"Nov. 26, 1847."

These dogs will attack a negro at their master's bidding and cling to him as the bull-dog will cling to a beast. Many are the speculations, as to whether the negro will be secured alive or dead, when these dogs once get on his track. A slave hunt took place near Natchez, a few days after Currer's arrival, which was calculated to give her no favourable opinion of the people. Two slaves had run off owing to severe punishment. The dogs were put upon their trail. The slaves went into the swamps, with the hope that the dogs when put on their scent would be unable to follow them through the water. The dogs soon took to the swamp, which lies between the highlands, which was now covered with water, waist deep: here these faithful animals, *swimming* nearly all the time, followed the zigzag course, the tortuous twistings and windings of these two fugitives, who, it was afterwards discovered, were lost; sometimes scenting the tree wherein they had found a temporary refuge from the mud and water; at other places where the deep mud had pulled off a shoe, and they had not taken time to put it on again. For two hours and a half, for four or five miles, did men and dogs wade through this bushy, dismal swamp, surrounded with grim-visaged alligators, who seemed to look on with jealous eye at this encroachment of their hereditary domain; now losing the trail—then slowly and dubiously taking it off again, until they triumphantly threaded it out, bringing them back to the river, where it was found that the negroes had crossed their own trail, near the place of starting. In the meantime a heavy shower had taken place, putting out the trail. The negroes were now at least four miles ahead.

It is well known to hunters that it requires the keenest scent and best blood to overcome such obstacles, and yet these persevering and sagacious animals conquered every difficulty. The slaves now made a straight course for the Baton Rouge and Bayou Sara road, about four miles distant.

Feeling hungry now, after their morning walk, and perhaps thirsty, too, they went about half a mile off the road, and ate a good, hearty, substantial breakfast. Negroes must eat, as well as other people, but the dogs will tell on them. Here, for a moment, the dogs are at fault, but soon unravel the mystery, and bring them back to the road again; and now what before was wonderful, becomes almost a miracle. Here, in this common highway—the thoroughfare for the whole country around—through mud and through mire, meeting waggons and teams, and different solitary wayfarers, and, what above all is most astonishing, actually running through a gang of negroes, their favourite game, who were working on the road, they pursue the track of the two negroes; they even ran for eight miles to the very edge of the plain—the slaves near them for the last mile. At first they would fain believe it some hunter chasing deer. Nearer and nearer the whimpering pack presses on; the delusion begins to dispel; all at once the truth flashes upon them like a glare of light; their hair stands on end; 'tis Tabor with his dogs. The scent becomes warmer and warmer. What was an irregular cry, now deepens into one ceaseless roar, as the relentless pack rolls on after its human prey. It puts one in mind of Actæon and his dogs. They grow desperate and leave the road, in the vain hope of shaking them off. Vain hope, indeed! The momentary cessation only adds new zest to the chase. The cry grows louder and louder; the yelp grows short and quick, sure indication that the game is at hand. It is a perfect rush upon the part of the hunters, while the negroes call upon their weary and jaded limbs to do their best, but they falter and stagger beneath them. The breath of the hounds is almost upon their very heels, and yet they have a vain hope of escaping these sagacious animals. They can run no longer; the dogs are upon them; they hastily attempt to climb a tree, and as the last one is nearly out of reach, the catch-dog seizes him by the leg, and brings him to the ground; he sings out lustily and the dogs are called off. After this man was secured, the one in the tree was ordered to come down; this, however, he refused to do, but a gun being pointed at him, soon caused him to change his mind. On reaching the ground, the fugitive made one more bound, and the chase again commenced. But it was of no use to run and he soon yielded. While being tied, he committed an unpardonable offence: he resisted, and for that he must be made an example on their arrival home. A mob was collected together, and a Lynch court was held, to determine what was best to be done with the negro who had had the impudence to raise his hand against a white man. The Lynch court decided that the negro should be burnt at the stake. A Natchez newspaper, the *Free Trader,* giving an account of it says,

"The body was taken and chained to a tree immediately on the banks of the Mississippi, on what is called Union Point. Faggots were then collected and piled around him, to which he appeared quite indifferent. When the work was completed, he was asked what he had to say. He then warned all to take example by him, and asked the prayers of all around; he then called for a drink of water, which was handed to him; he drank it, and said, 'Now set fire—I am ready to go in peace!' The torches were lighted, and placed in the pile, which soon ignited. He watched unmoved the curling flame that grew, until it began to entwine itself around and feed upon his body; then he sent forth cries of agony painful to the ear, begging some one to blow his brains out; at the same time surging with almost superhuman strength, until the staple with which the chain was fastened to the tree (not being well secured) drew out, and he leaped from the burning pile. At that moment the sharp ringing of several rifles was heard: the body of the negro fell a corpse on the ground. He was picked up by some two or three, and again thrown into the fire, and consumed, not a vestige remaining to show that such a being ever existed."

Nearly 4,000 slaves were collected from the plantations in the neighbourhood to witness this scene. Numerous speeches were made by the magistrates and ministers of religion to the large concourse of slaves, warning them, and telling them that the same fate awaited them, if they should prove rebellious to their owners. There are hundreds of negroes who run away and live in the woods. Some take refuge in the swamps, because they are less frequented by human beings. A Natchez newspaper gave the following account of the hiding-place of a slave who had been captured:—

"A runaway's den was discovered on Sunday, near the Washington Spring, in a little patch of woods, where it had been for several months so artfully concealed under ground, that it was detected only by accident, though in sight of two or three houses, and near the road and fields where there has been constant daily passing. The entrance was concealed by a pile of pine straw, representing a hog-bed, which being removed, discovered a trap-door and steps that led to a room about six feet square, comfortably ceiled with plank, containing a small fireplace, the flue of which was ingeniously conducted above ground and concealed by the straw. The inmates took the alarm, and made their escape; *but Mr. Adams and his excellent dogs being put upon the trail, soon run down and secured one of them,* which proved to be a negro-fellow who had been out about a year. He stated that the other occupant was a woman, who had been a runaway a still longer time. In the den was found a quantity of meal, bacon, corn, potatoes, &c. and various cooking utensils and wearing apparel."—*Vicksburgh Sentinel,* Dec. 6th, 1838.

Currer was one of those who witnessed the execution of the slave at the stake, and it gave her no very exalted opinion of the people of the cotton growing district.

IV. The Quadroon's Home

"How sweetly on the hill-side sleeps
  The sunlight with its quickening rays!
The verdant trees that crown the steeps,
  Grow greener in its quivering blaze."

ABOUT THREE miles from Richmond is a pleasant plain, with here and there a beautiful cottage surrounded by trees so as scarcely to be seen. Among them was one far retired from the public roads, and almost hidden among the trees. It was a perfect model of rural beauty. The piazzas that surrounded it were covered with clematis and passion flower. The pride of China mixed its oriental looking foliage with the majestic magnolia, and the air was redolent with the fragrance of flowers, peeping out of every nook and nodding upon you with a most unexpected welcome. The tasteful hand of art had not learned to imitate the lavish beauty and harmonious disorder of nature, but they lived together in loving amity, and spoke in accordant tones. The gateway rose in a gothic arch, with graceful tracery in iron work, surmounted by a cross, round which fluttered and played the mountain fringe, that lightest and most fragile of vines. This cottage was hired by Horatio Green for Clotel, and the quadroon girl soon found herself in her new home.

The tenderness of Clotel's conscience, together with the care her mother had with her and the high value she placed upon virtue, required an outward marriage; though she well knew that a union with her proscribed race was unrecognised by law, and therefore the ceremony would give her no legal hold on Horatio's constancy. But her high poetic nature regarded reality rather than the semblance of things; and when he playfully asked how she could keep him if he wished to run away, she

70

replied, "If the mutual love we have for each other, and the dictates of your own conscience do not cause you to remain my husband, and your affections fall from me, I would not, if I could, hold you by a single fetter." It was indeed a marriage sanctioned by heaven, although unrecognised on earth. There the young couple lived secluded from the world, and passed their time as happily as circumstances would permit. It was Clotel's wish that Horatio should purchase her mother and sister, but the young man pleaded that he was unable, owing to the fact that he had not come into possession of his share of property, yet he promised that when he did, he would seek them out and purchase them. Their first-born was named Mary, and her complexion was still lighter than her mother. Indeed she was not darker than other white children. As the child grew older, it more and more resembled its mother. The iris of her large dark eye had the melting mezzotinto, which remains the last vestige of African ancestry, and gives that plaintive expression, so often observed, and so appropriate to that docile and injured race. Clotel was still happier after the birth of her dear child; for Horatio, as might have been expected, was often absent day and night with his friends in the city, and the edicts of society had built up a wall of separation between the quadroon and them. Happy as Clotel was in Horatio's love, and surrounded by an outward environment of beauty, so well adapted to her poetic spirit, she felt these incidents with inexpressible pain. For herself she cared but little; for she had found a sheltered home in Horatio's heart, which the world might ridicule, but had no power to profane. But when she looked at her beloved Mary, and reflected upon the unavoidable and dangerous position which the tyranny of society had awarded her, her soul was filled with anguish. The rare loveliness of the child increased daily, and was evidently ripening into most marvellous beauty. The father seemed to rejoice in it with unmingled pride; but in the deep tenderness of the mother's eye, there was an indwelling sadness that spoke of anxious thoughts and fearful foreboding. Clotel now urged Horatio to remove to France or England, where both her and her child would be free, and where colour was not a crime. This request excited but little opposition, and was so attractive to his imagination, that he might have over-come all intervening obstacles, had not "a change come over the spirit of his dreams." He still loved Clotel; but he was now be-coming engaged in political and other affairs which kept him oftener and longer from the young mother; and ambition to become a statesman was slowly gaining the ascendancy over him.

Among those on whom Horatio's political success most de-pended was a very popular and wealthy man, who had an only daughter. His visits to the house were at first purely of a political nature; but the young lady was pleasing, and he fancied he dis-covered in her a sort of timid preference for himself. This ex-cited his vanity, and awakened thoughts of the great worldly advantages connected with a union. Reminiscences of his first love kept these vague ideas in check for several months; for with it was associated the idea of restraint. Moreover, Gertrude, though inferior in beauty, was yet a pretty contrast to her rival. Her light hair fell in silken ringlets down her shoulders, her blue eyes were gentle though inexpressive, and her healthy cheeks were like opening rosebuds. He had already become accus-tomed to the dangerous experiment of resisting his own inward convictions; and this new impulse to ambition, combined with the strong temptation of variety in love, met the ardent young man weakened in moral principle, and unfettered by laws of the land. The change wrought upon him was soon noticed by Clotel.

V. The Slave Market

"What! mothers from their children riven!
  What! God's own image bought and sold!
Americans to market driven,
  And barter'd as the brute for gold."—*Whittier.*

NOT far from Canal-street, in the city of New Orleans, stands a
large two story flat building surrounded by a stone wall twelve
feet high, the top of which is covered with bits of glass, and so
constructed as to prevent even the possibility of any one's passing over it without sustaining great injury. Many of the rooms
resemble cells in a prison. In a small room near the "office" are
to be seen any number of iron collars, hobbles, handcuffs,
thumbscrews, cowhides, whips, chains, gags, and yokes. A back
yard inclosed by a high wall looks something like the playground
attached to one of our large New England schools, and in which
are rows of benches and swings. Attached to the back premises
is a good-sized kitchen, where two old negresses are at work,
stewing, boiling, and baking, and occasionally wiping the sweat
from their furrowed and swarthy brows.

The slave-trader Walker, on his arrival in New Orleans, took
up his quarters at this slave pen with his gang of human cattle;
and the morning after, at ten o'clock, they were exhibited for
sale. There, first of all, was the beautiful Althesa, whose pale
countenance and dejected look told how many sad hours she
had passed since parting with her mother at Natchez. There was
a poor woman who had been separated from her husband and
five children. Another woman, whose looks and manner were
expressive of deep anguish, sat by her side. There, too, was
"Uncle Geemes," with his whiskers off, his face shaved clean,
and the grey hair plucked out, and ready to be sold for ten years

73

younger than he was. Toby was also there, with his face shaved and greased, ready for inspection. The examination commenced, and was carried on in a manner calculated to shock the feelings of any one not devoid of the milk of human kindness. "What are you wiping your eyes for?" inquired a fat, red-faced man, with a white hat set on one side of his head, and a cigar in his mouth, of a woman who sat on one of the stools. "I s'pose I have been crying." "Why do you cry?" "Because I have left my man behind." "Oh, if I buy you I will furnish you with a better man than you left. I have lots of young bucks on my farm." "I don't want, and will never have, any other man," replied the woman. "What's your name?" asked a man in a straw hat of a tall negro man, who stood with his arms folded across his breast, and leaning against the wall. "My name is Aaron, sir." "How old are you?" "Twenty-five." "Where were you raised?" "In old Virginny, sir." "How many men have owned you?" "Four." "Do you enjoy good health?" "Yes, sir." "How long did you live with your first owner?" "Twenty years." "Did you ever run away?" "No, sir." "Did you ever strike your master?" "No, sir." "Were you ever whipped much?" "No, sir, I s'pose I did not deserve it." "How long did you live with your second master?" "Ten years, sir." "Have you a good appetite?" "Yes, sir." "Can you eat your allowance?" "Yes, sir, when I can get it." "What were you employed at in Virginia?" "I worked in de terbacar feel." "In the tobacco field?" "Yes, sir." "How old did you say you were?" "I will be twenty-five if I live to see next sweet potater-digging time." "I am a cotton planter, and if I buy you, you will have to work in the cotton field. My men pick one hundred and fifty pounds a day, and the women one hundred and forty, and those who fail to pick their task receive five stripes from the cat for each pound that is wanting. Now, do you think you could keep up with the rest of the hands?" "I don't know, sir, I 'spec I'd have to." "How long did you live with your third master?" "Three years, sir." "Why, this makes you thirty-three, I thought you told me you was only twenty-five?" Aaron now looked first at the planter, then at the trader, and seemed perfectly bewildered. He had forgotten the lesson given him by Pompey as to his age, and the planter's circuitous talk (doubtless to find out the slave's real age) had the negro off his guard. "I must see your back, so as to know how much you have been whipped, before I think of buying," said the planter. Pompey, who had been standing by during the examination, thought that his services were now required, and stepping forward with a degree of officiousness, said to Aaron, "Don't you hear de gentman tell you he want to zamon your limbs. Come, unharness yeself, old boy, an don't be standing dar." Aaron was soon examined and pronounced "sound"; yet the conflicting statement about the age was not satisfactory.

Fortunate for Althesa she was spared the pain of undergoing such an examination. Mr. Crawford, a teller in one of the banks, had just been married, and wanted a maid-servant for his wife; and passing through the market in the early part of the day, was pleased with the young slave's appearance and purchased her, and in his dwelling the quadroon found a much better home than often falls to the lot of a slave sold in the New Orleans market. The heartrending and cruel traffic in slaves which has been so often described, is not confined to any particular class of persons. No one forfeits his or her character or standing in society, by buying or selling slaves; or even raising slaves for the market. The precise number of slaves carried from the slave-raising to the slave-consuming states, we have no means of knowing. But it must be very great, as more than forty thousand were sold and taken out of the state of Virginia in one year. Known to God only is the amount of human agony and suffering which sends its cry from the slave markets and negro pens, unheard and unheeded by man, up to his ear; mothers weeping for their children, breaking the night-silence with the shrieks of their breaking hearts. From some you will hear the burst of bitter lamentation, while from others the loud hysteric laugh, denoting still deeper agony. Most of them leave the market for cotton or rice plantations,

> "Where the slave-whip ceaseless swings,
> Where the noisome insect stings,
> Where the fever demon strews
> Poison with the falling dews,
> Where the sickly sunbeams glare
> Through the hot and misty air."

VI. The Religious Teacher

"What! preach and enslave men?
   Give thanks—and rob thy own afflicted poor?
   Talk of thy glorious liberty, and then
   Bolt hard the captive's door?"—*Whittier.*

THE REV. JOHN PECK was a native of the state of Connecticut, where he was educated for the ministry, in the Methodist persuasion. His father was a strict follower of John Wesley, and spared no pains in his son's education, with the hope that he would one day be as renowned as the great leader of his sect. John had scarcely finished his education at New Haven, when he was invited by an uncle, then on a visit to his father, to spend a few months at Natchez in the state of Mississippi. Young Peck accepted his uncle's invitation, and accompanied him to the South. Few young men, and especially clergymen, going fresh from a college to the South, but are looked upon as geniuses in a small way, and who are not invited to all the parties in the neighbourhood. Mr. Peck was not an exception to this rule. The society into which he was thrown on his arrival at Natchez was too brilliant for him not to be captivated by it; and, as might have been expected, he succeeded in captivating a plantation with seventy slaves, if not the heart of the lady to whom it belonged. Added to this, he became a popular preacher, had a large congregation with a snug salary. Like other planters, Mr. Peck confided the care of his farm to Ned Huckelby, an overseer of high reputation in his way. The Poplar Farm, as it was called, was situated in a beautiful valley nine miles from Natchez, and near the river Mississippi. The once unshorn face of nature had given way, and now the farm blossomed with a splendid harvest, the neat cottage stood in a grove where

Lombardy poplars lift their tufted tops almost to prop the skies; the willow, locust, and horse-chestnut spread their branches, and flowers never cease to blossom. This was the parson's country house, where the family spent only two months during the year.

The town residence was a fine villa, seated upon the brow of a hill at the edge of the city. It was in the kitchen of this house that Currer found her new home. Mr. Peck was, every inch of him, a democrat, and early resolved that his "people," as he called his slaves, should be well fed and not overworked, and therefore laid down the law and gospel to the overseer as well as the slaves.

"It is my wish," said he to Mr. Carlton, an old school-fellow, who was spending a few days with him, "it is my wish that a new system be adopted on the plantations in this estate. I believe that the sons of Ham should have the gospel, and I intend that my negroes shall. The gospel is calculated to make mankind better, and none should be without it." "What say you," replied Carlton, "about the right of man to his liberty?" "Now, Carlton, you have begun again to harp about man's rights; I really wish you could see this matter as I do. I have searched in vain for any authority for man's natural rights; if he had any, they existed before the fall. That is, Adam and Eve may have had some rights which God gave them, and which modern philosophy, in its pretended reverence for the name of God, prefers to call natural rights. I can imagine they had the right to eat of the fruit of the trees of the garden; they were restricted even in this by the prohibition of one. As far as I know without positive assertion, their liberty of action was confined to the garden. These were not 'inalienable rights,' however, for they forfeited both them and life with the first act of disobedience. Had they, after this, any rights? We cannot imagine them; they were condemned beings; they could have no rights, but by Christ's gift as king. These are the only rights man can have as an independent isolated being, if we choose to consider him in this impossible position, in which so many theorists have placed him. If he had no rights, he could suffer no wrongs. Rights and wrongs are therefore necessarily the creatures of society, such as man would establish himself in his gregarious state. They are, in this state, both artificial and voluntary. Though man has no rights, as thus considered, undoubtedly he has the power, by such arbitrary rules of right and wrong as his necessity enforces." "I regret I cannot see eye to eye with you," said Carlton. "I am a disciple of Rousseau, and have for years made the rights of man my study; and I must confess to you that I can see no difference between white men and black men as it regards liberty." "Now, my dear Carlton, would you really have the negroes enjoy the same rights with ourselves?" "I would, most certainly. Look at our great Declaration of Independence; look even at the constitution of our own Connecticut, and see what is said in these about liberty." "I regard all this talk about rights as mere humbug. The Bible is older than the Declaration of Independence, and there I take my stand. The Bible furnishes to us the armour of proof, weapons of heavenly temper and mould, whereby we can maintain our ground against all attacks. But this is true only when we obey its directions, as well as employ its sanctions. Our rights are there established, but it is always in connection with our duties. If we neglect the one we cannot make good the other. Our domestic institutions can be maintained against the world, if we but allow Christianity to throw its broad shield over them. But if we so act as to array the Bible against our social economy, they must fall. Nothing ever yet stood long against Christianity. Those who say that religious instruction is inconsistent with our peculiar civil polity, are the worst enemies of that polity. They would drive religious men from its defence. Sooner or later, if these views prevail, they will separate the religious portion of our community from the rest, and thus divided we shall become an easy prey. Why, is it not better that Christian men should hold slaves than unbelievers? We know how to value the bread of life, and will not keep it from our slaves."

"Well, every one to his own way of thinking," said Carlton, as he changed his position. "I confess," added he, "that I am no great admirer of either the Bible or slavery. My heart is my guide: my conscience is my Bible. I wish for nothing further to satisfy me of my duty to man. If I act rightly to mankind, I shall fear nothing." Carlton had drunk too deeply of the bitter waters of infidelity, and had spent too many hours over the writings of Rousseau, Voltaire, and Thomas Paine, to place that appreciation upon the Bible and its teachings that it demands. During this conversation there was another person in the room, seated by the window, who, although at work upon a fine piece of lace, paid every attention to what was said. This was Georgiana, the only daughter of the parson. She had just returned from Connecticut, where she had finished her education. She had had the opportunity of contrasting the spirit of Christianity and liberty in New England with that of slavery in her native state, and had learned to feel deeply for the injured negro. Georgiana was in her nineteenth year, and had been much benefited by a residence of five years at the North. Her form was tall and graceful; her features regular and well defined; and her complexion was illuminated by the freshness of youth, beauty, and health. The daughter differed from both the father and his visitor upon the subject which they had been discussing, and as soon as an opportunity offered, she gave it as her opinion, that the Bible was both the bulwark of Christianity and of liberty. With a smile she said, "Of course, papa will overlook my differing from him, for although I am a native of the South, I am by education and sympathy a Northerner." Mr. Peck laughed and appeared pleased, rather than otherwise, at the manner in which his daughter had expressed herself.

From this Georgiana took courage and said, "We must try the character of slavery, and our duty in regard to it, as we should try any other question of character and duty. To judge justly of the character of anything, we must know what it does. That which is good does good, and that which is evil does evil. And as to duty, God's designs indicate his claims. That which accomplishes the manifest design of God is right; that which counteracts it, wrong. Whatever, in its proper tendency and general effect, produces, secures, or extends human welfare, is according to the will of God, and is good; and our duty is to favour and promote, according to our power, that which God favours and promotes by the general law of his providence. On the other hand, whatever in its proper tendency and general effect destroys, abridges, or renders insecure, human welfare, is opposed to God's will, and is evil. And as whatever accords with the will of God, in any manifestation of it should be done and persisted in, so whatever opposes that will should not be done, and if done, should be abandoned. Can that then be right, be well doing—can that obey God's behest, which makes a man a slave? which dooms him and all his posterity, in limitless generations, to bondage, to unrequited toil through life? 'Thou shalt love thy neighbour as thyself.' This single passage of Scripture should cause us to have respect to the rights of the slave. True Christian love is of an enlarged, disinterested nature. It loves all who love the Lord Jesus Christ in sincerity, without regard to colour or condition." "Georgiana, my dear, you are an abolitionist; your talk is fanaticism," said Mr. Peck in rather a sharp tone; but the subdued look of the girl, and the presence of Carlton, caused the father to soften his language. Mr. Peck having lost his wife by consumption, and Georgiana being his only child, he loved her too dearly to say more, even if he felt displeased. A silence followed this exhortation from the young Christian. But her remarks had done a noble work. The father's heart was touched; and the sceptic, for the first time, was viewing Christianity in its true light.

"I think I must go out to your farm," said Carlton, as if to break the silence. "I shall be pleased to have you go," returned Mr. Peck. "I am sorry I can't go myself, but Huckelby will show you every attention; and I feel confident that when you return to Connecticut, you will do me the justice to say, that I am one who looks after my people, in a moral, social, and religious point of view." "Well, what do you say to my spending next Sunday there?" "Why, I think that a good move; you will then meet with Snyder, our missionary." "Oh, you have missionaries in these parts, have you?" "Yes," replied Mr. Peck; "Snyder is from New York, and is our missionary to the poor, and preaches to our 'people' on Sunday; you will no doubt like him; he is a capital fellow." "Then I shall go," said Carlton, "but only wish I had company." This last remark was intended for Miss Peck, for whom he had the highest admiration.

It was on a warm Sunday morning, in the month of May, that Miles Carlton found himself seated beneath a fine old apple tree, whose thick leaves entirely shaded the ground for some distance round. Under similar trees and near by, were gathered together all the "people" belonging to the plantation. Hontz Snyder was a man of about forty years of age, exceedingly low in stature, but of a large frame. He had been brought up in the Mohawk Valley, in the state of New York, and claimed relationship with the oldest Dutch families in that vicinity. He had once been a sailor, and had all the roughness of character that a seafaring man might expect to possess; together with the half-Yankee, half-German peculiarities of the people of the Mohawk Valley. It was nearly eleven o'clock when a one-horse waggon drove up in haste, and the low squatty preacher got out and took his place at the foot of one of the trees, where a sort of rough board table was placed, and took his books from his pocket and commenced.

"As it is rather late," said he, "we will leave the singing and praying for the last, and take our text, and commence immediately. I shall base my remarks on the following passage of Scripture, and hope to have that attention which is due to the cause of God:—'All things whatsoever ye would that men should do unto you, do ye even so unto them'; that is, do by all mankind just as you would desire they should do by you, if you were in their place and they in yours.

"Now, to suit this rule to your particular circumstances, suppose you were masters and mistresses, and had servants under you, would you not desire that your servants should do their business faithfully and honestly, as well when your back was turned as while you were looking over them? Would you not expect that they should take notice of what you said to them? that they should behave themselves with respect towards you and yours, and be as careful of every thing belonging to you as you would be yourselves? You are servants: do, therefore, as you would wish to be done by, and you will be both good servants to your masters and good servants to God, who requires this of you, and will reward you well for it, if you do it for the sake of conscience, in obedience to his commands.

"You are not to be eye-servants. Now, eye-servants are such as will work hard, and seem mighty diligent, while they think anybody is taking notice of them; but, when their masters' and mistresses' backs are turned they are idle, and neglect their business. I am afraid there are a great many such eye-servants among you, and that you do not consider how great a sin it is to be so, and how severely God will punish you for it. You may easily deceive your owners, and make them have an opinion of you that you do not deserve, and get the praise of men by it; but remember that you cannot deceive Almighty God, who sees your wickedness and deceit, and will punish you accordingly. For the rule is, that you must obey your masters in all things, and do the work they set you about with fear and trembling, in singleness of heart as unto Christ; not with eye-service, as men-pleasers, but as the servants of Christ, doing the will of God from the heart; with good-will doing service as to the Lord, and not as to men.

"*Take care that you do not fret or murmur, grumble or repine at your condition; for this will not only make your life uneasy, but will greatly offend Almighty God.* Consider that it is not yourselves, it is not the people that you belong to, it is not the men who have brought you to it, but *it is the will of God who hath by his providence made you servants, because, no doubt, he knew that condition would be best for you in this world, and help you the better towards heaven, if you would but do your duty in it.* So that any discontent at your not being free, or rich, or great, as you see some others, is quarrelling with your heavenly Master, and finding fault with God himself, who hath made you what you are, and hath promised you as large a share in the kingdom of heaven as the greatest man alive, if you will but behave yourself aright, and do the business he hath set you about in this world honestly and cheerfully. Riches and power have proved the ruin of many an unhappy soul, by drawing away the heart and affections from God, and fixing them on mean and sinful enjoyments; so that, when God, who knows our hearts better than we know them ourselves, sees that they would be hurtful to us, and therefore keeps them from us, it is the greatest mercy and kindness he could show us.

"You may perhaps fancy that, if you had riches and freedom, you could do your duty to God and man with greater pleasure

than you can now. But pray consider that, if you can but save
your souls through the mercy of God, you will have spent your
time to the best of purposes in this world; and he that at last can
get to heaven has performed a noble journey, let the road be
ever so rugged and difficult. Besides, you really have a great
advantage over most white people, who have not only the care
of their daily labour upon their hands, but the care of looking
forward and providing necessaries for to-morrow and next day,
and of clothing and bringing up their children, and of getting
food and raiment for as many of you as belong to their families,
which often puts them to great difficulties, and distracts their
minds so as to break their rest, and take off their thoughts from
the affairs of another world. Whereas you are quite eased from
all these cares, and have nothing but your daily labour to look
after, and, when that is done, take your needful rest. Neither is
it necessary for you to think of laying up anything against old
age, as white people are obliged to do; for the laws of the country have provided that you shall not be turned off when you are
past labour, but shall be maintained, while you live, by those you
belong to, whether you are able to work or not.

"There is only one circumstance which may appear grievous,
that I shall now take notice of, and that is correction.

"Now, when correction is given you, you either deserve it, or
you do not deserve it. But whether you really deserve it or not,
it is your duty, and Almighty God requires that you bear it patiently. You may perhaps think that this is hard doctrine; but, if
you consider it right, you must needs think otherwise of it.
Suppose, then, that you deserve correction, you cannot but say
that it is just and right you should meet with it. Suppose you do
not, or at least you do not deserve so much, or so severe a
correction, for the fault you have committed, you perhaps have
escaped a great many more, and are at last paid for all. Or suppose you are quite innocent of what is laid to your charge, and
suffer wrongfully in that particular thing, is it not possible you
may have done some other bad thing which was never discovered, and that Almighty God who saw you doing it would not let
you escape without punishment one time or another? And
ought you not, in such a case, to give glory to him, and be thank-

ful that he would rather punish you in this life for your wickedness than destroy your souls for it in the next life? But suppose
even this was not the case (a case hardly to be imagined), and
that you have by no means, known or unknown, deserved the
correction you suffered, there is this great comfort in it, that, if
you bear it patiently, and leave your cause in the hands of God,
he will reward you for it in heaven, and the punishment you suffer unjustly here shall turn to your exceeding great glory hereafter.

"Lastly, you should serve your masters faithfully, because of
their goodness to you. See to what trouble they have been on
your account. Your fathers were poor ignorant and barbarous
creatures in Africa, and the whites fitted out ships at great
trouble and expense and brought you from that benighted land
to Christian America, where you can sit under your own vine
and fig tree and no one molest or make you afraid. Oh, my dear
black brothers and sisters, you are indeed a fortunate and a
blessed people. Your masters have many troubles that you know
nothing about. If the banks break, your masters are sure to lose
something. If the crops turn out poor, they lose by it. If one of
you die, your master loses what he paid for you, while you lose
nothing. Now let me exhort you once more to be faithful."

Often during the delivery of the sermon did Snyder cast an
anxious look in the direction where Carlton was seated; no
doubt to see if he had found favour with the stranger. Huckelby,
the overseer, was also there, seated near Carlton. With all
Snyder's gesticulations, sonorous voice, and occasionally bringing his fist down upon the table with the force of a sledge hammer, he could not succeed in keeping the negroes all interested:
four or five were fast asleep, leaning against the trees; as many
more were nodding, while not a few were stealthily cracking and
eating hazelnuts. "Uncle Simon, you may strike up a hymn," said
the preacher as he closed his Bible. A moment more, and the
whole company (Carlton excepted) had joined in the well known
hymn, commencing with

> "When I can read my title clear
>   To mansions in the sky."

After the singing, Sandy closed with prayer, and the following
questions and answers read, and the meeting was brought to a
close.

"*Q*. What command has God given to servants concerning obedience to their masters?—*A*. 'Servants, obey in all things your masters
according to the flesh, not with eye-service as men-pleasers, but in
singleness of heart, fearing God.'

"*Q*. What does God mean by masters according to the flesh?—*A*.
'Masters in this world.'

"*Q*. What are servants to count their masters worthy of?—*A*. 'All
honour.'

"*Q*. How are they to do the service of their masters?—*A*. '*With good
will*, doing service as unto the Lord, and not unto men.'

"*Q*. How are they to try to please their masters?—*A*. 'Please him
well in all things, not answering again.'

"*Q*. Is a servant who is an eye-servant to his earthly master an eye-
servant to his heavenly master?—*A*. 'Yes.'

"*Q*. Is it right in a servant, when commanded to do any thing, to be
sullen and slow, and answer his master again?—*A*. 'No.'

"*Q*. If the servant professes to be a Christian, ought he not to be *as
a Christian servant,* an example to all other servants of love and obedience to his master?—*A*. 'Yes.'

"*Q*. And, should his master be a Christian also, ought he not on that
account specially to love and obey him?—*A*. 'Yes.'

"*Q*. But suppose the master is hard to please, and threatens and
punishes more than he ought, what is the servant to do?—*A*. 'Do his
best to please him.'

"*Q*. When the servant suffers *wrongfully* at the hands of his master,
and, to please God, takes it patiently, will God reward him for it?—*A*.
'Yes.'

"*Q*. Is it right for the servant to *run away*; or is it right to *harbour* a
runaway?—*A*. 'No.'

"*Q*. If a servant runs away, what should be done with him?—*A*. 'He
should be caught and brought back.'

"*Q*. When he is brought back, what should be done with him?—*A*.
'Whip him well.'

"*Q*. Why may not the whites be slaves as well as the blacks?—*A*.
'Because the Lord intended the negroes for slaves.'

"*Q*. Are they better calculated for servants than the whites?—*A*.

'Yes, their hands are large, the skin thick and tough, and they can stand the sun better than the whites.'

"Q. Why should servants not complain when they are whipped?—A. 'Because the Lord has commanded that they should be whipped.'

"Q. Where has He commanded it?—A. 'He says, He that knoweth his master's will, and doeth it not, shall be beaten with many stripes.'

"Q. Then is the master to blame for whipping his servant?—A. 'Oh, no! he is only doing his duty as a Christian.'"

Snyder left the ground in company with Carlton and Huckelby, and the three dined together in the overseer's dwelling.

"Well," said Joe, after the three white men were out of hearing, "Marser Snyder bin try hesef to-day." "Yes," replied Ned; "he want to show de strange gentman how good he can preach." "Dat's a new sermon he gib us to-day," said Sandy. "Dees white fokes is de very dibble," said Dick; "and all dey whole study is to try to fool de black people." "Didn't you like de sermon?" asked Uncle Simon. "No," answered four or five voices. "He rared and pitched enough," continued Uncle Simon.

Now Uncle Simon was himself a preacher, or at least he thought so, and was rather pleased than otherwise, when he heard others spoken of in a disparaging manner. "Uncle Simon can beat dat sermon all to pieces," said Ned, as he was filling his mouth with hazelnuts. "I got no notion of dees white fokes, no how," returned Aunt Dafney. "Dey all de time tellin' dat de Lord made us for to work for dem, and I don't believe a word of it." "Marser Peck give dat sermon to Snyder, I know," said Uncle Simon. "He jest de one for dat," replied Sandy. "I think de people dat made de Bible was great fools," said Ned. "Why?" Uncle Simon. "'Cause dey made such a great big book and put nuttin' in it, but servants obey yer masters." "Oh," replied Uncle Simon, "thars more in de Bible den dat, only Snyder never reads any other part to us; I use to hear it read in Maryland, and thar was more den what Snyder lets us hear." In the overseer's house there was another scene going on, and far different from what we have here described.

VII. The Poor Whites, South

"No seeming of logic can ever convince the American people, that thousands of our slave-holding brethren are not excellent, humane, and even Christian men, fearing God, and keeping His commandments."—*Rev. Dr. Joel Parker.*

"YOU LIKE these parts better than New York," said Carlton to Snyder, as they were sitting down to dinner in the overseer's dwelling. "I can't say that I do," was the reply; "I came here ten years ago as missionary, and Mr. Peck wanted me to stay, and I have remained. I travel among the poor whites during the week, and preach for the niggers on Sunday." "Are there many poor whites in this district?" "Not here, but about thirty miles from here, in the Sand Hill district; they are as ignorant as horses. Why it was no longer than last week I was up there, and really you would not believe it, that people were so poor off. In New England, and, I may say, in all the free states, they have free schools, and everybody gets educated. Not so here. In Connecticut there is only one out of every five hundred above twenty-one years that can neither read nor write. Here there is one out of every eight that can neither read nor write. There is not a single newspaper taken in five of the counties in this state. Last week I was at Sand Hill for the first time, and I called at a farmhouse. The man was out. It was a low log-hut, and yet it was the best house in that locality. The woman and nine children were there, and the geese, ducks, chickens, pigs, and children were all running about the floor. The woman seemed scared at me when I entered the house. I inquired if I could get a little dinner, and my horse fed. She said, yes, if I would only be good enough to feed him myself, as her 'gal,' as she called her

87

daughter, would be afraid of the horse. When I returned into the house again from the stable, she kept her eyes upon me all the time. At last she said, 'I s'pose you aint never bin in these parts afore?' 'No,' said I. 'Is you gwine to stay here long?' 'Not very long,' I replied. 'On business, I s'pose.' 'Yes,' said I, 'I am hunting up the lost sheep of the house of Israel.' 'Oh,' exclaimed she, 'hunting for lost sheep is you? Well, you have a hard time to find 'em here. My husband lost an old ram last week, and he aint found him yet, and he's hunted every day.' 'I am not looking for four-legged sheep,' said I, 'I am hunting for sinners.' 'Ah'; she said, 'then you are a preacher.' 'Yes,' said I. 'You are the first of that sort that's bin in these diggins for many a day.' Turning to her eldest daughter, she said in an excited tone, 'Clar out the pigs and ducks, and sweep up the floor; this is a preacher.' And it was some time before any of the children would come near me; one remained under the bed (which, by the by, was in the same room), all the while I was there. 'Well,' continued the woman, 'I was a tellin' my man only yesterday that I would like once more to go to meetin' before I died, and he said as he should like to do the same. But as you have come, it will save us the trouble of going out of the district.'" "Then you found some of the lost sheep," said Carlton. "Yes," replied Snyder, "I did not find anything else up there. The state makes no provision for educating the poor: they are unable to do it themselves, and they grow up in a state of ignorance and degradation. The men hunt and the women have to go in the fields and labour." "What is the cause of it?" inquired Carlton; "Slavery," answered Snyder, "slavery,—and nothing else. Look at the city of Boston; it pays more taxes for the support of the government than this entire state. The people of Boston do more business than the whole population of Mississippi put together. I was told some very amusing things while at Sand Hill. A farmer there told me a story about an old woman, who was very pious herself. She had a husband and three sons, who were sad characters, and she had often prayed for their conversion but to no effect. At last, one day while working in the corn-field, one of her sons was bitten by a rattlesnake. He had scarce reached home before he felt the poison, and in his agony called loudly on his Maker.

"The pious old woman, when she heard this, forgetful of her son's misery, and everything else but the glorious hope of his repentance, fell on her knees, and prayed as follows,—'Oh! Lord, I thank thee, that thou hast at last opened Jimmy's eyes to the error of his ways; and I pray that, in thy Divine mercy, thou wilt send a rattlesnake to bite the old man, and another to bite Tom, and another to bite Harry, for I am certain that nothing but a rattlesnake, or something of the kind, will ever turn them from their sinful ways, they are so hard-headed.' When returning home, and before I got out of the Sand Hill district, I saw a funeral, and thought I would fasten my horse to a post and attend. The coffin was carried in a common horse cart, and followed by fifteen or twenty persons very shabbily dressed, and attended by a man whom I took to be the religious man of the place. After the coffin had been placed near the grave, he spoke as follows,—

"'Friends and neighbours! you have congregated to see this lump of mortality put into a hole in the ground. You all know the deceased—a worthless, drunken, good-for-nothing vagabond. He lived in disgrace and infamy, and died in wretchedness. You all despised him—you all know his brother Joe, who lives on the hill? He's not a bit better though he has scrap'd together a little property by cheating his neighbours. His end will be like that of this loathsome creature, whom you will please put into the hole as soon as possible. I wont ask you to drop a tear, but brother Bohow will please raise a hymn while we fill up the grave.'"

"I am rather surprised to hear that any portion of the whites in this state are in so low a condition." "Yet it is true," returned Snyder.

"These are very onpleasant facts to be related to ye, Mr. Carlton," said Huckelby; "but I can bear witness to what Mr. Snyder has told ye." Huckelby was from Maryland, where many of the poor whites are in as sad a condition as the Sand Hillers of Mississippi. He was a tall man, of iron constitution, and could neither read nor write, but was considered one of the best overseers in the country. When about to break a slave in, to do a heavy task, he would make him work by his side all day; and if the new hand kept up with him, he was set down as an able bodied man. Huckelby had neither moral, religious, or political principles, and often boasted that conscience was a matter that never "cost" him a thought. "Mr. Snyder aint told ye half about the folks in these parts," continued he; "we who comes from more enlightened parts don't know how to put up with 'em down here. I find the people here knows mighty little indeed; in fact, I may say they are univarsaly onedicated. I goes out among none on 'em, 'cause they aint such as I have been used to 'sociate with. When I gits a little richer, so that I can stop work, I tend to go back to Maryland, and spend the rest of my days." "I wonder the negroes don't attempt to get their freedom by physical force." "It aint no use for 'em to try that, for if they do, we puts 'em through by daylight," replied Huckelby. "There are some desperate fellows among the slaves," said Snyder. "Indeed," remarked Carlton. "Oh, yes," replied the preacher. "A case has just taken place near here, where a neighbour of ours, Mr. J. Higgerson, attempted to correct a negro man in his employ, who resisted, drew a knife, and stabbed him (Mr. H.) in several places. Mr. J. C. Hobbs (a Tennessean) ran to his assistance. Mr. Hobbs stooped to pick up a stick to strike the negro, and, while in that position, the negro rushed upon him, and caused his immediate death. The negro then fled to the woods, but was pursued with dogs, and soon overtaken. He had stopped in a swamp to fight the dogs, when the party who were pursuing him came upon him, and commanded him to give up, which he refused to do. He then made several efforts to stab them. Mr. Roberson, one of the party, gave him several blows on the head with a rifle gun; but this, instead of subduing, only increased his desperate revenge. Mr. R. then discharged his gun at the negro, and missing him, the ball struck Mr. Boon in the face, and felled him to the ground. The negro, seeing Mr. Boon prostrated, attempted to rush up and stab him, but was prevented by the timely interference of some one of the party. He was then shot three times with a revolving pistol, and once with a rifle, and after having his throat cut, he still kept the knife firmly grasped in his hand, and tried to cut their legs when they approached to put an end to his life. This chastisement was given because the negro grumbled, and found fault with his master for flogging his wife." "Well, this is a bad state of affairs indeed, and especially the condition of the poor whites," said Carlton. "You see," replied Snyder, "no white man is respectable in these slave states who works for a living. No community can be prosperous, where honest labour is not honoured. No society can be rightly constituted, where the intellect is not fed. Whatever institution reflects discredit on industry, whatever institution forbids the general culture of the understanding, is palpably hostile to individual rights, and to social well-being. Slavery is the incubus that hangs over the Southern States." "Yes," interrupted Huckelby; "them's just my sentiments now, and no mistake. I think that, for the honour of our country, this slavery business should stop. I don't own any, no how, and I would not be an overseer if I wern't paid for it."

VIII. The Separation

"In many ways does the full heart reveal
    The presence of the love it would conceal;
    But in far more the estranged heart lets know
    The absence of the love, which yet it fain would show."

AT LENGTH the news of the approaching marriage of Horatio met the ear of Clotel. Her head grew dizzy, and her heart fainted within her; but, with a strong effort at composure, she inquired all the particulars, and her pure mind at once took its resolution. Horatio came that evening, and though she would fain have met him as usual, her heart was too full not to throw a deep sadness over her looks and tones. She had never complained of his decreasing tenderness, or of her own lonely hours; but he felt that the mute appeal of her heart-broken looks was more terrible than words. He kissed the hand she offered, and with a countenance almost as sad as her own, led her to a window in the recess shadowed by a luxuriant passion flower. It was the same seat where they had spent the first evening in this beautiful cottage, consecrated to their first loves. The same calm, clear moonlight looked in through the trellis. The vine then planted had now a luxuriant growth; and many a time had Horatio fondly twined its sacred blossoms with the glossy ringlets of her raven hair. The rush of memory almost overpowered poor Clotel; and Horatio felt too much oppressed and ashamed to break the long deep silence. At length, in words scarcely audible, Clotel said: "Tell me, dear Horatio, are you to be married next week?" He dropped her hand as if a rifle ball had struck him; and it was not until after long hesitation, that he began to make some reply about the necessity of circumstances. Mildly but earnestly the poor girl begged him to spare apologies. It was enough that he no longer loved her, and that they must bid farewell. Trusting to the yielding tenderness of her character, he ventured, in the most soothing accents, to suggest that as he still loved her better than all the world, she would ever be his real wife, and they might see each other frequently. He was not prepared for the storm of indignant emotion his words excited. True, she was his slave; her bones, and sinews had been purchased by his gold, yet she had the heart of a true woman, and hers was a passion too deep and absorbing to admit of partnership, and her spirit was too pure to form a selfish league with crime.

At length this painful interview came to an end. They stood together by the Gothic gate, where they had so often met and parted in the moonlight. Old remembrances melted their souls. "Farewell, dearest Horatio," said Clotel. "Give me a parting kiss." Her voice was choked for utterance, and the tears flowed freely, as she bent her lips toward him. He folded her convulsively in his arms, and imprinted a long impassioned kiss on that mouth, which had never spoken to him but in love and blessing. With efforts like a death-pang she at length raised her head from his heaving bosom, and turning from him with bitter sobs, "It is our last. To meet thus is henceforth crime. God bless you. I would not have you so miserable as I am. Farewell. A last farewell." "The last?" exclaimed he, with a wild shriek. "Oh God, Clotel, do not say that"; and covering his face with his hands, he wept like a child. Recovering from his emotion, he found himself alone. The moon looked down upon him mild, but very sorrowfully; as the Madonna seems to gaze upon her worshipping children, bowed down with consciousness of sin. At that moment he would have given worlds to have disengaged himself from Gertrude, but he had gone so far, that blame, disgrace, and duels with angry relatives would now attend any effort to obtain his freedom. Oh, how the moonlight oppressed him with its friendly sadness! It was like the plaintive eye of his forsaken one, like the music of sorrow echoed from an unseen world. Long and earnestly he gazed at that cottage, where he had so long known earth's purest foretaste of heavenly bliss. Slowly he walked away; then turned again to look on that charmed spot, the nestling-place of his early affections. He caught a glimpse of Clotel, weeping beside a magnolia, which commanded a long view of the path leading to the public road. He would have sprung toward her but she darted from him, and entered the cottage. That graceful figure, weeping in the moonlight, haunted him for years. It stood before his closing eyes, and greeted him with the morning dawn. Poor Gertrude, had she known all, what a dreary lot would hers have been; but fortunately she could not miss the impassioned tenderness she never experienced; and Horatio was the more careful in his kindness, because he was deficient in love. After Clotel had been separated from her mother and sister, she turned her attention to the subject of Christianity, and received that consolation from her Bible that is never denied to the children of God. Although it was against the laws of Virginia, for a slave to be taught to read, Currer had employed an old free negro, who lived near her, to teach her two daughters to read and write. She felt that the step she had taken in resolving never to meet Horatio again would no doubt expose her to his wrath, and probably cause her to be sold, yet her heart was too guileless for her to commit a crime, and therefore she had ten times rather have been sold as a slave than do wrong. Some months after the marriage of Horatio and Gertrude their barouche rolled along a winding road that skirted the forest near Clotel's cottage, when the attention of Gertrude was suddenly attracted by two figures among the trees by the wayside; and touching Horatio's arm, she exclaimed, "Do look at that beautiful child." He turned and saw Clotel and Mary. His lips quivered, and his face became deadly pale. His young wife looked at him intently, but said nothing. In returning home, he took another road; but his wife seeing this, expressed a wish to go back the way they had come. He objected, and suspicion was awakened in her heart, and she soon after learned that the mother of that lovely child bore the name of Clotel, a name which she had often heard Horatio murmur in uneasy slumbers. From gossiping tongues she soon learned more than she wished to know. She wept, but not as poor Clotel had done; for she never had loved, and been beloved like her, and her nature was more proud: henceforth a change came over her feelings and her manners, and Horatio had no further occasion to assume a tenderness in return for hers. Changed as he was by ambition, he felt the wintry chill of her polite propriety, and sometimes, in agony of heart, compared it with the gushing love of her who was indeed his wife. But these and all his emotions were a sealed book to Clotel, of which she could only guess the contents. With remittances for her and her child's support, there sometimes came earnest pleadings that she would consent to see him again; but these she never answered, though her heart yearned to do so. She pitied his young bride, and would not be tempted to bring sorrow into her household by any fault of hers. Her earnest prayer was, that she might not know of her existence. She had not looked on Horatio since she watched him under the shadow of the magnolia, until his barouche passed her in her rambles some months after. She saw the deadly paleness of his countenance, and had he dared to look back, he would have seen her tottering with faintness. Mary brought water from a rivulet, and sprinkled her face. When she revived, she clasped the beloved child to her heart with a vehemence that made her scream. Soothingly she kissed away her fears, and gazed into her beautiful eyes with a deep, deep sadness of expression, which poor Mary never forgot. Wild were the thoughts that passed round her aching heart, and almost maddened her poor brain; thoughts which had almost driven her to suicide the night of that last farewell. For her child's sake she had conquered the fierce temptation then; and for her sake, she struggled with it now. But the gloomy atmosphere of their once happy home overclouded the morning of Mary's life. Clotel perceived this, and it gave her unutterable pain.

> "Tis ever thus with woman's love,
>   True till life's storms have passed;
> And, like the vine around the tree,
>   It braves them to the last."

IX. The Man of Honour

"My tongue could never learn sweet soothing words,
  But now thy beauty is propos'd, my fee,
  My proud heart sues, and prompts my tongue to speak."
                                        Shakspeare.

JAMES CRAWFORD, the purchaser of Althesa, was from the green mountains of Vermont, and his feelings were opposed to the holding of slaves. But his young wife persuaded him into the idea that it was no worse to own a slave than to hire one and pay the money to another. Hence it was that he had been induced to purchase Althesa. Henry Morton, a young physician from the same state, and who had just commenced the practice of his profession in New Orleans, was boarding with Crawford when Althesa was brought home. The young physician had been in New Orleans but a few weeks, and had seen very little of slavery. In his own mountain home he had been taught that the slaves of the Southern states were negroes, if not from the coast of Africa, the descendants of those who had been imported. He was unprepared to behold with composure a beautiful young white girl of fifteen in the degraded position of a chattel slave. The blood chilled in his young heart as he heard Crawford tell how, by bantering with the trader, he had bought her for two hundred dollars less than he first asked. His very looks showed that the slave girl had the deepest sympathy of his heart. Althesa had been brought up by her mother to look after the domestic concerns of her cottage in Virginia, and knew well the duties imposed upon her. Mrs. Crawford was much pleased with her new servant, and often made mention of her in presence of Morton. The young man's sympathy ripened into love, which was reciprocated by the friendless and injured child of sorrow. There was but one course left; that was, to purchase the young girl and make her his wife, which he did six months after her arrival in Crawford's family. The young physician and his wife immediately took lodgings in another part of the city; a private teacher was called in, and the young wife taught some of those accomplishments which are necessary for one's taking a position in society. Dr. Morton soon obtained a large practice in his profession, and with it increased in wealth—but with all his wealth he never would own a slave. Mrs. Morton was now in a position to seek out and redeem her mother, whom she had not heard of since they parted at Natchez. An agent was immediately despatched to hunt out the mother and to see if she could be purchased. The agent had no trouble in finding out Mr. Peck: but all overtures were unavailable; he would not sell Currer. His excuse was, that she was such a good housekeeper that he could not spare her. Poor Althesa felt sad when she found that her mother could not be bought. However, she felt a consciousness of having done her duty in the matter, yet waited with the hope that the day might come when she should have her mother by her side.

X. The Young Christian

"Here we see *God dealing in slaves;* giving them to his own favourite child [Abraham], a man of superlative worth, and as a reward for his eminent goodness."—*Rev. Theodore Clapp, of New Orleans.*

ON CARLTON's return the next day from the farm, he was overwhelmed with questions from Mr. Peck, as to what he thought of the plantation, the condition of the negroes, Huckelby and Snyder; and especially how he liked the sermon of the latter. Mr. Peck was a kind of a patriarch in his own way. To begin with, he was a man of some talent. He not only had a good education, but was a man of great eloquence, and had a wonderful command of language. He too either had, or thought he had, poetical genius; and was often sending contributions to the *Natchez Free Trader,* and other periodicals. In the way of raising contributions for foreign missions, he took the lead of all others in his neighbourhood. Everything he did, he did for the "glory of God," as he said: he quoted Scripture for almost everything he did. Being in good circumstances, he was able to give to almost all benevolent causes to which he took a fancy. He was a most loving father, and his daughter exercised considerable influence over him, and, owing to her piety and judgment, that influence had a beneficial effect. Carlton, though a schoolfellow of the parson's, was nevertheless nearly ten years his junior; and though not an avowed infidel, was, however, a freethinker, and one who took no note of to-morrow. And for this reason Georgiana took peculiar interest in the young man, for Carlton was but little above thirty and unmarried. The young Christian felt that she would not be living up to that faith that she professed and believed in, if she did not exert herself to the utmost to save the thoughtless man from his downward career; and in this she succeeded to her most sanguine expectations. She not only converted him, but in placing the Scriptures before him in their true light, she redeemed those sacred writings from the charge of supporting the system of slavery, which her father had cast upon them in the discussion some days before.

Georgiana's first object, however, was to awaken in Carlton's breast a love for the Lord Jesus Christ. The young man had often sat under the sound of the gospel with perfect indifference. He had heard men talk who had grown grey bending over the Scriptures, and their conversation had passed by him unheeded; but when a young girl, much younger than himself, reasoned with him in that innocent and persuasive manner that woman is wont to use when she has entered with her whole soul upon an object, it was too much for his stout heart, and he yielded. Her next aim was to vindicate the Bible from sustaining the monstrous institution of slavery. She said, "'God has created of one blood all the nations of men, to dwell on all the face of the earth.' To claim, hold, and treat a human being as property is felony against God and man. The Christian religion is opposed to slaveholding in its spirit and its principles; it classes menstealers among murderers; and it is the duty of all who wish to meet God in peace, to discharge that duty in spreading these principles. Let us not deceive ourselves into the idea that slavery is right, because it is profitable to us. Slaveholding is the highest possible violation of the eighth commandment. To take from a man his earnings, is theft; but to take the earner is a compound, life-long theft; and we who profess to follow in the footsteps of our Redeemer, should do our utmost to extirpate slavery from the land. For my own part, I shall do all I can. When the Redeemer was about to ascend to the bosom of the Father, and resume the glory which he had with him before the world was, he promised his disciples that the power of the Holy Ghost should come upon them, and that they should be witnesses for him to the uttermost parts of the earth. What was the effect upon their minds? 'They all continued with one accord in prayer and supplication with the women.' Stimulated by the confident expectation that Jesus would fulfil his gracious promise, they poured out their hearts in fervent supplications, probably for strength to do the work which he had appointed them unto, for they felt that without him they could do nothing, and they consecrated themselves on the altar of God, to the great and glorious enterprise of preaching the unsearchable riches of Christ to a lost and perishing world. Have we less precious promises in the Scriptures of truth? May we not claim of our God the blessing promised unto those who consider the poor: the Lord will preserve them and keep them alive, and they shall be blessed upon the earth? Does not the language, 'Inasmuch as ye did it unto one of the least of these my brethren, ye did it unto me,' belong to all who are rightly engaged in endeavouring to unloose the bondman's fetters? Shall we not then do as the apostles did? Shall we not, in view of the two millions of heathen in our very midst, in view of the souls that are going down in an almost unbroken phalanx to utter perdition, continue in prayer and supplication, that God will grant us the supplies of his Spirit to prepare us for that work which he has given us to do? Shall not the wail of the mother as she surrenders her only child to the grasp of the ruthless kidnapper, or the trader in human blood, animate our devotions? Shall not the manifold crimes and horrors of slavery excite more ardent outpourings at the throne of grace to grant repentance to our guilty country, and permit us to aid in preparing the way for the glorious second advent of the Messiah, by preaching deliverance to the captives, and the opening of the prison doors to those who are bound?"

Georgiana had succeeded in rivetting the attention of Carlton during her conversation, and as she was finishing her last sentence, she observed the silent tear stealing down the cheek of the newly born child of God. At this juncture her father entered, and Carlton left the room. "Dear papa," said Georgiana, "will you grant me one favour; or, rather, make me a promise?" "I can't tell, my dear, till I know what it is," replied Mr. Peck. "If it is a reasonable request, I will comply with your wish," continued he. "I hope, my dear," answered she, "that papa would not think me capable of making an unreasonable request." "Well, well," returned he; "tell me what it is." "I hope," said she, "that in your future conversation with Mr. Carlton, on the subject of slavery, you will not speak of the Bible as sustaining it." "Why, Georgiana, my dear, you are mad, aint you?" exclaimed he, in an excited tone. The poor girl remained silent; the father saw in a moment that he had spoken too sharply; and taking her hand in his he said, "Now, my child, why do you make that request?" "Because," returned she, "I think he is on the stool of repentance, if he has not already been received among the elect. He, you know, was bordering upon infidelity, and if the Bible sanctions slavery, then he will naturally enough say that it is not from God; for the argument from internal evidence is not only refuted, but actually turned against the Bible. If the Bible sanctions slavery, then it misrepresents the character of God. Nothing would be more dangerous to the soul of a young convert than to satisfy him that the Scriptures favoured such a system of sin." "Don't you suppose that I understand the Scriptures better than you? I have been in the world longer." "Yes," said she, "you have been in the world longer, and amongst slaveholders so long that you do not regard it in the same light that those do who have not become so familiar with its every-day scenes as you. I once heard you say, that you were opposed to the institution, when you first came to the South." "Yes," answered he, "I did not know so much about it then." "With great deference to you, papa," replied Georgiana, "I don't think that the Bible sanctions slavery. The Old Testament contains this explicit condemnation of it, 'He that stealeth a man, and selleth him, or if he be found in his hand, he shall surely be put to death'; and 'Woe unto him that buildeth his house by unrighteousness, and his chambers by wrong; that useth his neighbour's service without wages, and giveth him not for his work'; when also the New Testament exhibits such words of rebuke as these, 'Behold the hire of the labourers who have reaped down your fields, which is of you kept back by fraud, crieth; and the cries of them who have reaped are entered into the ears of the Lord of Sabaoth.' 'The law is not made for a righteous man, but for the lawless and disobedient, for the ungodly and for sinners, for unholy and profane, for murderers of fathers and murderers of mothers, for manslayers, for whoremongers, for them that defile themselves with mankind, for *menstealers*, for liars, for perjured persons.' A more scathing denunciation of the sin in question is surely to be found on record in no other book. I am afraid," continued the daughter, "that the acts of the professed friends of Christianity in the South do more to spread infidelity than the writings of all the atheists which have ever been published. The infidel watches the religious world. He surveys the church, and, lo! thousands and tens of thousands of her accredited members actually hold slaves. Members 'in good and regular standing,' fellowshipped throughout Christendom except by a few anti-slavery churches generally despised as ultra and radical, reduce their fellow men to the condition of chattels, and by force keep them in that state of degradation. Bishops, ministers, elders, and deacons are engaged in this awful business, and do not consider their conduct as at all inconsistent with the precepts of either the Old or New Testaments. Moreover, those ministers and churches who do not themselves hold slaves, very generally defend the conduct of those who do, and accord to them a fair Christian character, and in the way of business frequently take mortgages and levy executions on the bodies of their fellow men, and in some cases of their fellow Christians.

"Now is it a wonder that infidels, beholding the practice and listening to the theory of professing Christians, should conclude that the Bible inculcates a morality not inconsistent with chattelising human beings? And must not this conclusion be strengthened, when they hear ministers of talent and learning declare that the Bible does sanction slaveholding, and that it ought not to be made a disciplinable offence in churches? And must not all doubt be dissipated, when one of the most learned professors in our theological seminaries asserts that the Bible 'recognises that the relation may still exist, *salva fide et salva ecclesia*' (without injury to the Christian faith or church) and that only 'the *abuse* of it is the essential and fundamental wrong?' Are not infidels bound to believe that these professors, ministers, and churches understand their own Bible, and that, consequently, notwithstanding solitary passages which appear to condemn slaveholding, the Bible sanctions it? When nothing can be further from the truth. And as for Christ, his whole life was a living testimony against slavery and all that it inculcates. When he designed to do us good, he took upon himself the form of a servant. He took his station at the bottom of society. He voluntarily identified himself with the poor and the despised. The warning voices of Jeremiah and Ezekiel were raised in olden time, against sin. Let us not forget what followed. 'Therefore, thus saith the Lord—ye have not hearkened unto me in proclaiming liberty every one to his brother, and every one to his neighbour—behold I proclaim a liberty for you saith the Lord, to the sword, to the pestilence, and to the famine.' Are we not virtually as a nation adopting the same impious language, and are we not exposed to the same tremendous judgments? Shall we not, in view of those things, use every laudable means to awaken our beloved country from the slumbers of death, and baptize all our efforts with tears and with prayers, that God may bless them? Then, should our labour fail to accomplish the end for which we pray, we shall stand acquitted at the bar of Jehovah, and although we may share in the national calamities which await unrepented sins, yet that blessed approval will be ours.—'Well done good and faithful servants, enter ye into the joy of your Lord.'"

"My dear Georgiana," said Mr. Peck, "I must be permitted to entertain my own views on this subject, and to exercise my own judgment."

"Believe me, dear papa," she replied, "I would not be understood as wishing to teach you, or to dictate to you in the least; but only grant my request, not to allude to the Bible as sanctioning slavery, when speaking with Mr. Carlton."

"Well," returned he, "I will comply with your wish."

The young Christian had indeed accomplished a noble work; and whether it was admitted by the father, or not, she was his superior and his teacher. Georgiana had viewed the right to enjoy perfect liberty as one of those inherent and inalienable rights which pertain to the whole human race, and of which they can never be divested, except by an act of gross injustice. And no one was more able than herself to impress those views upon the hearts of all with whom she came in contact. Modest and self-possessed, with a voice of great sweetness, and a most winning manner, she could, with the greatest ease to herself, engage their attention.

XI. The Parson Poet

"Unbind, unbind my galling chain,
    And set, oh! set me free:
No longer say that I'll disdain
    The gift of liberty."

THROUGH the persuasion of Mr. Peck, and fascinated with the charms of Georgiana, Carlton had prolonged his stay two months with his old school-fellow. During the latter part of the time he had been almost as one of the family. If Miss Peck was invited out, Mr. Carlton was, as a matter of course. She seldom rode out, unless with him. If Mr. Peck was absent, he took the head of the table; and, to the delight of the young lady, he had on several occasions taken part in the family worship. "I am glad," said Mr. Peck, one evening while at the tea table, "I am glad, Mr. Carlton, that my neighbour Jones has invited you to visit him at his farm. He is a good neighbour, but a very ungodly man; I want that you should see his people, and then, when you return to the North, you can tell how much better a Christian's slaves are situated than one who does nothing for the cause of Christ." "I hope, Mr. Carlton," said Georgiana, "that you will spend the Sabbath with him, and have a religious interview with the negroes." "Yes," replied the parson, "that's well thought of, Georgy." "Well, I think I will go up on Thursday next, and stay till Monday," said Carlton; "and I shall act upon your suggestion, Miss Peck," continued he; "and try to get a religious interview with the blacks. By-the-by," remarked Carlton, "I saw an advertisement in the *Free Trader* to-day that rather puzzled me. Ah, here it is now; and," drawing the paper from his pocket, "I will read it, and then you can tell me what it means:

104

'TO PLANTERS AND OTHERS.—*Wanted fifty negroes.* Any person having *sick negroes,* considered *incurable* by their respective physicians, (their owners of course,) and wishing to dispose of them, Dr. Stillman will pay cash for negroes affected with scrofula or king's evil, confirmed hypochondriacism, apoplexy, or diseases of the brain, kidneys, spleen, stomach and intestines, bladder and its appendages, diarrhœa, dysentery, &c. *The highest cash price will be paid as above.*'

When I read this to-day I thought that the advertiser must be a man of eminent skill as a physician, and that he intended to cure the sick negroes; but on second thought I find that some of the diseases enumerated are certainly incurable. What can he do with these sick negroes?" "You see," replied Mr. Peck, laughing, "that he is a doctor, and has use for them in his lectures. The doctor is connected with a small college. Look at his prospectus, where he invites students to attend, and that will explain the matter to you." Carlton turned to another column, and read the following:

"Some advantages of a peculiar character are connected with this institution, which it may be proper to point out. No place in the United States offers as great opportunities for the acquisition of anatomical knowledge. Subjects being obtained from among the coloured population in sufficient numbers *for every purpose,* and proper dissections carried on *without offending any individuals in the community!*"

"These are for dissection, then?" inquired Carlton with a trembling voice. "Yes," answered the parson. "Of course they wait till they die before they can use them." "They keep them on hand, and when they need one they bleed him to death," returned Mr. Peck. "Yes, but that's murder." "Oh, the doctors are licensed to commit murder, you know; and what's the difference, whether one dies owing to the loss of blood, or taking too many pills? For my own part, if I had to choose, I would rather submit to the former." "I have often heard what I considered hard stories in abolition meetings in New York about slavery; but now I shall begin to think that many of them are true." "The longer you remain here the more you will be convinced of the iniquity of the institution," remarked Georgiana. "Now, Georgy, my dear, don't give us another abolition lecture, if you please," said Mr.

Peck. "Here, Carlton," continued the parson, "I have written a short poem for your sister's album, as you requested me; it is a domestic piece, as you will see." "She will prize it the more for that," remarked Carlton; and taking the sheet of paper, he laughed as his eyes glanced over it. "Read it out, Mr. Carlton," said Georgiana, "and let me hear what it is; I know papa gets off some very droll things at times." Carlton complied with the young lady's request, and read aloud the following rare specimen of poetical genius:

"MY LITTLE NIG.

"I have a little nigger, the blackest thing alive,
  He'll be just four years old if he lives till forty-five;
  His smooth cheek hath a glossy hue, like a new polished boot,
  And his hair curls o'er his little head as black as any soot.
  His lips bulge from his countenance—his little ivories shine—
  His nose is what we call a little pug, but fashioned very fine:
  Although not quite a fairy, he is comely to behold,
  And I wouldn't sell him, 'pon my word, for a hundred all in gold.

"He gets up early in the morn, like all the other nigs,
  And runs off to the hog-lot, where he squabbles with the pigs—
  And when the sun gets out of bed, and mounts up in the sky,
  The warmest corner of the yard is where my nig doth lie.
  And there extended lazily, he contemplates and dreams,
  (I cannot qualify to this, but plain enough it seems;)
  Until 'tis time to take in grub, when you can't find him there,
  For, like a politician, he has gone to hunt his share.

"I haven't said a single word concerning my plantation,
  Though a prettier, I guess, cannot be found within the nation;
  When he gets a little bigger, I'll take and to him show it,
  And then I'll say, 'My little nig, now just prepare to go it!'
  I'll put a hoe into his hand—he'll soon know what it means,
  And every day for dinner, he shall have bacon and greens."

XII. A Night in the Parson's Kitchen

"And see the servants met,
   Their daily labour's o'er;
And with the jest and song they set
   The kitchen in a roar."

MR. PECK kept around him four servants besides Currer, of whom we have made mention: of these, Sam was considered the first. If a dinner-party was in contemplation, or any company to be invited to the parson's, after all the arrangements had been talked over by the minister and his daughter, Sam was sure to be consulted upon the subject by "Miss Georgy," as Miss Peck was called by the servants. If furniture, crockery, or anything else was to be purchased, Sam felt that he had been slighted if his opinion had not been asked. As to the marketing, he did it all. At the servants' table in the kitchen, he sat at the head, and was master of ceremonies. A single look from him was enough to silence any conversation or noise in the kitchen, or any other part of the premises. There is, in the Southern States, a great amount of prejudice against colour amongst the negroes themselves. The nearer the negro or mulatto approaches to the white, the more he seems to feel his superiority over those of a darker hue. This is, no doubt, the result of the prejudice that exists on the part of the whites towards both mulattoes and blacks. Sam was originally from Kentucky, and through the instrumentality of one of his young masters whom he had to take to school, he had learned to read so as to be well understood; and, owing to that fact, was considered a prodigy among the slaves, not only of his own master's, but those of the town who knew him. Sam had a great wish to follow in the footsteps of his master, and be a poet; and was, therefore, often heard singing doggrels of his own composition. But there was one great draw-back to Sam, and that was his colour. He was one of the blackest of his race. This he evidently regarded as a great misfortune. However, he made up for this in his dress. Mr. Peck kept his house servants well dressed; and as for Sam, he was seldom seen except in a ruffled shirt. Indeed, the washerwoman feared him more than all others about the house.

Currer, as we have already stated, was chief of the kitchen department, and had a general supervision of the household affairs. Alfred the coachman, Peter, and Hetty made up the remainder of the house servants. Besides these, Mr. Peck owned eight slaves who were masons. These worked in the city. Being mechanics, they were let out to greater advantage than to keep them on the farm. However, every Sunday night, Peck's servants, including the bricklayers, usually assembled in the kitchen, when the events of the week were freely discussed and commented on. It was on a Sunday evening, in the month of June, that there was a party at Mr. Peck's, and, according to custom in the Southern States, the ladies had their maid-servants with them. Tea had been served in "the house," and the servants, including the strangers, had taken their seats at the tea table in the kitchen. Sam, being a "single gentleman," was usually attentive to the "ladies" on this occasion. He seldom or ever let the day pass without spending at least an hour in combing and brushing up his "hair." Sam had an idea that fresh butter was better for his hair than any other kind of grease; and therefore, on churning days, half a pound of butter had always to be taken out before it was salted. When he wished to appear to great advantage, he would grease his face, to make it "shiny." On the evening of the party therefore, when all the servants were at the table, Sam cut a big figure. There he sat with his wool well combed and buttered, face nicely greased, and his ruffles extending five or six inches from his breast. The parson in his own drawing-room did not make a more imposing appearance than did his servant on this occasion. "I jist bin had my fortune told last Sunday night," said Sam, as he helped one of the girls to some sweet hash. "Indeed," cried half-a-dozen voices. "Yes," continued he; "Aunt Winny told me I is to hab de prettiest yaller gal in town, and dat I is to be free." All eyes were immediately turned toward Sally Johnson, who was seated near Sam. "I speck I see somebody blush at dat remark," said Alfred. "Pass dem pancakes and molasses up dis way, Mr. Alf, and none of your insinawaysion here," rejoined Sam. "Dat reminds me," said Currer, "dat Dorcas Simpson is gwine to git married." "Who to, I want to know?" inquired Peter. "To one of Mr. Darby's field-hands," answered Currer. "I should tink dat dat gal would not trow herself away in dat manner," said Sally. "She good enough looking to get a house servant, and not to put up wid a fiel' nigger," continued she. "Yes," said Sam, "dat's a wery insensible remark of yours, Miss Sally. I admire your judgment wery much, I assure you. Dah's plenty of suspectible and well-dressed house servants dat a gal of her looks can get, wid out taken up wid dem common darkies." "Is de man black or a mulatto?" inquired one of the company. "He's nearly white," replied Currer. "Well den, dat's some exchuse for her," remarked Sam; "for I don't like to see dis malgemation of blacks and mulattoes, no how," continued Sam. "If I had my rights I would be a mulatto too, for my mother was almost as light-coloured as Miss Sally," said he. Although Sam was one of the blackest men living, he nevertheless contended that his mother was a mulatto, and no one was more prejudiced against the blacks than he. A good deal of work, and the free use of fresh butter, had no doubt done wonders for his "hare" in causing it to grow long, and to this he would always appeal when he wished to convince others that he was part of an Anglo-Saxon. "I always thought you was not clear black, Mr. Sam," said Agnes. "You are right dahr, Miss Agnes. My hare tells what company I belong to," answered Sam. Here the whole company joined in the conversation about colour, which lasted for some time, giving unmistakeable evidence that caste is owing to ignorance. The evening's entertainment concluded by Sam's relating a little of his own experience while with his first master in old Kentucky.

Sam's former master was a doctor, and had a large practice among his neighbours, doctoring both masters and slaves. When Sam was about fifteen years of age, his old master set him to grinding up the ointment, then to making pills. As the young student grew older and became more practised in his profession, his services were of more importance to the doctor. The physician having a good business, and a large number of his patients being slaves, the most of whom had to call on the doctor when ill, he put Sam to bleeding, pulling teeth, and administering medicine to the slaves. Sam soon acquired the name amongst the slaves of the "Black Doctor." With this appellation he was delighted, and no regular physician could possibly have put on more airs than did the black doctor when his services were required. In bleeding, he must have more bandages, and rub and smack the arm more than the doctor would have thought of. We once saw Sam taking out a tooth for one of his patients, and nothing appeared more amusing. He got the poor fellow down on his back, and he got a straddle of the man's chest, and getting the turnkeys on the wrong tooth, he shut both eyes and pulled for his life. The poor man screamed as loud as he could, but to no purpose. Sam had him fast. After a great effort, out came the sound grinder, and the young doctor saw his mistake; but consoled himself with the idea that as the wrong tooth was out of the way, there was more room to get at the right one. Bleeding and a dose of calomel was always considered indispensable by the "Old Boss"; and, as a matter of course, Sam followed in his footsteps.

On one occasion the old doctor was ill himself, so as to be unable to attend to his patients. A slave, with pass in hand, called to receive medical advice, and the master told Sam to examine him and see what he wanted. This delighted him beyond measure, for although he had been acting his part in the way of giving out medicine as the master ordered it, he had never been called upon by the latter to examine a patient, and this seemed to convince him that, after all, he was no sham doctor. As might have been expected, he cut a rare figure in his first examination, placing himself directly opposite his patient, and folding his arms across his breast, and looking very knowingly, he began, "What's de matter wid you?" "I is sick." "Where is you sick?" "Here," replied the man, putting his hand upon his stomach. "Put out your tongue," continued the doctor. The man run out his tongue at full length. "Let me feel your pulse," at the same time taking his patient's hand in his, placing his fingers on his pulse, he said, "Ah, your case is a bad one; if I don't do something for you, and dat pretty quick, you 'ill be a gone coon, and dat's sartin." At this the man appeared frightened, and inquired what was the matter with him: in answer, Sam said, "I done told you dat your case is a bad one, and dat's enough." On Sam's returning to his master's bedside, the latter said, "Well, Sam, what do you think is the matter with him?" "His stomach is out of order, sir," he replied. "What do you think had best be done for him?" "I think I better bleed him and give him a dose of calomel," returned Sam. So to the latter's gratification the master let him have his own way. We need not further say, that the recital of Sam's experience as a physician gave him a high position amongst the servants that evening, and made him a decided favourite with the ladies, one of whom feigned illness, when the black doctor, to the delight of all, and certainly to himself, gave medical advice. Thus ended the evening amongst the servants in the parson's kitchen.

XIII. A Slave Hunting Parson

"'Tis too much prov'd—that with devotion's visage,
And pious action, we do sugar o'er the devil himself."
Shakspeare.

YOU WILL, no doubt, be well pleased with neighbour Jones,"
said Mr. Peck, as Carlton stepped into the chaise to pay his
promised visit to the "ungodly man." "Don't forget to have a
religious interview with the negroes," remarked Georgiana, as
she gave the last nod to her young convert. "I will do my best,"
returned Carlton, as the vehicle left the door. As might have
been expected, Carlton met with a cordial reception at the
hands of the proprietor of the Grove Farm. The servants in the
"Great House" were well dressed, and appeared as if they did
not want for food. Jones knew that Carlton was from the North,
and a non-slaveholder, and therefore did everything in his
power to make a favourable impression on his mind. "My negroes are well clothed, well fed, and not over worked," said the
slaveholder to his visitor, after the latter had been with him
nearly a week. "As far as I can see, your slaves appear to good
advantage," replied Carlton. "But," continued he, "if it is a fair
question, do you have preaching among your slaves on Sunday,
Mr. Jones?" "No, no," returned he, "I think that's all nonsense;
my negroes do their own preaching." "So you do permit them to
have meetings." "Yes, when they wish. There's some very intelligent and clever chaps among them." "As to-morrow is the
Sabbath," said Carlton, "if you have no objection, I will attend
meeting with them." "Most certainly you shall, if you will do the
preaching," returned the planter. Here the young man was
about to decline, but he remembered the parting words of

Georgiana, and he took courage and said, "Oh, I have no objection to give the negroes a short talk." It was then understood that Carlton was to have a religious interview with the blacks the next day, and the young man waited with a degree of impatience for the time.

In no part of the South are slaves in a more ignorant and degraded state than in the cotton, sugar, and rice districts.

If they are permitted to cease labour on the Sabbath, the time is spent in hunting, fishing, or lying beneath the shade of a tree, resting for the morrow. Religious instruction is unknown in the far South, except among such men as the Rev. C. C. Jones, John Peck, and some others who regard religious instruction, such as they impart to their slaves, as calculated to make them more trustworthy and valuable as property. Jones, aware that his slaves would make rather a bad show of intelligence if questioned by Carlton, resolved to have them ready for him, and therefore gave his driver orders with regard to their preparation. Consequently, after the day's labour was over, Dogget, the driver, assembled the negroes together and said, "Now, boys and gals, your master is coming down to the quarters to-morrow with his visitor, who is going to give you a preach, and I want you should understand what he says to you. Now many of you who came of Old Virginia and Kentuck, know what preaching is, and others who have been raised in these parts do not. Preaching is to tell you that you are mighty wicked and bad at heart. This, I suppose, you all know. But if the gentleman should ask you who made you, tell him the Lord; if he ask if you wish to go to heaven, tell him yes. Remember that you are all Christians, all love the Lord, all want to go to heaven, all love your masters, and all love me. Now, boys and gals, I want you to show yourselves smart to-morrow: be on your p's and q's, and, Monday morning, I will give you all a glass of whiskey bright and early." Agreeable to arrangement the slaves were assembled together on Sunday morning under the large trees near the great house, and after going through another drilling from the driver, Jones and Carlton made their appearance. "You see," said Jones to the negroes, as he approached them, "you see here's a gentleman that's come to talk to you about your souls, and I hope you 'ill all pay that attention that you ought." Jones then seated himself in one of the two chairs placed there for him and the stranger.

Carlton had already selected a chapter in the Bible to read to them, which he did, after first prefacing it with some remarks of his own. Not being accustomed to speak in public, he determined, after reading the Bible, to make it more of a conversational meeting than otherwise. He therefore began asking them questions. "Do you feel that you are a Christian?" asked he of a full-blooded negro that sat near him. "Yes, sir," was the response. "You feel, then, that you shall go to heaven." "Yes, sir." "Of course you know who made you?" The man put his hand to his head and began to scratch his wool; and, after a little hesitation, answered, "De overseer told us last night who made us, but indeed I forgot the gentmun's name." This reply was almost too much for Carlton, and his gravity was not a little moved. However, he bit his tongue, and turned to another man, who appeared, from his looks, to be more intelligent. "Do you serve the Lord?" asked he. "No, sir, I don't serve anybody but Mr. Jones; I neber belong to anybody else." To hide his feelings at this juncture, Carlton turned and walked to another part of the grounds, to where the women were seated, and said to a mulatto woman who had rather an anxious countenance, "Did you ever hear of John the Baptist?" "Oh yes, marser, John de Baptist; I know dat nigger bery well indeed; he libs in Old Kentuck, where I come from." Carlton's gravity here gave way, and he looked at the planter and laughed right out. The old woman knew a slave near her old master's farm in Kentucky, and was ignorant enough to suppose that he was the John the Baptist inquired about. Carlton occupied the remainder of the time in reading Scripture and talking to them. "My niggers aint shown off very well to-day," said Jones, as he and his visitor left the grounds. "No," replied Carlton. "You did not get hold of the bright ones," continued the planter. "So it seems," remarked Carlton. The planter evidently felt that his neighbour, Parson Peck, would have a nut to crack over the account that Carlton would give of the ignorance of the slaves, and said and did all in his power to remove the bad impression already made; but to no purpose. The report made by Carlton, on his return, amused the parson

very much. It appeared to him the best reason why professed
Christians like himself should be slave-holders. Not so with
Georgiana. She did not even smile when Carlton was telling his
story, but seemed sore at heart that such ignorance should prevail in their midst. The question turned upon the heathen of
other lands, and the parson began to expatiate upon his own efforts in foreign missions, when his daughter, with a child-like
simplicity, said,

> "Send Bibles to the heathen;
>   On every distant shore,
>   From light that's beaming o'er us,
>   Let streams increasing pour
>   But keep it from the millions
>   Down-trodden at our door.
>
> "Send Bibles to the heathen,
>   Their famished spirits feed;
>   Oh! haste, and join your efforts,
>   The priceless gift to speed;
>   Then flog the trembling negro
>   If he should learn to read."

"I saw a curiosity while at Mr. Jones's that I shall not forget
soon," said Carlton. "What was it?" inquired the parson. "A ken-
nel of bloodhounds; and such dogs I never saw before. They
were of a species between the bloodhound and the foxhound,
and were ferocious, gaunt, and savage-looking animals. They
were part of a stock imported from Cuba, he informed me. They
were kept in an iron cage, and fed on Indian corn bread. This
kind of food, he said, made them eager for their business.
Sometimes they would give the dogs meat, but it was always
after they had been chasing a negro." "Were those the dogs you
had, papa, to hunt Harry?" asked Georgiana. "No, my dear," was
the short reply: and the parson seemed anxious to change the
conversation to something else. When Mr. Peck had left the
room, Carlton spoke more freely of what he had seen, and spoke
more pointedly against slavery; for he well knew that Miss Peck
sympathised with him in all he felt and said.

"You mentioned about your father hunting a slave," said

Carlton, in an under tone. "Yes," replied she; "papa went with some slave-catchers and a parcel of those nasty negro-dogs, to hunt poor Harry. He belonged to papa and lived on the farm. His wife lives in town, and Harry had been to see her, and did not return quite as early as he should; and Huckelby was flogging him, and he got away and came here. I wanted papa to keep him in town, so that he could see his wife more frequently; but he said they could not spare him from the farm, and flogged him again, and sent him back. The poor fellow knew that the overseer would punish him over again, and instead of going back he went into the woods." "Did they catch him?" asked Carlton. "Yes," replied she. "In chasing him through the woods, he attempted to escape by swimming across a river, and the dogs were sent in after him, and soon caught him. But Harry had great courage and fought the dogs with a big club; and papa seeing the negro would escape from the dogs, shot at him, as he says, only to wound him, that he might be caught; but the poor fellow was killed." Overcome by relating this incident, Georgiana burst into tears.

Although Mr. Peck fed and clothed his house servants well, and treated them with a degree of kindness, he was, nevertheless, a most cruel master. He encouraged his driver to work the field-hands from early dawn till late at night; and the good appearance of the house-servants, and the preaching of Snyder to the field negroes, was to cause himself to be regarded as a Christian master. Being on a visit one day at the farm, and having with him several persons from the Free States, and wishing to make them believe that his slaves were happy, satisfied, and contented, the parson got out the whiskey and gave each one a dram, who in return had to drink the master's health, or give a toast of some kind. The company were not a little amused at some of the sentiments given, and Peck was delighted at every indication of contentment on the part of the blacks. At last it came to Jack's turn to drink, and the master expected something good from him, because he was considered the cleverest and most witty slave on the farm.

"Now," said the master, as he handed Jack the cup of whiskey; "now, Jack, give us something rich. You know," continued he, "we have raised the finest crop of cotton that's been seen in these parts for many a day. Now give us a toast on cotton; come, Jack, give us something to laugh at." The negro felt not a little elated at being made the hero of the occasion, and taking the whiskey in his right hand, put his left to his head and began to scratch his wool, and said,

> "The big bee flies high,
> The little bee make the honey;
> The black folks makes the cotton,
> And the white folks gets the money."

XIV. A Free Woman Reduced to Slavery

ALTHESA FOUND in Henry Morton a kind and affectionate husband; and his efforts to purchase her mother, although unsuccessful, had doubly endeared him to her. Having from the commencement resolved not to hold slaves, or rather not to own any, they were compelled to hire servants for their own use. Five years had passed away, and their happiness was increased by two lovely daughters. Mrs. Morton was seated, one bright afternoon, busily engaged with her needle, and near her sat Salome, a servant that she had just taken into her employ. The woman was perfectly white; so much so, that Mrs. Morton had expressed her apprehensions to her husband, when the woman first came, that she was not born a slave. The mistress watched the servant, as the latter sat sewing upon some coarse work, and saw the large silent tear in her eye. This caused an uneasiness to the mistress, and she said, "Salome, don't you like your situation here?" "Oh yes, madam," answered the woman in a quick tone, and then tried to force a smile. "Why is it that you often look sad, and with tears in your eyes?" The mistress saw that she had touched a tender chord, and continued, "I am your friend; tell me your sorrow, and, if I can, I will help you." As the last sentence was escaping the lips of the mistress, the slave woman put her check apron to her face and wept. Mrs. Morton saw plainly that there was cause for this expression of grief, and pressed the woman more closely. "Hear me, then," said the woman calming herself: "I will tell you why I sometimes weep. I was born in Germany, on the banks of the Rhine. Ten years ago my father came to this country, bringing with him my mother and myself. He was poor, and I, wishing to assist all I could, obtained a situ-

ation as nurse to a lady in this city. My father got employment
as a labourer on the wharf, among the steamboats; but he was
soon taken ill with the yellow fever, and died. My mother then
got a situation for herself, while I remained with my first employer. When the hot season came on, my master, with his wife,
left New Orleans until the hot season was over, and took me
with them. They stopped at a town on the banks of the
Mississippi river, and said they should remain there some
weeks. One day they went out for a ride, and they had not been
gone more than half an hour, when two men came into the room
and told me that they had bought me, and that I was their slave.
I was bound and taken to prison, and that night put on a steamboat and taken up the Yazoo river, and set to work on a farm. I
was forced to take up with a negro, and by him had three children. A year since my master's daughter was married, and I was
given to her. She came with her husband to this city, and I have
ever since been hired out."

"Unhappy woman," whispered Althesa, "why did you not tell
me this before?" "I was afraid," replied Salome, "for I was once
severely flogged for telling a stranger that I was not born a
slave." On Mr. Morton's return home, his wife communicated
to him the story which the slave woman had told her an hour
before, and begged that something might be done to rescue her
from the situation she was then in. In Louisiana as well as many
others of the slave states, great obstacles are thrown in the way
of persons who have been wrongfully reduced to slavery regaining their freedom. A person claiming to be free must prove his
right to his liberty. This, it will be seen, throws the burden of
proof upon the slave, who, in all probability, finds it out of his
power to procure such evidence. And if any free person shall
attempt to aid a freeman in regaining his freedom, he is compelled to enter into security in the sum of one thousand dollars,
and if the person claiming to be free shall fail to establish such
fact, the thousand dollars are forfeited to the state. This cruel
and oppressive law has kept many a freeman from espousing the
cause of persons unjustly held as slaves. Mr. Morton inquired
and found that the woman's story was true, as regarded the time
she had lived with her present owner; but the latter not only

denied that she was free, but immediately removed her from Morton's. Three months after Salome had been removed from Morton's and let out to another family, she was one morning cleaning the door steps, when a lady passing by, looked at the slave and thought she recognised some one that she had seen before. The lady stopped and asked the woman if she was a slave. "I am," said she. "Were you born a slave?" "No, I was born in Germany." "What's the name of the ship in which you came to this country?" inquired the lady. "I don't know," was the answer. "Was it the *Amazon?*" At the sound of this name, the slave woman was silent for a moment, and then the tears began to flow freely down her care-worn cheeks. "Would you know Mrs. Marshall, who was a passenger in the *Amazon,* if you should see her?" inquired the lady. At this the woman gazed at the lady with a degree of intensity that can be imagined better than described, and then fell at the lady's feet. The lady was Mrs. Marshall. She had crossed the Atlantic in the same ship with this poor woman. Salome, like many of her countrymen, was a beautiful singer, and had often entertained Mrs. Marshall and the other lady passengers on board the *Amazon.* The poor woman was raised from the ground by Mrs. Marshall, and placed upon the door step that she had a moment before been cleaning. "I will do my utmost to rescue you from the horrid life of a slave," exclaimed the lady, as she took from her pocket her pencil, and wrote down the number of the house, and the street in which the German woman was working as a slave.

After a long and tedious trial of many days, it was decided that Salome Miller was by birth a free woman, and she was set at liberty. The good and generous Althesa had contributed some of the money toward bringing about the trial, and had done much to cheer on Mrs. Marshall in her benevolent object. Salome Miller is free, but where are her three children? They are still slaves, and in all human probability will die as such.

This, reader, is no fiction; if you think so, look over the files of the New Orleans newspapers of the years 1845–6, and you will there see reports of the trial.

XV. To-day a Mistress, To-morrow a Slave

> "I promised thee a sister tale
> Of man's perfidious cruelty;
> Come, then, and hear what cruel wrong
> Befel the dark ladie."—*Coleridge.*

LET us return for a moment to the home of Clotel. While she was passing lonely and dreary hours with none but her darling child, Horatio Green was trying to find relief in that insidious enemy of man, the intoxicating cup. Defeated in politics, forsaken in love by his wife, he seemed to have lost all principle of honour, and was ready to nerve himself up to any deed, no matter how unprincipled. Clotel's existence was now well known to Horatio's wife, and both her and her father demanded that the beautiful quadroon and her child should be sold and sent out of the state. To this proposition he at first turned a deaf ear; but when he saw that his wife was about to return to her father's roof, he consented to leave the matter in the hands of his father-in-law. The result was, that Clotel was immediately sold to the slave-trader, Walker, who, a few years previous, had taken her mother and sister to the far South. But, as if to make her husband drink of the cup of humiliation to its very dregs, Mrs. Green resolved to take his child under her own roof for a servant. Mary was, therefore, put to the meanest work that could be found, and although only ten years of age, she was often compelled to perform labour, which, under ordinary circumstances, would have been thought too hard for one much older. One condition of the sale of Clotel to Walker was, that she should be taken out of the state, which was accordingly done. Most quadroon women who are taken to the lower countries to

121

be sold are either purchased by gentlemen for their own use, or sold for waiting-maids; and Clotel, like her sister, was fortunate enough to be bought for the latter purpose. The town of Vicksburgh stands on the left bank of the Mississippi, and is noted for the severity with which slaves are treated. It was here that Clotel was sold to Mr. James French, a merchant.

Mrs. French was severe in the extreme to her servants. Well dressed, but scantily fed, and overworked were all who found a home with her. The quadroon had been in her new home but a short time ere she found that her situation was far different from what it was in Virginia. What social virtues are possible in a society of which injustice is the primary characteristic? in a society which is divided into two classes, masters and slaves? Every married woman in the far South looks upon her husband as unfaithful, and regards every quadroon servant as a rival. Clotel had been with her new mistress but a few days, when she was ordered to cut off her long hair. The negro, constitutionally, is fond of dress and outward appearance. He that has short, woolly hair, combs it and oils it to death. He that has long hair, would sooner have his teeth drawn than lose it. However painful it was to the quadroon, she was soon seen with her hair cut as short as any of the full-blooded negroes in the dwelling.

Even with her short hair, Clotel was handsome. Her life had been a secluded one, and though now nearly thirty years of age, she was still beautiful. At her short hair, the other servants laughed, "Miss Clo needn't strut round so big, she got short nappy har well as I," said Nell, with a broad grin that showed her teeth. "She tinks she white, when she come here wid dat long har of hers," replied Mill. "Yes," continued Nell; "missus make her take down her wool so she no put it up to-day."

The fairness of Clotel's complexion was regarded with envy as well by the other servants as by the mistress herself. This is one of the hard features of slavery. To-day the woman is mistress of her own cottage; to-morrow she is sold to one who aims to make her life as intolerable as possible. And be it remembered, that the house servant has the best situation which a slave can occupy. Some American writers have tried to make the world believe that the condition of the labouring classes of England is as bad as the slaves of the United States.

The English labourer may be oppressed, he may be cheated, defrauded, swindled, and even starved; but it is not slavery under which he groans. He cannot be sold; in point of law he is equal to the prime minister. "It is easy to captivate the unthinking and the prejudiced, by eloquent declamation about the oppression of English operatives being worse than that of American slaves, and by exaggerating the wrongs on one side and hiding them on the other. But all informed and reflecting minds, knowing that bad as are the social evils of England, those of Slavery are immeasurably worse." But the degradation and harsh treatment that Clotel experienced in her new home was nothing compared with the grief she underwent at being separated from her dear child. Taken from her without scarcely a moment's warning, she knew not what had become of her. The deep and heartfelt grief of Clotel was soon perceived by her owners, and fearing that her refusal to take food would cause her death, they resolved to sell her. Mr. French found no difficulty in getting a purchaser for the quadroon woman, for such are usually the most marketable kind of property. Clotel was sold at private sale to a young man for a housekeeper; but even he had missed his aim.

XVI. Death of the Parson

CARLTON WAS above thirty years of age, standing on the last legs of a young man, and entering on the first of a bachelor. He had never dabbled in matters of love, and looked upon all women alike. Although he respected woman for her virtues, and often spoke of the goodness of heart of the sex, he had never dreamed of marriage. At first he looked upon Miss Peck as a pretty young woman, but after she became his religious teacher, he regarded her in that light, that every one will those whom they know to be their superiors. It was soon seen, however, that the young man not only respected and reverenced Georgiana for the incalculable service she had done him, in awakening him to a sense of duty to his soul, but he had learned to bow to the shrine of Cupid. He found, weeks after he had been in her company, that when he met her at table, or alone in the drawing-room, or on the piazza, he felt a shortness of breath, a palpitating of the heart, a kind of dizziness of the head; but he knew not its cause.

This was love in its first stage. Mr. Peck saw, or thought he saw, what would be the result of Carlton's visit, and held out every inducement in his power to prolong his stay. The hot season was just commencing, and the young Northerner was talking of his return home, when the parson was very suddenly taken ill. The disease was the cholera, and the physicians pronounced the case incurable. In less than five hours John Peck was a corpse. His love for Georgiana, and respect for her father, had induced Carlton to remain by the bedside of the dying man, although against the express orders of the physician. This act of kindness caused the young orphan henceforth to regard Carlton

124

as her best friend. He now felt it his duty to remain with the young woman until some of her relations should be summoned from Connecticut. After the funeral, the family physician advised that Miss Peck should go to the farm, and spend the time at the country seat; and also advised Carlton to remain with her, which he did.

At the parson's death his negroes showed little or no signs of grief. This was noticed by both Carlton and Miss Peck, and caused no little pain to the latter. "They are ungrateful," said Carlton, as he and Georgiana were seated on the piazza. "What," asked she, "have they to be grateful for?" "Your father was kind, was he not?" "Yes, as kind as most men who own slaves; but the kindness meted out to blacks would be unkindness if given to whites. We would think so, should we not?" "Yes," replied he. "If we would not consider the best treatment which a slave receives good enough for us, we should not think he ought to be grateful for it. Everybody knows that slavery in its best and mildest form is wrong. Whoever denies this, his lips libel his heart. Try him! Clank the chains in his ears, and tell him they are for him; give him an hour to prepare his wife and children for a life of slavery; bid him make haste, and get ready their necks for the yoke, and their wrists for the coffle chains; then look at his pale lips and trembling knees, and you have nature's testimony against slavery."

"Let's take a walk," said Carlton, as if to turn the conversation. The moon was just appearing through the tops of the trees, and the animals and insects in an adjoining wood kept up a continued din of music. The croaking of bull-frogs, buzzing of insects, cooing of turtle-doves, and the sound from a thousand musical instruments, pitched on as many different keys, made the welkin ring. But even all this noise did not drown the singing of a party of the slaves, who were seated near a spring that was sending up its cooling waters. "How prettily the negroes sing," remarked Carlton, as they were wending their way towards the place from whence the sound of the voices came. "Yes," replied Georgiana; "master Sam is there, I'll warrant you: he's always on hand when there's any singing or dancing. We must not let them see us, or they will stop singing." "Who makes their songs for them?" inquired the young man. "Oh, they make them up as they sing them; they are all impromptu songs." By this time they were near enough to hear distinctly every word; and, true enough, Sam's voice was heard above all others. At the conclusion of each song they all joined in a hearty laugh, with an expression of "Dats de song for me"; "Dems dems."

"Stop," said Carlton, as Georgiana was rising from the log upon which she was seated; "stop, and let's hear this one." The piece was sung by Sam, the others joining in the chorus, and was as follows:

Sam.
"Come, all my brethren, let us take a rest,
    While the moon shines so brightly and clear;
Old master is dead, and left us at last,
    And has gone at the Bar to appear.
Old master has died, and lying in his grave,
    And our blood will awhile cease to flow;
He will no more trample on the neck of the slave;
    For he's gone where the slaveholders go.

Chorus.
"Hang up the shovel and the hoe—
    Take down the fiddle and the bow—
    Old master has gone to the slaveholder's rest;
    He has gone where they all ought to go.

Sam.
"I heard the old doctor say the other night,
    As he passed by the dining-room door—
'Perhaps the old man may live through the night,
    But I think he will die about four.'
Young mistress sent me, at the peril of my life,
    For the parson to come down and pray,
For says she, 'Your old master is now about to die,'
    And says I, 'God speed him on his way.'

"Hang up the shovel, &c.

"At four o'clock at morn the family was called
    Around the old man's dying bed;

And oh! but I laughed to myself when I heard
   That the old man's spirit had fled.
Mr. Carlton cried, and so did I pretend;
   Young mistress very nearly went mad;
And the old parson's groans did the heavens fairly rend;
   But I tell you I felt mighty glad.

"Hang up the shovel, &c.

"We'll no more be roused by the blowing of his horn,
   Our backs no longer he will score;
He no more will feed us on cotton-seeds and corn;
   For his reign of oppression now is o'er.
He no more will hang our children on the tree,
   To be ate by the carrion crow;
He no more will send our wives to Tennessee;
   For he's gone where the slaveholders go.

"Hang up the shovel and the hoe,
Take down the fiddle and the bow,
We'll dance and sing,
And make the forest ring,
With the fiddle and the old banjo."

The song was not half finished before Carlton regretted that he had caused the young lady to remain and hear what to her must be anything but pleasant reflections upon her deceased parent. "I think we will walk," said he, at the same time extending his arm to Georgiana. "No," said she; "let's hear them out. It is from these unguarded expressions of the feelings of the negroes, that we should learn a lesson." At its conclusion they walked towards the house in silence: as they were ascending the steps, the young man said, "They are happy, after all. The negro, situated as yours are, is not aware that he is deprived of any just rights." "Yes, yes," answered Georgiana: "you may place the slave where you please; you may dry up to your utmost the fountains of his feelings, the springs of his thought; you may yoke him to your labour, as an ox which liveth only to work, and worketh only to live; you may put him under any process which, without destroying his value as a slave, will debase and crush him as a rational being; you may do this, and *the idea that he was*

born to be free will survive it all. It is allied to his hope of immortality; it is the ethereal part of his nature, which oppression
cannot reach; it is a torch lit up in his soul by the hand of Deity,
and never meant to be extinguished by the hand of man."

On reaching the drawing-room, they found Sam snuffing the
candles, and looking as solemn and as dignified as if he had
never sung a song or laughed in his life. "Will Miss Georgy have
de supper got up now?" asked the negro. "Yes," she replied.
"Well," remarked Carlton, "that beats anything I ever met with.
Do you think that was Sam we heard singing?" "I am sure of it,"
was the answer. "I could not have believed that that fellow was
capable of so much deception," continued he. "Our system of
slavery is one of deception; and Sam, you see, has only been a
good scholar. However, he is as honest a fellow as you will find
among the slave population here. If we would have them more
honest, we should give them their liberty, and then the inducement to be dishonest would be gone. I have resolved that these
creatures shall all be free." "Indeed!" exclaimed Carlton. "Yes, I
shall let them all go free, and set an example to those about me."
"I honour your judgment," said he. "But will the state permit
them to remain?" "If not, they can go where they can live in
freedom. I will not be unjust because the state is."

XVII. Retaliation

"I had a dream, a happy dream;
   I thought that I was free:
That in my own bright land again
   A home there was for me."

WITH THE deepest humiliation Horatio Green saw the daughter of Clotel, his own child, brought into his dwelling as a servant. His wife felt that she had been deceived, and determined to punish her deceiver. At first Mary was put to work in the kitchen, where she met with little or no sympathy from the other slaves, owing to the fairness of her complexion. The child was white, what should be done to make her look like other negroes, was the question Mrs. Green asked herself. At last she hit upon a plan: there was a garden at the back of the house over which Mrs. Green could look from her parlour window. Here the white slave-girl was put to work, without either bonnet or handkerchief upon her head. A hot sun poured its broiling rays on the naked face and neck of the girl, until she sank down in the corner of the garden, and was actually broiled to sleep. "Dat little nigger ain't working a bit, missus," said Dinah to Mrs. Green, as she entered the kitchen.

"She's lying in the sun, seasoning; she will work better by and by," replied the mistress. "Dees white niggers always tink dey sef good as white folks," continued the cook. "Yes, but we will teach them better; won't we, Dinah?" "Yes, missus, I don't like dees mularter niggers, no how; dey always want to set dey sef up for something big." The cook was black, and was not without that prejudice which is to be found among the negroes, as well as among the whites of the Southern States. The sun had the desired effect, for in less than a fortnight Mary's fair complexion had disappeared, and she was but little whiter than any other mulatto children running about the yard. But the close resemblance between the father and child annoyed the mistress more than the mere whiteness of the child's complexion. Horatio made proposition after proposition to have the girl sent away, for every time he beheld her countenance it reminded him of the happy days he had spent with Clotel. But his wife had commenced, and determined to carry out her unfeeling and fiendish designs. This child was not only white, but she was the granddaughter of Thomas Jefferson, the man who, when speaking against slavery in the legislature of Virginia, said,

"The whole commerce between master and slave is a perpetual exercise of the most boisterous passions; *the most unremitting despotism on the one part, and degrading submission on the other.* With what execration should the statesman be loaded who, permitting one half the citizens thus to trample on the rights of the other, transforms those into despots and these into enemies, destroys the morals of the one part, and the *amor patriæ* of the other! For if the slave can have a country in this world, it must be any other in preference to that in which he is born to live and labour for another; in which he must lock up the faculties of his nature, contribute as far as depends on his individual endeavours to the evanishment of the human race, or entail his own miserable condition on the endless generations proceeding from him. And can the liberties of a nation be thought secure when we have removed their only firm basis, a conviction in the minds of the people that these liberties are the gift of God? that they are not to be violated but with his wrath? Indeed, I tremble for my country when I reflect that God is just; that his justice cannot sleep for ever; that, considering numbers, nature, and natural means only, a revolution of the wheel of fortune, an exchange of situation, is among possible events; that it may become probable by supernatural interference! The Almighty has no attribute which can take side with us in such a contest.

• • •

"What an incomprehensible machine is man! Who can endure toil, famine, stripes, imprisonment, and death itself, in vindication of his own liberty, and the next moment be deaf to all those motives, whose power supported him through his trial, and inflict on his fellow-men a bondage, *one hour of which is fraught with more misery than ages of that which he rose in rebellion to oppose!* But we must wait with patience the workings of an overruling Providence, and hope that that is preparing the deliverance of these our suffering brethren. When the measure of their tears shall be full—when their tears shall have involved heaven itself in darkness—doubtless a God of justice will awaken to their distress, and by diffusing light and liberality among their oppressors, or at length by his exterminating thunder, manifest his attention to things of this world, and that they are not left to the guidance of blind fatality."

The same man, speaking of the probability that the slaves might some day attempt to gain their liberties by a revolution, said,

"I tremble for my country, when I recollect that God is just, and that His justice cannot sleep for ever. The Almighty has no attribute that can take sides with us in such a struggle."

But, sad to say, Jefferson is not the only American statesman who has spoken high-sounding words in favour of freedom, and then left his own children to die slaves.

XVIII. The Liberator

"We hold these truths to be self-evident, that all men are created free and equal; that they are endowed by their Creator with certain inalienable rights; among these are life, *liberty,* and the pursuit of happiness." —*Declaration of American Independence.*

THE DEATH of the parson was the commencement of a new era in the history of his slaves. Only a little more than eighteen years of age, Georgiana could not expect to carry out her own wishes in regard to the slaves, although she was sole heir to her father's estate. There were distant relations whose opinions she had at least to respect. And both law and public opinion in the state were against any measure of emancipation that she might think of adopting; unless, perhaps, she might be permitted to send them to Liberia. Her uncle in Connecticut had already been written to, to come down and aid in settling up the estate. He was a Northern man, but she knew him to be a tight-fisted yankee, whose whole counsel would go against liberating the negroes. Yet there was one way in which the thing could be done. She loved Carlton, and she well knew that he loved her; she read it in his countenance every time they met, yet the young man did not mention his wishes to her. There were many reasons why he should not. In the first place, her father was just deceased, and it seemed only right that he should wait a reasonable time. Again, Carlton was poor, and Georgiana was possessed of a large fortune; and his high spirit would not, for a moment, allow him to place himself in a position to be regarded as a fortune-hunter. The young girl hinted, as best she could, at the probable future; but all to no purpose. He took nothing to himself. True, she had read much of "woman's rights"; and had even attended a meet-

ing, while at the North, which had been called to discuss the
wrongs of woman; but she could not nerve herself up to the point
of putting the question to Carlton, although she felt sure that she
should not be rejected. She waited, but in vain. At last, one evening, she came out of her room rather late, and was walking on
the piazza for fresh air. She passed near Carlton's room, and
heard the voice of Sam. The negro had just come in to get the
young man's boots, and had stopped, as he usually did, to have
some talk. "I wish," said Sam, "dat Marser Carlton an Miss
Georgy would get married; den, I 'spec, we'd have good times."
"I don't think your mistress would have me," replied the young
man. "What make tink dat, Marser Carlton?" "Your mistress
would marry no one, Sam, unless she loved them." "Den I wish
she would lub you, cause I tink we have good times den. All our
folks is de same 'pinion like me," returned the negro, and then
left the room with the boots in his hands. During the conversation between the Anglo-Saxon and the African, one word had
been dropped by the former that haunted the young lady the
remainder of the night—"Your mistress would marry no one
unless she loved them." That word awoke her in the morning,
and caused her to decide upon this important subject. Love and
duty triumphed over the woman's timid nature, and that day
Georgiana informed Carlton that she was ready to become his
wife. The young man, with grateful tears, accepted and kissed
the hand that was offered to him. The marriage of Carlton and
Miss Peck was hailed with delight by both the servants in the
house and the negroes on the farm. New rules were immediately
announced for the working and general treatment of the slaves
on the plantation. With this, Huckelby, the overseer, saw his
reign coming to an end; and Snyder, the Dutch preacher, felt
that his services would soon be dispensed with, for nothing was
more repugnant to the feelings of Mrs. Carlton than the sermons
preached by Snyder to the slaves. She regarded them as something intended to make them better satisfied with their condition, and more valuable as pieces of property, without preparing
them for the world to come. Mrs. Carlton found in her husband
a congenial spirit, who entered into all her wishes and plans for
bettering the condition of their slaves. Mrs. Carlton's views and

sympathies were all in favour of immediate emancipation; but then she saw, or thought she saw, a difficulty in that. If the slaves were liberated, they must be sent out of the state. This, of course, would incur additional expense; and if they left the state, where had they better go? "Let's send them to Liberia," said Carlton. "Why should they go to Africa, any more than to the Free States or to Canada?" asked the wife. "They would be in their native land," he answered. "Is not this their native land? What right have we, more than the negro, to the soil here, or to style ourselves native Americans? Indeed it is as much their home as ours, and I have sometimes thought it was more theirs. The negro has cleared up the lands, built towns, and enriched the soil with his blood and tears; and in return, he is to be sent to a country of which he knows nothing. Who fought more bravely for American independence than the blacks? A negro, by the name of Attucks, was the first that fell in Boston at the commencement of the revolutionary war; and, throughout the whole of the struggles for liberty in this country, the negroes have contributed their share. In the last war with Great Britain, the country was mainly indebted to the blacks in New Orleans for the achievement of the victory at that place; and even General Jackson, the commander in chief, called the negroes together at the close of the war, and addressed them in the following terms:—

"'Soldiers!—When on the banks of the Mobile I called you to take up arms, inviting you to partake the perils and glory of your *white fellow citizens, I expected much from you;* for I was not ignorant that you possessed qualities most formidable to an invading enemy. I knew with what fortitude you could endure hunger and thirst, and all the fatigues of a campaign. *I knew well how you loved your native country,* and that you, as well as ourselves, had to defend what *man* holds most dear—his parents, wife, children, and property. *You have done more than I expected.* In addition to the previous qualities I before knew you to possess, I found among you a noble enthusiasm, which leads to the performance of great things.

"'Soldiers! The President of the United States shall hear how praiseworthy was your conduct in the hour of danger, and the representatives of the American people will give you the praise your exploits entitle you to. Your general anticipates them in applauding your noble ardour.'

"And what did these noble men receive in return for their courage, their heroism? Chains and slavery. Their good deeds have been consecrated only in their own memories. Who rallied with more alacrity in response to the summons of danger? If in that hazardous hour, when our homes were menaced with the horrors of war, we did not disdain to call upon the negro to assist in repelling invasion, why should we, now that the danger is past, deny him a home in his native land?" "I see," said Carlton, "you are right, but I fear you will have difficulty in persuading others to adopt your views." "We will set the example," replied she, "and then hope for the best; for I feel that the people of the Southern States will one day see their error. Liberty has always been our watchword, as far as profession is concerned. Nothing has been held so cheap as our common humanity, on a national average. If every man had his aliquot proportion of the injustice done in this land, by law and violence, the present freemen of the northern section would many of them commit suicide in self-defence, and would court the liberties awarded by Ali Pasha of Egypt to his subjects. Long ere this we should have tested, in behalf of our bleeding and crushed American brothers of every hue and complexion, every new constitution, custom, or practice, by which inhumanity was supposed to be upheld, the injustice and cruelty they contained, emblazoned before the great tribunal of mankind for condemnation; and the good and available power they possessed, for the relief, deliverance and elevation of oppressed men, permitted to shine forth from under the cloud, for the refreshment of the human race."

Although Mr. and Mrs. Carlton felt that immediate emancipation was the right of the slave and the duty of the master, they resolved on a system of gradual emancipation, so as to give them time to accomplish their wish, and to prepare the negro for freedom. Huckelby was one morning told that his services would no longer be required. The negroes, ninety-eight in number, were called together and told that the whip would no longer be used, and that they would be allowed a certain sum for every bale of cotton produced. Sam, whose long experience in the cotton-field before he had been taken into the house, and whose general intelligence justly gave him the first place amongst the

negroes on the Poplar Farm, was placed at their head. They
were also given to understand that the money earned by them
would be placed to their credit; and when it amounted to a certain sum, they should all be free.

The joy with which this news was received by the slaves,
showed their grateful appreciation of the boon their benefactors
were bestowing upon them. The house servants were called and
told that wages would be allowed them, and what they earned
set to their credit, and they too should be free. The next were the
bricklayers. There were eight of these, who had paid their master two dollars per day, and boarded and clothed themselves. An
arrangement was entered into with them, by which the money
they earned should be placed to their credit; and they too should
be free, when a certain amount should be accumulated; and
great was the change amongst all these people. The bricklayers
had been to work but a short time, before their increased industry was noticed by many. They were no longer apparently the
same people. A sedateness, a care, an economy, an industry, took
possession of them, to which there seemed to be no bounds but
in their physical strength. They were never tired of labouring,
and seemed as though they could never effect enough. They
became temperate, moral, religious, setting an example of innocent, unoffending lives to the world around them, which was
seen and admired by all. Mr. Parker, a man who worked nearly
forty slaves at the same business, was attracted by the manner in
which these negroes laboured. He called on Mr. Carlton, some
weeks after they had been acting on the new system, and offered
2,000 dollars for the head workman, Jim. The offer was, of
course, refused. A few days after the same gentleman called
again, and made an offer of double the sum that he had on the
former occasion. Mr. Parker, finding that no money would purchase either of the negroes, said, "Now, Mr. Carlton, pray tell
me what it is that makes your negroes work so? What kind of
people are they?" "I suppose," observed Carlton, "that they are
like other people, flesh and blood." "Why, sir," continued Parker,
"I have never seen such people; building as they are next door to
my residence, I see and have my eye on them from morning till
night. You are never there, for I have never met you, or seen you

once at the building. Why, sir, I am an early riser, getting up before day; and do you think that I am not awoke every morning in my life by the noise of their trowels at work, and their singing and noise before day; and do you suppose, sir, that they stop or leave off work at sundown? No, sir, but they work as long as they can see to lay a brick, and then they carry up brick and mortar for an hour or two afterward, to be ahead of their work the next morning. And again, sir, do you think that they walk at their work? No, sir, they run all day. You see, sir, those immensely long ladders, five stories in height; do you suppose they walk up them? No, sir, they run up and down them like so many monkeys all day long. I never saw such people as these in my life. I don't know what to make of them. Were a white man with them and over them with a whip, then I should see and understand the cause of the running and incessant labour; but I cannot comprehend it; there is something in it, sir. Great man, sir, that Jim; great man; I should like to own him." Carlton here informed Parker that their liberties depended upon their work; when the latter replied, "If niggers can work so for the promise of freedom, they ought to be made to work without it." This last remark was in the true spirit of the slaveholder, and reminds us of the fact that, some years since, the overseer of General Wade Hampton offered the niggers under him a suit of clothes to the one that picked the most cotton in one day; and after that time that day's work was given as a task to the slaves on that plantation; and, after a while, was adopted by other planters.

The negroes on the farm, under "Marser Sam," were also working in a manner that attracted the attention of the planters round about. They no longer feared Huckelby's whip, and no longer slept under the preaching of Snyder. On the Sabbath, Mr. and Mrs. Carlton read and explained the Scriptures to them; and the very great attention paid by the slaves showed plainly that they appreciated the gospel when given to them in its purity. The death of Currer, from yellow fever, was a great trial to Mrs. Carlton; for she had not only become much attached to her, but had heard with painful interest the story of her wrongs, and would, in all probability, have restored her to her daughter in New Orleans.

XIX. Escape of Clotel

"The fetters galled my weary soul—
    A soul that seemed but thrown away;
I spurned the tyrant's base control,
    Resolved at least the man to play."

NO COUNTRY has produced so much heroism in so short a time, connected with escapes from peril and oppression, as has occurred in the United States among fugitive slaves, many of whom show great shrewdness in their endeavours to escape from this land of bondage. A slave was one day seen passing on the high road from a border town in the interior of the state of Virginia to the Ohio river. The man had neither hat upon his head or coat upon his back. He was driving before him a very nice fat pig, and appeared to all who saw him to be a labourer employed on an adjoining farm. "No negro is permitted to go at large in the Slave States without a written pass from his or her master, except on business in the neighbourhood." "Where do you live, my boy?" asked a white man of the slave, as he passed a white house with green blinds. "Jist up de road, sir," was the answer. "That's a fine pig." "Yes, sir, marser like dis choat berry much." And the negro drove on as if he was in great haste. In this way he and the pig travelled more than fifty miles before they reached the Ohio river. Once at the river they crossed over; the pig was sold; and nine days after the runaway slave passed over the Niagara river, and, for the first time in his life, breathed the air of freedom. A few weeks later, and, on the same road, two slaves were seen passing; one was on horseback, the other was walking before him with his arms tightly bound, and a long rope leading from the man on foot to the one on horseback.

"Oh, ho, that's a runaway rascal, I suppose," said a farmer, who met them on the road. "Yes, sir, he bin runaway, and I got him fast. Marser will tan his jacket for him nicely when he gets him." "You are a trustworthy fellow, I imagine," continued the farmer. "Oh yes, sir; marser puts a heap of confidence in dis nigger." And the slaves travelled on. When the one on foot was fatigued they would change positions, the other being tied and driven on foot. This they called "ride and tie." After a journey of more than two hundred miles they reached the Ohio river, turned the horse loose, told him to go home, and proceeded on their way to Canada. However they were not to have it all their own way. There are men in the Free States, and especially in the states adjacent to the Slave States, who make their living by catching the runaway slave, and returning him for the reward that may be offered. As the two slaves above mentioned were travelling on towards the land of freedom, led by the North Star, they were set upon by four of these slave-catchers, and one of them unfortunately captured. The other escaped. The captured fugitive was put under the torture, and compelled to reveal the name of his owner and his place of residence. Filled with delight, the kidnappers started back with their victim. Overjoyed with the prospect of receiving a large reward, they gave themselves up on the third night to pleasure. They put up at an inn. The negro was chained to the bed-post, in the same room with his captors. At dead of night, when all was still, the slave arose from the floor upon which he had been lying, looked around, and saw that the white men were fast asleep. The brandy punch had done its work. With palpitating heart and trembling limbs he viewed his position. The door was fast, but the warm weather had compelled them to leave the window open. If he could but get his chains off, he might escape through the window to the piazza, and reach the ground by one of the posts that supported the piazza. The sleeper's clothes hung upon chairs by the bedside; the slave thought of the padlock key, examined the pockets and found it. The chains were soon off, and the negro stealthily making his way to the window: he stopped and said to himself, "These men are villains, they are enemies to all who like me are trying to be free. Then why not I teach them a lesson?" He then undressed himself, took the clothes of one of the men, dressed himself in them, and escaped through the window, and, a moment more, he was on the high road to Canada. Fifteen days later, and the writer of this gave him a passage across Lake Erie, and saw him safe in her Britannic Majesty's dominions.

We have seen Clotel sold to Mr. French in Vicksburgh, her hair cut short, and everything done to make her realise her position as a servant. Then we have seen her re-sold, because her owners feared she would die through grief. As yet her new purchaser treated her with respectful gentleness, and sought to win her favour by flattery and presents, knowing that whatever he gave her he could take back again. But she dreaded every moment lest the scene should change, and trembled at the sound of every footfall. At every interview with her new master Clotel stoutly maintained that she had left a husband in Virginia, and would never think of taking another. The gold watch and chain, and other glittering presents which he purchased for her, were all laid aside by the quadroon, as if they were of no value to her. In the same house with her was another servant, a man, who had from time to time hired himself from his master. William was his name. He could feel for Clotel, for he, like her, had been separated from near and dear relatives, and often tried to console the poor woman. One day the quadroon observed to him that her hair was growing out again. "Yes," replied William, "you look a good deal like a man with your short hair." "Oh," rejoined she, "I have often been told that I would make a better looking man than a woman. If I had the money," continued she, "I would bid farewell to this place." In a moment more she feared that she had said too much, and smilingly remarked, "I am always talking nonsense." William was a tall, full-bodied negro, whose very countenance beamed with intelligence. Being a mechanic, he had, by his own industry, made more than what he paid his owner; this he laid aside, with the hope that some day he might get enough to purchase his freedom. He had in his chest one hundred and fifty dollars. His was a heart that felt for others, and he had again and again wiped the tears from his eyes as he heard the story of Clotel as related by herself. "If she can get free with a little money, why not give her what I have?"

thought he, and then he resolved to do it. An hour after, he
came into the quadroon's room, and laid the money in her lap,
and said, "There, Miss Clotel, you said if you had the means you
would leave this place; there is money enough to take you to
England, where you will be free. You are much fairer than many
of the white women of the South, and can easily pass for a free
white lady." At first Clotel feared that it was a plan by which the
negro wished to try her fidelity to her owner; but she was soon
convinced by his earnest manner, and the deep feeling with
which he spoke, that he was honest. "I will take the money only
on one condition," said she; "and that is, that I effect your escape as well as my own." "How can that be done?" he inquired.
"I will assume the disguise of a gentleman and you that of a
servant, and we will take passage on a steamboat and go to
Cincinnati, and thence to Canada." Here William put in several
objections to the plan. He feared detection, and he well knew
that, when a slave is once caught when attempting to escape, if
returned is sure to be worse treated than before. However,
Clotel satisfied him that the plan could be carried out if he
would only play his part.

The resolution was taken, the clothes for her disguise procured, and before night everything was in readiness for their
departure. That night Mr. Cooper, their master, was to attend a
party, and this was their opportunity. William went to the wharf
to look out for a boat, and had scarcely reached the landing ere
he heard the puffing of a steamer. He returned and reported
the fact. Clotel had already packed her trunk, and had only to
dress and all was ready. In less than an hour they were on board
the boat. Under the assumed name of "Mr. Johnson," Clotel
went to the clerk's office and took a private state room for herself, and paid her own and servant's fare. Besides being attired
in a neat suit of black, she had a white silk handkerchief tied
round her chin, as if she was an invalid. A pair of green glasses
covered her eyes; and fearing that she would be talked to too
much and thus render her liable to be detected, she assumed to
be very ill. On the other hand, William was playing his part well
in the servants' hall; he was talking loudly of his master's wealth.
Nothing appeared as good on the boat as in his master's fine

mansion. "I don't like dees steam-boats no how," said William; "I hope when marser goes on a journey agin he will take de carriage and de hosses." Mr. Johnson (for such was the name by which Clotel now went) remained in his room, to avoid, as far as possible, conversation with others. After a passage of seven days they arrived at Louisville, and put up at Gough's Hotel. Here they had to await the departure of another boat for the North. They were now in their most critical position. They were still in a slave state, and John C. Calhoun, a distinguished slave-owner, was a guest at this hotel. They feared, also, that trouble would attend their attempt to leave this place for the North, as all persons taking negroes with them have to give bail that such negroes are not runaway slaves. The law upon this point is very stringent: all steamboats and other public conveyances are liable to a fine for every slave that escapes by them, besides paying the full value for the slave. After a delay of four hours, Mr. Johnson and servant took passage on the steamer Rodolph, for Pittsburgh. It is usual, before the departure of the boats, for an officer to examine every part of the vessel to see that no slave secretes himself on board. "Where are you going?" asked the officer of William, as he was doing his duty on this occasion. "I am going with marser," was the quick reply. "Who is your master?" "Mr. Johnson, sir, a gentleman in the cabin." "You must take him to the office and satisfy the captain that all is right, or you can't go on this boat." William informed his master what the officer had said. The boat was on the eve of going, and no time could be lost, yet they knew not what to do. At last they went to the office, and Mr. Johnson, addressing the captain, said, "I am informed that my boy can't go with me unless I give security that he belongs to me." "Yes," replied the captain, "that is the law." "A very strange law indeed," rejoined Mr. Johnson, "that one can't take his property with him." After a conversation of some minutes, and a plea on the part of Johnson that he did not wish to be delayed owing to his illness, they were permitted to take their passage without farther trouble, and the boat was soon on its way up the river. The fugitives had now passed the Rubicon, and the next place at which they would land would be in a Free State. Clotel called William to her room, and said to him, "We are now free, you can go on your way to Canada, and I shall go to Virginia in search of my daughter." The announcement that she was going to risk her liberty in a Slave State was unwelcome news to William. With all the eloquence he could command, he tried to persuade Clotel that she could not escape detection, and was only throwing her freedom away. But she had counted the cost, and made up her mind for the worst. In return for the money he had furnished, she had secured for him his liberty, and their engagement was at an end.

After a quick passage the fugitives arrived at Cincinnati, and there separated. William proceeded on his way to Canada, and Clotel again resumed her own apparel, and prepared to start in search of her child. As might have been expected, the escape of those two valuable slaves created no little sensation in Vicksburgh. Advertisements and messages were sent in every direction in which the fugitives were thought to have gone. It was soon, however, known that they had left the town as master and servant; and many were the communications which appeared in the newspapers, in which the writers thought, or pretended, that they had seen the slaves in their disguise. One was to the effect that they had gone off in a chaise; one as master, and the other as servant. But the most probable was an account given by a correspondent of one of the Southern newspapers, who happened to be a passenger in the same steamer in which the slaves escaped, and which we here give:—

"One bright starlight night, in the month of December last, I found myself in the cabin of the steamer Rodolph, then lying in the port of Vicksburgh, and bound to Louisville. I had gone early on board, in order to select a good berth, and having got tired of reading the papers, amused myself with watching the appearance of the passengers as they dropped in, one after another, and I being a believer in physiognomy, formed my own opinion of their characters.

"The second bell rang, and as I yawningly returned my watch to my pocket, my attention was attracted by the appearance of a young man who entered the cabin supported by his servant, a strapping negro.

"The man was bundled up in a capacious overcoat; his face was bandaged with a white handkerchief, and its expression entirely hid by a pair of enormous spectacles.

"There was something so mysterious and unusual about the young man as he sat restless in the corner, that curiosity led me to observe him more closely.

"He appeared anxious to avoid notice, and before the steamer had fairly left the wharf, requested, in a low, womanly voice, to be shown his berth, as he was an invalid, and must retire early: his name he gave as Mr. Johnson. His servant was called, and he was put quietly to bed. I paced the deck until Tybee light grew dim in the distance, and then went to my berth.

"I awoke in the morning with the sun shining in my face; we were then just passing St. Helena. It was a mild beautiful morning, and most of the passengers were on deck, enjoying the freshness of the air, and stimulating their appetites for breakfast. Mr. Johnson soon made his appearance, arrayed as on the night before, and took his seat quietly upon the guard of the boat.

"From the better opportunity afforded by daylight, I found that he was a slight built, apparently handsome young man, with black hair and eyes, and of a darkness of complexion that betokened Spanish extraction. Any notice from others seemed painful to him; so to satisfy my curiosity, I questioned his servant, who was standing near, and gained the following information.

"His master was an invalid—he had suffered for a long time under a complication of diseases, that had baffled the skill of the best physicians in Mississippi; he was now suffering principally with the 'rheumatism,' and he was scarcely able to walk or help himself in any way. He came from Vicksburgh, and was now on his way to Philadelphia, at which place resided his uncle, a celebrated physician, and through whose means he hoped to be restored to perfect health.

"This information, communicated in a bold, off-hand manner, enlisted my sympathies for the sufferer, although it occurred to me that he walked rather too gingerly for a person afflicted with so many ailments."

After thanking Clotel for the great service she had done him in bringing him out of slavery, William bade her farewell. The prejudice that exists in the Free States against coloured persons, on account of their colour, is attributable solely to the influence of slavery, and is but another form of slavery itself. And even the slave who escapes from the Southern plantations, is surprised when he reaches the North, at the amount and withering influ-

ence of this prejudice. William applied at the railway station for
a ticket for the train going to Sandusky, and was told that if he
went by that train he would have to ride in the luggage-van.
"Why?" asked the astonished negro. "We don't send a Jim Crow
carriage but once a day, and that went this morning." The "Jim
Crow" carriage is the one in which the blacks have to ride.
Slavery is a school in which its victims learn much shrewdness,
and William had been an apt scholar. Without asking any more
questions, the negro took his seat in one of the first-class carriages. He was soon seen and ordered out. Afraid to remain in
the town longer, he resolved to go by that train; and consequently seated himself on a goods' box in the luggage-van. The
train started at its proper time, and all went on well. Just before
arriving at the end of the journey, the conductor called on
William for his ticket. "I have none," was the reply. "Well, then,
you can pay your fare to me," said the officer. "How much is it?"
asked the black man. "Two dollars." "What do you charge those
in the passenger-carriage?" "Two dollars." "And do you charge
me the same as you do those who ride in the best carriages?"
asked the negro. "Yes," was the answer. "I shan't pay it," returned the man. "You black scamp, do you think you can ride on
this road without paying your fare?" "No, I don't want to ride for
nothing; I only want to pay what's right." "Well, launch out two
dollars, and that's right." "No, I shan't; I will pay what I ought,
and won't pay any more." "Come, come, nigger, your fare and
be done with it," said the conductor, in a manner that is never
used except by Americans to blacks. "I won't pay you two dollars, and that enough," said William. "Well, as you have come all
the way in the luggage-van, pay me a dollar and a half and you
may go." "I shan't do any such thing." "Don't you mean to pay
for riding?" "Yes, but I won't pay a dollar and a half for riding
up here in the freight-van. If you had let me come in the carriage where others ride, I would have paid you two dollars."
"Where were you raised? You seem to think yourself as good as
white folks." "I want nothing more than my rights." "Well, give
me a dollar, and I will let you off." "No, sir, I shan't do it." "What
do you mean to do then—don't you wish to pay anything?" "Yes,
sir, I want to pay you the full price." "What do you mean by full

price?" "What do you charge per hundred-weight for goods?" inquired the negro with a degree of gravity that would have astonished Diogenes himself. "A quarter of a dollar per hundred," answered the conductor. "I weigh just one hundred and fifty pounds," returned William, "and will pay you three-eighths of a dollar." "Do you expect that you will pay only thirty-seven cents for your ride?" "This, sir, is your own price. I came in a luggage-van, and I'll pay for luggage." After a vain effort to get the negro to pay more, the conductor took the thirty-seven cents, and noted in his cash-book, "Received for one hundred and fifty pounds of luggage, thirty-seven cents." This, reader, is no fiction; it actually occurred in the railway above described.

Thomas Corwin, a member of the American Congress, is one of the blackest white men in the United States. He was once on his way to Congress, and took passage in one of the Ohio river steamers. As he came just at the dinner hour, he immediately went into the dining saloon, and took his seat at the table. A gentleman with his whole party of five ladies at once left the table. "Where is the captain," cried the man in an angry tone. The captain soon appeared, and it was sometime before he could satisfy the old gent. that Governor Corwin was not a nigger. The newspapers often have notices of mistakes made by innkeepers and others who undertake to accommodate the public, one of which we give below.

On the 6th inst., the Hon. Daniel Webster and family entered Edgartown, on a visit for health and recreation. Arriving at the hotel, without alighting from the coach, the landlord was sent for to see if suitable accommodation could be had. That dignitary appearing, and surveying Mr. Webster, while the hon. senator addressed him, seemed woefully to mistake the dark features of the traveller as he sat back in the corner of the carriage, and to suppose him a *coloured man,* particularly as there were two coloured servants of Mr. W. outside. So he promptly declared that there was no room for him and his family, and he could not be accommodated there—at the same time suggesting that he might perhaps find accommodation at some of the huts "up back," to which he pointed. So deeply did the prejudice of looks possess him, that he appeared not to notice that the stranger introduced himself to him as Daniel Webster, or to be so ignorant as not to have heard of such a personage; and turning away, he expressed to the driver his astonishment that he should bring *black* people there for *him* to take in. It was not till he had been repeatedly assured and made to understand that the said Daniel Webster was a real live senator of the United States, that he perceived his awkward mistake and the distinguished honour which he and his house were so near missing.

In most of the Free States, the coloured people are disfranchised on account of their colour. The following scene, which we take from a newspaper in the state of Ohio, will give some idea of the extent to which this prejudice is carried.

"The whole of Thursday last was occupied by the Court of Common Pleas for this county in trying to find out whether one Thomas West was of the VOTING COLOUR, as some had very *constitutional doubts* as to whether his colour was orthodox, and whether his hair was of the official crisp! Was it not a dignified business? Four profound judges, four acute lawyers, twelve grave jurors, and I don't know how many venerable witnesses, making in all about thirty men, perhaps, all engaged in the profound, laborious, and illustrious business, of finding out whether a man who pays tax, works on the road, and is an industrious farmer, has been born according to the republican, Christian constitution of Ohio—so that he can vote! And they wisely, gravely, and 'JUDGMATICALLY' decided that he should not vote! What wisdom—what research it must have required to evolve this truth! It was left for the Court of Common Pleas for Columbian county, Ohio, in the United States of North America, to find out what Solomon never dreamed of—the courts of all civilised, heathen, or Jewish countries, never contemplated. Lest the wisdom of our courts should be circumvented by some such men as might be named, who are so near being born constitutionally that they might be taken for white by sight, I would suggest that our court be invested with SMELLING powers, and that if a man don't exhale the constitutional smell, he shall not vote! This would be an additional security to our liberties."

William found, after all, that liberty in the so-called Free States was more a name than a reality; that prejudice followed the coloured man into every place that he might enter. The temples erected for the worship of the living God are no exception. The finest Baptist church in the city of Boston has the following paragraph in the deed that conveys its seats to pew-holders:

"And it is a further condition of these presents, that if the owner or owners of said pew shall determine hereafter to sell the same, it shall first be offered, in writing, to the standing committee of said society for the time being, at such price as might otherwise be obtained for it; and the said committee shall have the right, for ten days after such offer, to purchase said pew for said society, at that price, first deducting therefrom all taxes and assessments on said pew then remaining unpaid. And if the said committee shall not so complete such purchase within said ten days, then the pew may be sold by the owner or owners thereof (after payment of all such arrears) to any one respectable *white person,* but upon the same conditions as are contained in this instrument; and immediate notice of such sale shall be given in writing, by the vendor, to the treasurer of said society."

Such are the conditions upon which the Rowe Street Baptist Church, Boston, disposes of its seats. The writer of this is able to put that whole congregation, minister and all, to flight, by merely putting his coloured face in that church. We once visited a church in New York that had a place set apart for the sons of Ham. It was a dark, dismal looking place in one corner of the gallery, grated in front like a hen-coop, with a black border around it. It had two doors; over one was B. M.—black men; over the other B. W.—black women.

XX. A True Democrat

"Who can, with patience, for a moment see
  The medley mass of pride and misery,
  Of whips and charters, manacles and rights,
  Of slaving blacks and democratic whites,
  And all the piebald policy that reigns
  In free confusion o'er Columbia's plains?
  To think that man, thou just and gentle God!
  Should stand before thee with a tyrant's rod,
  O'er creatures like himself, with souls from thee,
  Yet dare to boast of perfect liberty!"—*Thomas Moore.*

EDUCATED IN a free state, and marrying a wife who had been a victim to the institution of slavery, Henry Morton became strongly opposed to the system. His two daughters, at the age of twelve years, were sent to the North to finish their education, and to receive that refinement that young ladies cannot obtain in the Slave States. Although he did not publicly advocate the abolition of slavery, he often made himself obnoxious to private circles, owing to the denunciatory manner in which he condemned the "peculiar institution." Being one evening at a party, and hearing one of the company talking loudly of the glory and freedom of American institutions, he gave it as his opinion that, unless slavery was speedily abolished, it would be the ruin of the Union. "It is not our boast of freedom," said he, "that will cause us to be respected abroad. It is not our loud talk in favour of liberty that will cause us to be regarded as friends of human freedom; but our acts will be scrutinised by the people of other countries. We say much against European despotism; let us look to ourselves. That government is despotic where the rulers govern subjects by their own mere will—by decrees and laws emanating from their uncontrolled will, in the enactment and execution of which the ruled have no voice, and under which they have no right except at the will of the rulers. Despotism does not depend upon the number of the rulers, or the number of the subjects. It may have one ruler or many. Rome was a despotism under Nero; so she was under the triumvirate. Athens was a despotism under Thirty Tyrants; under her Four Hundred Tyrants; under her Three Thousand Tyrants. It has been generally observed that despotism increases in severity with the number of despots; the responsibility is more divided, and the claims more numerous. The triumvirs each demanded his victims. The smaller the number of subjects in proportion to the tyrants, the more cruel the oppression, because the less danger from rebellion. In this government, the free white citizens are the rulers—the sovereigns, as we delight to be called. All others are subjects. There are, perhaps, some sixteen or seventeen millions of sovereigns, and four millions of subjects.

"The rulers and the ruled are of all colours, from the clear white of the Caucasian tribes to the swarthy Ethiopian. The former, by courtesy, are all called white, the latter black. In this government the subject has no rights, social, political, or personal. He has no voice in the laws which govern him. He can hold no property. His very wife and children are not his. His labour is another's. He, and all that appertain to him, are the absolute property of his rulers. He is governed, bought, sold, punished, executed, by laws to which he never gave his assent, and by rulers whom he never chose. He is not a serf merely, with half the rights of men like the subjects of despotic Russia; but a native slave, stripped of every right which God and nature gave him, and which the high spirit of our revolution declared inalienable—which he himself could not surrender, and which man could not take from him. Is he not then the subject of despotic sway?

"The slaves of Athens and Rome were free in comparison. They had some rights—could acquire some property; could choose their own masters, and purchase their own freedom;

and, when free, could rise in social and political life. The slaves of America, then, lie under the most absolute and grinding despotism that the world ever saw. But who are the despots? The rulers of the country—the sovereign people! Not merely the slaveholder who cracks the lash. He is but the instrument in the hands of despotism. That despotism is the government of the Slave States, and the United States, consisting of all its rulers—all the free citizens. Do not look upon this as a paradox, because you and I and the sixteen millions of rulers are free. The rulers of every despotism are free. Nicholas of Russia is free. The grand Sultan of Turkey is free. The butcher of Austria is free. Augustus, Anthony, and Lepidus were free, while they drenched Rome in blood. The Thirty Tyrants—the Four Hundred—the Three Thousand, were free while they bound their countrymen in chains. You, and I, and the sixteen millions are free, while we fasten iron chains, and rivet manacles on four millions of our fellowmen—take their wives and children from them—separate them—sell them, and doom them to perpetual, eternal bondage. Are we not then despots—despots such as history will brand and God abhor?

"We, as individuals, are fast losing our reputation for honest dealing. Our nation is losing its character. The loss of a firm national character, or the degradation of a nation's honour, is the inevitable prelude to her destruction. Behold the once proud fabric of a Roman empire—an empire carrying its arts and arms into every part of the Eastern continent; the monarchs of mighty kingdoms dragged at the wheels of her triumphal chariots; her eagle waving over the ruins of desolated countries;— where is her splendour, her wealth, her power, her glory? Extinguished for ever. Her mouldering temples, the mournful vestiges of her former grandeur, afford a shelter to her muttering monks. Where are her statesmen, her sages, her philosophers, her orators, generals? Go to their solitary tombs and inquire. She lost her national character, and her destruction followed. The ramparts of her national pride were broken down, and Vandalism desolated her classic fields. Then let the people of our country take warning ere it is too late. But most of us say to ourselves,

"'Who questions the right of mankind to be free?
Yet, what are the rights of the *negro* to me?
I'm well fed and clothed, I have plenty of pelf—
I'll care for the blacks when I turn black myself.'

"New Orleans is doubtless the most immoral place in the United States. The theatres are open on the Sabbath. Bull-fights, horse-racing, and other cruel amusements are carried on in this city to an extent unknown in any other part of the Union. The most stringent laws have been passed in that city against negroes, yet a few years since the State Legislature passed a special act to enable a white man to marry a coloured woman, on account of her being possessed of a large fortune. And, very recently, the following paragraph appeared in the city papers:—

"'There has been quite a stir recently in this city, in consequence of a marriage of a white man, named Buddington, a teller in the Canal Bank, to the negro daughter of one of the wealthiest merchants. Buddington, before he could be married, was obliged to swear that he had negro blood in his veins, and to do this he made an incision in his arm, and put some of her blood in the cut. The ceremony was performed by a Catholic clergyman, and the bridegroom has received with his wife a fortune of fifty or sixty thousand dollars.'

"It seems that the fifty or sixty thousand dollars entirely covered the negro woman's black skin, and the law prohibiting marriage between blacks and whites was laid aside for the occasion."

Althesa felt proud, as well she might, at her husband's taking such high ground in a slaveholding city like New Orleans.

XXI. The Christian's Death

"O weep, ye friends of freedom weep!
Your harps to mournful measures sweep."

ON THE LAST DAY of November, 1620, on the confines of the Grand Bank of Newfoundland, lo! we behold one little solitary tempest-tost and weather-beaten ship; it is all that can be seen on the length and breadth of the vast intervening solitudes, from the melancholy wilds of Labrador and New England's iron-bound shores, to the western coasts of Ireland and the rock-defended Hebrides, but one lonely ship greets the eye of angels or of men, on this great thoroughfare of nations in our age. Next in moral grandeur, was this ship, to the great discoverer's: Columbus found a continent; the May-flower brought the seed-wheat of states and empire. That is the May-flower, with its servants of the living God, their wives and little ones, hastening to lay the foundations of nations in the occidental lands of the setting-sun. Hear the voice of prayer to God for his protection, and the glorious music of praise, as it breaks into the wild tempest of the mighty deep, upon the ear of God. Here in this ship are great and good men. Justice, mercy, humanity, respect for the rights of all; each man honoured, as he was useful to himself and others; labour respected, law-abiding men, constitution-making and respecting men; men, whom no tyrant could conquer, or hardship overcome, with the high commission sealed by a Spirit divine, to establish religious and political liberty for all. This ship had the embryo elements of all that is useful, great, and grand in Northern institutions; it was the great type of goodness and wisdom, illustrated in two and a quarter centuries gone by; it was the good genius of America.

But look far in the South-east, and you behold on the same day, in 1620, a low rakish ship hastening from the tropics, solitary and alone, to the New World. What is she? She is freighted with the elements of unmixed evil. Hark! hear those rattling chains, hear that cry of despair and wail of anguish, as they die away in the unpitying distance. Listen to those shocking oaths, the crack of that flesh-cutting whip. Ah! it is the first cargo of slaves on their way to Jamestown, Virginia. Behold the May-flower anchored at Plymouth Rock, the slave-ship in James River. Each a parent, one of the prosperous, labour-honouring, law-sustaining institutions of the North; the other the mother of slavery, idleness, lynch-law, ignorance, unpaid labour, poverty, and duelling, despotism, the ceaseless swing of the whip, and the peculiar institutions of the South. These ships are the representation of good and evil in the New World, even to our day. When shall one of those parallel lines come to an end?

The origin of American slavery is not lost in the obscurity of by-gone ages. It is a plain historical fact, that it owes its birth to the African slave trade, now pronounced by every civilised community the greatest crime ever perpetrated against humanity. Of all causes intended to benefit mankind, the abolition of chattel slavery must necessarily be placed amongst the first, and the negro hails with joy every new advocate that appears in his cause. Commiseration for human suffering and human sacrifices awakened the capacious mind, and brought into action the enlarged benevolence, of Georgiana Carlton. With respect to her philosophy—it was of a noble cast. It was, that all men are by nature equal; that they are wisely and justly endowed by the Creator with certain rights, which are irrefragable; and that, however human pride and human avarice may depress and debase, still God is the author of good to man—and of evil, man is the artificer to himself and to his species. Unlike Plato and Socrates, her mind was free from the gloom that surrounded theirs; her philosophy was founded in the school of Christianity; though a devoted member of her father's church, she was not a sectarian.

We learn from Scripture, and it is a little remarkable that it is the only exact definition of religion found in the sacred volume, that "pure religion and undefiled before God, even the Father, is this, to visit the fatherless and widows in their affliction, and to keep oneself unspotted from the world." "Look not every man on his own things, but every man also on the things of others." "Remember them that are in bonds as bound with them." "Whatsoever ye would that others should do to you, do ye even so to them."

This was her view of Christianity, and to this end she laboured with all her energies to convince her slaveholding neighbours that the negro could not only take care of himself, but that he also appreciated liberty, and was willing to work and redeem himself. Her most sanguine wishes were being realized when she suddenly fell into a decline. Her mother had died of consumption, and her physician pronounced this to be her disease. She was prepared for this sad intelligence, and received it with the utmost composure. Although she had confidence in her husband that he would carry out her wishes in freeing the negroes after her death, Mrs. Carlton resolved upon their immediate liberation. Consequently the slaves were all summoned before the noble woman, and informed that they were no longer bondsmen. "From this hour," said she, "you are free, and all eyes will be fixed upon you. I dare not predict how far your example may affect the welfare of your brethren yet in bondage. If you are temperate, industrious, peaceable, and pious, you will show to the world that slaves can be emancipated without danger. Remember what a singular relation you sustain to society. The necessities of the case require not only that you should behave as well as the whites, but better than the whites; and for this reason: if you behave no better than they, your example will lose a great portion of its influence. Make the Lord Jesus Christ your refuge and exemplar. His is the only standard around which you can successfully rally. If ever there was a people who needed the consolations of religion to sustain them in their grievous afflictions, you are that people. You had better trust in the Lord than to put confidence in man. Happy is that people whose God is the Lord. Get as much education as possible for yourselves and your children. An ignorant people can never occupy any other than a degraded station in society; they can never be truly free until they are intelligent. In a few days you will start for the state of Ohio, where land will be purchased for some of you who have families, and where I hope you will all prosper. We have been urged to send you to Liberia, but we think it wrong to send you from your native land. We did not wish to encourage the Colonization Society, for it originated in hatred of the free coloured people. Its pretences are false, its doctrines odious, its means contemptible. Now, whatever may be your situation in life, 'Remember those in bonds as bound with them.' You must get ready as soon as you can for your journey to the North."

Seldom was there ever witnessed a more touching scene than this. There sat the liberator,—pale, feeble, emaciated, with death stamped upon her countenance, surrounded by the sons and daughters of Africa; some of whom had in former years been separated from all that they had held near and dear, and the most of whose backs had been torn and gashed by the negro whip. Some were upon their knees at the feet of their benefactress; others were standing round her weeping. Many begged that they might be permitted to remain on the farm and work for wages, for some had wives and some husbands on other plantations in the neighbourhood, and would rather remain with them.

But the laws of the state forbade any emancipated negroes remaining, under penalty of again being sold into slavery. Hence the necessity of sending them out of the state. Mrs. Carlton was urged by her friends to send the emancipated negroes to Africa. Extracts from the speeches of Henry Clay, and other distinguished Colonization Society men, were read to her to induce her to adopt this course. Some thought they should be sent away because the blacks are vicious; others because they would be missionaries to their brethren in Africa. "But," said she, "if we send away the negroes because they are profligate and vicious, what sort of missionaries will they make? Why not send away the vicious among the whites for the same reason, and the same purpose?"

Death is a leveller, and neither age, sex, wealth, nor usefulness can avert when he is permitted to strike. The most beautiful flowers soon fade, and droop, and die; this is also the case with man; his days are uncertain as the passing breeze. This hour he glows in the blush of health and vigour, but the next he may be counted with the number no more known on earth.

Although in a low state of health, Mrs. Carlton had the pleasure of seeing all her slaves, except Sam and three others, start for a land of freedom. The morning they were to go on board the steamer, bound for Louisville, they all assembled on the large grass plot, in front of the drawing-room window, and wept while they bid their mistress farewell. When they were on the boat, about leaving the wharf, they were heard giving the charge to those on shore—"Sam, take care of Misus, take care of Marser, as you love us, and hope to meet us in de Hio (Ohio), and in heben; be sure and take good care of Misus and Marser."

In less than a week after her emancipated people had started for Ohio, Mrs. Carlton was cold in death. Mr. Carlton felt deeply, as all husbands must who love their wives, the loss of her who had been a lamp to his feet, and a light to his path. She had converted him from infidelity to Christianity; from the mere theory of liberty to practical freedom. He had looked upon the negro as an ill-treated distant link of the human family; he now regarded them as a part of God's children. Oh, what a silence pervaded the house when the Christian had been removed. His indeed was a lonesome position.

> "'Twas midnight, and he sat alone—
> The husband of the dead,
> That day the dark dust had been thrown
> Upon the buried head."

In the midst of the buoyancy of youth, this cherished one had drooped and died. Deep were the sounds of grief and mourning heard in that stately dwelling, when the stricken friends, whose office it had been to nurse and soothe the weary sufferer, beheld her pale and motionless in the sleep of death.

Oh what a chill creeps through the breaking heart when we look upon the insensible form, and feel that it no longer contains the spirit we so dearly loved! How difficult to realise that the eye which always glowed with affection and intelligence—that the ear which had so often listened to the sounds of sorrow and gladness—that the voice whose accents had been to us like sweet music, and the heart, the habitation of benevolence and truth, are now powerless and insensate as the bier upon which the form rests. Though faith be strong enough to penetrate the cloud of gloom which hovers near, and to behold the freed spirit safe, *for ever,* safe in its home in heaven, yet the thoughts *will* linger sadly and cheerlessly upon the grave.

Peace to her ashes! she fought the fight, obtained the Christian's victory, and wears the crown. But if it were that departed spirits are permitted to note the occurrences of this world, with what a frown of disapprobation would hers view the effort being made in the United States to retard the work of emancipation for which she laboured and so wished to see brought about.

In what light would she consider that hypocritical priesthood who gave their aid and sanction to the infamous "Fugitive Slave Law." If true greatness consists in doing good to mankind, then was Georgiana Carlton an ornament to human nature. Who can think of the broken hearts made whole, of sad and dejected countenances now beaming with contentment and joy, of the mother offering her free-born babe to heaven, and of the father whose cup of joy seems overflowing in the presence of his family, where none can molest or make him afraid. Oh, that God may give more such persons to take the whip-scarred negro by the hand, and raise him to a level with our common humanity! May the professed lovers of freedom in the new world see that true liberty is freedom for all! and may every American continually hear it sounding in his ear:—

> "Shall every flap of England's flag
>   Proclaim that all around are free,
> From 'farthest Ind' to each blue crag
>   That beetles o'er the Western Sea?
> And shall we scoff at Europe's kings,
>   When Freedom's fire is dim with us,
> And round our country's altar clings
>   The damning shade of Slavery's curse?"

XXII. A Ride in a Stage-Coach

WE SHALL now return to Cincinnati, where we left Clotel preparing to go to Richmond in search of her daughter. Tired of the disguise in which she had escaped, she threw it off on her arrival at Cincinnati. But being assured that not a shadow of safety would attend her visit to a city in which she was well known, unless in some disguise, she again resumed men's apparel on leaving Cincinnati. This time she had more the appearance of an Italian or Spanish gentleman. In addition to the fine suit of black cloth, a splendid pair of dark false whiskers covered the sides of her face, while the curling moustache found its place upon the upper lip. From practice she had become accustomed to high-heeled boots, and could walk without creating any suspicion as regarded her sex. It was on a cold evening that Clotel arrived at Wheeling, and took a seat in the coach going to Richmond. She was already in the state of Virginia, yet a long distance from the place of her destination.

A ride in a stage-coach, over an American road, is unpleasant under the most favourable circumstances. But now that it was winter, and the roads unusually bad, the journey was still more dreary. However, there were eight passengers in the coach, and I need scarcely say that such a number of genuine Americans could not be together without whiling away the time somewhat pleasantly. Besides Clotel, there was an elderly gentleman with his two daughters—one apparently under twenty years, the other a shade above. The pale, spectacled face of another slim, tall man, with a white neckerchief, pointed him out as a minister. The rough featured, dark countenance of a stout looking man, with a white hat on one side of his head, told that he was from the sunny South. There was nothing remarkable about the other two, who might pass for ordinary American gentlemen. It was on the eve of a presidential election, when every man is thought to be a politician. Clay, Van Buren, and Harrison were the men who expected the indorsement of the Baltimore Convention. "Who does this town go for?" asked the old gent. with the ladies, as the coach drove up to an inn, where groups of persons were waiting for the latest papers. "We are divided," cried the rough voice of one of the outsiders. "Well, who do you think will get the majority here?" continued the old gent. "Can't tell very well; I go for 'Old Tip,'" was the answer from without. This brought up the subject fairly before the passengers, and when the coach again started a general discussion commenced, in which all took a part except Clotel and the young ladies. Some were for Clay, some for Van Buren, and others for "Old Tip." The coach stopped to take in a real farmer-looking man, who no sooner entered than he was saluted with "Do you go for Clay?" "No," was the answer. "Do you go for Van Buren?" "No." "Well, then, of course you will go for Harrison." "No." "Why, don't you mean to work for any of them at the election?" "No." "Well, who will you work for?" asked one of the company. "I work for Betsy and the children, and I have a hard job of it at that," replied the farmer, without a smile. This answer, as a matter of course, set the new comer down as one upon whom the rest of the passengers could crack their jokes with the utmost impunity. "Are you an Odd Fellow?" asked one. "No, sir, I've been married more than a month." "I mean, do you belong to the order of Odd Fellows?" "No, no; I belong to the order of married men." "Are you a mason?" "No, I am a carpenter by trade." "Are you a Son of Temperance?" "Bother you, no; I am a son of Mr. John Gosling." After a hearty laugh in which all joined, the subject of Temperance became the theme for discussion. In this the spectacled gent. was at home. He soon showed that he was a New Englander, and went the whole length of the "Maine Law." The minister was about having it all his own way, when the Southerner, in the white hat, took the opposite side of the question. "I don't bet a red cent on these teetotlars," said he, and at the same time looking round to see if he had the approbation of the rest of the company. "Why?"

asked the minister. "Because they are a set who are afraid to spend a cent. They are a bad lot, the whole on 'em." It was evident that the white hat gent. was an uneducated man. The minister commenced in full earnest, and gave an interesting account of the progress of temperance in Connecticut, the state from which he came, proving, that a great portion of the prosperity of the state was attributable to the disuse of intoxicating drinks. Every one thought the white hat had got the worst of the argument, and that he was settled for the remainder of the night. But not he; he took fresh courage and began again. "Now," said he, "I have just been on a visit to my uncle's in Vermont, and I guess I knows a little about these here teetotlars. You see, I went up there to make a little stay of a fortnight. I got there at night, and they seemed glad to see me, but they didn't give me a bit of anything to drink. Well, thinks I to myself, the jig's up: I sha'n't get any more liquor till I get out of the state." We all sat up till twelve o'clock that night, and I heard nothing but talk about the 'Juvinal Temperance Army,' the 'Band of Hope,' the 'Rising Generation,' the 'Female Dorcas Temperance Society,' 'The None Such,' and I don't know how many other names they didn't have. As I had taken several pretty large 'Cock Tails' before I entered the state, I thought upon the whole that I would not spile for the want of liquor. The next morning, I commenced writing back to my friends, and telling them what's what. Aunt Polly said, 'Well, Johnny, I s'pose you are given 'em a pretty account of us all here.' 'Yes,' said I; 'I am tellin' 'em if they want anything to drink when they come up here, they had better bring it with 'em.' 'Oh,' said aunty, 'they would search their boxes; can't bring any spirits in the state.' Well, as I was saying, jist as I got my letters finished, and was going to the post office (for uncle's house was two miles from the town), aunty says, 'Johnny, I s'pose you'll try to get a little somethin' to drink in town won't you?' Says I, 'I s'pose it's no use.' 'No,' said she, 'you can't; it aint to be had no how, for love nor money.' So jist as I was puttin' on my hat, 'Johnny,' cries out aunty, 'What,' says I. 'Now I'll tell you, I don't want you to say nothin' about it, but I keeps a little rum to rub my head with, for I am troubled with the headache; now I don't want you to mention it for the world, but I'll give you a little taste, the old man is such a teetotaller, that I should never hear the last of it, and I would not like for the boys to know it, they are members of the "Cold Water Army."'

"Aunty now brought out a black bottle and gave me a cup, and told me to help myself, which I assure you I did. I now felt ready to face the cold. As I was passing the barn I heard uncle thrashing oats, so I went to the door and spoke to him. 'Come in, John,' says he. 'No,' said I; 'I am goin' to post some letters,' for I was afraid that he would smell my breath if I went too near to him. 'Yes, yes, come in.' So I went in, and says he, 'It's now eleven o'clock; that's about the time you take your grog, I s'pose, when you are at home.' 'Yes,' said I. 'I am sorry for you, my lad; you can't get anything up here; you can't even get it at the chemist's, except as medicine, and then you must let them mix it and you take it in their presence.' 'This is indeed hard,' replied I; 'Well, it can't be helped,' continued he: 'and it ought not to be if it could. It's best for society; people's better off without drink. I recollect when your father and I, thirty years ago, used to go out on a spree and spend more than half a dollar in a night. Then here's the rising generation; there's nothing like settin' a good example. Look how healthy your cousins are—there's Benjamin, he never tasted spirits in his life. Oh, John, I would you were a teetotaller.' 'I suppose,' said I, 'I'll have to be one till I leave the state.' 'Now,' said he, 'John, I don't want you to mention it, for your aunt would go into hysterics if she thought there was a drop of intoxicating liquor about the place, and I would not have the boys to know it for anything, but I keep a little brandy to rub my joints for the rheumatics, and being it's you, I'll give you a little dust.' So the old man went to one corner of the barn, took out a brown jug and handed it to me, and I must say it was a little the best cognac that I had tasted for many a day. Says I, 'Uncle, you are a good judge of brandy.' 'Yes,' said he, 'I learned when I was young.' So off I started for the post office. In returnin' I thought I'd jist go through the woods where the boys were chopping wood, and wait and go to the house with them when they went to dinner. I found them hard at work, but as merry as crickets. 'Well, cousin John, are you done writing?' 'Yes,' answered I. 'Have you posted them?' 'Yes.' 'Hope you didn't go to any place inquiring for grog.'

'No, I knowed it was no good to do that.' 'I suppose a cock-tail would taste good now.' 'Well, I guess it would,' says I. The three boys then joined in a hearty laugh. 'I suppose you have told 'em that we are a dry set up here?' 'Well, I aint told 'em anything else.' 'Now, cousin John,' said Edward, 'if you wont say anything, we will give you a small taste. For mercy's sake don't let father or mother know it; they are such rabid teetotallers, that they would not sleep a wink to-night if they thought there was any spirits about the place.' 'I am mum,' says I. And the boys took a jug out of a hollow stump, and gave me some first-rate peach brandy. And during the fortnight that I was in Vermont, with my teetotal relations, I was kept about as well corned as if I had been among my hot water friends in Tennessee."

This narrative, given by the white hat man, was received with unbounded applause by all except the pale gent. in spectacles, who showed, by the way in which he was running his fingers between his cravat and throat, that he did not intend to "give it up so." The white hat gent. was now the lion of the company.

"Oh, you did not get hold of the right kind of teetotallers," said the minister. "I can give you a tale worth a dozen of yours," continued he. "Look at society in the states where temperance views prevail, and you will there see real happiness. The people are taxed less, the poor houses are shut up for want of occupants, and extreme destitution is unknown. Every one who drinks at all is liable to become an habitual drunkard. Yes, I say boldly, that no man living who uses intoxicating drinks, is free from the danger of at least occasional, and if of occasional, ultimately of habitual excess. There seems to be no character, position, or circumstances that free men from the danger. *I have known* many young men of the finest promise, led by the drinking habit into vice, ruin, and early death. *I have known* many tradesmen whom it has made bankrupt. *I have known* Sunday scholars whom it has led to prison—teachers, and even superintendents, whom it has dragged down to profligacy. *I have known* ministers of high academic honours, of splendid eloquence, nay, of vast usefulness, whom it has fascinated, and hurried over the precipice of public infamy with their eyes open, and gazing with horror on their fate. *I have known* men of the strongest and clearest intellect and of vigorous resolution, whom it has made weaker than children and fools—gentlemen of refinement and taste whom it has debased into brutes—poets of high genius whom it has bound in a bondage worse than the galleys, and ultimately cut short their days. *I have known* statesmen, lawyers, and judges whom it has killed—kind husbands and fathers whom it has turned into monsters. *I have known* honest men whom it has made villains—elegant and Christian *ladies* whom it has *converted into bloated sots.*"

"But you talk too fast," replied the white hat man. "You don't give a feller a chance to say nothin'." "I heard you," continued the minister, "and now you hear me out. It is indeed wonderful how people become lovers of strong drink. Some years since, before I became a teetotaller I kept spirits about the house, and I had a servant who was much addicted to strong drink. He used to say that he could not make my boots shine, without mixing the blacking with whiskey. So to satisfy myself that the whiskey was put in the blacking, one morning I made him bring the dish in which he kept the blacking, and poured in the whiskey myself. And now, sir, what do you think?" "Why, I s'pose your boots shined better than before," replied the white hat. "No," continued the minister. "He took the blacking out, and I watched him, and he drank down the whiskey, blacking, and all."

This turned the joke upon the advocate of strong drink, and he began to put his wits to work for arguments. "You are from Connecticut, are you?" asked the Southerner. "Yes, and we are an orderly, pious, peaceable people. Our holy religion is respected, and we do more for the cause of Christ than the whole Southern States put together." "I don't doubt it," said the white hat gent. "You sell wooden nutmegs and other spurious articles enough to do some good. You talk of your 'holy religion'; but your robes' righteousness are woven at Lowell and Manchester; your paradise is high per centum on factory stocks; your palms of victory and crowns of rejoicing are triumphs over a rival party in politics, on the questions of banks and tariffs. If you could, you would turn heaven into Birmingham, make every angel a weaver, and with the eternal din of looms and spindles drown all the anthems of the morning stars. Ah! I know you Connecticut people like a

book. No, no, all hoss; you can't come it on me." This last speech
of the rough featured man again put him in the ascendant, and
the spectacled gent. once more ran his fingers between his cravat
and throat. "You live in Tennessee, I think," said the minister.
"Yes," replied the Southerner, "I used to live in Orleans, but now
I claim to be a Tennessean." "Your people of New Orleans are
the most ungodly set in the United States," said the minister.
Taking a New Orleans newspaper from his pocket he continued,
"Just look here, there are not less than three advertisements of
bull fights to take place on the Sabbath. You people of the Slave
States have no regard for the Sabbath, religion, morality or anything else intended to make mankind better." Here Clotel could
have borne ample testimony, had she dared to have taken sides
with the Connecticut man. Her residence in Vicksburgh had
given her an opportunity of knowing something of the character
of the inhabitants of the far South. "Here is an account of a grand
bull fight that took place in New Orleans a week ago last Sunday.
I will read it to you." And the minister read aloud the following:

"Yesterday, pursuant to public notice, came off at Gretna, opposite
the Fourth District, the long heralded fight between the famous griz-
zly bear, General Jackson (victor in fifty battles), and the Attakapas
bull, Santa Anna.

"The fame of the coming conflict had gone forth to the four winds,
and women and children, old men and boys, from all parts of the city,
and from the breezy banks of Lake Pontchartrain and Borgne, brushed
up their Sunday suit, and prepared to see the fun. Long before the
published hour, the quiet streets of the rural Gretna were filled with
crowds of anxious denizens, flocking to the arena, and before the fight
commenced, such a crowd had collected as Gretna had not seen, nor
will be likely to see again.

"The arena for the sports was a cage, twenty feet square, built upon
the ground, and constructed of heavy timbers and iron bars. Around it
were seats, circularly placed, and intended to accommodate many
thousands. About four or five thousand persons assembled, covering
the seats as with a cloud, and crowding down around the cage, were
within reach of the bars.

"The bull selected to sustain the honour and verify the pluck of
Attakapas on this trying occasion was a black animal from the
Opelousas, lithe and sinewy as a four year old courser, and with eyes

like burning coals. His horns bore the appearance of having been filed at the tips, and wanted that keen and slashing appearance so common with others of his kith and kin; otherwise it would have been 'all day' with Bruin at the first pass, and no mistake.

"The bear was an animal of note, and called General Jackson, from the fact of his licking up everything that came in his way, and taking 'the responsibility' on all occasions. He was a wicked looking beast, very lean and unamiable in aspect, with hair all standing the wrong way. He had fought some fifty bulls (so they said), always coming out victorious, but that either one of the fifty had been an Attakapas bull, the bills of the performances did not say. Had he tackled Attakapas first it is likely his fifty battles would have remained unfought.

"About half past four o'clock the performances commenced.

"The bull was first seen, standing in the cage alone, with head erect, and looking a very monarch in his capacity. At an appointed signal, a cage containing the bear was placed alongside the arena, and an opening being made, bruin stalked into the battle ground—not, however, without sundry stirrings up with a ten foot pole, he being experienced in such matters, and backwards in raising a row.

"Once on the battle-field, both animals stood, like wary champions, eyeing each other, the bear cowering low, with head upturned and fangs exposed, while Attakapas stood wondering, with his eye dilated, lashing his sides with his long and bushy tail, and pawing up the earth in very wrath.

"The bear seemed little inclined to begin the attack, and the bull, standing a moment, made steps first backward and then forward, as if measuring his antagonist, and meditating where to plant a blow. Bruin wouldn't come to the scratch no way, till one of the keepers, with an iron rod, tickled his ribs and made him move. Seeing this, Attakapas took it as a hostile demonstration, and, gathering his strength, dashed savagely at the enemy, catching him on the points of his horns, and doubling him up like a sack of bran against the bars. Bruin 'sung out' at this, and made a dash for his opponent's nose.

"Missing this, the bull turned to the 'about face,' and the bear caught him by the ham, inflicting a ghastly wound. But Attakapas with a kick shook him off, and renewing the attack, went at him again, head on and with a rush. This time he was not so fortunate, for the bear caught him above the eye, burying his fangs in the tough hide, and holding him as in a vice. It was now the bull's turn to 'sing out,' and he did it, bellowing forth with a voice more hideous than that of all the bulls of Bashan. Some minutes stood matters thus, and the cries of the

which spread over the surface of the body. If, then, a happy
crisis came not, all hope was gone. Soon the breath infected the
air with a fetid odour, the lips were glazed, despair painted itself
in the eyes, and sobs, with long intervals of silence, formed the
only language. From each side of the mouth spread foam, tinged
with black and burnt blood. Blue streaks mingled with the yellow all over the frame. All remedies were useless. This was the
Yellow Fever. The disorder spread alarm and confusion throughout the city. On an average, more than 400 died daily. In the
midst of disorder and confusion, death heaped victims on victims. Friend followed friend in quick succession. The sick were
avoided from the fear of contagion, and for the same reason the
dead were left unburied. Nearly 2000 dead bodies lay uncov-
ered in the burial-ground, with only here and there a little lime
thrown over them, to prevent the air becoming infected.

The negro, whose home is in a hot climate, was not proof
against the disease. Many plantations had to suspend their work
for want of slaves to take the places of those carried off by the
fever. Henry Morton and wife were among the thirteen thousand swept away by the raging disorder that year. Like too
many, Morton had been dealing extensively in lands and stocks;
and though apparently in good circumstances was, in reality,
deeply involved in debt. Althesa, although as white as most
white women in a southern clime, was, as we already know, born
a slave. By the laws of all the Southern States the children follow
the condition of the mother. If the mother is free the children
are free; if a slave, they are slaves. Morton was unacquainted
with the laws of the land; and although he had married Althesa,
it was a marriage which the law did not recognise; and therefore
she whom he thought to be his wife was, in fact, nothing more
than his slave. What would have been his feelings had he known
this, and also known that his two daughters, Ellen and Jane,
were his slaves? Yet such was the fact. After the disappearance
of the disease with which Henry Morton had so suddenly been
removed, his brother went to New Orleans to give what aid he
could in settling up the affairs. James Morton, on his arrival in
New Orleans, felt proud of his nieces, and promised them a
home with his own family in Vermont; little dreaming that his

brother had married a slave woman, and that his nieces were slaves. The girls themselves had never heard that their mother had been a slave, and therefore knew nothing of the danger hanging over their heads. An inventory of the property was made out by James Morton, and placed in the hands of the creditors; and the young ladies, with their uncle, were about leaving the city to reside for a few days on the banks of Lake Pontchartrain, where they could enjoy a fresh air that the city could not afford. But just as they were about taking the train, an officer arrested the whole party; the young ladies as slaves, and the uncle upon the charge of attempting to conceal the property of his deceased brother. Morton was overwhelmed with horror at the idea of his nieces being claimed as slaves, and asked for time, that he might save them from such a fate. He even offered to mortgage his little farm in Vermont for the amount which young slave women of their ages would fetch. But the creditors pleaded that they were "an extra article," and would sell for more than common slaves; and must, therefore, be sold at auction. They were given up, but neither ate nor slept, nor separated from each other, till they were taken into the New Orleans slave market, where they were offered to the highest bidder. There they stood, trembling, blushing, and weeping; compelled to listen to the grossest language, and shrinking from the rude hands that examined the graceful proportions of their beautiful frames.

After a fierce contest between the bidders, the young ladies were sold, one for 2,300 dollars, and the other for 3,000 dollars. We need not add that had those young girls been sold for mere house servants or field hands, they would not have brought one half the sums they did. The fact that they were the granddaughters of Thomas Jefferson, no doubt, increased their value in the market. Here were two of the softer sex, accustomed to the fondest indulgence, surrounded by all the refinements of life, and with all the timidity that such a life could produce, bartered away like cattle in Smithfield market. Ellen, the eldest, was sold to an old gentleman, who purchased her, as he said, for a housekeeper. The girl was taken to his residence, nine miles from the city. She soon, however, knew for what purpose she had been bought; and an educated and cultivated mind and taste, which made her see and understand how great was her degradation, now armed her hand with the ready means of death. The morning after her arrival, she was found in her chamber, a corpse. She had taken poison. Jane was purchased by a dashing young man, who had just come into the possession of a large fortune. The very appearance of the young Southerner pointed him out as an unprincipled profligate; and the young girl needed no one to tell her of her impending doom. The young maid of fifteen was immediately removed to his country seat, near the junction of the Mississippi river with the sea. This was a most singular spot, remote, in a dense forest spreading over the summit of a cliff that rose abruptly to a great height above the sea; but so grand in its situation, in the desolate sublimity which reigned around, in the reverential murmur of the waves that washed its base, that, though picturesque, it was a forest prison. Here the young lady saw no one, except an old negress who acted as her servant. The smiles with which the young man met her were indignantly spurned. But she was the property of another, and could hope for justice and mercy only through him.

Jane, though only in her fifteenth year, had become strongly attached to Volney Lapuc, a young Frenchman, a student in her father's office. The poverty of the young man, and the youthful age of the girl, had caused their feelings to be kept from the young lady's parents. At the death of his master, Volney had returned to his widowed mother at Mobile, and knew nothing of the misfortune that had befallen his mistress, until he received a letter from her. But how could he ever obtain a sight of her, even if he wished, locked up as she was in her master's mansion? After several days of what her master termed "obstinacy" on her part, the young girl was placed in an upper chamber, and told that that would be her home, until she should yield to her master's wishes. There she remained more than a fortnight, and with the exception of a daily visit from her master, she saw no one but the old negress who waited upon her. One bright moonlight evening as she was seated at the window, she perceived the figure of a man beneath her window. At first, she thought it was her master; but the tall figure of the stranger soon convinced her that it was another. Yes, it was Volney! He had no sooner received her letter, than he set out for New Orleans; and finding on his arrival there, that his mistress had been taken away, resolved to follow her. There he was; but how could she communicate with him? She dared not trust the old negress with her secret, for fear that it might reach her master. Jane wrote a hasty note and threw it out of the window, which was eagerly picked up by the young man, and he soon disappeared in the woods. Night passed away in dreariness to her, and the next morning she viewed the spot beneath her window with the hope of seeing the footsteps of him who had stood there the previous night. Evening returned, and with it the hope of again seeing the man she loved. In this she was not disappointed; for daylight had scarcely disappeared, and the moon once more rising through the tops of the tall trees, when the young man was seen in the same place as on the previous night. He had in his hand a rope ladder. As soon as Jane saw this, she took the sheets from her bed, tore them into strings, tied them together, and let one end down the side of the house. A moment more, and one end of the rope ladder was in her hand, and she fastened it inside the room. Soon the young maiden was seen descending, and the enthusiastic lover, with his arms extended, waiting to receive his mistress. The planter had been out on an hunting excursion, and returning home, saw his victim as her lover was receiving her in his arms. At this moment the sharp sound of a rifle was heard, and the young man fell weltering in his blood, at the feet of his mistress. Jane fell senseless by his side. For many days she had a confused consciousness of some great agony, but knew not where she was, or by whom surrounded. The slow recovery of her reason settled into the most intense melancholy, which gained at length the compassion even of her cruel master. The beautiful bright eyes, always pleading in expression, were now so heart-piercing in their sadness, that he could not endure their gaze. In a few days the poor girl died of a broken heart, and was buried at night at the back of the garden by the negroes; and no one wept at the grave of her who had been so carefully cherished, and so tenderly beloved.

This, reader, is an unvarnished narrative of one doomed by the laws of the Southern States to be a slave. It tells not only its own story of grief, but speaks of a thousand wrongs and woes beside, which never see the light; all the more bitter and dreadful, because no help can relieve, no sympathy can mitigate, and no hope can cheer.

XXIV. The Arrest

"The fearful storm—it threatens lowering,
    Which God in mercy long delays;
Slaves yet may see their masters cowering,
    While whole plantations smoke and blaze!"
                                                            Carter.

IT WAS LATE in the evening when the coach arrived at
Richmond, and Clotel once more alighted in her native city. She
had intended to seek lodging somewhere in the outskirts of the
town, but the lateness of the hour compelled her to stop at one
of the principal hotels for the night. She had scarcely entered
the inn, when she recognised among the numerous black servants one to whom she was well known; and her only hope was,
that her disguise would keep her from being discovered. The
imperturbable calm and entire forgetfulness of self which induced Clotel to visit a place from which she could scarcely hope
to escape, to attempt the rescue of a beloved child, demonstrate
that over-willingness of woman to carry out the promptings of
the finer feelings of her heart. True to woman's nature, she had
risked her own liberty for another.

She remained in the hotel during the night, and the next
morning, under the plea of illness, she took her breakfast alone.
That day the fugitive slave paid a visit to the suburbs of the
town, and once more beheld the cottage in which she had spent
so many happy hours. It was winter, and the clematis and passion flower were not there; but there were the same walks she
had so often pressed with her feet, and the same trees which
had so often shaded her as she passed through the garden at the

back of the house. Old remembrances rushed upon her memory, and caused her to shed tears freely. Clotel was now in her native town, and near her daughter; but how could she communicate with her? How could she see her? To have made herself known, would have been a suicidal act; betrayal would have followed, and she arrested. Three days had passed away, and Clotel still remained in the hotel at which she had first put up; and yet she had got no tidings of her child. Unfortunately for Clotel, a disturbance had just broken out amongst the slave population in the state of Virginia, and all strangers were eyed with suspicion.

The evils consequent on slavery are not lessened by the incoming of one or two rays of light. If the slave only becomes aware of his condition, and conscious of the injustice under which he suffers, if he obtains but a faint idea of these things, he will seize the first opportunity to possess himself of what he conceives to belong to him. The infusion of Anglo-Saxon with African blood has created an insurrectionary feeling among the slaves of America hitherto unknown. Aware of their blood connection with their owners, these mulattoes labour under the sense of their personal and social injuries; and tolerate, if they do not encourage in themselves, low and vindictive passions. On the other hand, the slave owners are aware of their critical position, and are ever watchful, always fearing an outbreak among the slaves.

True, the Free States are equally bound with the Slave States to suppress any insurrectionary movement that may take place among the slaves. The Northern freemen are bound by their constitutional obligations to aid the slaveholder in keeping his slaves in their chains. Yet there are, at the time we write, four millions of bond slaves in the United States. The insurrection to which we now refer was headed by a full-blooded negro, who had been born and brought up a slave. He had heard the twang of the driver's whip, and saw the warm blood streaming from the negro's body; he had witnessed the separation of parents and children, and was made aware, by too many proofs, that the slave could expect no justice at the hand of the slave owner. He went by the name of "Nat Turner." He was a preacher amongst the negroes, and distinguished for his eloquence, respected by the whites, and loved and venerated by the negroes. On the discovery of the plan for the outbreak, Turner fled to the swamps, followed by those who had joined in the insurrection. Here the revolted negroes numbered some hundreds, and for a time bade defiance to their oppressors. The Dismal Swamps cover many thousands of acres of wild land, and a dense forest, with wild animals and insects, such as are unknown in any other part of Virginia. Here runaway negroes usually seek a hiding place, and some have been known to reside here for years. The revolters were joined by one of these. He was a large, tall, full-blooded negro, with a stern and savage countenance; the marks on his face showed that he was from one of the barbarous tribes in Africa, and claimed that country as his native land; his only covering was a girdle around his loins, made of skins of wild beasts which he had killed; his only token of authority among those that he led, was a pair of epaulettes made from the tail of a fox, and tied to his shoulder by a cord. Brought from the coast of Africa when only fifteen years of age to the island of Cuba, he was smuggled from thence into Virginia. He had been two years in the swamps, and considered it his future home. He had met a negro woman who was also a runaway; and, after the fashion of his native land, had gone through the process of oiling her as the marriage ceremony. They had built a cave on a rising mound in the swamp; this was their home. His name was Picquilo. His only weapon was a sword, made from the blade of a scythe, which he had stolen from a neighbouring plantation. His dress, his character, his manners, his mode of fighting, were all in keeping with the early training he had received in the land of his birth. He moved about with the activity of a cat, and neither the thickness of the trees, nor the depth of the water could stop him. He was a bold, turbulent spirit; and from revenge imbrued his hands in the blood of all the whites he could meet. Hunger, thirst, fatigue, and loss of sleep he seemed made to endure as if by peculiarity of constitution. His air was fierce, his step oblique, his look sanguinary. Such was the character of one of the leaders in the Southampton insurrection. All negroes were arrested who were found beyond their master's threshold, and all strange whites watched with a great degree of alacrity.

Such was the position in which Clotel found affairs when she returned to Virginia in search of her Mary. Had not the slave-owners been watchful of strangers, owing to the outbreak, the fugitive could not have escaped the vigilance of the police; for advertisements, announcing her escape and offering a large reward for her arrest, had been received in the city previous to her arrival, and the officers were therefore on the look-out for the runaway slave. It was on the third day, as the quadroon was seated in her room at the inn, still in the disguise of a gentleman, that two of the city officers entered the room, and informed her that they were authorised to examine all strangers, to assure the authorities that they were not in league with the revolted negroes. With trembling heart the fugitive handed the key of her trunk to the officers. To their surprise, they found nothing but woman's apparel in the box, which raised their curiosity, and caused a further investigation that resulted in the arrest of Clotel as a fugitive slave. She was immediately conveyed to prison, there to await the orders of her master. For many days, uncheered by the voice of kindness, alone, hopeless, desolate, she waited for the time to arrive when the chains were to be placed on her limbs, and she returned to her inhuman and unfeeling owner.

The arrest of the fugitive was announced in all the newspapers, but created little or no sensation. The inhabitants were too much engaged in putting down the revolt among the slaves; and although all the odds were against the insurgents, the whites found it no easy matter, with all their caution. Every day brought news of fresh outbreaks. Without scruple and without pity, the whites massacred all blacks found beyond their owners' plantations: the negroes, in return, set fire to houses, and put those to death who attempted to escape from the flames. Thus carnage was added to carnage, and the blood of the whites flowed to avenge the blood of the blacks. These were the ravages of slavery. No graves were dug for the negroes; their dead bodies became food for dogs and vultures, and their bones, partly calcined by the sun, remained scattered about, as if to mark the mournful fury of servitude and lust of power. When the slaves were subdued, except a few in the swamps, bloodhounds were put in this dismal place to hunt out the remaining revolters. Among the captured negroes was one of whom we shall hereafter make mention.

XXV. Death is Freedom

"I asked but freedom, and ye gave
    Chains, and the freedom of the grave."—*Snelling.*

THERE ARE, in the district of Columbia, several slave prisons, or "negro pens," as they are termed. These prisons are mostly occupied by persons to keep their slaves in, when collecting their gangs together for the New Orleans market. Some of them belong to the government, and one, in particular, is noted for having been the place where a number of free coloured persons have been incarcerated from time to time. In this district is situated the capitol of the United States. Any free coloured persons visiting Washington, if not provided with papers asserting and proving their right to be free, may be arrested and placed in one of these dens. If they succeed in showing that they are free, they are set at liberty, provided they are able to pay the expenses of their arrest and imprisonment; if they cannot pay these expenses, they are sold out. Through this unjust and oppressive law, many persons born in the Free States have been consigned to a life of slavery on the cotton, sugar, or rice plantations of the Southern States. By order of her master, Clotel was removed from Richmond and placed in one of these prisons, to await the sailing of a vessel for New Orleans. The prison in which she was put stands midway between the capitol at Washington and the President's house. Here the fugitive saw nothing but slaves brought in and taken out, to be placed in ships and sent away to the same part of the country to which she herself would soon be compelled to go. She had seen or heard nothing of her daughter while in Richmond, and all hope of seeing her now had fled. If she was carried back to New Orleans, she could expect no mercy from her master.

At the dusk of the evening previous to the day when she was to be sent off, as the old prison was being closed for the night, she suddenly darted past her keeper, and ran for her life. It is not a great distance from the prison to the Long Bridge, which passes from the lower part of the city across the Potomac, to the extensive forests and woodlands of the celebrated Arlington Place, occupied by that distinguished relative and descendant of the immortal Washington, Mr. George W. Curtis. Thither the poor fugitive directed her flight. So unexpected was her escape, that she had quite a number of rods the start before the keeper had secured the other prisoners, and rallied his assistants in pursuit. It was at an hour when, and in a part of the city where, horses could not be readily obtained for the chase; no bloodhounds were at hand to run down the flying woman; and for once it seemed as though there was to be a fair trial of speed and endurance between the slave and the slave-catchers. The keeper and his forces raised the hue and cry on her pathway close behind; but so rapid was the flight along the wide avenue, that the astonished citizens, as they poured forth from their dwellings to learn the cause of alarm, were only able to comprehend the nature of the case in time to fall in with the motley mass in pursuit, (as many a one did that night,) to raise an anxious prayer to heaven, as they refused to join in the pursuit, that the panting fugitive might escape, and the merciless soul dealer for once be disappointed of his prey. And now with the speed of an arrow— having passed the avenue—with the distance between her and her pursuers constantly increasing, this poor hunted female gained the *"Long Bridge,"* as it is called, where interruption seemed improbable, and already did her heart begin to beat high with the hope of success. She had only to pass three-fourths of a mile across the bridge, and she could bury herself in a vast forest, just at the time when the curtain of night would close around her, and protect her from the pursuit of her enemies.

But God by his Providence had otherwise determined. He had determined that an appalling tragedy should be enacted that night, within plain sight of the President's house and the capitol of the Union, which should be an evidence wherever it should be known, of the unconquerable love of liberty the heart may inherit; as well as a fresh admonition to the slave dealer, of the cruelty and enormity of his crimes. Just as the pursuers crossed the high draw for the passage of sloops, soon after entering upon the bridge, they beheld three men slowly approaching from the Virginia side. They immediately called to them to arrest the fugitive, whom they proclaimed a runaway slave. True to their Virginian instincts as she came near, they formed in line across the narrow bridge, and prepared to seize her. Seeing escape impossible in that quarter, she stopped suddenly, and turned upon her pursuers. On came the profane and ribald crew, faster than ever, already exulting in her capture, and threatening punishment for her flight. For a moment she looked wildly and anxiously around to see if there was no hope of escape. On either hand, far down below, rolled the deep foamy waters of the Potomac, and before and behind the rapidly approaching step and noisy voices of pursuers, showing how vain would be any further effort for freedom. Her resolution was taken. She clasped her *hands* convulsively, and raised *them,* as she at the same time raised her *eyes* towards heaven, and begged for that mercy and compassion *there,* which had been denied her on earth; and then, with a single bound, she vaulted over the railings of the bridge, and sunk for ever beneath the waves of the river!

Thus died Clotel, the daughter of Thomas Jefferson, a president of the United States; a man distinguished as the author of the Declaration of American Independence, and one of the first statesmen of that country.

Had Clotel escaped from oppression in any other land, in the disguise in which she fled from the Mississippi to Richmond, and reached the United States, no honour within the gift of the American people would have been too good to have been heaped upon the heroic woman. But she was a slave, and therefore out of the pale of their sympathy. They have tears to shed over Greece and Poland; they have an abundance of sympathy for "poor Ireland"; they can furnish a ship of war to convey the Hungarian refugees from a Turkish prison to the "land of the free and home of the brave." They boast that America is the "cradle of liberty"; if it is, I fear they have rocked the child to death. The body of Clotel was picked up from the bank of the river, where it had been washed by the strong current, a hole dug in the sand, and there deposited, without either inquest being held over it, or religious service being performed. Such was the life and such the death of a woman whose virtues and goodness of heart would have done honour to one in a higher station of life, and who, if she had been born in any other land but that of slavery, would have been honoured and loved. A few days after the death of Clotel, the following poem appeared in one of the newspapers:

> "Now, rest for the wretched! the long day is past,
>   And night on yon prison descendeth at last.
>   Now lock up and bolt! Ha, jailor, look there!
>   Who flies like a wild bird escaped from the snare?
>   A woman, a slave—up, out in pursuit,
>   While linger some gleams of day!
>   Let thy call ring out!—now a rabble rout
>   Is at thy heels—speed away!
>
> "A bold race for freedom!—On, fugitive, on!
>   Heaven help but the right, and thy freedom is won.
>   How eager she drinks the free air of the plains;
>   Every limb, every nerve, every fibre she strains;
>   From Columbia's glorious capitol,
>   Columbia's daughter flees
>   To the sanctuary God has given—
>   The sheltering forest trees.
>
> "Now she treads the Long Bridge—joy lighteth her eye—
>   Beyond her the dense wood and darkening sky—
>   Wild hopes thrill her heart as she neareth the shore:
>   O, despair! there are *men* fast advancing before!
>   Shame, shame on their manhood! they hear, they heed
>   The cry, her flight to stay,
>   And like demon forms with their outstretched arms,
>   They wait to seize their prey!

"She pauses, she turns! Ah, will she flee back?
  Like wolves, her pursuers howl loud on their track;
  She lifteth to Heaven one look of despair—
  Her anguish breaks forth in one hurried prayer—
      Hark! her jailor's yell! like a bloodhound's bay
        On the low night wind it sweeps!
      Now, death or the chain! to the stream she turns,
        And she leaps! O God, she leaps!

"The dark and the cold, yet merciful wave,
  Receives to its bosom the form of the slave:
  She rises—earth's scenes on her dim vision gleam,
  Yet she struggleth not with the strong rushing stream:
      And low are the death-cries her woman's heart gives,
        As she floats adown the river,
      Faint and more faint grows the drowning voice,
        And her cries have ceased for ever!

"Now back, jailor, back to thy dungeons, again,
  To swing the red lash and rivet the chain!
  The form thou would'st fetter—returned to its God;
      The universe holdeth no realm of night
        More drear than her slavery—
      More merciless fiends than here stayed her flight—
        Joy! the hunted slave is free!

"That bond-woman's corpse—let Potomac's proud wave
  Go bear it along *by our Washington's grave,*
  And heave it high up on that hallowed strand,
  To tell of the freedom he won for our land.
      A weak woman's corpse, by freemen chased down;
        Hurrah for our country! hurrah!
      To freedom she leaped, through drowning and death—
        Hurrah for our country! hurrah!"

XXVI. The Escape

"No refuge is found on our unhallowed ground,
  For the wretched in Slavery's manacles bound;
  While our star-spangled banner in vain boasts to wave
  O'er the land of the free and the home of the brave!"

WE LEFT MARY, the daughter of Clotel, in the capacity of a servant in her own father's house, where she had been taken by her mistress for the ostensible purpose of plunging her husband into the depths of humiliation. At first the young girl was treated with great severity; but after finding that Horatio Green had lost all feeling for his child, Mrs. Green's own heart became touched for the offspring of her husband, and she became its friend. Mary had grown still more beautiful, and, like most of her sex in that country, was fast coming to maturity.

The arrest of Clotel, while trying to rescue her daughter, did not reach the ears of the latter till her mother had been removed from Richmond to Washington. The mother had passed from time to eternity before the daughter knew that she had been in the neighbourhood. Horatio Green was not in Richmond at the time of Clotel's arrest; had he been there, it is not probable but he would have made an effort to save her. She was not his slave, and therefore was beyond his power, even had he been there and inclined to aid her. The revolt amongst the slaves had been brought to an end, and most of the insurgents either put to death or sent out of the state. One, however, remained in prison. He was the slave of Horatio Green, and had been a servant in his master's dwelling. He, too, could boast that his father was an American statesman. His name was George. His mother had been employed as a servant in one of the principal hotels in

Washington, where members of Congress usually put up. After George's birth his mother was sold to a slave trader, and he to an agent of Mr. Green, the father of Horatio. George was as white as most white persons. No one would suppose that any African blood coursed through his veins. His hair was straight, soft, fine, and light; his eyes blue, nose prominent, lips thin, his head well formed, forehead high and prominent; and he was often taken for a free white person by those who did know him. This made his condition still more intolerable; for one so white seldom ever receives fair treatment at the hands of his fellow slaves; and the whites usually regard such slaves as persons who, if not often flogged, and otherwise ill treated, to remind them of their condition, would soon "forget" that they were slaves, and "think themselves as good as white folks." George's opportunities were far greater than most slaves. Being in his master's house, and waiting on educated white people, he had become very familiar with the English language. He had heard his master and visitors speak of the down-trodden and oppressed Poles; he heard them talk of going to Greece to fight for Grecian liberty, and against the oppressors of that ill-fated people. George, fired with the love of freedom, and zeal for the cause of his enslaved countrymen, joined the insurgents, and with them had been defeated and captured. He was the only one remaining of these unfortunate people, and he would have been put to death with them but for a circumstance that occurred some weeks before the outbreak. The court house had, by accident, taken fire, and was fast consuming. The engines could not be made to work, and all hope of saving the building seemed at an end. In one of the upper chambers there was a small box containing some valuable deeds belonging to the city; a ladder was placed against the house, leading from the street to the window of the room in which the box stood. The wind blew strong, and swept the flames in that direction. Broad sheets of fire were blown again and again over that part of the building, and then the wind would lift the pall of smoke, which showed that the work of destruction was not yet accomplished. While the doomed building was thus exposed, and before the destroying element had made its final visit, as it did soon after, George was standing by, and hearing that much depended on the contents of the box, and seeing no one disposed to venture through the fiery element to save the treasure, mounted the ladder and made his way to the window, entered the room, and was soon seen descending with the much valued box. Three cheers rent the air as the young slave fell from the ladder when near the ground; the white men took him up in their arms, to see if he had sustained any injury. His hair was burnt, eyebrows closely singed, and his clothes smelt strongly of smoke; but the heroic young slave was unhurt. The city authorities, at their next meeting, passed a vote of thanks to George's master for the lasting benefit that the slave had rendered the public, and commanded the poor boy to the special favour of his owner. When George was on trial for participating in the revolt, this "meritorious act," as they were pleased to term it, was brought up in his favour. His trial was put off from session to session, till he had been in prison more than a year. At last, however, he was convicted of high treason, and sentenced to be hanged within ten days of that time. The judge asked the slave if he had anything to say why sentence of death should not be passed on him. George stood for a moment in silence, and then said, "As I cannot speak as I should wish, I will say nothing." "You may say what you please," said the judge. "You had a good master," continued he, "and still you were dissatisfied; you left your master and joined the negroes who were burning our houses and killing our wives." "As you have given me permission to speak," remarked George, "I will tell you why I joined the revolted negroes. I have heard my master read in the Declaration of Independence 'that all men are created free and equal,' and this caused me to inquire of myself why I was a slave. I also heard him talking with some of his visitors about the war with England, and he said, all wars and fightings for freedom were just and right. If so, in what am I wrong? The grievances of which your fathers complained, and which caused the Revolutionary War, were trifling in comparison with the wrongs and sufferings of those who were engaged in the late revolt. Your fathers were never slaves, ours are; your fathers were never bought and sold like cattle, never shut out from the light of knowledge and religion, never subjected to the lash of brutal task-masters. For the crime of having a dark skin, my people suffer the pangs of hunger, the infliction of stripes, and the ignominy of brutal servitude. We are kept in heathenish darkness by laws expressly enacted to make our instruction a criminal offence. What right has one man to the bones, sinews, blood, and nerves of another? Did not one God make us all? You say your fathers fought for freedom—so did we. You tell me that I am to be put to death for violating the laws of the land. Did not the American revolutionists violate the laws when they struck for liberty? They were revolters, but their success made them patriots—we were revolters, and our failure makes us rebels. Had we succeeded, we would have been patriots too. Success makes all the difference. You make merry on the 4th of July; the thunder of cannon and ringing of bells announce it as the birthday of American independence. Yet while these cannons are roaring and bells ringing, one-sixth of the people of this land are in chains and slavery. You boast that this is the 'Land of the Free'; but a traditionary freedom will not save you. It will not do to praise your fathers and build their sepulchres. Worse for you that you have such an inheritance, if you spend it foolishly and are unable to appreciate its worth. Sad if the genius of a true humanity, beholding you with tearful eyes from the mount of vision, shall fold his wings in sorrowing pity, and repeat the strain, 'O land of Washington, how often would I have gathered thy children together, as a hen doth gather her brood under her wings, and ye would not; behold your house is left unto you desolate.' This is all I have to say; I have done." Nearly every one present was melted to tears; even the judge seemed taken by surprise at the intelligence of the young slave. But George was a slave, and an example must be made of him, and therefore he was sentenced. Being employed in the same house with Mary, the daughter of Clotel, George had become attached to her, and the young lovers fondly looked forward to the time when they should be husband and wife.

After George had been sentenced to death, Mary was still more attentive to him, and begged and obtained leave of her mistress to visit him in his cell. The poor girl paid a daily visit to him to whom she had pledged her heart and hand. At one of these meetings, and only four days from the time fixed for the execution, while Mary was seated in George's cell, it occurred to her that she might yet save him from a felon's doom. She revealed to him the secret that was then occupying her thoughts, viz. that George should exchange clothes with her, and thus attempt his escape in disguise. But he would not for a single moment listen to the proposition. Not that he feared detection; but he would not consent to place an innocent and affectionate girl in a position where she might have to suffer for him. Mary pleaded, but in vain—George was inflexible. The poor girl left her lover with a heavy heart, regretting that her scheme had proved unsuccessful.

Towards the close of the next day, Mary again appeared at the prison door for admission, and was soon by the side of him whom she so ardently loved. While there the clouds which had overhung the city for some hours broke, and the rain fell in torrents amid the most terrific thunder and lightning. In the most persuasive manner possible, Mary again importuned George to avail himself of her assistance to escape from an ignominious death. After assuring him that she, not being the person condemned, would not receive any injury, he at last consented, and they began to exchange apparel. As George was of small stature, and both were white, there was no difficulty in his passing out without detection; and as she usually left the cell weeping, with handkerchief in hand, and sometimes at her face, he had only to adopt this mode and his escape was safe. They had kissed each other, and Mary had told George where he would find a small parcel of provisions which she had placed in a secluded spot, when the prison-keeper opened the door and said, "Come, girl, it is time for you to go." George again embraced Mary, and passed out of the jail. It was already dark, and the street lamps were lighted, so that our hero in his new dress had no dread of detection. The provisions were sought out and found, and poor George was soon on the road towards Canada. But neither of them had once thought of a change of dress for George when he should have escaped, and he had walked but a short distance before he felt that a change of his apparel would facilitate his progress. But he dared not go amongst even his coloured associ-

ates for fear of being betrayed. However, he made the best of
his way on towards Canada, hiding in the woods during the day,
and travelling by the guidance of the North Star at night.

With the poet he could truly say,

> "Star of the North! while blazing day
>   Pours round me its full tide of light,
> And hides thy pale but faithful ray,
>   I, too, lie hid, and long for night."

One morning, George arrived on the banks of the Ohio river,
and found his journey had terminated, unless he could get some
one to take him across the river in a secret manner, for he would
not be permitted to cross in any of the ferry boats, it being a
penalty for crossing a slave, besides the value of the slave. He
concealed himself in the tall grass and weeds near the river, to
see if he could embrace an opportunity to cross. He had been in
his hiding place but a short time, when he observed a man in a
small boat, floating near the shore, evidently fishing. His first
impulse was to call out to the man and ask him to take him over
to the Ohio side, but the fear that the man was a slaveholder, or
one who might possibly arrest him, deterred him from it. The
man after rowing and floating about for some time fastened the
boat to the root of a tree, and started to a neighbouring farmhouse.

This was George's moment, and he seized it. Running down
the bank, he unfastened the boat, jumped in, and with all the
expertness of one accustomed to a boat, rowed across the river
and landed on the Ohio side.

Being now in a Free State, he thought he might with perfect
safety travel on towards Canada. He had, however, gone but a
very few miles when he discovered two men on horseback coming behind him. He felt sure that they could not be in pursuit of
him, yet he did not wish to be seen by them, so he turned into
another road leading to a house near by. The men followed, and
were but a short distance from George, when he ran up to a
farmhouse, before which was standing a farmer-looking man, in
a broad-brimmed hat and straight-collared coat, whom he implored to save him from the "slave-catchers." The farmer told

him to go into the barn near by; he entered by the front door, the farmer following, and closing the door behind George, but remaining outside, and gave directions to his hired man as to what should be done with George. The slaveholders by this time had dismounted, and were in front of the barn demanding admittance, and charging the farmer with secreting their slave woman, for George was still in the dress of a woman. The Friend, for the farmer proved to be a member of the Society of Friends, told the slave-owners that if they wished to search his barn, they must first get an officer and a search warrant. While the parties were disputing, the farmer began nailing up the front door, and the hired man served the back door in the same way. The slaveholders, finding that they could not prevail on the Friend to allow them to get the slave, determined to go in search of an officer. One was left to see that the slave did not escape from the barn, while the other went off at full speed to Mount Pleasant, the nearest town. George was not the slave of either of these men, nor were they in pursuit of him, but they had lost a woman who had been seen in that vicinity, and when they saw poor George in the disguise of a female, and attempting to elude pursuit, they felt sure they were close upon their victim. However, if they had caught him, although he was not their slave, they would have taken him back and placed him in jail, and there he would have remained until his owner arrived.

After an absence of nearly two hours, the slave-owner returned with an officer and found the Friend still driving large nails into the door. In a triumphant tone and with a corresponding gesture, he handed the search-warrant to the Friend, and said, "There, sir, now I will see if I can't get my nigger." "Well," said the Friend, "thou hast gone to work according to law, and thou canst now go into my barn." "Lend me your hammer that I may get the door open," said the slaveholder. "Let me see the warrant again." And after reading it over once more, he said, "I see nothing in this paper which says I must supply thee with tools to open my door; if thou wishest to go in, thou must get a hammer elsewhere." The sheriff said, "I will go to a neighbouring farm and borrow something which will introduce us to Miss Dinah"; and he immediately went in search of tools. In a short time the officer returned, and they commenced an assault and battery upon the barn door, which soon yielded; and in went the slaveholder and officer, and began turning up the hay and using all other means to find the lost property; but, to their astonishment, the slave was not there. After all hope of getting Dinah was gone, the slave-owner in a rage said to the Friend, "My nigger is not here." "I did not tell thee there was any one here." "Yes, but I saw her go in, and you shut the door behind her, and if she was not in the barn, what did you nail the door for?" "Can't I do what I please with my own barn door? Now I will tell thee; thou need trouble thyself no more, for the person thou art after entered the front door and went out at the back door, and is a long way from here by this time. Thou and thy friend must be somewhat fatigued by this time; won't thou go in and take a little dinner with me?" We need not say that this cool invitation of the good Quaker was not accepted by the slaveholders. George in the meantime had been taken to a friend's dwelling some miles away, where, after laying aside his female attire, and being snugly dressed up in a straight collared coat, and pantaloons to match, was again put on the right road towards Canada.

The fugitive now travelled by day, and laid by during night. After a fatiguing and dreary journey of two weeks, the fugitive arrived in Canada, and took up his abode in the little town of St. Catherine's, and obtained work on the farm of Colonel Street. Here he attended a night-school, and laboured for his employer during the day. The climate was cold, and wages small, yet he was in a land where he was free, and this the young slave prized more than all the gold that could be given to him. Besides doing his best to obtain education for himself, he imparted what he could to those of his fellow-fugitives about him, of whom there were many.

XXVII. The Mystery

GEORGE, however, did not forget his promise to use all the means in his power to get Mary out of slavery. He, therefore, laboured with all his might to obtain money with which to employ some one to go back to Virginia for Mary. After nearly six months' labour at St. Catherine's, he employed an English missionary to go and see if the girl could be purchased, and at what price. The missionary went accordingly, but returned with the sad intelligence that, on account of Mary's aiding George to escape, the court had compelled Mr. Green to sell her out of the state, and she had been sold to a negro trader, and taken to the New Orleans market. As all hope of getting the girl was now gone, George resolved to quit the American continent for ever. He immediately took passage in a vessel laden with timber, bound for Liverpool, and in five weeks from that time he was standing on the quay of the great English seaport. With little or no education, he found many difficulties in the way of getting a respectable living. However he obtained a situation as porter in a large house in Manchester, where he worked during the day, and took private lessons at night. In this way he laboured for three years, and was then raised to the situation of clerk. George was so white as easily to pass for a white man, and being somewhat ashamed of his African descent, he never once mentioned the fact of his having been a slave. He soon became a partner in the firm that employed him, and was now on the road to wealth.

In the year 1842, just ten years after George Green (for he adopted his master's name) arrived in England, he visited France, and spent some days at Dunkirk. It was towards sunset, on a warm day in the month of October, that Mr. Green, after strolling some distance from the Hotel de Leon, entered a burial ground, and wandered long alone among the silent dead, gazing upon the many green graves and marble tombstones of those who once moved on the theatre of busy life, and whose sounds of gaiety once fell upon the ear of man. All nature around was hushed in silence, and seemed to partake of the general melancholy which hung over the quiet resting-place of departed mortals. After tracing the varied inscriptions which told the characters or conditions of the departed, and viewing the mounds beneath which the dust of mortality slumbered, he had now reached a secluded spot, near to where an aged weeping willow bowed its thick foliage to the ground, as though anxious to hide from the scrutinising gaze of curiosity the grave beneath it. Mr. Green seated himself upon a marble tomb, and began to read Roscoe's *Leo X.*, a copy of which he had under his arm. It was then about twilight, and he had scarcely gone through half a page, when he observed a lady in black, leading a boy, some five years old, up one of the paths; and as the lady's black veil was over her face, he felt somewhat at liberty to eye her more closely. While looking at her, the lady gave a scream, and appeared to be in a fainting position, when Mr. Green sprang from his seat in time to save her from falling to the ground. At this moment, an elderly gentleman was seen approaching with a rapid step, who, from his appearance, was evidently the lady's father, or one intimately connected with her. He came up, and, in a confused manner, asked what was the matter. Mr. Green explained as well as he could. After taking up the smelling bottle which had fallen from her hand, and holding it a short time to her face, she soon began to revive. During all this time the lady's veil had so covered her face, that Mr. Green had not seen it. When she had so far recovered as to be able to raise her head, she again screamed, and fell back into the arms of the old man. It now appeared quite certain, that either the countenance of George Green, or some other object, was the cause of these fits of fainting; and the old gentleman, thinking it was the former, in rather a petulant tone said, "I will thank you, sir, if you will leave us alone." The child whom the lady was leading, had now set up a squall; and amid the death-like appearance of the lady, the harsh look of the old man, and the cries of the boy, Mr. Green left the grounds, and returned to his hotel.

Whilst seated by the window, and looking out upon the crowded street, with every now and then the strange scene in the grave-yard vividly before him, Mr. Green thought of the book he had been reading, and, remembering that he had left it on the tomb, where he had suddenly dropped it when called to the assistance of the lady, he immediately determined to return in search of it. After a walk of some twenty minutes, he was again over the spot where he had been an hour before, and from which he had been so unceremoniously expelled by the old man. He looked in vain for the book; it was nowhere to be found: nothing save the bouquet which the lady had dropped, and which lay half-buried in the grass from having been trodden upon, indicated that any one had been there that evening. Mr. Green took up the bunch of flowers, and again returned to the hotel.

After passing a sleepless night, and hearing the clock strike six, he dropped into a sweet sleep, from which he did not awake until roused by the rap of a servant, who, entering his room, handed him a note which ran as follows:—"Sir,—I owe you an apology for the inconvenience to which you were subjected last evening, and if you will honour us with your presence to dinner to-day at four o'clock, I shall be most happy to give you due satisfaction. My servant will be in waiting for you at half-past three. I am, sir, your obedient servant, J. Devenant. October 23. To George Green, Esq."

The servant who handed this note to Mr. Green, informed him that the bearer was waiting for a reply. He immediately resolved to accept the invitation, and replied accordingly. Who this person was, and how his name and the hotel where he was stopping had been found out, was indeed a mystery. However, he waited impatiently for the hour when he was to see this new acquaintance, and get the mysterious meeting in the grave-yard solved.

XXVIII. The Happy Meeting

"Man's love is of man's life, a thing apart;
'Tis woman's whole existence."—*Byron.*

THE CLOCK on a neighbouring church had scarcely ceased striking three, when the servant announced that a carriage had called for Mr. Green. In less than half an hour he was seated in a most sumptuous barouche, drawn by two beautiful iron greys, and rolling along over a splendid gravel road completely shaded by large trees, which appeared to have been the accumulating growth of many centuries. The carriage soon stopped in front of a low villa, and this too was embedded in magnificent trees covered with moss. Mr. Green alighted and was shown into a superb drawing room, the walls of which were hung with fine specimens from the hands of the great Italian painters, and one by a German artist representing a beautiful monkish legend connected with "The Holy Catherine," an illustrious lady of Alexandria. The furniture had an antique and dignified appearance. High backed chairs stood around the room; a venerable mirror stood on the mantle shelf; rich curtains of crimson damask hung in folds at either side of the large windows; and a rich Turkey carpet covered the floor. In the centre stood a table covered with books, in the midst of which was an old-fashioned vase filled with fresh flowers, whose fragrance was exceedingly pleasant. A faint light, together with the quietness of the hour, gave beauty beyond description to the whole scene.

Mr. Green had scarcely seated himself upon the sofa, when the elderly gentleman whom he had met the previous evening made his appearance, followed by the little boy, and introduced himself as Mr. Devenant. A moment more, and a lady—a beau-

tiful brunette—dressed in black, with long curls of a chesnut
colour hanging down her cheeks, entered the room. Her eyes
were of a dark hazel, and her whole appearance indicated that
she was a native of a southern clime. The door at which she
entered was opposite to where the two gentlemen were seated.
They immediately rose; and Mr. Devenant was in the act of introducing her to Mr. Green, when he observed that the latter
had sunk back upon the sofa, and the last word that he remembered to have heard was, "It is her." After this, all was dark and
dreamy: how long he remained in this condition it was for another to tell. When he awoke, he found himself stretched upon
the sofa, with his boots off, his neckerchief removed, shirt collar
unbuttoned, and his head resting upon a pillow. By his side sat
the old man, with the smelling bottle in the one hand, and a
glass of water in the other, and the little boy standing at the foot
of the sofa. As soon as Mr. Green had so far recovered as to be
able to speak, he said, "Where am I, and what does this mean?"
"Wait a while," replied the old man, "and I will tell you all."
After a lapse of some ten minutes he rose from the sofa, ad-
justed his apparel, and said, "I am now ready to hear anything
you have to say." "You were born in America?" said the old man.
"Yes," he replied. "And you were acquainted with a girl named
Mary?" continued the old man. "Yes, and I loved her as I can
love none other." "The lady whom you met so mysteriously last
evening is Mary," replied Mr. Devenant. George Green was silent, but the fountains of mingled grief and joy stole out from
beneath his eyelashes, and glistened like pearls upon his pale
and marble-like cheeks. At this juncture the lady again entered
the room. Mr. Green sprang from the sofa, and they fell into
each other's arms, to the surprise of the old man and little
George, and to the amusement of the servants who had crept up
one by one, and were hid behind the doors, or loitering in the
hall. When they had given vent to their feelings, they resumed
their seats, and each in turn related the adventures through
which they had passed. "How did you find out my name and
address?" asked Mr. Green. "After you had left us in the grave-
yard, our little George said, 'O, mamma, if there aint a book!'
and picked it up and brought it to us. Papa opened it, and said,

'The gentleman's name is written in it, and here is a card of the Hotel de Leon, where I suppose he is stopping.' Papa wished to leave the book, and said it was all a fancy of mine that I had ever seen you before, but I was perfectly convinced that you were my own George Green. Are you married?" "No, I am not." "Then, thank God!" exclaimed Mrs. Devenant. "And are you single now?" inquired Mr. Green. "Yes," she replied. "This is indeed the Lord's doings," said Mr. Green, at the same time bursting into a flood of tears. Mr. Devenant was past the age when men should think upon matrimonial subjects, yet the scene brought vividly before his eyes the days when he was a young man, and had a wife living. After a short interview, the old man called their attention to the dinner, which was then waiting. We need scarcely add, that Mr. Green and Mrs. Devenant did very little towards diminishing the dinner that day.

After dinner the lovers (for such we have to call them) gave their experience from the time that George left the jail dressed in Mary's clothes. Up to that time Mr. Green's was substantially as we have related it. Mrs. Devenant's was as follows:—"The night after you left the prison," said she, "I did not shut my eyes in sleep. The next morning, about eight o'clock, Peter the gardener came to the jail to see if I had been there the night before, and was informed that I had, and that I had left a little after dark. About an hour after, Mr. Green came himself, and I need not say that he was much surprised on finding me there, dressed in your clothes. This was the first tidings they had of your escape." "What did Mr. Green say when he found that I had fled?" "Oh!" continued Mrs. Devenant, "he said to me when no one was near, I hope George will get off, but I fear you will have to suffer in his stead. I told him that if it must be so I was willing to die if you could live." At this moment George Green burst into tears, threw his arms around her neck, and exclaimed, "I am glad I have waited so long, with the hope of meeting you again."

Mrs. Devenant again resumed her story:—"I was kept in jail three days, during which time I was visited by the magistrates, and two of the judges. On the third day I was taken out, and master told me that I was liberated, upon condition that I should be immediately sent out of the state. There happened to be just at the time in the neighbourhood a negro-trader, and he purchased me, and I was taken to New Orleans. On the steamboat we were kept in a close room, where slaves are usually confined, so that I saw nothing of the passengers on board, or the towns we passed. We arrived at New Orleans, and were all put into the slave-market for sale. I was examined by many persons, but none seemed willing to purchase me, as all thought me too white, and said I would run away and pass as a free white woman. On the second day, while in the slave-market, and while planters and others were examining slaves and making their purchases, I observed a tall young man, with long black hair, eyeing me very closely, and then talking to the trader. I felt sure that my time had now come, but the day closed without my being sold. I did not regret this, for I had heard that foreigners made the worst of masters, and I felt confident that the man who eyed me so closely was not an American.

"The next day was the Sabbath. The bells called the people to the different places of worship. Methodists sang, and Baptists immersed, and Presbyterians sprinkled, and Episcopalians read their prayers, while the ministers of the various sects preached that Christ died for all; yet there were some twenty-five or thirty of us poor creatures confined in the 'Negro Pen,' awaiting the close of the holy Sabbath, and the dawn of another day, to be again taken into the market, there to be examined like so many beasts of burden. I need not tell you with what anxiety we waited for the advent of another day. On Monday we were again brought out and placed in rows to be inspected; and, fortunately for me, I was sold before we had been on the stand an hour. I was purchased by a gentleman residing in the city, for a waiting-maid for his wife, who was just on the eve of starting for Mobile, to pay a visit to a near relation. I was then dressed to suit the situation of a maid-servant; and upon the whole, I thought that, in my new dress, I looked as much the lady as my mistress.

"On the passage to Mobile, who should I see among the passengers but the tall, long-haired man that had eyed me so closely in the slave-market a few days before. His eyes were again on me, and he appeared anxious to speak to me, and I as reluctant to be spoken to. The first evening after leaving New Orleans,

soon after twilight had let her curtain down, and pinned it with
a star, and while I was seated on the deck of the boat near the
ladies' cabin, looking upon the rippled waves, and the reflection
of the moon upon the sea, all at once I saw the tall young man
standing by my side. I immediately rose from my seat, and was
in the act of returning to the cabin, when he in a broken accent
said, 'Stop a moment; I wish to have a word with you. I am your
friend.' I stopped and looked him full in the face, and he said, 'I
saw you some days since in the slave-market, and I intended to
have purchased you to save you from the condition of a slave. I
called on Monday, but you had been sold and had left the market. I inquired and learned who the purchaser was, and that you
had to go to Mobile, so I resolved to follow you. If you are willing I will try and buy you from your present owner, and you shall
be free.' Although this was said in an honest and off-hand manner, I could not believe the man to be sincere in what he said.
'Why should you wish to set *me* free?' I asked. 'I had an only
sister,' he replied, 'who died three years ago in France, and you
are so much like her that had I not known of her death, I would
most certainly have taken you for her.' 'However much I may
resemble your sister, you are aware that I am not her, and why
take so much interest in one whom you never saw before?' 'The
love,' said he, 'which I had for my sister is transferred to you.' I
had all along suspected that the man was a knave, and this profession of love confirmed me in my former belief, and I turned
away and left him.

"The next day, while standing in the cabin and looking
through the window, the French gentleman (for such he was)
came to the window while walking on the guards, and again
commenced as on the previous evening. He took from his
pocket a bit of paper and put it into my hand, at the same time
saying, 'Take this, it may some day be of service to you; remember it is from a friend,' and left me instantly. I unfolded the
paper, and found it to be a 100 dollars bank note, on the United
States Branch Bank, at Philadelphia. My first impulse was to
give it to my mistress, but, upon a second thought, I resolved to
seek an opportunity, and to return the hundred dollars to the
stranger.

"Therefore I looked for him, but in vain; and had almost given up the idea of seeing him again, when he passed me on the guards of the boat and walked towards the stem of the vessel. It being now dark, I approached him and offered the money to him. He declined, saying at the same time, 'I gave it to you—keep it.' 'I do not want it,' I said. 'Now,' said he, 'you had better give your consent for me to purchase you, and you shall go with me to France.' 'But you cannot buy me now,' I replied, 'for my master is in New Orleans, and he purchased me not to sell, but to retain in his own family.' 'Would you rather remain with your present mistress than be free?' 'No,' said I. 'Then fly with me to-night; we shall be in Mobile in two hours from this, and when the passengers are going on shore, you can take my arm, and you can escape unobserved. The trader who brought you to New Orleans exhibited to me a certificate of your good character, and one from the minister of the church to which you were attached in Virginia; and upon the faith of these assurances, and the love I bear you, I promise before high heaven that I will marry you as soon as it can be done.' This solemn promise, coupled with what had already transpired, gave me confidence in the man; and rash as the act may seem, I determined in an instant to go with him. My mistress had been put under the charge of the captain; and as it would be past ten o'clock when the steamer would land, she accepted an invitation of the captain to remain on board with several other ladies till morning. I dressed myself in my best clothes, and put a veil over my face, and was ready on the landing of the boat. Surrounded by a number of passengers, we descended the stage leading to the wharf, and were soon lost in the crowd that thronged the quay. As we went on shore we encountered several persons announcing the names of hotels, the starting of boats for the interior, and vessels bound for Europe. Among these was the ship Utica, Captain Pell, bound for Havre. 'Now,' said Mr. Devenant, 'this is our chance.' The ship was to sail at twelve o'clock that night, at high tide; and following the men who were seeking passengers, we went immediately on board. Devenant told the captain of the ship that I was his sister, and for such we passed during the voyage. At the hour of twelve the Utica set sail, and we were soon out at sea.

"The morning after we left Mobile, Devenant met me as I came from my state-room, and embraced me for the first time. I loved him, but it was only that affection which we have for one who has done us a lasting favour: it was the love of gratitude rather than that of the heart. We were five weeks on the sea, and yet the passage did not seem long, for Devenant was so kind. On our arrival at Havre we were married and came to Dunkirk, and I have resided here ever since."

At the close of this narrative, the clock struck ten, when the old man, who was accustomed to retire at an early hour, rose to take leave, saying at the same time, "I hope you will remain with us to-night." Mr. Green would fain have excused himself, on the ground that they would expect him and wait at the hotel, but a look from the lady told him to accept the invitation. The old man was the father of Mrs. Devenant's deceased husband, as you will no doubt long since have supposed. A fortnight from the day on which they met in the grave-yard, Mr. Green and Mrs. Devenant were joined in holy wedlock; so that George and Mary, who had loved each other so ardently in their younger days, were now husband and wife.

A celebrated writer has justly said of woman, "A woman's whole life is a history of the affections. The heart is her world; it is there her ambition strives for empire; it is there her avarice seeks for hidden treasures. She sends forth her sympathies on adventure; she embarks her whole soul in the traffic of affection; and, if shipwrecked, her case is hopeless, for it is a bankruptcy of the heart."

Mary had every reason to believe that she would never see George again; and although she confesses that the love she bore him was never transferred to her first husband, we can scarcely find fault with her for marrying Mr. Devenant. But the adherence of George Green to the resolution never to marry, unless to his Mary, is, indeed, a rare instance of the fidelity of man in the matter of love. We can but blush for our country's shame when we recall to mind the fact, that while George and Mary Green, and numbers of other fugitives from American slavery, can receive protection from any of the governments of Europe, they cannot return to their native land without becoming slaves.

XXIX. Conclusion

MY NARRATIVE has now come to a close. I may be asked, and no doubt shall, Are the various incidents and scenes related founded in truth? I answer, Yes. I have personally participated in many of those scenes. Some of the narratives I have derived from other sources; many from the lips of those who, like myself, have run away from the land of bondage. Having been for nearly nine years employed on Lake Erie, I had many opportunities for helping the escape of fugitives, who, in return for the assistance they received, made me the depositary of their sufferings and wrongs. Of their relations I have made free use. To Mrs. Child, of New York, I am indebted for part of a short story. American Abolitionist journals are another source from whence some of the characters appearing in my narrative are taken. All these combined have made up my story. Having thus acknowledged my resources, I invite the attention of my readers to the following statement, from which I leave them to draw their own conclusions:—"It is estimated that in the United States, members of the Methodist church own 219,363 slaves; members of the Baptist church own 226,000 slaves; members of the Episcopalian church own 88,000 slaves; members of the Presbyterian church own 77,000 slaves; members of all other churches own 50,000 slaves; in all, 660,563 slaves owned by members of the Christian church in this pious democratic republic!"

May these facts be pondered over by British Christians, and at the next anniversaries of the various religious denominations in London may their influence be seen and felt! The religious bodies of American Christians will send their delegates to these meetings. Let British feeling be publicly manifested. Let British sympathy express itself in tender sorrow for the condition of my unhappy race. Let it be understood, unequivocally understood, that no fellowship can be held with slaveholders professing the same common Christianity as yourselves. And until this stain from America's otherwise fair escutcheon be wiped away, let no Christian association be maintained with those who traffic in the blood and bones of those whom God has made of one flesh as yourselves. Finally, let the voice of the whole British nation be heard across the Atlantic, and throughout the length and breadth of the land of the Pilgrim Fathers, beseeching their descendants, as they value *the* common salvation, which knows no distinction between the bond and the free, to proclaim the Year of Jubilee. Then shall the "earth indeed yield her increase, and God, even our own God, shall bless us; and all the ends of the earth shall fear Him."

Our Nig;
or,
Sketches from the Life of a Free Black

HARRIET E. WILSON

Contents

Preface

IN OFFERING to the public the following pages, the writer confesses her inability to minister to the refined and cultivated, the pleasure supplied by abler pens. It is not for such these crude narrations appear. Deserted by kindred, disabled by failing health, I am forced to some experiment which shall aid me in maintaining myself and child without extinguishing this feeble life. I would not from these motives even palliate slavery at the South, by disclosures of its appurtenances North. My mistress was wholly imbued with *southern* principles. I do not pretend to divulge every transaction in my own life, which the unprejudiced would declare unfavorable in comparison with treatment of legal bondmen; I have purposely omitted what would most provoke shame in our good anti-slavery friends at home.

My humble position and frank confession of errors will, I hope, shield me from severe criticism. Indeed, defects are so apparent it requires no skilful hand to expose them.

I sincerely appeal to my colored brethren universally for patronage, hoping they will not condemn this attempt of their sister to be erudite, but rally around me a faithful band of supporters and defenders.

H. E. W.

I. Mag Smith, My Mother

Oh, Grief beyond all other griefs, when fate
First leaves the young heart lone and desolate
In the wide world, without that only tie
For which it loved to live or feared to die;
Lorn as the hung-up lute, that ne'er hath spoken
Since the sad day its master-chord was broken!

Moore.

LONELY MAG SMITH! See her as she walks with downcast eyes
and heavy heart. It was not always thus. She *had* a loving, trusting heart. Early deprived of parental guardianship, far removed
from relatives, she was left to guide her tiny boat over life's
surges alone and inexperienced. As she merged into womanhood, unprotected, uncherished, uncared for, there fell on her
ear the music of love, awakening an intensity of emotion long
dormant. It whispered of an elevation before unaspired to; of
ease and plenty her simple heart had never dreamed of as hers.
She knew the voice of her charmer, so ravishing, sounded far
above her. It seemed like an angel's, alluring her upward and
onward. She thought she could ascend to him and become an
equal. She surrendered to him a priceless gem, which he
proudly garnered as a trophy, with those of other victims, and
left her to her fate. The world seemed full of hateful deceivers
and crushing arrogance. Conscious that the great bond of union
to her former companions was severed, that the disdain of others would be insupportable, she determined to leave the few
friends she possessed, and seek an asylum among strangers. Her
offspring came unwelcomed, and before its nativity numbered

weeks, it passed from earth, ascending to a purer and better
life.

"God be thanked," ejaculated Mag, as she saw its breathing
cease; "no one can taunt *her* with my ruin."

Blessed release! may we all respond. How many pure, innocent children not only inherit a wicked heart of their own, claiming life-long scrutiny and restraint, but are heirs also of parental
disgrace and calumny, from which only long years of patient
endurance in paths of rectitude can disencumber them.

Mag's new home was soon contaminated by the publicity of
her fall; she had a feeling of degradation oppressing her; but she
resolved to be circumspect, and try to regain in a measure what
she had lost. Then some foul tongue would jest of her shame,
and averted looks and cold greetings disheartened her. She saw
she could not bury in forgetfulness her misdeed, so she resolved
to leave her home and seek another in the place she at first fled
from.

Alas, how fearful are we to be first in extending a helping
hand to those who stagger in the mires of infamy; to speak the
first words of hope and warning to those emerging into the sunlight of morality! Who can tell what numbers, advancing just far
enough to hear a cold welcome and join in the reserved con-
verse of professed reformers, disappointed, disheartened, have
chosen to dwell in unclean places, rather than encounter these
"holier-than-thou" of the great brotherhood of man!

Such was Mag's experience; and disdaining to ask favor or
friendship from a sneering world, she resolved to shut herself
up in a hovel she had often passed in better days, and which she
knew to be untenanted. She vowed to ask no favors of familiar
faces; to die neglected and forgotten before she would be dependent on any. Removed from the village, she was seldom
seen except as upon your introduction, gentle reader, with
downcast visage, returning her work to her employer, and thus
providing herself with the means of subsistence. In two years
many hands craved the same avocation; foreigners who cheap-
ened toil and clamored for a livelihood, competed with her, and
she could not thus sustain herself. She was now above no
drudgery. Occasionally old acquaintances called to be favored

with help of some kind, which she was glad to bestow for the sake of the money it would bring her; but the association with them was such a painful reminder of by-gones, she returned to her hut morose and revengeful, refusing all offers of a better home than she possessed. Thus she lived for years, hugging her wrongs, but making no effort to escape. She had never known plenty, scarcely competency; but the present was beyond comparison with those innocent years when the coronet of virtue was hers.

Every year her melancholy increased, her means diminished. At last no one seemed to notice her, save a kind-hearted African, who often called to inquire after her health and to see if she needed any fuel, he having the responsibility of furnishing that article, and she in return mending or making garments.

"How much you earn dis week, Mag?" asked he one Saturday evening.

"Little enough, Jim. Two or three days without any dinner. I washed for the Reeds, and did a small job for Mrs. Bellmont; that's all. I shall starve soon, unless I can get more to do. Folks seem as afraid to come here as if they expected to get some awful disease. I don't believe there is a person in the world but would be glad to have me dead and out of the way."

"No, no, Mag! don't talk so. You shan't starve so long as I have barrels to hoop. Peter Greene boards me cheap. I'll help you, if nobody else will."

A tear stood in Mag's faded eye. "I'm glad," she said, with a softer tone than before, "if there is *one* who isn't glad to see me suffer. I b'lieve all Singleton wants to see me punished, and feel as if they could tell when I've been punished long enough. It's a long day ahead they'll set it, I reckon."

After the usual supply of fuel was prepared, Jim returned home. Full of pity for Mag, he set about devising measures for her relief. "By golly!" said he to himself one day—for he had become so absorbed in Mag's interest that he had fallen into a habit of musing aloud—"By golly! I wish she'd *marry* me."

"Who?" shouted Pete Greene, suddenly starting from an unobserved corner of the rude shop.

"Where you come from, you sly nigger!" exclaimed Jim.

"Come, tell me, who is't?" said Pete; "Mag Smith, you want to marry?"

"Git out, Pete! and when you come in dis shop again, let a nigger know it. Don't steal in like a thief."

Pity and love know little severance. One attends the other. Jim acknowledged the presence of the former, and his efforts in Mag's behalf told also of a finer principle.

This sudden expedient which he had unintentionally disclosed, roused his thinking and inventive powers to study upon the best method of introducing the subject to Mag.

He belted his barrels, with many a scheme revolving in his mind, none of which quite satisfied him, or seemed, on the whole, expedient. He thought of the pleasing contrast between her fair face and his own dark skin; the smooth, straight hair, which he had once, in expression of pity, kindly stroked on her now wrinkled but once fair brow. There was a tempest gathering in his heart, and at last, to ease his pent-up passion, he exclaimed aloud, "By golly!" Recollecting his former exposure, he glanced around to see if Pete was in hearing again. Satisfied on this point, he continued: "She'd be as much of a prize to me as she'd fall short of coming up to the mark with white folks. I don't care for past things. I've done things 'fore now I's 'shamed of. She's good enough for me, any how."

One more glance about the premises to be sure Pete was away.

The next Saturday night brought Jim to the hovel again. The cold was fast coming to tarry its apportioned time. Mag was nearly despairing of meeting its rigor.

"How's the wood, Mag?" asked Jim.

"All gone; and no more to cut, any how," was the reply.

"Too bad!" Jim said. His truthful reply would have been, I'm glad.

"Anything to eat in the house?" continued he.

"No," replied Mag.

"Too bad!" again, orally, with the same *inward* gratulation as before.

"Well, Mag," said Jim, after a short pause, "you's down low

enough. I don't see but I've got to take care of ye. 'Sposin' we marry!"

Mag raised her eyes, full of amazement, and uttered a sonorous "What?"

Jim felt abashed for a moment. He knew well what were her objections.

"You's had trial of white folks any how. They run off and left ye, and now none of 'em come near ye to see if you's dead or alive. I's black outside, I know, but I's got a white heart inside. Which you rather have, a black heart in a white skin, or a white heart in a black one?"

"Oh, dear!" sighed Mag; "Nobody on earth cares for *me*—"

"I do," interrupted Jim.

"I can do but two things," said she, "beg my living, or get it from you."

"Take me, Mag. I can give you a better home than this, and not let you suffer so."

He prevailed; they married. You can philosophize, gentle reader, upon the impropriety of such unions, and preach dozens of sermons on the evils of amalgamation. Want is a more powerful philosopher and preacher. Poor Mag. She has sundered another bond which held her to her fellows. She has descended another step down the ladder of infamy.

II. My Father's Death

Misery! we have known each other,
Like a sister and a brother,
Living in the same lone home
Many years—we must live some
Hours or ages yet to come.
                    Shelley.

JIM, proud of his treasure,—a white wife,—tried hard to fulfil
his promises; and furnished her with a more comfortable dwelling, diet, and apparel. It was comparatively a comfortable winter
she passed after her marriage. When Jim could work, all went
on well. Industrious, and fond of Mag, he was determined she
should not regret her union to him. Time levied an additional
charge upon him, in the form of two pretty mulattos, whose in-
fantile pranks amply repaid the additional toil. A few years, and
a severe cough and pain in his side compelled him to be an idler
for weeks together, and Mag had thus a reminder of by-gones.
She cared for him only as a means to subserve her own comfort;
yet she nursed him faithfully and true to marriage vows till
death released her. He became the victim of consumption. He
loved Mag to the last. So long as life continued, he stifled his
sensibility to pain, and toiled for her sustenance long after he
was able to do so.

A few expressive wishes for her welfare; a hope of better days
for her; an anxiety lest they should not all go to the "good place";
brief advice about their children; a hope expressed that Mag
would not be neglected as she used to be; the manifestation of
Christian patience; these were *all* the legacy of miserable Mag.

216

A feeling of cold desolation came over her, as she turned from the grave of one who had been truly faithful to her.

She was now expelled from companionship with white people; this last step—her union with a black—was the climax of repulsion.

Seth Shipley, a partner in Jim's business, wished her to remain in her present home; but she declined, and returned to her hovel again, with obstacles threefold more insurmountable than before. Seth accompanied her, giving her a weekly allowance which furnished most of the food necessary for the four inmates. After a time, work failed; their means were reduced.

How Mag toiled and suffered, yielding to fits of desperation, bursts of anger, and uttering curses too fearful to repeat. When both were supplied with work, they prospered; if idle, they were hungry together. In this way their interests became united; they planned for the future together. Mag had lived an outcast for years. She had ceased to feel the gushings of penitence; she had crushed the sharp agonies of an awakened conscience. She had no longings for a purer heart, a better life. Far easier to descend lower. She entered the darkness of perpetual infamy. She asked not the rite of civilization or Christianity. Her will made her the wife of Seth. Soon followed scenes familiar and trying.

"It's no use," said Seth one day; "we must give the children away, and try to get work in some other place."

"Who'll take the black devils?" snarled Mag.

"They're none of mine," said Seth; "what you growling about?"

"Nobody will want any thing of mine, or yours either," she replied.

"We'll make 'em, p'r'aps," he said. "There's Frado's six years old, and pretty, if she is yours, and white folks'll say so. She'd be a prize somewhere," he continued, tipping his chair back against the wall, and placing his feet upon the rounds, as if he had much more to say when in the right position.

Frado, as they called one of Mag's children, was a beautiful mulatto, with long, curly black hair, and handsome, roguish eyes, sparkling with an exuberance of spirit almost beyond restraint.

Hearing her name mentioned, she looked up from her play, to see what Seth had to say of her.

"Wouldn't the Bellmonts take her?" asked Seth.

"Bellmonts?" shouted Mag. "His wife is a right she-devil! and if—"

"Hadn't they better be all together?" interrupted Seth, reminding her of a like epithet used in reference to her little ones.

Without seeming to notice him, she continued, "She can't keep a girl in the house over a week; and Mr. Bellmont wants to hire a boy to work for him, but he can't find one that will live in the house with her; she's so ugly, they can't."

"Well, we've got to make a move soon," answered Seth; "if you go with me, we shall go right off. Had you rather spare the other one?" asked Seth, after a short pause.

"One's as bad as t'other," replied Mag. "Frado is such a wild, frolicky thing, and means to do jest as she's a mind to; she won't go if she don't want to. I don't want to tell her she is to be given away."

"I will," said Seth. "Come here, Frado?"

The child seemed to have some dim foreshadowing of evil, and declined.

"Come here," he continued; "I want to tell you something."

She came reluctantly. He took her hand and said: "We're going to move, by-'m-bye; will you go?"

"No!" screamed she; and giving a sudden jerk which destroyed Seth's equilibrium, left him sprawling on the floor, while she escaped through the open door.

"She's a hard one," said Seth, brushing his patched coat sleeve. "I'd risk her at Bellmont's."

They discussed the expediency of a speedy departure. Seth would first seek employment, and then return for Mag. They would take with them what they could carry, and leave the rest with Pete Greene, and come for them when they were wanted. They were long in arranging affairs satisfactorily, and were not a little startled at the close of their conference to find Frado missing. They thought approaching night would bring her. Twilight passed into darkness, and she did not come. They thought she had understood their plans, and had, perhaps, permanently withdrawn. They could not rest without making some effort to ascertain her retreat. Seth went in pursuit, and returned without her. They rallied others when they discovered that another little colored girl was missing, a favorite playmate of Frado's. All effort proved unavailing. Mag felt sure her fears were realized, and that she might never see her again. Before her anxieties became realities, both were safely returned, and from them and their attendant they learned that they went to walk, and not minding the direction soon found themselves lost. They had climbed fences and walls, passed through thickets and marshes, and when night approached selected a thick cluster of shrubbery as a covert for the night. They were discovered by the person who now restored them, chatting of their prospects, Frado attempting to banish the childish fears of her companion. As they were some miles from home, they were kindly cared for until morning. Mag was relieved to know her child was not driven to desperation by their intentions to relieve themselves of her, and she was inclined to think severe restraint would be healthful.

The removal was all arranged; the few days necessary for such migrations passed quickly, and one bright summer morning they bade farewell to their Singleton hovel, and with budgets and bundles commenced their weary march. As they neared the village, they heard the merry shouts of children gathered around the schoolroom, awaiting the coming of their teacher.

"Halloo!" screamed one, "Black, white and yeller!" "Black, white and yeller," echoed a dozen voices.

It did not grate so harshly on poor Mag as once it would. She did not even turn her head to look at them. She had passed into an insensibility no childish taunt could penetrate, else she would have reproached herself as she passed familiar scenes, for extending the separation once so easily annihilated by steadfast integrity. Two miles beyond lived the Bellmonts, in a large, old fashioned, two-story white house, environed by fruitful acres, and embellished by shrubbery and shade trees. Years ago a youthful couple consecrated it as home; and after many little feet had worn paths to favorite fruit trees, and over its green hills, and mingled at last with brother man in the race which belongs neither to the swift or strong, the sire became grey-haired and decrepit, and went to his last repose. His aged consort soon followed him. The old homestead thus passed into the hands of a son, to whose wife Mag had applied the epithet "she-devil," as may be remembered. John, the son, had not in his family arrangements departed from the example of the father. The pastimes of his boyhood were ever freshly revived by witnessing the games of his own sons as they rallied about the same goal his youthful feet had often won; as well as by the amusements of his daughters in their imitations of maternal duties.

At the time we introduce them, however, John is wearing the badge of age. Most of his children were from home; some seeking employment; some were already settled in homes of their own. A maiden sister shared with him the estate on which he resided, and occupied a portion of the house.

Within sight of the house, Seth seated himself with his bundles and the child he had been leading, while Mag walked onward to the house leading Frado. A knock at the door brought Mrs. Bellmont, and Mag asked if she would be willing to let that child stop there while she went to the Reed's house to wash, and when she came back she would call and get her. It seemed a novel request, but she consented. Why the impetuous child entered the house, we cannot tell; the door closed, and Mag hastily departed. Frado waited for the close of day, which was to bring back her mother. Alas! it never came. It was the last time she ever saw or heard of her mother.

III. A New Home For Me

Oh! did we but know of the shadows so nigh,
   The world would indeed be a prison of gloom;
All light would be quenched in youth's eloquent eye,
   And the prayer-lisping infant would ask for the tomb.

For if Hope be a star that may lead us astray,
   And "deceiveth the heart," as the aged ones preach;
Yet 'twas Mercy that gave it, to beacon our way,
   Though its halo illumes where it never can reach.
                                        Eliza Cook.

AS THE DAY closed and Mag did not appear, surmises were expressed by the family that she never intended to return. Mr. Bellmont was a kind, humane man, who would not grudge hospitality to the poorest wanderer, nor fail to sympathize with any sufferer, however humble. The child's desertion by her mother appealed to his sympathy, and he felt inclined to succor her. To do this in opposition to Mrs. Bellmont's wishes, would be like encountering a whirlwind charged with fire, daggers and spikes. She was not as susceptible of fine emotions as her spouse. Mag's opinion of her was not without foundation. She was self-willed, haughty, undisciplined, arbitrary and severe. In common parlance, she was a *scold,* a thorough one. Mr. B. remained silent during the consultation which follows, engaged in by mother, Mary and John, or Jack, as he was familiarly called.

"Send her to the County House," said Mary, in reply to the query what should be done with her, in a tone which indicated self-importance in the speaker. She was indeed the idol of her mother, and more nearly resembled her in disposition and manners than the others.

Jane, an invalid daughter, the eldest of those at home, was reclining on a sofa apparently uninterested.

"Keep her," said Jack. "She's real handsome and bright, and not very black, either."

"Yes," rejoined Mary; "that's just like you, Jack. She'll be of no use at all these three years, right under foot all the time."

"Poh! Miss Mary; if she should stay, it wouldn't be two days before you would be telling the girls about *our* nig, *our* nig!" retorted Jack.

"I don't want a nigger 'round *me,* do you, mother?" asked Mary.

"I don't mind the nigger in the child. I should like a dozen better than one," replied her mother. "If I could make her do my work in a few years, I would keep her. I have so much trouble with girls I hire, I am almost persuaded if I have one to train up in my way from a child, I shall be able to keep them awhile. I am tired of changing every few months."

"Where could she sleep?" asked Mary. "I don't want her near me."

"In the L chamber," answered the mother.

"How'll she get there?" asked Jack. "She'll be afraid to go through that dark passage, and she can't climb the ladder safely."

"She'll have to go there; it's good enough for a nigger," was the reply.

Jack was sent on horseback to ascertain if Mag was at her home. He returned with the testimony of Pete Greene that they were fairly departed, and that the child was intentionally thrust upon their family.

The imposition was not at all relished by Mrs. B., or the pert, haughty Mary, who had just glided into her teens.

"Show the child to bed, Jack," said his mother. "You seem most pleased with the little nigger, so you may introduce her to her room."

He went to the kitchen, and, taking Frado gently by the hand, told her he would put her in bed now; perhaps her mother would come the next night after her.

It was not yet quite dark, so they ascended the stairs without any light, passing through nicely furnished rooms, which were a source of great amazement to the child. He opened the door which connected with her room by a dark, unfinished passageway. "Don't bump your head," said Jack, and stepped before to open the door leading into her apartment,—an unfinished chamber over the kitchen, the roof slanting nearly to the floor, so that the bed could stand only in the middle of the room. A small half window furnished light and air. Jack returned to the sitting room with the remark that the child would soon outgrow those quarters.

"When she *does,* she'll outgrow the house," remarked the mother.

"What can she do to help you?" asked Mary. "She came just in the right time, didn't she? Just the very day after Bridget left," continued she.

"I'll see what she can do in the morning," was the answer.

While this conversation was passing below, Frado lay, revolving in her little mind whether she would remain or not until her mother's return. She was of wilful, determined nature, a stranger to fear, and would not hesitate to wander away should she decide to. She remembered the conversation of her mother with Seth, the words "given away" which she heard used in reference to herself; and though she did not know their full import, she thought she should, by remaining, be in some relation to white people she was never favored with before. So she resolved to tarry, with the hope that mother would come and get her some time. The hot sun had penetrated her room, and it was long before a cooling breeze reduced the temperature so that she could sleep.

Frado was called early in the morning by her new mistress. Her first work was to feed the hens. She was shown how it was *always* to be done, and in no other way; any departure from this rule to be punished by a whipping. She was then accompanied by Jack to drive the cows to pasture, so she might learn the way. Upon her return she was allowed to eat her breakfast, consisting of a bowl of skimmed milk, with brown bread crusts, which she was told to eat, standing, by the kitchen table, and must not be over ten minutes about it. Meanwhile the family were taking their morning meal in the dining-room. This over, she was placed on a cricket to wash the common dishes; she was to be in waiting always to bring wood and chips, to run hither and thither from room to room.

A large amount of dish-washing for small hands followed dinner. Then the same after tea and going after the cows finished her first day's work. It was a new discipline to the child. She found some attractions about the place, and she retired to rest at night more willing to remain. The same routine followed day after day, with slight variation; adding a little more work, and spicing the toil with "words that burn," and frequent blows on her head. These were great annoyances to Frado, and had she known where her mother was, she would have gone at once to her. She was often greatly wearied, and silently wept over her sad fate. At first she wept aloud, which Mrs. Bellmont noticed by applying a rawhide, always at hand in the kitchen. It was a symptom of discontent and complaining which must be "nipped in the bud," she said.

Thus passed a year. No intelligence of Mag. It was now certain Frado was to become a permanent member of the family. Her labors were multiplied; she was quite indispensable, although but seven years old. She had never learned to read, never heard of a school until her residence in the family.

Mrs. Bellmont was in doubt about the utility of attempting to educate people of color, who were incapable of elevation. This subject occasioned a lengthy discussion in the family. Mr. Bellmont, Jane and Jack arguing for Frado's education; Mary and her mother objecting. At last Mr. Bellmont declared decisively that she *should* go to school. He was a man who seldom decided controversies at home. The word once spoken admitted of no appeal; so, notwithstanding Mary's objection that she would have to attend the same school she did, the word became law.

It was to be a new scene to Frado, and Jack had many queries and conjectures to answer. He was himself too far advanced to attend the summer school, which Frado regretted, having had too many opportunities of witnessing Miss Mary's temper to feel safe in her company alone.

The opening day of school came. Frado sauntered on far in the rear of Mary, who was ashamed to be seen "walking with a nigger." As soon as she appeared, with scanty clothing and bared feet, the children assembled, noisily published her approach: "See that nigger," shouted one. "Look! look!" cried another. "I won't play with her," said one little girl. "Nor I neither," replied another.

Mary evidently relished these sharp attacks, and saw a fair prospect of lowering Nig where, according to her views, she belonged. Poor Frado, chagrined and grieved, felt that her anticipations of pleasure at such a place were far from being realized. She was just deciding to return home, and never come there again, when the teacher appeared, and observing the downcast looks of the child, took her by the hand, and led her into the school-room. All followed, and, after the bustle of securing seats was over, Miss Marsh inquired if the children knew "any cause for the sorrow of that little girl?" pointing to Frado. It was soon all told. She then reminded them of their duties to the poor and friendless; their cowardice in attacking a young innocent child; referred them to one who looks not on outward appearances, but on the heart. "She looks like a good girl; I think *I* shall love her, so lay aside all prejudice, and vie with each other in shewing kindness and good-will to one who seems different from you," were the closing remarks of the kind lady. Those kind words! The most agreeable sound which ever meets the ear of sorrowing, grieving childhood.

Example rendered her words efficacious. Day by day there was a manifest change of deportment towards "Nig." Her speeches often drew merriment from the children; no one could do more to enliven their favorite pastimes than Frado. Mary could not endure to see her thus noticed, yet knew not how to prevent it. She could not influence her schoolmates as she wished. She had not gained their affections by winning ways and yielding points of controversy. On the contrary, she was self-willed, domineering; every day reported "mad" by some of her companions. She availed herself of the only alternative, abuse and taunts, as they returned from school. This was not satisfactory; she wanted to use physical force "to subdue her," to "keep her down."

There was, on their way home, a field intersected by a stream over which a single plank was placed for a crossing. It occurred to Mary that it would be a punishment to Nig to compel her to cross over; so she dragged her to the edge, and told her authoritatively to go over. Nig hesitated, resisted. Mary placed herself behind the child, and, in the struggle to force her over, lost her footing and plunged into the stream. Some of the larger scholars being in sight, ran, and thus prevented Mary from drowning and Frado from falling. Nig scampered home fast as possible, and Mary went to the nearest house, dripping, to procure a change of garments. She came loitering home, half crying, exclaiming, "Nig pushed me into the stream!" She then related the particulars. Nig was called from the kitchen. Mary stood with anger flashing in her eyes. Mr. Bellmont sat quietly reading his paper. He had witnessed too many of Miss Mary's outbreaks to be startled. Mrs. Bellmont interrogated Nig.

"I didn't do it! I didn't do it!" answered Nig, passionately, and then related the occurrence truthfully.

The discrepancy greatly enraged Mrs. Bellmont. With loud accusations and angry gestures she approached the child. Turning to her husband, she asked,

"Will you sit still, there, and hear that black nigger call Mary a liar?"

"How do we know but she has told the truth? I shall not punish her," he replied, and left the house, as he usually did when a tempest threatened to envelop him. No sooner was he out of sight than Mrs. B. and Mary commenced beating her inhumanly; then propping her mouth open with a piece of wood, shut her up in a dark room, without any supper. For employment, while the tempest raged within, Mr. Bellmont went for the cows, a task belonging to Frado, and thus unintentionally prolonged her pain. At dark Jack came in, and seeing Mary, accosted her with, "So you thought you'd vent your spite on Nig, did you? Why can't you let her alone? It was good enough for you to get a ducking, only you did not stay in half long enough."

"Stop!" said his mother. "You shall never talk so before me.

You would have that little nigger trample on Mary, would you?
She came home with a lie; it made Mary's story false."

"What was Mary's story?" asked Jack.

It was related.

"Now," said Jack, sallying into a chair, "the school-children
happened to see it all, and they tell the same story Nig does.
Which is most likely to be true, what a dozen agree they saw, or
the contrary?"

"It is very strange you will believe what others say against
your sister," retorted his mother, with flashing eye. "I think it is
time your father subdued you."

"Father is a sensible man," argued Jack. "He would not wrong
a dog. Where *is* Frado?" he continued.

"Mother gave her a good whipping and shut her up," replied
Mary.

Just then Mr. Bellmont entered, and asked if Frado was "shut
up yet."

The knowledge of her innocence, the perfidy of his sister,
worked fearfully on Jack. He bounded from his chair, searched
every room till he found the child; her mouth wedged apart, her
face swollen, and full of pain.

How Jack pitied her! He relieved her jaws, brought her some
supper, took her to her room, comforted her as well as he knew
how, sat by her till she fell asleep, and then left for the sitting
room. As he passed his mother, he remarked, "If that was the
way Frado was to be treated, he hoped she would never wake
again!" He then imparted her situation to his father, who
seemed untouched, till a glance at Jack exposed a tearful eye.
Jack went early to her next morning. She awoke sad, but re-
freshed. After breakfast Jack took her with him to the field, and
kept her through the day. But it could not be so generally. She
must return to school, to her household duties. He resolved to
do what he could to protect her from Mary and his mother. He
bought her a dog, which became a great favorite with both. The
invalid, Jane, would gladly befriend her; but she had not the
strength to brave the iron will of her mother. Kind words and
affectionate glances were the only expressions of sympathy she
could safely indulge in. The men employed on the farm were

always glad to hear her prattle; she was a great favorite with them. Mrs. Bellmont allowed them the privilege of talking with her in the kitchen. She did not fear but she should have ample opportunity of subduing her when they were away. Three months of schooling, summer and winter, she enjoyed for three years. Her winter over-dress was a cast-off overcoat, once worn by Jack, and a sun-bonnet. It was a source of great merriment to the scholars, but Nig's retorts were so mirthful, and their satisfaction so evident in attributing the selection to "Old Granny Bellmont," that it was not painful to Nig or pleasurable to Mary. Her jollity was not to be quenched by whipping or scolding. In Mrs. Bellmont's presence she was under restraint; but in the kitchen, and among her schoolmates, the pent up fires burst forth. She was ever at some sly prank when unseen by her teacher, in school hours; not unfrequently some outburst of merriment, of which she was the original, was charged upon some innocent mate, and punishment inflicted which she merited. They enjoyed her antics so fully that any of them would suffer wrongfully to keep open the avenues of mirth. She would venture far beyond propriety, thus shielded and countenanced.

The teacher's desk was supplied with drawers, in which were stored his books and other *et ceteras* of the profession. The children observed Nig very busy there one morning before school, as they flitted in occasionally from their play outside. The master came; called the children to order; opened a drawer to take the book the occasion required; when out poured a volume of smoke. "Fire! fire!" screamed he, at the top of his voice. By this time he had become sufficiently acquainted with the peculiar odor, to know he was imposed upon. The scholars shouted with laughter to see the terror of the dupe, who, feeling abashed at the needless fright, made no very strict investigation, and Nig once more escaped punishment. She had provided herself with cigars, and puffing, puffing away at the crack of the drawer, had filled it with smoke, and then closed it tightly to deceive the teacher, and amuse the scholars. The interim of terms was filled up with a variety of duties new and peculiar. At home, no matter how powerful the heat when sent to rake hay or guard the grazing herd, she was never permitted to shield her skin from the sun. She was not many shades darker than Mary now; what a calamity it would be ever to hear the contrast spoken of. Mrs. Bellmont was determined the sun should have full power to darken the shade which nature had first bestowed upon her as best befitting.

IV. A Friend For Nig

"Hours of my youth! when nurtured in my breast,
  To love a stranger, friendship made me blest;—
Friendship, the dear peculiar bond of youth,
When every artless bosom throbs with truth;
Untaught by worldly wisdom how to feign;
And check each impulse with prudential reign;
When all we feel our honest souls disclose—
In love to friends, in open hate to foes;
No varnished tales the lips of youth repeat,
No dear-bought knowledge purchased by deceit."
                                          —*Byron*

WITH WHAT differing emotions have the denizens of earth
awaited the approach of to-day. Some sufferer has counted the
vibrations of the pendulum impatient for its dawn, who, now
that it has arrived, is anxious for its close. The votary of pleasure,
conscious of yesterday's void, wishes for power to arrest time's
haste till a few more hours of mirth shall be enjoyed. The unfortunate are yet gazing in vain for golden-edged clouds they fancied would appear in their horizon. The good man feels that he
has accomplished too little for the Master, and sighs that another day must so soon close. Innocent childhood, weary of its
stay, longs for another morrow; busy manhood cries, hold! hold!
and pursues it to another's dawn. All are dissatisfied. All crave
some good not yet possessed, which time is expected to bring
with all its morrows.

Was it strange that, to a disconsolate child, three years should
seem a long, long time? During school time she had rest from
Mrs. Bellmont's tyranny. She was now nine years old; time, her
mistress said, such privileges should cease.

She could now read and spell, and knew the elementary steps in grammar, arithmetic, and writing. Her education completed, as *she* said, Mrs. Bellmont felt that her time and person belonged solely to her. She was under her in every sense of the word. What an opportunity to indulge her vixen nature! No matter what occurred to ruffle her, or from what source provocation came, real or fancied, a few blows on Nig seemed to relieve her of a portion of ill-will.

These were days when Fido was the entire confidant of Frado. She told him her griefs as though he were human; and he sat so still, and listened so attentively, she really believed he knew her sorrows. All the leisure moments she could gain were used in teaching him some feat of dog-agility, so that Jack pronounced him very knowing, and was truly gratified to know he had furnished her with a gift answering his intentions.

Fido was the constant attendant of Frado, when sent from the house on errands, going and returning with the cows, out in the fields, to the village. If ever she forgot her hardships it was in his company.

Spring was now retiring. James, one of the absent sons, was expected home on a visit. He had never seen the last acquisition to the family. Jack had written faithfully of all the merits of his colored *protegé,* and hinted plainly that mother did not always treat her just right. Many were the preparations to make the visit pleasant, and as the day approached when he was to arrive, great exertions were made to cook the favorite viands, to prepare the choicest table-fare.

The morning of the arrival day was a busy one. Frado knew not who would be of so much importance; her feet were speeding hither and thither so unsparingly. Mrs. Bellmont seemed a trifle fatigued, and her shoes which had, early in the morning, a methodic squeak, altered to an irregular, peevish snap.

"Get some little wood to make the fire burn," said Mrs. Bellmont, in a sharp tone. Frado obeyed, bringing the smallest she could find.

Mrs. Bellmont approached her, and, giving her a box on her ear, reiterated the command.

The first the child brought was the smallest to be found; of course, the second must be a trifle larger. She well knew it was, as she threw it into a box on the hearth. To Mrs. Bellmont it was a greater affront, as well as larger wood, so she "taught her" with the raw-hide, and sent her the third time for "little wood."

Nig, weeping, knew not what to do. She had carried the smallest; none left would suit her mistress; of course further punishment awaited her; so she gathered up whatever came first, and threw it down on the hearth. As she expected, Mrs. Bellmont, enraged, approached her, and kicked her so forcibly as to throw her upon the floor. Before she could rise, another foiled the attempt, and then followed kick after kick in quick succession and power, till she reached the door. Mr. Bellmont and Aunt Abby, hearing the noise, rushed in, just in time to see the last of the performance. Nig jumped up, and rushed from the house, out of sight.

Aunt Abby returned to her apartment, followed by John, who was muttering to himself.

"What were you saying?" asked Aunt Abby.

"I said I hoped the child never would come into the house again."

"What would become of her? You cannot mean *that*," continued his sister.

"I do mean it. The child does as much work as a woman ought to; and just see how she is kicked about!"

"Why do you have it so, John?" asked his sister.

"How am I to help it? Women rule the earth, and all in it."

"I think I should rule my own house, John,"—

"And live in hell meantime," added Mr. Bellmont.

John now sauntered out to the barn to await the quieting of the storm.

Aunt Abby had a glimpse of Nig as she passed out of the yard; but to arrest her, or shew her that *she* would shelter her, in Mrs. Bellmont's presence, would only bring reserved wrath on her defenceless head. Her sister-in-law had great prejudices against her. One cause of the alienation was that she did not give her right in the homestead to John, and leave it forever; another was that she was a professor of religion, (so was Mrs. Bellmont;) but Nab, as she called her, did not live according to her profession;

another, that she *would* sometimes give Nig cake and pie, which she was never allowed to have at home. Mary had often noticed and spoken of her inconsistencies.

The dinner hour passed. Frado had not appeared. Mrs. B. made no inquiry or search. Aunt Abby looked long, and found her concealed in an outbuilding. "Come into the house with me," implored Aunt Abby.

"I ain't going in any more," sobbed the child.

"What will you do?" asked Aunt Abby.

"I've got to stay out here and die. I ha'n't got no mother, no home. I wish I was dead."

"Poor thing," muttered Aunt Abby; and slyly providing her with some dinner, left her to her grief.

Jane went to confer with her Aunt about the affair; and learned from her the retreat. She would gladly have concealed her in her own chamber, and ministered to her wants; but she was dependent on Mary and her mother for care, and any displeasure caused by attention to Nig, was seriously felt.

Toward night the coach brought James. A time of general greeting, inquiries for absent members of the family, a visit to Aunt Abby's room, undoing a few delicacies for Jane, brought them to the tea hour.

"Where's Frado?" asked Mr. Bellmont, observing she was not in her usual place, behind her mistress' chair.

"I don't know, and I don't care. If she makes her appearance again, I'll take the skin from her body," replied his wife.

James, a fine looking young man, with a pleasant countenance, placid, and yet decidedly serious, yet not stern, looked up confounded. He was no stranger to his mother's nature; but years of absence had erased the occurrences once so familiar, and he asked, "Is this that pretty little Nig, Jack writes to me about, that you are so severe upon, mother?"

"I'll not leave much of her beauty to be seen, if she comes in sight; and now, John," said Mrs. B., turning to her husband, "you need not think you are going to learn her to treat me in this way; just see how saucy she was this morning. She shall learn her place."

Mr. Bellmont raised his calm, determined eye full upon her,

and said, in a decisive manner: "You shall not strike, or scald, or skin her, as you call it, if she comes back again. Remember!" and he brought his hand down upon the table. "I have searched an hour for her now, and she is not to be found on the premises. Do *you* know where she is? Is she *your* prisoner?"

"No! I have just told you I did not know where she was. Nab has her hid somewhere, I suppose. Oh, dear! I did not think it would come to this; that my own husband would treat me so." Then came fast flowing tears, which no one but Mary seemed to notice. Jane crept into Aunt Abby's room; Mr. Bellmont and James went out of doors, and Mary remained to condole with her parent.

"Do you know where Frado is?" asked Jane of her aunt.

"No," she replied. "I have hunted everywhere. She has left her first hiding-place. I cannot think what has become of her. There comes Jack and Fido; perhaps he knows"; and she walked to a window near, where James and his father were conversing together.

The two brothers exchanged a hearty greeting, and then Mr. Bellmont told Jack to eat his supper; afterward he wished to send him away. He immediately went in. Accustomed to all the phases of indoor storms, from a whine to thunder and lightning, he saw at a glance marks of disturbance. He had been absent through the day, with the hired men.

"What's the fuss?" asked he, rushing into Aunt Abby's.

"Eat your supper," said Jane; "go home, Jack."

Back again through the dining-room, and out to his father.

"What's the fuss?" again inquired he of his father.

"Eat your supper, Jack, and see if you can find Frado. She's not been seen since morning, and then she was kicked out of the house."

"I shan't eat my supper till I find her," said Jack, indignantly. "Come, James, and see the little creature mother treats so."

They started, calling, searching, coaxing, all their way along. No Frado. They returned to the house to consult. James and Jack declared they would not sleep till she was found.

Mrs. Bellmont attempted to dissuade them from the search. "It was a shame a little *nigger* should make so much trouble."

Just then Fido came running up, and Jack exclaimed, "Fido knows where she is, I'll bet."

"So I believe," said his father; "but we shall not be wiser unless we can outwit him. He will not do what his mistress forbids him."

"I know how to fix him," said Jack. Taking a plate from the table, which was still waiting, he called, "Fido! Fido! Frado wants some supper. Come!" Jack started, the dog followed, and soon capered on before, far, far into the fields, over walls and through fences, into a piece of swampy land. Jack followed close, and soon appeared to James, who was quite in the rear, coaxing and forcing Frado along with him.

A frail child, driven from shelter by the cruelty of his mother, was an object of interest to James. They persuaded her to go home with them, warmed her by the kitchen fire, gave her a good supper, and took her with them into the sitting-room.

"Take that nigger out of my sight," was Mrs. Bellmont's command, before they could be seated.

James led her into Aunt Abby's, where he knew they were welcome. They chatted awhile until Frado seemed cheerful; then James led her to her room, and waited until she retired.

"Are you glad I've come home?" asked James.

"Yes; if you won't let me be whipped tomorrow."

"You won't be whipped. You must try to be a good girl," counselled James.

"If I do, I get whipped," sobbed the child. "They won't believe what I say. Oh, I wish I had my mother back; then I should not be kicked and whipped so. Who made me so?"

"God;" answered James.

"Did God make you?"

"Yes."

"Who made Aunt Abby?"

"God."

"Who made your mother?"

"God."

"Did the same God that made her make me?"

"Yes."

"Well, then, I don't like him."

"Why not?"

"Because he made her white, and me black. Why didn't he make us *both* white?"

"I don't know; try to go to sleep, and you will feel better in the morning," was all the reply he could make to her knotty queries. It was a long time before she fell asleep; and a number of days before James felt in a mood to visit and entertain old associates and friends.

V. Departures

Life is a strange avenue of various trees and flowers;
Lightsome at commencement, but darkening to its end in a distant,
     massy portal.
It beginneth as a little path, edged with the violet and primrose,
A little path of lawny grass and soft to tiny feet.
Soon, spring thistles in the way.

                                Tupper.

JAMES' VISIT CONCLUDED. Frado had become greatly attached to him, and with sorrow she listened and joined in the farewells which preceded his exit. The remembrance of his kindness cheered her through many a weary month, and an occasional word to her in letters to Jack, were like "cold waters to a thirsty soul." Intelligence came that James would soon marry; Frado hoped he would, and remove her from such severe treatment as she was subject to. There had been additional burdens laid on her since his return. She must now *milk* the cows, she had then only to drive. Flocks of sheep had been added to the farm, which daily claimed a portion of her time. In the absence of the men, she must harness the horse for Mary and her mother to ride, go to mill, in short, do the work of a boy, could one be procured to endure the tirades of Mrs. Bellmont. She was first up in the morning, doing what she could towards breakfast. Occasionally, she would utter some funny thing for Jack's benefit, while she was waiting on the table, provoking a sharp look from his mother, or expulsion from the room.

On one such occasion, they found her on the roof of the barn. Some repairs having been necessary, a staging had been erected, and was not wholly removed. Availing herself of ladders, she was

mounted in high glee on the topmost board. Mr. Bellmont
called sternly for her to come down; poor Jane nearly fainted
from fear. Mrs. B. and Mary did not care if she "broke her
neck," while Jack and the men laughed at her fearlessness.
Strange, one spark of playfulness could remain amid such constant toil; but her natural temperament was in a high degree
mirthful, and the encouragement she received from Jack and
the hired men, constantly nurtured the inclination. When she
had none of the family around to be merry with, she would
amuse herself with the animals. Among the sheep was a willful
leader, who always persisted in being first served, and many
times in his fury he had thrown down Nig, till, provoked, she
resolved to punish him. The pasture in which the sheep grazed
was bounded on three sides by a wide stream, which flowed on
one side at the base of precipitous banks. The first spare moments at her command, she ran to the pasture with a dish in her
hand, and mounting the highest point of land nearest the
stream, called the flock to their mock repast. Mr. Bellmont, with
his laborers, were in sight, though unseen by Frado. They
paused to see what she was about to do. Should she by any mis-
hap lose her footing, she must roll into the stream, and, without
aid, must drown. They thought of shouting; but they feared an
unexpected salute might startle her, and thus ensure what they
were anxious to prevent. They watched in breathless silence.
The willful sheep came furiously leaping and bounding far in
advance of the flock. Just as he leaped for the dish, she suddenly
jumped to one side, when down he rolled into the river, and
swimming across, remained alone till night. The men lay down,
convulsed with laughter at the trick, and guessed at once its
object. Mr. Bellmont talked seriously to the child for exposing
herself to such danger; but she hopped about on her toes, and
with laughable grimaces replied, she knew she was quick
enough to "give him a slide."

But to return. James married a Baltimorean lady of wealthy
parentage, an indispensable requisite, his mother had always
taught him. He did not marry her wealth, though; he loved *her*,
sincerely. She was not unlike his sister Jane, who had a social,

gentle, loving nature, rather *too* yielding, her brother thought. His Susan had a firmness which Jane needed to complete her character, but which her ill health may in a measure have failed to produce. Although an invalid, she was not excluded from society. Was it strange *she* should seem a desirable companion, a treasure as a wife?

Two young men seemed desirous of possessing her. One was a neighbor, Henry Reed, a tall, spare young man, with sandy hair, and blue, sinister eyes. He seemed to appreciate her wants, and watch with interest her improvement or decay. His kindness she received, and by it was almost won. Her mother wished her to encourage his attentions. She had counted the acres which were to be transmitted to an only son; she knew there was silver in the purse; she would not have Jane too sentimental.

The eagerness with which he amassed wealth, was repulsive to Jane; he did not spare his person or beasts in its pursuit. She felt that to such a man she should be considered an incumbrance; she doubted if he would desire her, if he did not know she would bring a handsome patrimony. Her mother, full in favor with the parents of Henry, commanded her to accept him. She engaged herself, yielding to her mother's wishes, because she had not strength to oppose them; and sometimes, when witness of her mother's and Mary's tyranny, she felt any change would be preferable, even such a one as this. She knew her husband should be the man of her own selecting, one she was conscious of preferring before all others. She could not say this of Henry.

In this dilemma, a visitor came to Aunt Abby's; one of her boy-favorites, George Means, from an adjoining State. Sensible, plain looking, agreeable, talented, he could not long be a stranger to any one who wished to know him. Jane was accustomed to sit much with Aunt Abby always; her presence now seemed necessary to assist in entertaining this youthful friend. Jane was more pleased with him each day, and silently wished Henry possessed more refinement, and the polished manners of George. She felt dissatisfied with her relation to him. His calls while George was there, brought their opposing qualities vividly before her, and she found it disagreeable to force herself into those attentions belonging to him. She received him apparently only as a neighbor.

George returned home, and Jane endeavored to stifle the risings of dissatisfaction, and had nearly succeeded, when a letter came which needed but one glance to assure her of its birthplace; and she retired for its perusal. Well was it for her that her mother's suspicion was not aroused, or her curiosity startled to inquire who it came from. After reading it, she glided into Aunt Abby's, and placed it in her hands, who was no stranger to Jane's trials.

George could not rest after his return, he wrote, until he had communicated to Jane the emotions her presence awakened, and his desire to love and possess her as his own. He begged to know if his affections were reciprocated, or could be; if she would permit him to write to her; if she was free from all obligation to another.

"What would mother say?" queried Jane, as she received the letter from her aunt.

"Not much to comfort you."

"Now, aunt, George is just such a man as I could really love, I think, from all I have seen of him; you know I never could say that of Henry"—

"Then don't marry him," interrupted Aunt Abby.

"Mother will make me."

"Your father won't."

"Well, aunt, what can I do? Would you answer the letter, or not?"

"Yes, answer it. Tell him your situation."

"I shall not tell him all my feelings."

Jane answered that she had enjoyed his company much; she had seen nothing offensive in his manner or appearance; that she was under no obligations which forbade her receiving letters from him as a friend and acquaintance. George was puzzled by the reply. He wrote to Aunt Abby, and from her learned all. He could not see Jane thus sacrificed, without making an effort to rescue her. Another visit followed. George heard Jane say she preferred *him*. He then conferred with Henry at his home. It was not a pleasant subject to talk upon. To be thus supplanted, was not to be thought of. He would sacrifice everything but his inheritance to secure his betrothed.

"And so you are the cause of her late coldness towards me. Leave! I will talk no more about it; the business is settled between us; there it will remain," said Henry.

"Have you no wish to know the real state of Jane's affections towards you?" asked George.

"No! Go, I say! go!" and Henry opened the door for him to pass out.

He retired to Aunt Abby's. Henry soon followed, and presented his cause to Mrs. Bellmont.

Provoked, surprised, indignant, she summoned Jane to her presence, and after a lengthy tirade upon Nab, and her satanic influence, told her she could not break the bonds which held her to Henry; she should not. George Means was rightly named; he was, truly, mean enough; she knew his family of old; his father had four wives, and five times as many children.

"Go to your room, Miss Jane," she continued. "Don't let me know of your being in Nab's for one while."

The storm was now visible to all beholders. Mr. Bellmont sought Jane. She told him her objections to Henry; showed him George's letter; told her answer, the occasion of his visit. He bade her not make herself sick; he would see that she was not compelled to violate her free choice in so important a transaction. He then sought the two young men; told them he could not as a father see his child compelled to an uncongenial union; a free, voluntary choice was of such importance to one of her health. She must be left free to her own choice.

Jane sent Henry a letter of dismission; he her one of a legal bearing, in which he balanced his disappointment by a few hundreds.

To brave her mother's fury, nearly overcame her, but the consolations of a kind father and aunt cheered her on. After a suitable interval she was married to George, and removed to his home in Vermont. Thus another light disappeared from Nig's horizon. Another was soon to follow. Jack was anxious to try his skill in providing for his own support; so a situation as clerk in a store was procured in a Western city, and six months after Jane's departure, was Nig abandoned to the tender mercies of Mary and her mother. As if to remove the last vestige of earthly joy, Mrs. Bellmont sold the companion and pet of Frado, the dog Fido.

VI. Varieties

"Hard are life's early steps; and but that youth is buoyant, confident, and strong in hope, men would behold its threshold and despair."

THE SORROW of Frado was very great for her pet, and Mr. Bellmont by great exertion obtained it again, much to the relief of the child. To be thus deprived of all her sources of pleasure was a sure way to exalt their worth, and Fido became, in her estimation, a more valuable presence than the human beings who surrounded her.

James had now been married a number of years, and frequent requests for a visit from the family were at last accepted, and Mrs. Bellmont made great preparations for a fall sojourn in Baltimore. Mary was installed housekeeper—in name merely, for Nig was the only moving power in the house. Although suffering from their joint severity, she felt safer than to be thrown wholly upon an ardent, passionate, unrestrained young lady, whom she always hated and felt it hard to be obliged to obey. The trial she must meet. Were Jack or Jane at home she would have some refuge; one only remained; good Aunt Abby was still in the house.

She saw the fast receding coach which conveyed her master and mistress with regret, and begged for one favor only, that James would send for her when they returned, a hope she had confidently cherished all these five years.

She was now able to do all the washing, ironing, baking, and the common *et cetera* of household duties, though but fourteen. Mary left all for her to do, though she affected great responsibility. She would show herself in the kitchen long enough to relieve herself of some command, better withheld; or insist upon

243

some compliance to her wishes in some department which she was very imperfectly acquainted with, very much less than the person she was addressing; and so impetuous till her orders were obeyed, that to escape the turmoil, Nig would often go contrary to her own knowledge to gain a respite.

Nig was taken sick! What could be done? The *work*, certainly, but not by Miss Mary. So Nig would work while she could remain erect, then sink down upon the floor, or a chair, till she could rally for a fresh effort. Mary would look in upon her, chide her for her laziness, threaten to tell mother when she came home, and so forth.

"Nig!" screamed Mary, one of her sickest days, "come here, and sweep these threads from the carpet." She attempted to drag her weary limbs along, using the broom as support. Impatient of delay, she called again, but with a different request. "Bring me some wood, you lazy jade, quick." Nig rested the broom against the wall, and started on the fresh behest.

Too long gone. Flushed with anger, she rose and greeted her with, "What are you gone so long for? Bring it in quick, I say."

"I am coming as quick as I can," she replied, entering the door.

"Saucy, impudent nigger, you! is this the way you answer me?" and taking a large carving knife from the table, she hurled it, in her rage, at the defenceless girl.

Dodging quickly, it fastened in the ceiling a few inches from where she stood. There rushed on Mary's mental vision a picture of bloodshed, in which she was the perpetrator, and the sad consequences of what was so nearly an actual occurrence.

"Tell anybody of this, if you dare. If you tell Aunt Abby, I'll certainly kill you," said she, terrified. She returned to her room, brushed her threads herself; was for a day or two more guarded, and so escaped deserved and merited penalty.

Oh, how long the weeks seemed which held Nig in subjection to Mary; but they passed like all earth's sorrows and joys. Mr. and Mrs. B. returned delighted with their visit, and laden with rich presents for Mary. No word of hope for Nig. James was quite unwell, and would come home the next spring for a visit.

This, thought Nig, will be my time of release. I shall go back with him.

From early dawn until after all were retired, was she toiling, overworked, disheartened, longing for relief.

Exposure from heat to cold, or the reverse, often destroyed her health for short intervals. She wore no shoes until after frost, and snow even, appeared; and bared her feet again before the last vestige of winter disappeared. These sudden changes she was so illy guarded against, nearly conquered her physical system. Any word of complaint was severely repulsed or cruelly punished.

She was told she had much more than she deserved. So that manual labor was not in reality her only burden; but such an incessant torrent of scolding and boxing and threatening, was enough to deter one of maturer years from remaining within sound of the strife.

It is impossible to give an impression of the manifest enjoyment of Mrs. B. in these kitchen scenes. It was her favorite exercise to enter the apartment noisily, vociferate orders, give a few sudden blows to quicken Nig's pace, then return to the sitting room with *such* a satisfied expression, congratulating herself upon her thorough house-keeping qualities.

She usually rose in the morning at the ringing of the bell for breakfast; if she were heard stirring before that time, Nig knew well there was an extra amount of scolding to be borne.

No one now stood between herself and Frado, but Aunt Abby. And if *she* dared to interfere in the least, she was ordered back to her "own quarters." Nig would creep slyly into her room, learn what she could of her regarding the absent, and thus gain some light in the thick gloom of care and toil and sorrow in which she was immersed.

The first of spring a letter came from James, announcing declining health. He must try northern air as a restorative; so Frado joyfully prepared for this agreeable increase of the family, this addition to her cares.

He arrived feeble, lame, from his disease, so changed Frado wept at his appearance, fearing he would be removed from her forever. He kindly greeted her, took her to the parlor to see his wife and child, and said many things to kindle smiles on her sad face.

Frado felt so happy in his presence, so safe from maltreatment! He was to her a shelter. He observed, silently, the ways of the house a few days; Nig still took her meals in the same manner as formerly, having the same allowance of food. He, one day, bade her not remove the food, but sit down to the table and eat.

"She *will,* mother," said he, calmly, but imperatively; I'm determined; she works hard; I've watched her. Now, while I stay, she is going to sit down *here,* and eat such food as we eat."

A few sparks from the mother's black eyes were the only reply; she feared to oppose where she knew she could not prevail. So Nig's standing attitude, and selected diet vanished.

Her clothing was yet poor and scanty; she was not blessed with a Sunday attire; for she was never permitted to attend church with her mistress. "Religion was not meant for niggers," *she* said; when the husband and brothers were absent, she would drive Mrs. B. and Mary there, then return, and go for them at the close of the service, but never remain. Aunt Abby would take her to evening meetings, held in the neighborhood, which Mrs. B. never attended; and impart to her lessons of truth and grace as they walked to the place of prayer.

Many of less piety would scorn to present so doleful a figure; Mrs. B. had shaved her glossy ringlets; and, in her coarse cloth gown and ancient bonnet, she was anything but an enticing object. But Aunt Abby looked within. She saw a soul to save, an immortality of happiness to secure.

These evenings were eagerly anticipated by Nig; it was such a pleasant release from labor.

Such perfect contrast in the melody and prayers of these good people to the harsh tones which fell on her ears during the day.

Soon she had all their sacred songs at command, and enlivened her toil by accompanying it with this melody.

James encouraged his aunt in her efforts. He had found the *Saviour,* he wished to have Frado's desolate heart gladdened, quieted, sustained, by *His* presence. He felt sure there were elements in her heart which, transformed and purified by the gospel, would make her worthy the esteem and friendship of the world. A kind, affectionate heart, native wit, and common sense, and the pertness she sometimes exhibited, he felt if restrained properly, might become useful in originating a self-reliance which would be of service to her in after years.

Yet it was not possible to compass all this, while she remained where she was. He wished to be cautious about pressing too closely her claims on his mother, as it would increase the burdened one he so anxiously wished to relieve. He cheered her on with the hope of returning with his family, when he recovered sufficiently.

Nig seemed awakened to new hopes and aspirations, and realized a longing for the future, hitherto unknown.

To complete Nig's enjoyment, Jack arrived unexpectedly. His greeting was as hearty to herself as to any of the family.

"Where are your curls, Fra?" asked Jack, after the usual salutation.

"Your mother cut them off."

"Thought you were getting handsome, did she? Same old story, is it; knocks and bumps? Better times coming; never fear, Nig."

How different this appellative sounded from him; he said it in such a tone, with such a rogueish look!

She laughed, and replied that he had better take her West for a housekeeper.

Jack was pleased with James's innovations of table discipline, and would often tarry in the dining-room, to see Nig in her new place at the family table. As he was thus sitting one day, after the family had finished dinner, Frado seated herself in her mistress' chair, and was just reaching for a clean dessert plate which was on the table, when her mistress entered.

"Put that plate down; you shall not have a clean one; eat from mine," continued she. Nig hesitated. To eat after James, his wife or Jack, would have been pleasant; but to be commanded to do what was disagreeable by her mistress, *because* it was disagreeable, was trying. Quickly looking about, she took the plate, called Fido to wash it, which he did to the best of his ability; then, wiping her knife and fork on the cloth, she proceeded to eat her dinner.

Nig never looked toward her mistress during the process. She had Jack near; she did not fear her now.

Insulted, full of rage, Mrs. Bellmont rushed to her husband, and commanded him to notice this insult; to whip that child; if he would not do it, James ought.

James came to hear the kitchen version of the affair. Jack was boiling over with laughter. He related all the circumstances to James, and pulling a bright, silver half-dollar from his pocket, he threw it at Nig, saying, "There, take that; 'twas worth paying for."

James sought his mother; told her he "would not excuse or palliate Nig's impudence; but she should not be whipped or be punished at all. You have not treated her, mother, so as to gain her love; she is only exhibiting your remissness in this matter."

She only smothered her resentment until a convenient opportunity offered. The first time she was left alone with Nig, she gave her a thorough beating, to bring up arrearages; and threatened, if she ever exposed her to James, she would "cut her tongue out."

James found her, upon his return, sobbing; but fearful of revenge, she dared not answer his queries. He guessed their cause, and longed for returning health to take her under his protection.

VII. Spiritual Condition of Nig

"What are our joys but dreams? and what our hopes
But goodly shadows in the summer cloud?"

H. K. W.

JAMES DID NOT improve as was hoped. Month after month passed away, and brought no prospect of returning health. He could not walk far from the house for want of strength; but he loved to sit with Aunt Abby in her quiet room, talking of unseen glories, and heart-experiences, while planning for the spiritual benefit of those around them. In these confidential interviews, Frado was never omitted. They would discuss the prevalent opinion of the public, that people of color are really inferior; incapable of cultivation and refinement. They would glance at the qualities of Nig, which promised so much if rightly directed. "I wish you would take her, James, when you are well, home with *you*," said Aunt Abby, in one of these seasons.

"Just what I am longing to do, Aunt Abby. Susan is just of my mind, and we intend to take her; I have been wishing to do so for years."

"She seems much affected by what she hears at the evening meetings, and asks me many questions on serious things; seems to love to read the Bible; I feel hopes of her."

"I hope she *is* thoughtful; no one has a kinder heart, one capable of loving more devotedly. But to think how prejudiced the world are towards her people; that she must be reared in such ignorance as to drown all the finer feelings. When I think of what she might be, of what she will be, I feel like grasping time till opinions change, and thousands like her rise into a noble freedom. I have seen Frado's grief, because she is black, amount

249

to agony. It makes me sick to recall these scenes. Mother pretends to think she don't know enough to sorrow for anything; but if she could see her as I have, when she supposed herself entirely alone, except her little dog Fido, lamenting her loneliness and complexion, I think, if she is not past feeling, she would retract. In the summer I was walking near the barn, and as I stood I heard sobs. 'Oh! oh!' I heard, 'why was I made? why can't I die? Oh, what have I to live for? No one cares for me only to get my work. And I feel sick; who cares for that? Work as long as I can stand, and then fall down and lay there till I can get up. No mother, father, brother or sister to care for me, and then it is, You lazy nigger, lazy nigger—all because I am black! Oh, if I could die!'

"I stepped into the barn, where I could see her. She was crouched down by the hay with her faithful friend Fido, and as she ceased speaking, buried her face in her hands, and cried bitterly; then, patting Fido, she kissed him, saying, 'You love me, Fido, don't you? but we must go work in the field.' She started on her mission; I called her to me, and told her she need not go, the hay was doing well.

"She has such confidence in me that she will do just as I tell her; so we found a seat under a shady tree, and there I took the opportunity to combat the notions she seemed to entertain respecting the loneliness of her condition and want of sympathizing friends. I assured her that mother's views were by no means general; that in our part of the country there were thousands upon thousands who favored the elevation of her race, disapproving of oppression in all its forms; that she was not unpitied, friendless, and utterly despised; that she might hope for better things in the future. Having spoken these words of comfort, I rose with the resolution that if I recovered my health I would take her home with me, whether mother was willing or not."

"I don't know what your mother would do without her; still, I wish she was away."

Susan now came for her long absent husband, and they returned home to their room.

The month of November was one of great anxiety on James's account. He was rapidly wasting away.

A celebrated physician was called, and performed a surgical operation, as a last means. Should this fail, there was no hope. Of course he was confined wholly to his room, mostly to his bed. With all his bodily suffering, all his anxiety for his family, whom he might not live to protect, he did not forget Frado. He shielded her from many beatings, and every day imparted religious instructions. No one, but his wife, could move him so easily as Frado; so that in addition to her daily toil she was often deprived of her rest at night.

Yet she insisted on being called; she wished to show her love for one who had been such a friend to her. Her anxiety and grief increased as the probabilities of his recovery became doubtful.

Mrs. Bellmont found her weeping on his account, shut her up, and whipped her with the raw-hide, adding an injunction never to be seen snivelling again because she had a little work to do. She was very careful never to shed tears on his account, in her presence, afterwards.

VIII. Visitor and Departure

—"Other cares engross me, and my tired soul with emulative haste,
  Looks to its God."

THE BROTHER associated with James in business, in Baltimore,
was sent for to confer with one who might never be able to see
him there.

James began to speak of life as closing; of heaven, as of a place
in immediate prospect; of aspirations, which waited for fruition
in glory. His brother, Lewis by name, was an especial favorite of
sister Mary; more like her, in disposition and preferences than
James or Jack.

He arrived as soon as possible after the request, and saw with
regret the sure indications of fatality in his sick brother, and
listened to his admonitions—admonitions to a Christian life—
with tears, and uttered some promises of attention to the subject
so dear to the heart of James.

How gladly he would have extended healing aid. But, alas! it
was not in his power; so, after listening to his wishes and arrangements for his family and business, he decided to return
home.

Anxious for company home, he persuaded his father and
mother to permit Mary to attend him. She was not at all needed
in the sick room; she did not choose to be useful in the kitchen,
and then she was fully determined to go.

So all the trunks were assembled and crammed with the best
selections from the wardrobe of herself and mother, where the
last-mentioned articles could be appropriated.

"Nig was never so helpful before," Mary remarked, and wondered what had induced such a change in place of former sullenness.

Nig was looking further than the present, and congratulating herself upon some days of peace, for Mary never lost opportunity of informing her mother of Nig's delinquencies, were she otherwise ignorant.

Was it strange if she were officious, with such relief in prospect?

The parting from the sick brother was tearful and sad. James prayed in their presence for their renewal in holiness; and urged their immediate attention to eternal realities, and gained a promise that Susan and Charlie should share their kindest regards.

No sooner were they on their way, than Nig slyly crept round to Aunt Abby's room, and tiptoeing and twisting herself into all shapes, she exclaimed,—

"She's gone, Aunt Abby, she's gone, fairly gone"; and jumped up and down, till Aunt Abby feared she would attract the notice of her mistress by such demonstrations.

"Well, she's gone, gone, Aunt Abby. I hope she'll never come back again."

"No! no! Frado, that's wrong! you would be wishing her dead; that won't do."

"Well, I'll bet she'll never come back again; somehow, I feel as though she wouldn't."

"She is James's sister," remonstrated Aunt Abby.

"So is our cross sheep just as much, that I ducked in the river; I'd like to try my hand at curing *her* too."

"But you forget what our good minister told us last week, about doing good to those that hate us."

"Didn't I do good, Aunt Abby, when I washed and ironed and packed her old duds to get rid of her, and helped her pack her trunks, and run here and there for her?"

"Well, well, Frado; you must go finish your work, or your mistress will be after you, and remind you severely of Miss Mary, and some others beside."

Nig went as she was told, and her clear voice was heard as she went, singing in joyous notes the relief she felt at the removal of one of her tormentors.

Day by day the quiet of the sick man's room was increased. He was helpless and nervous; and often wished change of position, thereby hoping to gain momentary relief. The calls upon Frado were consequently more frequent, her nights less tranquil. Her health was impaired by lifting the sick man, and by drudgery in the kitchen. Her ill health she endeavored to conceal from James, fearing he might have less repose if there should be a change of attendants; and Mrs. Bellmont, she well knew, would have no sympathy for her. She was at last so much reduced as to be unable to stand erect for any great length of time. She would *sit* at the table to wash her dishes; if she heard the well-known step of her mistress, she would rise till she returned to her room, and then sink down for further rest. Of course she was longer than usual in completing the services assigned her. This was a subject of complaint to Mrs. Bellmont; and Frado endeavored to throw off all appearance of sickness in her presence.

But it was increasing upon her, and she could no longer hide her indisposition. Her mistress entered one day, and finding her seated, commanded her to go to work. "I am sick," replied Frado, rising and walking slowly to her unfinished task, "and cannot stand long, I feel so bad."

Angry that she should venture a reply to her command, she suddenly inflicted a blow which lay the tottering girl prostrate on the floor. Excited by so much indulgence of a dangerous passion, she seemed left to unrestrained malice; and snatching a towel, stuffed the mouth of the sufferer, and beat her cruelly.

Frado hoped she would end her misery by whipping her to death. She bore it with the hope of a martyr, that her misery would soon close. Though her mouth was muffled, and the sounds much stifled, there was a sensible commotion, which James' quick ear detected.

"Call Frado to come here," he said faintly, "I have not seen her to-day."

Susan retired with the request to the kitchen, where it was evident some brutal scene had just been enacted.

Mrs. Bellmont replied that she had "some work to do just now; when that was done, she might come."

Susan's appearance confirmed her husband's fears, and he requested his father, who sat by the bedside, to go for her. This was a messenger, as James well knew, who could not be denied; and the girl entered the room, sobbing and faint with anguish.

James called her to him, and inquired the cause of her sorrow. She was afraid to expose the cruel author of her misery, lest she should provoke new attacks. But after much entreaty, she told him all, much which had escaped his watchful ear. Poor James shut his eyes in silence, as if pained to forgetfulness by the recital. Then turning to Susan, he asked her to take Charlie, and walk out; "she needed the fresh air," he said. "And say to mother I wish Frado to sit by me till you return. I think you are fading, from staying so long in this sick room." Mr. B. also left, and Frado was thus left alone with her friend. Aunt Abby came in to make her daily visit, and seeing the sick countenance of the attendant, took her home with her to administer some cordial. She soon returned, however, and James kept her with him the rest of the day; and a comfortable night's repose following, she was enabled to continue, as usual, her labors. James insisted on her attending religious meetings in the vicinity with Aunt Abby.

Frado, under the instructions of Aunt Abby and the minister, became a believer in a future existence—one of happiness or misery. Her doubt was, *is* there a heaven for the black? She knew there was one for James, and Aunt Abby, and all good white people; but was there any for blacks? She had listened attentively to all the minister said, and all Aunt Abby had told her; but then it was all for white people.

As James approached that blessed world, she felt a strong desire to follow, and be with one who was such a dear, kind friend to her.

While she was exercised with these desires and aspirations, she attended an evening meeting with Aunt Abby, and the good man urged all, young or old, to accept the offers of mercy, to receive a compassionate Jesus as their Saviour. "Come to Christ," he urged, "all, young or old, white or black, bond or free, come all to Christ for pardon; repent, believe."

This was the message she longed to hear; it seemed to be spoken for her. But he had told them to repent; "what was that?" she asked. She knew she was unfit for any heaven, made for whites or blacks. She would gladly repent, or do anything which would admit her to share the abode of James.

Her anxiety increased; her countenance bore marks of solicitude unseen before; and though she said nothing of her inward contest, they all observed a change.

James and Aunt Abby hoped it was the springing of good seed sown by the Spirit of God. Her tearful attention at the last meeting encouraged his aunt to hope that her mind was awakened, her conscience aroused. Aunt Abby noticed that she was particularly engaged in reading the Bible; and this strengthened her conviction that a heavenly Messenger was striving with her. The neighbors dropped in to inquire after the sick, and also if Frado was *"serious?"* They noticed she seemed very thoughtful and tearful at the meetings. Mrs. Reed was very inquisitive; but Mrs. Bellmont saw no appearance of change for the better. She did not feel responsible for her spiritual culture, and hardly believed she had a soul.

Nig was in truth suffering much; her feelings were very intense on any subject, when once aroused. She read her Bible carefully, and as often as an opportunity presented, which was when entirely secluded in her own apartment, or by Aunt Abby's side, who kindly directed her to Christ, and instructed her in the way of salvation.

Mrs. Bellmont found her one day quietly reading her Bible. Amazed and half crediting the reports of officious neighbors, she felt it was time to interfere. Here she was, reading and shedding tears over the Bible. She ordered her to put up the book, and go to work, and not be snivelling about the house, or stop to read again.

But there was one little spot seldom penetrated by her mistress' watchful eye: this was her room, uninviting and comfortless; but to herself a safe retreat. Here she would listen to the pleadings of a Saviour, and try to penetrate the veil of doubt and sin which clouded her soul, and long to cast off the fetters of sin, and rise to the communion of saints.

Mrs. Bellmont, as we before said, did not trouble herself about the future destiny of her servant. If she did what she desired for *her* benefit, it was all the responsibility she acknowledged. But she seemed to have great aversion to the notice Nig would attract should she become pious. How could she meet this case? She resolved to make her complaint to John. Strange, when she was always foiled in this direction, she should resort to him. It was time something was done; she had begun to read the Bible openly.

The night of this discovery, as they were retiring, Mrs. Bellmont introduced the conversation, by saying:

"I want your attention to what I am going to say. I have let Nig go out to evening meetings a few times, and, if you will believe it, I found her reading the Bible to-day, just as though she expected to turn pious nigger, and preach to white folks. So now you see what good comes of sending her to school. If she should get converted she would have to go to meeting: at least, as long as James lives. I wish he had not such queer notions about her. It seems to trouble him to know he must die and leave her. He says if he should get well he would take her home with him, or educate her here. Oh, how awful! What can the child mean? So careful, too, of her! He says we shall ruin her health making her work so hard, and sleep in such a place. O, John! do you think he is in his right mind?"

"Yes, yes; she is slender."

"Yes, *yes!*" she repeated sarcastically, "you know these niggers are just like black snakes; you *can't* kill them. If she wasn't tough she would have been killed long ago. There was never one of my girls could do half the work."

"Did they ever try?" interposed her husband. "I think she can do more than all of them together."

"What a man!" said she, peevishly. "But I want to know what is going to be done with her about getting pious?"

"Let her do just as she has a mind to. If it is a comfort to her, let her enjoy the privilege of being good. I see no objection."

"I should think *you* were crazy, sure. Don't you know that every night she will want to go toting off to meeting? and Sundays, too? and you know we have a great deal of company Sundays, and she can't be spared."

"I thought you Christians held to going to church," remarked Mr. B.

"Yes, but who ever thought of having a nigger go, except to drive others there? Why, according to you and James, we should very soon have her in the parlor, as smart as our own girls. It's of no use talking to you or James. If you should go on as you would like, it would not be six months before she would be leaving me; and that won't do. Just think how much profit she was to us last summer. We had no work hired out; she did the work of two girls—"

"And got the whippings for two with it!" remarked Mr. Bellmont.

"I'll beat the money out of her, if I can't get her worth any other way," retorted Mrs. B. sharply. While this scene was passing, Frado was trying to utter the prayer of the publican, "God be merciful to me a sinner."

IX. Death

We have now
But a small portion of what men call time,
To hold communion.

SPRING OPENED, and James, instead of rallying, as was hoped, grew worse daily. Aunt Abby and Frado were the constant allies of Susan. Mrs. Bellmont dared not lift him. She was not "strong enough," she said.

It was very offensive to Mrs. B. to have Nab about James so much. She had thrown out many a hint to detain her from so often visiting the sick-room; but Aunt Abby was too well accustomed to her ways to mind them. After various unsuccessful efforts, she resorted to the following expedient. As she heard her cross the entry below, to ascend the stairs, she slipped out and held the latch of the door which led into the upper entry.

"James does not want to see you, or any one else," she said.

Aunt Abby hesitated, and returned slowly to her own room; wondering if it were really James' wish not to see her. She did not venture again that day, but still felt disturbed and anxious about him. She inquired of Frado, and learned that he was no worse. She asked her if James did not wish her to come and see him; what could it mean?

Quite late next morning, Susan came to see what had become of her aunt.

"Your mother said James did not wish to see me, and I was afraid I tired him."

"Why, aunt, that is a mistake, I *know*. What could mother mean?" asked Susan.

The next time she went to the sitting-room she asked her mother,—

"Why does not Aunt Abby visit James as she has done? Where is she?"

"At home. I hope that she will stay there," was the answer.

"I should think she would come in and see James," continued Susan.

"I told her he did not want to see her, and to stay out. You need make no stir about it; remember:" she added, with one of her fiery glances.

Susan kept silence. It was a day or two before James spoke of her absence. The family were at dinner, and Frado was watching beside him. He inquired the cause of her absence, and *she* told him all. After the family returned he sent his wife for her. When she entered, he took her hand, and said, "Come to me often, Aunt. Come any time,—I am always glad to see you. I have but a little longer to be with you,—come often, Aunt. Now please help lift me up, and see if I can rest a little."

Frado was called in, and Susan and Mrs. B. all attempted; Mrs. B. was too weak; she did not feel able to lift so much. So the three succeeded in relieving the sufferer.

Frado returned to her work. Mrs. B. followed. Seizing Frado, she said she would "cure her of tale-bearing," and, placing the wedge of wood between her teeth, she beat her cruelly with the raw-hide. Aunt Abby heard the blows, and came to see if she could hinder them.

Surprised at her sudden appearance, Mrs. B. suddenly stopped, but forbade her removing the wood till she gave her permission, and commanded Nab to go home.

She was thus tortured when Mr. Bellmont came in, and, making inquiries which she did not, because she could not, answer, approached her; and seeing her situation, quickly removed the instrument of torture, and sought his wife. Their conversation we will omit; suffice it to say, a storm raged which required many days to exhaust its strength.

Frado was becoming seriously ill. She had no relish for food, and was constantly overworked, and then she had such solicitude about the future. She wished to pray for pardon. She did try to pray. Her mistress had told her it would "do no good for her to attempt prayer; prayer was for whites, not for blacks. If she minded her mistress, and did what she commanded, it was all that was required of her."

This did not satisfy her, or appease her longings. She knew her instructions did not harmonize with those of the man of God or Aunt Abby's. She resolved to persevere. She said nothing on the subject, unless asked. It was evident to all her mind was deeply exercised. James longed to speak with her alone on the subject. An opportunity presented soon, while the family were at tea. It was usual to summon Aunt Abby to keep company with her, as his death was expected hourly.

As she took her accustomed seat, he asked, "Are you afraid to stay with me alone, Frado?"

"No," she replied, and stepped to the window to conceal her emotion.

"Come here, and sit by me; I wish to talk with you."

She approached him, and, taking her hand, he remarked:

"How poor you are, Frado! I want to tell you that I fear I shall never be able to talk with you again. It is the last time, perhaps, I shall *ever* talk with you. You are old enough to remember my dying words and profit by them. I have been sick a long time; I shall die pretty soon. My Heavenly Father is calling me home. Had it been his will to let me live I should take you to live with me; but, as it is, I shall go and leave you. But, Frado, if you will be a good girl, and love and serve God, it will be but a short time before we are in a *heavenly* home together. There will never be any sickness or sorrow there."

Frado, overcome with grief, sobbed, and buried her face in his pillow. She expected he would die; but to hear him speak of his departure himself was unexpected.

"Bid me good bye, Frado."

She kissed him, and sank on her knees by his bedside; his hand rested on her head; his eyes were closed; his lips moved in prayer for this disconsolate child.

His wife entered, and interpreting the scene, gave him some restoratives, and withdrew for a short time.

It was a great effort for Frado to cease sobbing; but she dared not be seen below in tears; so she choked her grief, and descended to her usual toil. Susan perceived a change in her husband. She felt that death was near.

He tenderly looked on her, and said, "Susan, my wife, our farewells are all spoken. I feel prepared to go. I shall meet you in heaven. Death is indeed creeping fast upon me. Let me see them all once more. Teach Charlie the way to heaven; lead him up as you come."

The family all assembled. He could not talk as he wished to them. He seemed to sink into unconsciousness. They watched him for hours. He had labored hard for breath some time, when he seemed to awake suddenly, and exclaimed, "Hark! do you hear it?"

"Hear what, my son?" asked the father.

"Their call. Look, look, at the shining ones! Oh, let me go and be at rest!"

As if waiting for this petition, the Angel of Death severed the golden thread, and he was in heaven. At midnight the messenger came.

They called Frado to see his last struggle. Sinking on her knees at the foot of his bed, she buried her face in the clothes, and wept like one inconsolable. They led her from the room. She seemed to be too much absorbed to know it was necessary for her to leave. Next day she would steal into the chamber as often as she could, to weep over his remains, and ponder his last words to her. She moved about the house like an automaton. Every duty performed—but an abstraction from all, which shewed her thoughts were busied elsewhere. Susan wished her to attend his burial as one of the family. Lewis and Mary and Jack it was not thought best to send for, as the season would not allow them time for the journey. Susan provided her with a dress for the occasion, which was her first intimation that she would be allowed to mingle her grief with others.

The day of the burial she was attired in her mourning dress; but Susan, in her grief, had forgotten a bonnet.

She hastily ransacked the closets, and found one of Mary's, trimmed with bright pink ribbon.

It was too late to change the ribbon, and she was unwilling to leave Frado at home; she knew it would be the wish of James she should go with her. So tying it on, she said, "Never mind, Frado, you shall see where our dear James is buried." As she passed out, she heard the whispers of the by-standers, "Look there! see there! how that looks,—a black dress and a pink ribbon!"

Another time, such remarks would have wounded Frado. She had now a sorrow with which such were small in comparison.

As she saw his body lowered in the grave she wished to share it; but she was not fit to die. She could not go where he was if she did. She did not love God; she did not serve him or know how to.

She retired at night to mourn over her unfitness for heaven, and gaze out upon the stars, which, she felt, studded the entrance of heaven, above which James reposed in the bosom of Jesus, to which her desires were hastening. She wished she could see God, and ask him for eternal life. Aunt Abby had taught her that He was ever looking upon her. Oh, if she could see him, or hear him speak words of forgiveness. Her anxiety increased; her health seemed impaired, and she felt constrained to go to Aunt Abby and tell her all about her conflicts.

She received her like a returning wanderer; seriously urged her to accept of Christ; explained the way; read to her from the Bible, and remarked upon such passages as applied to her state. She warned her against stifling that voice which was calling her to heaven; echoed the farewell words of James, and told her to come to her with her difficulties, and not to delay a duty so important as attention to the truths of religion, and her soul's interests.

Mrs. Bellmont would occasionally give instruction, though far different. She would tell her she could not go where James was; she need not try. If she should get to heaven at all, she would never be as high up as he.

He was the attraction. Should she "want to go there if she could not see him?"

Mrs. B. seldom mentioned her bereavement, unless in such allusion to Frado. She donned her weeds from custom; kept close her crape veil for so many Sabbaths, and abated nothing of her characteristic harshness.

The clergyman called to minister consolation to the afflicted widow and mother. Aunt Abby seeing him approach the dwelling, knew at once the object of his visit, and followed him to the parlor, unasked by Mrs. B! What a daring affront! The good man dispensed the consolations, of which he was steward, to the apparently grief-smitten mother, who talked like one schooled in a heavenly atmosphere. Such resignation expressed, as might have graced the trial of the holiest. Susan, like a mute sufferer, bared her soul to his sympathy and godly counsel, but only replied to his questions in short syllables. When he offered prayer, Frado stole to the door that she might hear of the heavenly bliss of one who was her friend on earth. The prayer caused profuse weeping, as any tender reminder of the heaven-born was sure to. When the good man's voice ceased, she returned to her toil, carefully removing all trace of sorrow. Her mistress soon followed, irritated by Nab's impudence in presenting herself unasked in the parlor, and upbraided her with indolence, and bade her apply herself more diligently. Stung by unmerited rebuke, weak from sorrow and anxiety, the tears rolled down her dark face, soon followed by sobs, and then losing all control of herself, she wept aloud. This was an act of disobedience. Her mistress grasping her raw-hide, caused a longer flow of tears, and wounded a spirit that was craving healing mercies.

X. Perplexities—Another Death

Neath the billows of the ocean,
Hidden treasures wait the hand,
That again to light shall raise them
With the diver's magic wand.
                                        G. W. Cook.

THE FAMILY, gathered by James' decease, returned to their homes. Susan and Charles returned to Baltimore. Letters were received from the absent, expressing their sympathy and grief. The father bowed like a "bruised reed," under the loss of his beloved son. He felt desirous to die the death of the righteous; also, conscious that he was unprepared, he resolved to start on the narrow way, and some time solicit entrance through the gate which leads to the celestial city. He acknowledged his too ready acquiescence with Mrs. B., in permitting Frado to be deprived of her only religious privileges for weeks together. He accordingly asked his sister to take her to meeting once more, which she was ready at once to do.

The first opportunity they once more attended meeting together. The minister conversed faithfully with every person present. He was surprised to find the little colored girl so solicitous, and kindly directed her to the flowing fountain where she might wash and be clean. He inquired of the origin of her anxiety, of her progress up to this time, and endeavored to make Christ, instead of James, the attraction of Heaven. He invited her to come to his house, to speak freely her mind to him, to pray much, to read her Bible often.

The neighbors, who were at meeting,—among them Mrs. Reed,—discussed the opinions Mrs. Bellmont would express on the subject. Mrs. Reed called and informed Mrs. B. that her colored girl "related her experience the other night at the meeting."

"What experience?" asked she, quickly, as if she expected to hear the number of times she had whipped Frado, and the number of lashes set forth in plain Arabic numbers.

"Why, you know she is serious, don't you? She told the minister about it."

Mrs. B. made no reply, but changed the subject adroitly. Next morning she told Frado she "should not go out of the house for one while, except on errands; and if she did not stop trying to be religious, she would whip her to death."

Frado pondered; her mistress was a professor of religion; was *she* going to heaven? then she did not wish to go. If she should be near James, even, she could not be happy with those fiery eyes watching her ascending path. She resolved to give over all thought of the future world, and strove daily to put her anxiety far from her.

Mr. Bellmont found himself unable to do what James or Jack could accomplish for her. He talked with her seriously, told her he had seen her many times punished undeservedly; he did not wish to have her saucy or disrespectful, but when she was *sure* she did not deserve a whipping, to avoid it if she could. "You are looking sick," he added, "you cannot endure beating as you once could."

It was not long before an opportunity offered of profiting by his advice. She was sent for wood, and not returning as soon as Mrs. B. calculated, she followed her, and, snatching from the pile a stick, raised it over her.

"Stop!" shouted Frado, "strike me, and I'll never work a mite more for you"; and throwing down what she had gathered, stood like one who feels the stirring of free and independent thoughts.

By this unexpected demonstration, her mistress, in amazement, dropped her weapon, desisting from her purpose of chastisement. Frado walked towards the house, her mistress following with the wood she herself was sent after. She did not know, before, that she had a power to ward off assaults. Her triumph in seeing her enter the door with *her* burden, repaid her for much of her former suffering.

It was characteristic of Mrs. B. never to rise in her majesty, unless she was sure she should be victorious.

This affair never met with an "after clap," like many others.

Thus passed a year. The usual amount of scolding, but fewer whippings. Mrs. B. longed once more for Mary's return, who had been absent over a year; and she wrote imperatively for her to come quickly to her. A letter came in reply, announcing that she would comply as soon as she was sufficiently recovered from an illness which detained her.

No serious apprehensions were cherished by either parent, who constantly looked for notice of her arrival, by mail. Another letter brought tidings that Mary was seriously ill; her mother's presence was solicited.

She started without delay. Before she reached her destination, a letter came to the parents announcing her death.

No sooner was the astounding news received, than Frado rushed into Aunt Abby's, exclaiming:—

"She's dead, Aunt Abby!"

"Who?" she asked, terrified by the unprefaced announcement.

"Mary; they've just had a letter."

As Mrs. B. was away, the brother and sister could freely sympathize, and she sought him in this fresh sorrow, to communicate such solace as she could, and to learn particulars of Mary's untimely death, and assist him in his journey thither.

It seemed a thanksgiving to Frado. Every hour or two she would pop in into Aunt Abby's room with some strange query:

"She got into the *river* again, Aunt Abby, didn't she; the Jordan is a big one to tumble into, any how. S'posen she goes to hell, she'll be as black as I am. Wouldn't mistress be mad to see her a nigger!" and others of a similar stamp, not at all acceptable to the pious, sympathetic dame; but she could not evade them.

The family returned from their sorrowful journey, leaving the dead behind. Nig looked for a change in her tyrant; what could subdue her, if the loss of her idol could not?

Never was Mrs. B. known to shed tears so profusely, as when

she reiterated to one and another the sad particulars of her darling's sickness and death. There was, indeed, a season of quiet grief; it was the lull of the fiery elements. A few weeks revived the former tempests, and so at variance did they seem with chastisement sanctified, that Frado felt them to be unbearable. She determined to flee. But where? Who would take her? Mrs. B. had always represented her ugly. Perhaps every one thought her so. Then no one would take her. She was black, no one would love her. She might have to return, and then she would be more in her mistress' power than ever.

She remembered her victory at the wood-pile. She decided to remain to do as well as she could; to assert her rights when they were trampled on; to return once more to her meeting in the evening, which had been prohibited. She had learned how to conquer; she would not abuse the power while Mr. Bellmont was at home.

But had she not better run away? Where? She had never been from the place far enough to decide what course to take. She resolved to speak to Aunt Abby. *She* mapped the dangers of her course, her liability to fail in finding so good friends as John and herself. Frado's mind was busy for days and nights. She contemplated administering poison to her mistress, to rid herself and the house of so detestable a plague.

But she was restrained by an overruling Providence; and finally decided to stay contentedly through her period of service, which would expire when she was eighteen years of age.

In a few months Jane returned home with her family, to relieve her parents, upon whom years and affliction had left the marks of age. The years intervening since she had left her home, had, in some degree, softened the opposition to her unsanctioned marriage with George. The more Mrs. B. had about her, the more energetic seemed her directing capabilities, and her fault-finding propensities. Her own, she had full power over; and Jane after vain endeavors, became disgusted, weary, and perplexed, and decided that, though her mother might suffer, she could not endure her home. They followed Jack to the West. Thus vanished all hopes of sympathy or relief from this source to Frado. There seemed no one capable of enduring the oppressions of the house but her. She turned to the darkness of the future with the determination previously formed, to remain until she should be eighteen. Jane begged her to follow her so soon as she should be released; but so wearied out was she by her mistress, she felt disposed to flee from any and every one having her similitude of name or feature.

XI. Marriage Again

Crucified the hopes that cheered me,
All that to the earth endeared me;
Love of wealth and fame and power,
Love,—all have been crucified.

C. E.

DARKNESS before day. Jane left, but Jack was now to come again. After Mary's death he visited home, leaving a wife behind. An orphan whose home was with a relative, gentle, loving, the true mate of kind, generous Jack. His mother was a stranger to her, of course, and had perfect right to interrogate:

"Is she good looking, Jack?" asked his mother.

"Looks well to me," was the laconic reply.

"Was her *father* rich?"

"Not worth a copper, as I know of; I never asked him," answered Jack.

"Hadn't she any property? What did you marry her for," asked his mother.

"Oh, she's *worth a million* dollars, mother, though not a cent of it is in money."

"Jack! what do you want to bring such a poor being into the family, for? You'd better stay here, at home, and let your wife go. Why couldn't you try to do better, and not disgrace your parents?"

"Don't judge, till you see her," was Jack's reply, and immediately changed the subject. It was no recommendation to his mother, and she did not feel prepared to welcome her cordially now he was to come with his wife. He was indignant at his mother's advice to desert her. It rankled bitterly in his soul, the bare suggestion. He had more to bring. He now came with a child also. He decided to leave the West, but not his family.

Upon their arrival, Mrs. B. extended a cold welcome to her new daughter, eyeing her dress with closest scrutiny. Poverty was to her a disgrace, and she could not associate with any thus dishonored. This coldness was felt by Jack's worthy wife, who only strove the harder to recommend herself by her obliging, winning ways.

Mrs. B. could never let Jack be with her alone without complaining of this or that deficiency in his wife.

He cared not so long as the complaints were piercing his own ears. He would not have Jenny disquieted. He passed his time in seeking employment.

A letter came from his brother Lewis, then at the South, soliciting his services. Leaving his wife, he repaired thither.

Mrs. B. felt that great restraint was removed, that Jenny was more in her own power. She wished to make her feel her inferiority; to relieve Jack of his burden if he would not do it himself. She watched her incessantly, to catch at some act of Jenny's which might be construed into conjugal unfaithfulness.

Near by were a family of cousins, one a young man of Jack's age, who, from love to his cousin, proffered all needful courtesy to his stranger relative. Soon news reached Jack that Jenny was deserting her covenant vows, and had formed an illegal intimacy with his cousin. Meantime Jenny was told by her mother-in-law that Jack did not marry her untrammelled. He had another love whom he would be glad, even now, if he could, to marry. It was very doubtful if he ever came for her.

Jenny would feel pained by her unwelcome gossip, and, glancing at her child, she decided, however true it might be, she had a pledge which would enchain him yet. Ere long, the mother's inveterate hate crept out into some neighbor's enclosure, and, caught up hastily, they passed the secret round till it became none, and Lewis was sent for, the brother by whom Jack was employed. The neighbors saw her fade in health and spirits; they found letters never reached their destination when sent by either. Lewis arrived with the joyful news that he had come to take Jenny home with him.

What a relief to her to be freed from the gnawing taunts of her adversary.

Jenny retired to prepare for the journey, and Mrs. B. and Lewis had a long interview. Next morning he informed Jenny that new clothes would be necessary, in order to make her presentable to Baltimore society, and he should return without her, and she must stay till she was suitably attired.

Disheartened, she rushed to her room, and, after relief from weeping, wrote to Jack to come; to have pity on her, and take her to him. No answer came. Mrs. Smith, a neighbor, watchful and friendly, suggested that she write away from home, and employ some one to carry it to the office who would elude Mrs. B., who, they very well knew, had intercepted Jenny's letter, and influenced Lewis to leave her behind. She accepted the offer, and Frado succeeded in managing the affair so that Jack soon came to the rescue, angry, wounded, and forever after alienated from his early home and his mother. Many times would Frado steal up into Jenny's room, when she knew she was tortured by her mistress' malignity, and tell some of her own encounters with her, and tell her she might "be sure it wouldn't kill her, for she should have died long before at the same treatment."

Susan and her child succeeded Jenny as visitors. Frado had merged into womanhood, and, retaining what she had learned, in spite of the few privileges enjoyed formerly, was striving to enrich her mind. Her school-books were her constant companions, and every leisure moment was applied to them. Susan was delighted to witness her progress, and some little book from her was a reward sufficient for any task imposed, however difficult. She had her book always fastened open near her, where she could glance from toil to soul refreshment. The approaching spring would close the term of years which Mrs. B. claimed as the period of her servitude. Often as she passed the waymarks of former years did she pause to ponder on her situation, and wonder if she *could* succeed in providing for her own wants. Her health was delicate, yet she resolved to try.

Soon she counted the time by days which should release her. Mrs. B. felt that she could not well spare one who could so well adapt herself to all departments—man, boy, housekeeper, domestic, etc. She begged Mrs. Smith to talk with her, to show her how ungrateful it would appear to leave a home of such comfort—how wicked it was to be ungrateful! But Frado replied that she had had enough of such comforts; she wanted some new ones; and as it was so wicked to be ungrateful, she would go from temptation; Aunt Abby said "we mustn't put ourselves in the way of temptation."

Poor little Fido! She shed more tears over him than over all beside.

The morning for departure dawned. Frado engaged to work for a family a mile distant. Mrs. Bellmont dismissed her with the assurance that she would soon wish herself back again, and a present of a silver half dollar.

Her wardrobe consisted of one decent dress, without any superfluous accompaniments. A Bible from Susan she felt was her greatest treasure.

Now was she alone in the world. The past year had been one of suffering resulting from a fall, which had left her lame.

The first summer passed pleasantly, and the wages earned were expended in garments necessary for health and cleanliness. Though feeble, she was well satisfied with her progress. Shut up in her room, after her toil was finished, she studied what poor samples of apparel she had, and, for the first time, prepared her own garments.

Mrs. Moore, who employed her, was a kind friend to her, and attempted to heal her wounded spirit by sympathy and advice, burying the past in the prospects of the future. But her failing health was a cloud no kindly human hand could dissipate. A little light work was all she could accomplish. A clergyman, whose family was small, sought her, and she was removed there. Her engagement with Mrs. Moore finished in the fall. Frado was anxious to keep up her reputation for efficiency, and often pressed far beyond prudence. In the winter she entirely gave up work, and confessed herself thoroughly sick. Mrs. Hale, soon overcome by additional cares, was taken sick also, and now it became necessary to adopt some measures for Frado's comfort, as well as to relieve Mrs. Hale. Such dark forebodings as visited her as she lay, solitary and sad, no moans or sighs could relieve.

The family physician pronounced her case one of doubtful issue. Frado hoped it was final. She could not feel relentings that her former home was abandoned, and yet, should she be in need of succor could she obtain it from one who would now so grudgingly bestow it? The family were applied to, and it was decided to take her there. She was removed to a room built out from the main building, used formerly as a workshop, where cold and rain found unobstructed access, and here she fought with bitter reminiscences and future prospects till she became reckless of her faith and hopes and person, and half wished to end what nature seemed so tardily to take.

Aunt Abby made her frequent visits, and at last had her removed to her own apartment, where she might supply her wants, and minister to her once more in heavenly things.

Then came the family consultation.

"What is to be done with her," asked Mrs. B., "after she is moved there with Nab?"

"Send for the Dr., your brother," Mr. B. replied.

"When?"

"To-night."

"To-night! and for her! Wait till morning," she continued.

"She has waited too long now; I think something should be done soon."

"I doubt if she is much sick," sharply interrupted Mrs. B.

"Well, we'll see what our brother thinks."

His coming was longed for by Frado, who had known him well during her long sojourn in the family; and his praise of her nice butter and cheese, from which his table was supplied, she knew he felt as well as spoke.

"You're sick, very sick," he said, quickly, after a moment's pause. "Take good care of her, Abby, or she'll never get well. All broken down."

"Yes, it was at Mrs. Moore's," said Mrs. B., "all this was done. She did but little the latter part of the time she was here."

"It was commenced longer ago than last summer. Take good care of her; she may never get well," remarked the Dr.

"We sha'n't pay you for doctoring her; you may look to the town for that, sir," said Mrs. B., and abruptly left the room.

"Oh dear! oh dear!" exclaimed Frado, and buried her face in the pillow.

A few kind words of consolation, and she was once more alone in the darkness which enveloped her previous days. Yet she felt sure they owed her a shelter and attention, when disabled, and she resolved to feel patient, and remain till she could help herself. Mrs. B. would not attend her, nor permit her domestic to stay with her at all. Aunt Abby was her sole comforter. Aunt Abby's nursing had the desired effect, and she slowly improved. As soon as she was able to be moved, the kind Mrs. Moore took her to her home again, and completed what Aunt Abby had so well commenced. Not that she was well, or ever would be; but she had recovered so far as rendered it hopeful she might provide for her own wants. The clergyman at whose house she was taken sick, was now seeking some one to watch his sick children, and as soon as he heard of her recovery, again asked for her services.

What seemed so light and easy to others, was too much for Frado; and it became necessary to ask once more where the sick should find an asylum.

All felt that the place where her declining health began, should be the place of relief; so they applied once more for a shelter.

"No," exclaimed the indignant Mrs. B., "she shall never come under this roof again; never! never!" she repeated, as if each repetition were a bolt to prevent admission.

One only resource; the public must pay the expense. So she was removed to the home of two maidens, (old,) who had principle enough to be willing to earn the money a charitable public disburses.

Three years of weary sickness wasted her, without extinguishing a life apparently so feeble. Two years had these maidens watched and cared for her, and they began to weary, and finally to request the authorities to remove her.

Mrs. Hoggs was a lover of gold and silver, and she asked the favor of filling her coffers by caring for the sick. The removal caused severe sickness.

By being bolstered in the bed, after a time she could use her hands, and often would ask for sewing to beguile the tedium. She had become very expert with her needle the first year of her release from Mrs. B., and she had forgotten none of her skill. Mrs. H. praised her, and as she improved in health, was anxious to employ her. She told her she could in this way replace her clothes, and as her board would be paid for, she would thus gain something.

Many times her hands wrought when her body was in pain; but the hope that she might yet help herself, impelled her on.

Thus she reckoned her store of means by a few dollars, and was hoping soon to come in possession, when she was startled by the announcement that Mrs. Hoggs had reported her to the physician and town officers as an impostor. That she was, in truth, able to get up and go to work.

This brought on a severe sickness of two weeks, when Mrs. Moore again sought her, and took her to her home. She had formerly had wealth at her command, but misfortune had deprived her of it, and unlocked her heart to sympathies and favors she had never known while it lasted. Her husband, defrauded of his last means by a branch of the Bellmont family, had supported them by manual labor, gone to the West, and left his wife and four young children. But she felt humanity required her to give a shelter to one she knew to be worthy of a hospitable reception. Mrs. Moore's physician was called, and pronounced her a very sick girl, and encouraged Mrs. M. to keep her and care for her, and he would see that the authorities were informed of Frado's helplessness, and pledged assistance.

Here she remained till sufficiently restored to sew again. Then came the old resolution to take care of herself, to cast off the unpleasant charities of the public.

She learned that in some towns in Massachusetts, girls make straw bonnets—that it was easy and profitable. But how should *she*, black, feeble and poor, find any one to teach her. But God prepares the way, when human agencies see no path. Here was found a plain, poor, simple woman, who could see merit beneath a dark skin; and when the invalid mulatto told her sorrows, she opened her door and her heart, and took the stranger in. Expert with the needle, Frado soon equalled her instructress; and she sought also to teach her the value of useful books; and while one read aloud to the other of deeds historic and names renowned, Frado experienced a new impulse. She felt herself capable of elevation; she felt that this book information supplied an undefined dissatisfaction she had long felt, but could not express. Every leisure moment was carefully applied to self-improvement, and a devout and Christian exterior invited confidence from the villagers. Thus she passed months of quiet, growing in the confidence of her neighbors and new found friends.

XII. The Winding Up of the Matter

Nothing new under the sun.
Solomon.

A FEW YEARS AGO, within the compass of my narrative, there appeared often in some of our New England villages, professed fugitives from slavery, who recounted their personal experience in homely phrase, and awakened the indignation of non-slaveholders against brother Pro. Such a one appeared in the new home of Frado; and as people of color were rare there, was it strange she should attract her dark brother; that he should inquire her out; succeed in seeing her; feel a strange sensation in his heart towards her; that he should toy with her shining curls, feel proud to provoke her to smile and expose the ivory concealed by thin, ruby lips; that her sparkling eyes should fascinate; that he should propose; that they should marry? A short acquaintance was indeed an objection, but she saw him often, and thought she knew him. He never spoke of his enslavement to her when alone, but she felt that, like her own oppression, it was painful to disturb oftener than was needful.

He was a fine, straight negro, whose back showed no marks of the lash, erect as if it never crouched beneath a burden. There was a silent sympathy which Frado felt attracted her, and she opened her heart to the presence of love—that arbitrary and inexorable tyrant.

She removed to Singleton, her former residence, and there was married. Here were Frado's first feelings of trust and repose on human arm. She realized, for the first time, the relief of looking to another for comfortable support. Occasionally he would leave her to "lecture."

Those tours were prolonged often to weeks. Of course he had little spare money. Frado was again feeling her self-dependence, and was at last compelled to resort alone to that. Samuel was kind to her when at home, but made no provision for his absence, which was at last unprecedented.

He left her to her fate—embarked at sea, with the disclosure that he had never seen the South, and that his illiterate harangues were humbugs for hungry abolitionists. Once more alone! Yet not alone. A still newer companionship would soon force itself upon her. No one wanted her with such prospects. Herself was burden enough; who would have an additional one?

The horrors of her condition nearly prostrated her, and she was again thrown upon the public for sustenance. Then followed the birth of her child. The long absent Samuel unexpectedly returned, and rescued her from charity. Recovering from her expected illness, she once more commenced toil for herself and child, in a room obtained of a poor woman, but with better fortune. One so well known would not be wholly neglected. Kind friends watched her when Samuel was from home, prevented her from suffering, and when the cold weather pinched the warmly clad, a kind friend took them in, and thus preserved them. At last Samuel's business became very engrossing, and after long desertion, news reached his family that he had become a victim of yellow fever, in New Orleans.

So much toil as was necessary to sustain Frado, was more than she could endure. As soon as her babe could be nourished without his mother, she left him in charge of a Mrs. Capon, and procured an agency, hoping to recruit her health, and gain an easier livelihood for herself and child. This afforded her better maintenance than she had yet found. She passed into the various towns of the State she lived in, then into Massachusetts. Strange were some of her adventures. Watched by kidnappers, maltreated by professed abolitionists, who didn't want slaves at the South, nor niggers in their own houses, North. Faugh! to lodge one; to eat with one; to admit one through the front door; to sit next one; awful!

Traps slyly laid by the vicious to ensnare her, she resolutely

avoided. In one of her tours, Providence favored her with a
friend who, pitying her cheerless lot, kindly provided her with
a valuable recipe, from which she might herself manufacture a
useful article for her maintenance. This proved a more agreeable, and an easier way of sustenance.

And thus, to the present time, may you see her busily employed in preparing her merchandise; then sallying forth to encounter many frowns, but some kind friends and purchasers.
Nothing turns her from her steadfast purpose of elevating herself. Reposing on God, she has thus far journeyed securely. Still
an invalid, she asks your sympathy, gentle reader. Refuse not,
because some part of her history is unknown, save by the
Omniscient God. Enough has been unrolled to demand your
sympathy and aid.

Do you ask the destiny of those connected with her *early*
history? A few years only have elapsed since Mr. and Mrs. B.
passed into another world. As age increased, Mrs. B. became
more irritable, so that no one, even her own children, could
remain with her; and she was accompanied by her husband to
the home of Lewis, where, after an agony in death unspeakable,
she passed away. Only a few months since, Aunt Abby entered
heaven. Jack and his wife rest in heaven, disturbed by no intrud-
ers; and Susan and her child are yet with the living. Jane has
silver locks in place of auburn tresses, but she has the early love
of George still, and has never regretted her exchange of lovers.
Frado has passed from their memories, as Joseph from the but-
ler's, but she will never cease to track them till beyond mortal
vision.

Appendix

"Truth is stranger than fiction"; and whoever reads the narrative of Alfrado, will find the assertion verified.

About eight years ago I became acquainted with the author of this book, and I feel it a privilege to speak a few words in her behalf. Through the instrumentality of an itinerant colored lecturer, she was brought to W——, Mass. This is an ancient town, where the mothers and daughters seek, not "wool and flax," but *straw*,—working willingly with their hands! Here she was introduced to the family of Mrs. Walker, who kindly consented to receive her as an inmate of her household, and immediately succeeded in procuring work for her as a "straw sewer." Being very ingenious, she soon acquired the art of making hats; but on account of former hard treatment, her constitution was greatly impaired, and she was subject to seasons of sickness. On this account Mrs. W. gave her a room joining her own chamber, where she could hear her faintest call. Never shall I forget the expression of her "black, but comely" face, as she came to me one day, exclaiming, "O, aunt J——, I have at last found a *home*,—and not only a home, but a *mother*. My cup runneth over. What shall I render to the Lord for all his benefits?"

Months passed on, and she was *happy*—truly happy. Her health began to improve under the genial sunshine in which she lived, and she even looked forward with *hope*—joyful hope to the future. But, alas, "it is not in man that walketh to direct his steps." One beautiful morning in the early spring of 1842, as she was taking her usual walk, she chanced to meet her old friend, the "lecturer," who brought her to W——, and with him was a fugitive slave. Young, well-formed and very handsome, he said he had been a *house*servant, which seemed to account in some measure for his gentlemanly manners and pleasing address. The meeting was entirely accidental; but it was a sad occurrence for poor Alfrado, as her own sequel tells. Suffice it to say, an acquaintance and attachment was formed, which, in due time, resulted in marriage. In a few days she left W——, and *all* her home comforts, and took up her abode in New Hampshire. For a while everything went on well, and she dreamed not of danger; but in an evil hour he left his young and trusting wife, and embarked for sea. She knew nothing of all this, and waited for his return. But she waited in vain. Days passed, weeks passed, and he came not; then her heart failed her. She felt herself deserted at a time, when, of all others, she most needed the care and soothing attentions of a devoted husband. For a time she tried to sustain *herself,* but this was impossible. She had friends, but they were mostly of that class who are poor in the things of earth, but "rich in faith." The charity on which she depended failed at last, and there was nothing to save her from the "County House"; *go she must.* But her feelings on her way thither, and after her arrival, can be given better in her own language; and I trust it will be no breach of confidence if I here insert part of a letter she wrote her mother Walker, concerning the matter.

* * * "The evening before I left for my dreaded journey to the 'house' which was to be my abode, I packed my trunk, carefully placing in it every little memento of affection received from *you* and my friends in W——, among which was the portable inkstand, pens and paper. My beautiful little Bible was laid aside, as a place nearer my heart was reserved for that. I need not tell you I slept not a moment that night. My home, my peaceful, quiet home with you, was before me. I could see my dear little room, with its pleasant eastern window opening to the morning; but more than all, I beheld *you,* my mother, gliding softly in and kneeling by my bed to read, as no one but you *can* read, 'The Lord is my shepherd,—I shall not want.' But I cannot go on, for tears blind me. For a description of the morning, and of the scant breakfast, I must wait until another time.

"We started. The man who came for me was kind as he could be,—helped me carefully into the wagon, (for I had no strength,) and drove on. For miles I spoke not a word. Then the silence would be broken by the driver uttering some sort of word the horse seemed to understand; for he invariably quickened his pace. And so, just before nightfall, we halted at the institution, prepared for the *homeless*. With cold civility the matron received me, and bade one of the inmates shew me my room. She did so; and I followed up two flights of stairs. I crept as I was able; and when she said, 'Go in there,' I obeyed, asking for my trunk, which was soon placed by me. My room was furnished some like the 'prophet's chamber,' except there was no 'candle-stick'; so when I could creep down I begged for a light, and it was granted. Then I flung myself on the bed and cried, until I could cry no longer. I rose up and tried to pray; the Saviour seemed near. I opened my precious little Bible, and the first verse that caught my eye was—'I am poor and needy, yet the Lord thinketh upon me.' O, my mother, could I tell you the comfort this was to me. I sat down, calm, almost happy, took my pen and wrote on the inspiration of the moment—

> "O, holy Father, by thy power,
>   Thus far in life I'm brought;
> And now in this dark, trying hour,
>   O God, forsake me not.
>
> "Dids't thou not nourish and sustain
>   My infancy and youth?
> Have I not testimonials plain,
>   Of thy unchanging truth?
>
> "Though I've no home to call my own,
>   My heart shall not repine;
> The saint may live on earth unknown,
>   And yet in glory shine.
>
> "When my Redeemer dwelt below,
>   He chose a lowly lot;
> He came unto his own, but lo!
>   His own received him not.
>
> "Oft was the mountain his abode,
>   The cold, cold earth his bed;
> The midnight moon shone softly down
>   On his unsheltered head.

"But *my* head *was sheltered,* and I tried to feel thankful."

• • •

Two or three letters were received after this by her friends in W——, and then all was silent. No one of us knew whether she still lived or had gone to her home on high. But it seems she remained in this house until after the birth of her babe; then her faithless husband returned, and took her to some town in New Hampshire, where, for a time, he supported her and his little son decently well. But again he left her as before—suddenly and unexpectedly, and she saw him no more. Her efforts were again successful in a measure in securing a meagre maintenance for a time; but her struggles with poverty and sickness were severe. At length, a door of hope was opened. A kind gentleman and lady took her little boy into their own family, and provided everything necessary for his good; and all this without the hope of remuneration. But let them know, they shall be "recompensed at the resurrection of the just." God is not unmindful of this work,—this labor of love. As for the afflicted mother, she too has been remembered. The heart of a stranger was moved with compassion, and bestowed a recipe upon her for restoring gray hair to its former color. She availed herself of this great help, and has been quite successful; but her health is again falling, and she has felt herself obliged to resort to another method of procuring her bread—that of writing an Autobiography.

I trust she will find a ready sale for her interesting work; and let all the friends who purchase a volume, remember they are doing good to one of the most worthy, and I had almost said most unfortunate, of the human family. I will only add in conclusion, a few lines, calculated to comfort and strengthen this sorrowful, homeless one. "I will help thee, saith the Lord."

> "I will help thee," promise kind,
>   Made by our High Priest above;
> Soothing to the troubled mind,
>   Full of tenderness and love.
>
> "I will help thee" when the storm
>   Gathers dark on every side;

Safely from impending harm,
 In my sheltering bosom hide.

"I will help thee," weary saint,
 Cast thy burdens *all on me;*
Oh, how cans't thou tire or faint,
 While my arm encircles thee.

I have pitied every tear,
 Heard and *counted* every sigh;
Ever lend a gracious ear
 To thy supplicating cry.

What though thy wounded bosom bleed,
 Pierced by affliction's dart;
Do I not all thy sorrows heed,
 And bear thee on my heart?

Soon will the lowly grave become
 Thy quiet resting place;
Thy spirit find a peaceful home
 In mansions *near my face.*

There are thy robes and glittering crown,
 Outshining yonder sun;
Soon shalt thou lay the body down,
 And put those glories on.

Long has thy golden lyre been strung,
 Which angels cannot move;
No song to this is ever sung,
 But bleeding, dying Love.

ALLIDA.

TO THE FRIENDS OF OUR DARK-COMPLEXIONED BRETHREN
AND SISTERS, THIS NOTE IS INTENDED.

Having known the writer of this book for a number of years,
and knowing the many privations and mortifications she has had
to pass through, I the more willingly add my testimony to the
truth of her assertions. She is one of that class, who by some are
considered not only as little lower than the angels, but far beneath them; but I have long since learned that we are not to look

at the color of the hair, the eyes, or the skin, for the man or woman; their life is the criterion we are to judge by. The writer of this book has seemed to be a child of misfortune.

Early in life she was deprived of her parents, and all those endearing associations to which childhood clings. Indeed, she may be said not to have had that happy period; for, being taken from home so young, and placed where she had nothing to love or cling to, I often wonder she had not grown up a *monster;* and those very people calling themselves Christians, (the good Lord deliver me from such,) and they likewise ruined her health by hard work, both in the field and house. She was indeed a slave, in every sense of the word; and a lonely one, too.

But she has found some friends in this degraded world, that were willing to do by others as they would have others do by them; that were willing she should live, and have an existence on the earth with them. She has never enjoyed any degree of comfortable health since she was eighteen years of age, and a great deal of the time has been confined to her room and bed. She is now trying to write a book; and I hope the public will look favorably on it, and patronize the same, for she is a worthy woman.

Her own health being poor, and having a child to care for, (for, by the way, she has been married,) and she wishes to educate him; in her sickness he has been taken from her, and sent to the county farm, because she could not pay his board every week; but as soon as she was able, she took him from that *place,* and now he has a home where he is contented and happy, and where he is considered as good as those he is with. He is an intelligent, smart boy, and no doubt will make a smart man, if he is rightly managed. He is beloved by his playmates, and by all the friends of the family; for the family do not recognize those as friends who do not include him in their family, or as one of them, and his mother as a daughter—for they treat her as such; and she certainly deserves all the affection and kindness that is bestowed upon her, and they are always happy to have her visit them whenever she will. They are not wealthy, but the latch-string is always out when suffering humanity needs a shelter; the last loaf they are willing to divide with those more needy than themselves, remembering these words, Do good as we have opportunity; and we can always find opportunity, if we have the disposition.

And now I would say, I hope those who call themselves friends of our dark-skinned brethren, will lend a helping hand, and assist our sister, not in giving, but in buying a book; the expense is trifling, and the reward of doing good is great. Our duty is to our fellow-beings, and when we let an opportunity pass, we know not what we lose. Therefore we should do with all our might what our hands find to do; and remember the words of Him who went about doing good, that inasmuch as ye have done a good deed to one of the least of these my brethren, ye have done it to me; and even a cup of water is not forgotten. Therefore, let us work while the day lasts, and we shall in no wise lose our reward.

MARGARETTA THORN.

MILFORD, JULY 20th, 1859.

Feeling a deep interest in the welfare of the writer of this book, and hoping that its circulation will be extensive, I wish to say a few words in her behalf. I have been acquainted with her for several years, and have always found her worthy the esteem of all friends of humanity; one whose soul is alive to the work to which she puts her hand. Although her complexion is a little darker than my own, I esteem it a privilege to associate with her, and assist her whenever an opportunity presents itself. It is with this motive that I write these few lines, knowing this book must be interesting to all who have any knowledge of the writer's character, or wish to have. I hope no one will refuse to aid her in her work, as she is worthy the sympathy of all Christians, and those who have a spark of humanity in their breasts.

Thinking it unnecessary for me to write a long epistle, I will close by bidding her God speed.

C. D. S.

A CATALOG OF SELECTED
DOVER BOOKS
IN ALL FIELDS OF INTEREST

A CATALOG OF SELECTED DOVER

BOOKS IN ALL FIELDS OF INTEREST

CONCERNING THE SPIRITUAL IN ART, Wassily Kandinsky. Pioneering work by father of abstract art. Thoughts on color theory, nature of art. Analysis of earlier masters. 12 illustrations. 80pp. of text. $5^{3}/_{8}$ x $8^{1}/_{2}$.   0-486-23411-8

CELTIC ART: The Methods of Construction, George Bain. Simple geometric techniques for making Celtic interlacements, spirals, Kells-type initials, animals, humans, etc. Over 500 illustrations. 160pp. 9 x 12. (Available in U.S. only.)   0-486-22923-8

AN ATLAS OF ANATOMY FOR ARTISTS, Fritz Schider. Most thorough reference work on art anatomy in the world. Hundreds of illustrations, including selections from works by Vesalius, Leonardo, Goya, Ingres, Michelangelo, others. 593 illustrations. 192pp. $7^{1}/_{8}$ x $10^{1}/_{4}$.   0-486-20241-0

CELTIC HAND STROKE-BY-STROKE (Irish Half-Uncial from "The Book of Kells"): An Arthur Baker Calligraphy Manual, Arthur Baker. Complete guide to creating each letter of the alphabet in distinctive Celtic manner. Covers hand position, strokes, pens, inks, paper, more. Illustrated. 48pp. $8^{1}/_{4}$ x 11.   0-486-24336-2

EASY ORIGAMI, John Montroll. Charming collection of 32 projects (hat, cup, pelican, piano, swan, many more) specially designed for the novice origami hobbyist. Clearly illustrated easy-to-follow instructions insure that even beginning papercrafters will achieve successful results. 48pp. $8^{1}/_{4}$ x 11.   0-486-27298-2

BLOOMINGDALE'S ILLUSTRATED 1886 CATALOG: Fashions, Dry Goods and Housewares, Bloomingdale Brothers. Famed merchants' extremely rare catalog depicting about 1,700 products: clothing, housewares, firearms, dry goods, jewelry, more. Invaluable for dating, identifying vintage items. Also, copyright-free graphics for artists, designers. Co-published with Henry Ford Museum & Greenfield Village. 160pp. $8^{1}/_{4}$ x 11.

0-486-25780-0

THE ART OF WORLDLY WISDOM, Baltasar Gracian. "Think with the few and speak with the many," "Friends are a second existence," and "Be able to forget" are among this 1637 volume's 300 pithy maxims. A perfect source of mental and spiritual refreshment, it can be opened at random and appreciated either in brief or at length. 128pp. $5^{5}/_{8}$ x $8^{1}/_{2}$.

0-486-44034-6

JOHNSON'S DICTIONARY: A Modern Selection, Samuel Johnson (E. L. McAdam and George Milne, eds.). This modern version reduces the original 1755 edition's 2,300 pages of definitions and literary examples to a more manageable length, retaining the verbal pleasure and historical curiosity of the original. 480pp. $5^{3}/_{16}$ x $8^{1}/_{4}$.

0-486-44089-3

ADVENTURES OF HUCKLEBERRY FINN, Mark Twain, Illustrated by E. W. Kemble. A work of eternal richness and complexity, a source of ongoing critical debate, and a literary landmark, Twain's 1885 masterpiece about a barefoot boy's journey of self-discovery has enthralled readers around the world. This handsome clothbound reproduction of the first edition features all 174 of the original black-and-white illustrations. 368pp. $5^{3}/_{8}$ x $8^{1}/_{2}$.   0-486-44322-1

FRENCH STORIES/CONTES FRANÇAIS: A Dual-Language Book, Wallace Fowlie. Ten stories by French masters, Voltaire to Camus: "Micromegas" by Voltaire; "The Atheist's Mass" by Balzac; "Minuet" by de Maupassant; "The Guest" by Camus, six more. Excellent English translations on facing pages. Also French-English vocabulary list, exercises, more. 352pp. $5^3/_8$ x $8^1/_2$. 0-486-26443-2

CHICAGO AT THE TURN OF THE CENTURY IN PHOTOGRAPHS: 122 Historic Views from the Collections of the Chicago Historical Society, Larry A. Viskochil. Rare large-format prints offer detailed views of City Hall, State Street, the Loop, Hull House, Union Station, many other landmarks, circa 1904-1913. Introduction. Captions. Maps. 144pp. $9^3/_8$ x $12^1/_4$. 0-486-24656-6

OLD BROOKLYN IN EARLY PHOTOGRAPHS, 1865–1929, William Lee Younger. Luna Park, Gravesend race track, construction of Grand Army Plaza, moving of Hotel Brighton, etc. 157 previously unpublished photographs. 165pp. $8^7/_8$ x $11^3/_4$.
0-486-23587-4

THE MYTHS OF THE NORTH AMERICAN INDIANS, Lewis Spence. Rich anthology of the myths and legends of the Algonquins, Iroquois, Pawnees and Sioux, prefaced by an extensive historical and ethnological commentary. 36 illustrations. 480pp. $5^3/_8$ x $8^1/_2$.
0-486-25967-6

AN ENCYCLOPEDIA OF BATTLES: Accounts of Over 1,560 Battles from 1479 B.C. to the Present, David Eggenberger. Essential details of every major battle in recorded history from the first battle of Megiddo in 1479 B.C. to Grenada in 1984. List of Battle Maps. New Appendix covering the years 1967–1984. Index. 99 illustrations. 544pp. $6^1/_2$ x $9^1/_4$.
0-486-24913-1

SAILING ALONE AROUND THE WORLD, Captain Joshua Slocum. First man to sail around the world, alone, in small boat. One of the great feats of seamanship told in delightful manner. 67 illustrations. 294pp. $5^3/_8$ x $8^1/_2$. 0-486-20326-3

ANARCHISM AND OTHER ESSAYS, Emma Goldman. Powerful, penetrating, prophetic essays on direct action, role of minorities, prison reform, puritan hypocrisy, violence, etc. 271pp. $5^3/_8$ x $8^1/_2$. 0-486-22484-8

MYTHS OF THE HINDUS AND BUDDHISTS, Ananda K. Coomaraswamy and Sister Nivedita. Great stories of the epics; deeds of Krishna, Shiva, taken from puranas, Vedas, folk tales; etc. 32 illustrations. 400pp. $5^3/_8$ x $8^1/_2$. 0-486-21759-0

MY BONDAGE AND MY FREEDOM, Frederick Douglass. Born a slave, Douglass became outspoken force in antislavery movement. The best of Douglass' autobiographies. Graphic description of slave life. 464pp. $5^3/_8$ x $8^1/_2$. 0-486-22457-0

FOLLOWING THE EQUATOR: A Journey Around the World, Mark Twain. Fascinating humorous account of 1897 voyage to Hawaii, Australia, India, New Zealand, etc. Ironic, bemused reports on peoples, customs, climate, flora and fauna, politics, much more. 197 illustrations. 720pp. $5^3/_8$ x $8^1/_2$. 0-486-26113-1

GREAT SPEECHES BY AMERICAN WOMEN, edited by James Daley. Here are 21 legendary speeches from the country's most inspirational female voices, including Sojourner Truth, Susan B. Anthony, Eleanor Roosevelt, Hillary Rodham Clinton, Nancy Pelosi, and many others. 192pp. $5^3/_{16}$ x $8^1/_4$. 0-486-46141-6

THE MYTHS OF GREECE AND ROME, H. A. Guerber. A classic of mythology, generously illustrated, long prized for its simple, graphic, accurate retelling of the principal myths of Greece and Rome, and for its commentary on their origins and significance. With 64 illustrations by Michelangelo, Raphael, Titian, Rubens, Canova, Bernini and others. 480pp. $5^3/_8$ x $8^1/_2$. 0-486-27584-1

PSYCHOLOGY OF MUSIC, Carl E. Seashore. Classic work discusses music as a medium from psychological viewpoint. Clear treatment of physical acoustics, auditory apparatus, sound perception, development of musical skills, nature of musical feeling, host of other topics. 88 figures. 408pp. 5³/₈ x 8¹/₂.   0-486-21851-1

LIFE IN ANCIENT EGYPT, Adolf Erman. Fullest, most thorough, detailed older account with much not in more recent books, domestic life, religion, magic, medicine, commerce, much more. Many illustrations reproduce tomb paintings, carvings, hieroglyphs, etc. 597pp. 5³/₈ x 8¹/₂.   0-486-22632-8

SUNDIALS, Their Theory and Construction, Albert Waugh. Far and away the best, most thorough coverage of ideas, mathematics concerned, types, construction, adjusting anywhere. Simple, nontechnical treatment allows even children to build several of these dials. Over 100 illustrations. 230pp. 5³/₈ x 8¹/₂.   0-486-22947-5

GREAT SPEECHES BY AFRICAN AMERICANS: Frederick Douglass, Sojourner Truth, Dr. Martin Luther King, Jr., Barack Obama, and Others, edited by James Daley. Tracing the struggle for freedom and civil rights across two centuries, this anthology comprises speeches by Martin Luther King, Jr., Marcus Garvey, Malcolm X, Barack Obama, and many other influential figures. 160pp. 5³/₁₆ x 8¹/₄.   0-486-44761-8

OLD-TIME VIGNETTES IN FULL COLOR, Carol Belanger Grafton (ed.). Over 390 charming, often sentimental illustrations, selected from archives of Victorian graphics— pretty women posing, children playing, food, flowers, kittens and puppies, smiling cherubs, birds and butterflies, much more. All copyright-free. 48pp. 9¹/₄ x 12¹/₄.   0-486-27269-9

PERSPECTIVE FOR ARTISTS, Rex Vicat Cole. Depth, perspective of sky and sea, shadows, much more, not usually covered. 391 diagrams, 81 reproductions of drawings and paintings. 279pp. 5³/₈ x 8¹/₂.   0-486-22487-2

DRAWING THE LIVING FIGURE, Joseph Sheppard. Innovative approach to artistic anatomy focuses on specifics of surface anatomy, rather than muscles and bones. Over 170 drawings of live models in front, back and side views, and in widely varying poses. Accompanying diagrams. 177 illustrations. Introduction. Index. 144pp. 8³/₈ x 11¹/₄.
                                0-486-26723-7

GOTHIC AND OLD ENGLISH ALPHABETS: 100 Complete Fonts, Dan X. Solo. Add power, elegance to posters, signs, other graphics with 100 stunning copyright- free alphabets: Blackstone, Dolbey, Germania, 97 more—including many lower-case, numerals, punctuation marks. 104pp. 8¹/₈ x 11.   0-486-24695-7

THE BOOK OF WOOD CARVING, Charles Marshall Sayers. Finest book for beginners discusses fundamentals and offers 34 designs. "Absolutely first rate . . . well thought out and well executed."—E. J. Tangerman. 118pp. 7³/₄ x 10⁵/₈.   0-486-23654-4

ILLUSTRATED CATALOG OF CIVIL WAR MILITARY GOODS: Union Army Weapons, Insignia, Uniform Accessories, and Other Equipment, Schuyler, Hartley, and Graham. Rare, profusely illustrated 1846 catalog includes Union Army uniform and dress regulations, arms and ammunition, coats, insignia, flags, swords, rifles, etc. 226 illustrations. 160pp. 9 x 12.   0-486-24939-5

WOMEN'S FASHIONS OF THE EARLY 1900s: An Unabridged Republication of "New York Fashions, 1909," National Cloak & Suit Co. Rare catalog of mail-order fashions documents women's and children's clothing styles shortly after the turn of the century. Captions offer full descriptions, prices. Invaluable resource for fashion, costume historians. Approximately 725 illustrations. 128pp. 8³/₈ x 11¹/₄.   0-486-27276-1

LIGHT AND SHADE: A Classic Approach to Three-Dimensional Drawing, Mrs. Mary P. Merrifield. Handy reference clearly demonstrates principles of light and shade by revealing effects of common daylight, sunshine, and candle or artificial light on geometrical solids. 13 plates. 64pp. 5³/₈ x 8¹/₂. 0-486-44143-1

ASTROLOGY AND ASTRONOMY: A Pictorial Archive of Signs and Symbols, Ernst and Johanna Lehner. Treasure trove of stories, lore, and myth, accompanied by more than 300 rare illustrations of planets, the Milky Way, signs of the zodiac, comets, meteors, and other astronomical phenomena. 192pp. 8³/₈ x 11. 0-486-43981-X

JEWELRY MAKING: Techniques for Metal, Tim McCreight. Easy-to-follow instructions and carefully executed illustrations describe tools and techniques, use of gems and enamels, wire inlay, casting, and other topics. 72 line illustrations and diagrams. 176pp. 8¹/₄ x 10⁷/₈. 0-486-44043-5

MAKING BIRDHOUSES: Easy and Advanced Projects, Gladstone Califf. Easy-to-follow instructions include diagrams for everything from a one-room house for bluebirds to a forty-two-room structure for purple martins. 56 plates; 4 figures. 80pp. 8³/₄ x 6³/₈.
0-486-44183-0

LITTLE BOOK OF LOG CABINS: How to Build and Furnish Them, William S. Wicks. Handy how-to manual, with instructions and illustrations for building cabins in the Adirondack style, fireplaces, stairways, furniture, beamed ceilings, and more. 102 line drawings. 96pp. 8³/₄ x 6³/₈. 0-486-44259-4

THE SEASONS OF AMERICA PAST, Eric Sloane. From "sugaring time" and strawberry picking to Indian summer and fall harvest, a whole year's activities described in charming prose and enhanced with 79 of the author's own illustrations. 160pp. 8¹/₄ x 11.
0-486-44220-9

THE METROPOLIS OF TOMORROW, Hugh Ferriss. Generous, prophetic vision of the metropolis of the future, as perceived in 1929. Powerful illustrations of towering structures, wide avenues, and rooftop parks—all features in many of today's modern cities. 59 illustrations. 144pp. 8¹/₄ x 11. 0-486-43727-2

THE PATH TO ROME, Hilaire Belloc. This 1902 memoir abounds in lively vignettes from a vanished time, recounting a pilgrimage on foot across the Alps and Apennines in order to "see all Europe which the Christian Faith has saved." 77 of the author's original line drawings complement his sparkling prose. 272pp. 5³/₈ x 8¹/₂. 0-486-44001-X

THE HISTORY OF RASSELAS: Prince of Abissinia, Samuel Johnson. Distinguished English writer attacks eighteenth-century optimism and man's unrealistic estimates of what life has to offer. 112pp. 5³/₈ x 8¹/₂. 0-486-44094-X

A VOYAGE TO ARCTURUS, David Lindsay. A brilliant flight of pure fancy, where wild creatures crowd the fantastic landscape and demented torturers dominate victims with their bizarre mental powers. 272pp. 5³/₈ x 8¹/₂. 0-486-44198-9